Rise
of the
Summerfields

The Books of Nancy Moser

HISTORICAL NOVELS

- *The Pattern Artist*
- *Love of the Summerfields* (Book 1 of Manor House Series)
- *Bride of the Summerfields* (Book 2 of Manor House Series)
- *Rise of the Summerfields* (Book 3 of Manor House Series)
- *Mozart's Sister* (biographical novel of Nannerl Mozart)
- *Just Jane* (biographical novel of Jane Austen)
- *Washington's Lady* (bio-novel of Martha Washington)
- *How Do I Love Thee?* (bio-novel of Elizabeth Barrett Browning)
- *Masquerade*
- *An Unlikely Suitor*
- *The Journey of Josephine Cain*
- *A Patchwork Christmas* (novella collection)
- *A Basket Brigade Christmas* (novella collection)

CONTEMPORARY BOOKS

- *The Invitation* (Book 1 of Mustard Seed Series)
- *The Quest* (Book 2 of Mustard Seed Series)
- *The Temptation* (Book 3 of Mustard Seed Series)
- *The Seat Beside Me* (Book 1 of Steadfast Series)
- *A Steadfast Surrender* (Book 2 of Steadfast Series)
- *The Ultimatum* (Book 3 of Steadfast Series)
- *The Sister Circle* (Book 1 of Sister Circle Series)
- *Round the Corner* (Book 2 of Sister Circle Series)
- *An Undivided Heart* (Book 3 of Sister Circle Series)
- *A Place to Belong* (Book 4 of Sister Circle Series)
- *Time Lottery* (Book 1 of Time Lottery Series)
- *Second Time Around* (Book 2 of Time Lottery Series)
- *John 3:16*
- *The Good Nearby*
- *Solemnly Swear*
- *Weave of the World*

Read excerpts at www.nancymoser.com

Rise of the Summerfields

a novel

Book Three
of the
Manor House Series

Nancy Moser

Overland Park, Kansas

Rise of the Summerfields

ISBN-13: 978-0-9975398-0-6

Published by:
Mustard Seed Press
PO Box 23002
Overland Park, KS 66283

This story is a work of fiction. Any resemblances to actual people, places, or events are purely coincidental.

All Scripture quotations are taken from The Holy Bible, King James Version.

Cover design by Mustard Seed Press

Printed and bound in the United States of America

Dedication

To my family
Life is all about rising up — no matter what.
I'm so proud of you.

Love of the Summerfields: 1880

The Weston family has lived in Summerfield Manor for centuries. **Frederick Weston** is the Earl of Summerfield. His wife, **Ruth**, is the Countess. They have two children, **Clarissa**—a willful, dramatic young lady, and **George**, an adolescent keen on horses and not much else. Also living in the Manor is the widowed **Dowager Countess, Adelaide Weston** (Frederick's mother). She is strong, dutiful, and intimidating—which has caused Ruth to become a recluse, rarely venturing from her room, letting the dowager handle her duties. Ruth's loyal lady's maid, **Molly**, cares for her. Molly is in love with **Morgan Hayward**, whose family runs the village mercantile.

In the mercantile are the Haywards: **Jack** and **Fidelia**, and their two grown children, Morgan and **Lila**. Jack is a saint to tolerate his wife, because Fidelia is contentious, demanding, never-happy, and a horrible gossip. Jack's mother comes to live with them (**Mary Hayward**—**Nana**.)

Another visitor to Summerfield is **Colonel Grady Cummings** who was the dowager's one true love. When they were young (they're both in their sixties now) she'd been forced to marry the Earl of Summerfield rather than Grady, her parents choosing wealth and a title over poverty and love. But now—forty-six years later—he's back to claim his Addie.

He does a good job of wooing her, and they marry and move into the old caretaker's cottage on the Summerfield grounds. This is an enormous culture change for Addie, who is used to servants, fine dresses, lavish meals, and being in control. Now she must learn to fish and make her own tea. Yet eventually Addie embraces this simpler life with her lovely Grady. She even has some of her dresses simplified so she can better work in the garden. No one is more surprised than Addie regarding her ability to leave duty and privilege behind. Love changes everything.

The secret that lurks in the shadows of both families—that is ready to jump out at any moment—is that Jack is actually Frederick's older brother. Addie and her husband, the earl, had two sons: Alexander and Frederick, but Alexander was drowned in a nearby river when he was small.

Or was he drowned?

Forty-some years ago Mary Hayward and her ne'er do well husband lived in the woods near Summerfield. Mary lost many babies and longed for a child. So her husband got her one, snatching little Alexander from the woods near the river while his nanny slept under a tree. He told Mary the child was abandoned, and they quickly moved to London where they raised their son—they named him Jack—to be a good man, who learned how to run a mercantile.

Jack married Fidelia and moved to Summerfield when the local mercantile was up for sale. There, they had their two children.

Fidelia is one of the first people to learn the secret that her husband is actually the earl and she is actually the Countess of Summerfield. But in her excitement to lord it over the Westons (whom she hates) she falls down some stairs and dies. Actually—sadly—Jack his children are more relieved than saddened by her passing.

Other than Fidelia, the Haywards have no knowledge of Jack's true heritage until…

Mary Hayward befriends Addie (not knowing she's the dowager) and hears Addie's story of a long-lost son who had a star birthmark on his arm. Jack has such a birthmark! Mary realizes Jack is Alexander.

Choices are made that have life-changing repercussions. When the truth is revealed, Jack becomes the earl, Morgan becomes the heir, and Lila is now Lady Lila.

The existing Westons in Summerfield Manor are all demoted. Frederick is now the second son, and Ruth is no longer the countess—which suits her just fine. George doesn't care that he's not the heir anymore as long as he can ride horses, but Clarissa is angry at her demotion (and Lila's promotion), and runs off to London.

During the course of this family drama (before the secret is revealed) Lila falls in love with **Joseph Kidd**, the son of a viscount in nearby Crompton Hall. And he with her. Yet because she is just a shopkeeper's daughter, their match isn't possible. To make matters worse, Joseph's father arranges for him to marry Clarissa—who doesn't love him. Yet Clarissa doesn't want him to marry anyone else either.

In the end, with the Haywards elevated to a title, Lila is free to marry Joseph, the man she loves. And Joseph is free to marry his lovely Lila.

And Molly—who loved Morgan, the son of a shopkeeper? As a servant she has no chance to marry him now that he's become the heir to the earldom of Summerfield. Heartbroken, Molly runs away.

Bride of the Summerfields: 1882

Molly has made a life for herself in London, making hats. **Clarissa** has led a secret life on the stage as Clara West. Her parents think she's traveling with family friends, when in actuality, she lives in dire poverty. Molly has to go back to Summerfield because her mother (who is a servant there) has had a stroke.

Back in Summerfield Manor, **Morgan** is betrothed to marry an American heiress, **Genevieve Farrow**. Genevieve and her bossy mother arrive from New York City. She's a sweet girl, and has fallen in love with Morgan through his letters. With Molly suddenly showing up—his past love interest—Morgan is torn between Molly and Genevieve. He knows where his duty lies— as the estate needs the influx of Genevieve's family money. But first love dies hard.

A new addition to the Weston family is **Tilda Cavendish**, the goddaughter of **Grady** (the colonel.) Tilda has led a hard life. Her mother ran away after she was born and she was raised by an inept soldier father who's recently died. She is streetwise and has been cleaning the houses of soldiers to make ends meet. She's also used to stealing a bit here and there.

Tilda comes to the Manor with two chaperones, **Mr. and Mrs. White**, who have ulterior motives. Mr. White used to work at the Manor and blackmails the Westons, saying *he* is Morgan's father (not the earl, **Jack**) that *he* had his way with Fidelia years back. The Westons pay up to keep him silent, not wanting there to be any question about Morgan's claim to the earldom, especially in light of his betrothal to Genevieve. Tilda is lured into the nastiness, but in the end, Mr. White has a change of heart and admits he was never intimate with Fidelia. All is well. Morgan is the legitimate heir. And Tilda is left to apologize for her part in the mess. Yet facing her lesser side makes Tilda grow up. She realizes what a blessing it is to be with the Westons. She will not hurt them again.

In London, Clarissa befriends a little girl who lives on the stairs of her building. **Beth** is twelve and all alone, fending for herself on the streets of London. Clarissa lets her try on pretty hats and shows her kindness — revealing a foreign aspect of her character. But when Clarissa loses her job at the theatre and gets kicked out of her apartment for non-payment of rent, all her belongings are cast out on the street. Clarissa has no choice but to go back to Summerfield and take her lumps for lying to her family about her whereabouts and her secret life.

But she's not ready to return to the Manor and takes refuge at Crompton Hall with **Lila** and **Joseph**. She hears about Tilda, and is jealous of her because Tilda seems to have taken over her place in the family, including becoming close to Clarissa's mother, Ruth.

Clarissa is haunted by thoughts of Beth, back on the streets. Is she all right? She elicits the help of a village carpenter, **Timothy Billings**, to go find her. They bring Beth back to Summerfield. *Now* Clarissa is ready to go home to the Manor where she presents herself to her family after nearly two years' absence. They are thrilled to see her, but are naturally surprised at the presence of Beth. Clarissa informs them she is going to raise Beth as her daughter — which negates any chance of Clarissa marrying well. So be it. Beth is worth it.

Morgan's indecision regarding Molly and Genevieve comes to a head, and he rightfully chooses Genevieve. They are married and seem destined for a happy life.

Molly is resigned to his choice, and even agrees with it. During the tense time at the Manor, Molly has gained the kind attention of **Dr. Peter**, who's been caring for her mother. They are a good pair as she has a talent for nursing. She realizes their friendship is actually love.

All has worked out as it should.

The Families in *Rise of the Summerfields*

SUMMERFIELD MANOR:

ADELAIDE CUMMINGS: the dowager Countess of Summerfield, married to **COLONEL GRADY CUMMINGS**

Her sons:

JACK WESTON: the Earl of Summerfield (his wife **FIDELIA** died.)

Jack's children:

- **MORGAN,** married to **GENEVIEVE FARROW**, Children: twins **MAX** and **MAY**
- **LILA,** married to **JOSEPH KIDD**, Child: **HENRIETTA**

FREDERICK WESTON: Jack's younger brother, married to **RUTH**

Frederick's children:

- **CLARISSA** and adopted daughter **BETH**
- **GEORGE**

TILDA CAVENDISH: goddaughter of Colonel Cummings

CROMPTON HALL:

IAN KIDD: the Viscount Newley (his wife died when Joseph was born)

Ian's son:

- **JOSEPH,** married to **LILA WESTON**, Child: **HENRIETTA**
- Ian's sister: **LADY SILVEY (SYLVIA)** widowed baroness
- Ian's nephew: **LORD SILVEY (DAMON)**

The Village:

- **MOLLY EVERS** (*né* Wallace): former Summerfield maid, married to **DR. PETER EVERS**
- **MARY HAYWARD (NANA):** Jack's adoptive mother, grandmother to Lila and Morgan
- **TIMOTHY BILLINGS:** Local carpenter and dear friend to Lila, Clarissa, and Beth

Prologue

Summer 1883

"It's a boy!"

Genevieve grabbed a fresh breath and forced herself to open her eyes. She saw the bedroom of Summerfield Manor, the doctor, and her mother with her hands clasped to her chin. But she didn't see the one thing in the world she wanted to see—had to see. "Let me see him!"

Dr. Peter held him up for inspection. The baby screamed.

Genevieve's mother grasped her hand. "He has good lungs on him, that's for certain."

"Can I hold him?"

"Shortly," the doctor said. "Let us get him cleaned up."

Genevieve was vaguely aware of the doctor and his wife, Molly, taking care of her son.

Her son! She was a moth—

Her happy thoughts were interrupted by another contraction. "Ahhh!"

"What's going on, doctor?" asked her mother.

He returned to Genevieve and examined her. "Oh my! We have another one!"

Another one?

"You're going to have to do it again, Mrs. Weston."

Genevieve knew that without having to be told. Her body was demanding. *It* was in charge and all she could do was submit.

The here and now was consumed with pain. She heard voices but they floated outside her consciousness. She and the baby were one, focused on a common goal.

"Push!"

There was no alternative. Her mother and Molly supported her on either side, and with a primal scream she pushed the baby into its new life.

"It's a girl!"

Fully spent, Genevieve fell back on the pillows. "One of each?"

Her mother kissed her cheek. "One of each, my girl. How marvelous!"

She heard a door opening, and Morgan's voice. "I heard the scream. Is she all right?"

"Morgan . . ." Genevieve held out her hand and he rushed by her side, his eyes trying to take in everything around him.

"What? Two?" He pulled her hand to his lips.

"A boy and a girl."

His eyes welled with tears as he kissed her. "Well done, my darling!"

After a few minutes, Dr. Peter passed her their son, and Genevieve cradled him in her right arm. "He is beautiful."

"And here, Mr. Weston, here is your daughter."

Morgan sat on the bed and took the little girl into his arms. He gently touched her chin and stroked her head. "Oh dear. Oh my. I am smitten."

"Let me see her. Let me see my babies, together," Genevieve asked.

He placed their daughter upon her left arm. The two babies snuggled and wriggled and cooed, making a myriad of expressions. "Our joy is complete," she said.

Morgan beamed down at them. "Our joy is just beginning."

Chapter One

Autumn 1883

In the early morning moments between sleep and awakening, Clarissa Weston remembered.

They left me.

Yet even in her tenuous state she was savvy enough to know "left" was too small a word. Her family hadn't *left* her. They had abandoned her.

To counter a cloud of loneliness she threw back the covers and got out of bed. The chill of the autumn morning fully awakened her and the pain of being left behind dimmed. So much so, that she told herself to stop this pathetic foolishness, get back in bed, and sleep another hour or two like every other woman of her social set.

But Clarissa had never subscribed to being like other women. Her main point of distinction lay in the fact that she knew no other lady of twenty-three who was the mother of a thirteen-year-old girl. Other than the flagrant detail that it was not physically possible, Clarissa knew of no other lady who had the gumption and courage to adopt a child in need, saving her from the harsh and evil streets of London.

She needed to see her daughter right now.

Clarissa ignored the niceties of slippers and her dressing gown. She carefully opened her bedroom door and took a look right and left before exiting. Yet, once in the hallway, she realized she could run up and back and knock on each of the twenty-five bedrooms and only bother five people.

Five people left her. With five others left behind.

She crossed the hall to Beth's room and entered without a knock. The room glowed in the early light of dawn. Unlike the rest of them, Beth slept with her draperies open, saying she liked to see the stars and the moon. She also didn't mind the sun waking her early.

This morning Clarissa would be her sun.

She quietly clicked the door shut behind her and moved to Beth's bed, slipping under the covers.

Beth murmured, then scooted over. "What's wrong?"

"I woke up early and decided to get up."

Beth adjusted the covers. "You never get up early."

"I can. If I want to."

"So you want to?"

"No." Clarissa sighed, lay on her back, and adjusted a pillow. "My family abandoned me and went to India as a happy gaggle, never thinking twice about leaving me behind."

Beth yawned. "Didn't they invite you to go?"

She let a memory flit by. "Mother might of mentioned it."

"You chose to stay."

"It's too early for truth, Beth."

Beth turned on her side to face her. "The truth is you stayed behind because of me."

"You could have gone along too."

"I like being home. I like helping Genevieve with the twins."

"They have Nanny Colleen."

"And me. They have me."

True. "Your skill with the babies has surprised us all."

"And me. I've never been around babies before now." Beth stretched out next to Clarissa, draping her arms over the top of the coverlet. "They're so helpless."

"Like you were in London?"

"Maybe that's it. I know what it's like to have no one to care for me. I don't want May and Max to ever feel like I did."

Clarissa found her hand and squeezed it. Beth embodied everything good. Although it was true Clarissa did a good deed in taking her in, Beth's good was a virtue that was rooted deep, in spite of her difficult past. Because of it?

Clarissa knew that her own moments of good often seemed like feeble and infrequent offerings that happened in spite of her character, not because of it.

"I miss my family," she said.

"They just left yesterday."

Logic didn't help.

"Did you miss them when you were in London for over a year?" Beth asked.

"I *chose* to leave. I wasn't left."

"I suppose that matters?"

"It does. And honestly, in London I was too busy to miss them."

"Then get busy again, here in Summerfield."

Which came full circle to her initial feeling of abandonment. She turned on her side and Beth did the same, facing her. The radiance of the early light let Clarissa see her daughter's soft features, her porcelain skin and vivid blue eyes. "When I was out in the hallway just now I realized how empty the Manor is. No Mother, no Father, and no George. And Grandmamma and Colonel Grady are gone from their cottage. Other than you, my entire family is gone."

"Uncle Jack is your family. Morgan and Genevieve are your family."

"Once removed. They are Lila's family, Lila's father and brother. Lila's sister-in-law."

Clarissa's thoughts turned to Lila, her cousin and nemesis. Clarissa had been rude to Lila at the going-away party two days previous. And people had noticed. Grandmamma had scolded her—blessedly, in private— which added to Clarissa's personal loathing. Why did seeing Lila and her husband Joseph still annoy her? They'd been married two years.

Beth interrupted her inner chastening. "Tilda is here too."

Speaking of an annoyance. "Tilda isn't family." Clarissa sat up, moving the pillows against the headboard, forcing Beth to do the same if she didn't want to lose the warmth of the covers. "Tilda is Grady's god-daughter. So why didn't they take her with them?" *Why leave her here to torment me?* "I'm sure Mother would have loved having her along as her surrogate daughter. They took George, why not take Tilda?"

Beth hesitated. "Uncle Grady said *because* George was going they didn't want to take Tilda. You know the romantic sparks that flew between them when she first came. They're sixteen. The family doesn't want them to become romantically involved. Traveling all the way to India together and being gone for months and months might cause a problem."

"So *we* are left with the problem."

"Tilda's not a problem, Mum. She's nice. She's very good with the babies too."

"Then leave her to the babies. Let her be the nanny. She should be a servant. She's not one of the family. She doesn't deserve to be treated as such."

"You can't still be mad she borrowed some of your clothes."

"I have a right to be. While I was away she all but slept in my room. She was in my jewelry box—touching and wearing family jewels."

"She's just a girl who likes pretty things and wasn't used to them. I'm a girl who likes pretty things too, and I'm not used to them."

Whoops. "That's different. You're my Beth."

"Now. But I came from lesser roots than Tilda. Her father was a soldier. I don't even know who my father was. Just like Tilda's mum, my mother left me to fend for myself. I lived on the stairs of your building, Mum. I deserve less standing than Tilda."

Clarissa was sorry she'd started this conversation. She didn't want Beth to feel unworthy of the life Clarissa was happy to give her. "You have good character and deserve the world."

"So does she. Tell me why you still hold this grudge against her. It's been a year."

If only I could. Tilda had grown up among soldiers who treated her like a pet to be used for their amusement. She was cleaning houses for the families of soldiers before she came to Summerfield. Clarissa *should* feel compassion for her, not contempt.

"Don't you know why?" Beth asked.

"I don't." She pulled her knees close and adjusted the covers. "I know it's illogical. I know what I *should* feel but can't seem to get there. When everyone was home I didn't have to think about it. But now that they've abandoned me, and left *her*..." Clarissa wanted to snuggle down and pull the covers over her shame. Instead, she leaned her head back until it touched the headboard. "Oh, Beth. Why do you see through me like no one else?"

"Because we saved each other. I'm here for you and you're here for me."

"You're my daughter." That one amazing face made it possible for Clarissa to endure her own faults.

Beth looked towards the window. The halo of the sunrise was just touching the tops of the trees in the distance. "You don't have to say that to people."

"Say what?"

"Say that I'm your daughter. I appreciate you treating me like it's true, but you don't need to say it publicly. I'm not a child any more. I can see how you're ruining your chances for marriage. No gentleman is going to marry you when you have a thirteen-year-old, low-born daughter."

"Who needs them?"

"You do. You need to choose whether to get married — or not — because of love, not because of me."

Clarissa put an arm around her shoulders and kissed her head. "I have you. That is enough."

"For now. But what if one day it's not?"

"We're in this together, forever and always."

Beth shrugged away from her touch and faced her. "I've thought about this a lot lately, and I have an idea. Why don't you let me be a ward of the family? I get to live here as I do now, but you are free."

"But I'm proud to call you my daughter."

"In a better world it wouldn't matter, but in this world of titles and rules and station, it does. Think about it, Mum. Let me live with the family as a ward. That would leave you clear to be happy and find love."

"I am happy and I have found love. I love you."

"It's not the same."

It wasn't the same, but raising Beth as her daughter hadn't been a decision made lightly. Clarissa had many faults, but going back on her word wasn't one of them.

"Enough, Beth. I am very content with how things are."

Beth laughed. "So it was contentment that brought you to my room before sunrise?"

Caught again. Clarissa whipped the covers off and got up. "Go back to sleep and I'll do the same."

But Beth got out of bed too. "I think I'll get dressed and go help Nanny Colleen. Getting two babies up in the morning is a chore."

Once again, Clarissa was struck by Beth's generous nature.

"You could come with me," Beth said.

She could...

Yet old habits were as hard to break as old attitudes. So Clarissa went back to bed, leaving good deeds in the care of others.

In the early morning moments between sleep and awakening, Tilda Cavendish remembered.

They left me.

Yet even in her tenuous state Tilda was savvy enough to know "left" was too small a word. The Westons hadn't *left* her, they'd abandoned her like the orphan she was.

Tilda turned on her side and pulled a pillow to her chest. She'd have to get used to the pillow being the only semblance of a hug she'd get anymore.

She would miss her godfather the most. She'd come to Summerfield because of him. Uncle Grady was kind and wise. But she wasn't his first concern. That designation fell to the dowager countess, Adelaide. Although the two of them had been married three years, and though they were both nearly seventy years of age, they still acted like the newlyweds they should have been fifty years earlier when parents and station had kept them apart. Tilda hoped to find an everlasting love like that someday.

That love would *not* be with George Weston.

By taking George with them to India, and not taking her...Tilda had asked Uncle Grady about it. He'd explained that it was often traditional for a young man George's age to be shown the world.

Not so much young ladies. Unspoken was the added truth: *especially young ladies who aren't family.*

Yet Uncle Grady and George were not the people she would miss the most. That honor went to Aunt Ruth, the mother of Clarissa and George.

Aunt Ruth had taken Tilda under her wing, caring for her, listening to her, encouraging her drawing, and being the mother she'd never had. Her soldier father had done his best to raise her, but not enough. Tilda had been exposed to pubs, drinking songs, and rough language.

During this last year at the Manor she'd worked very hard to use the right words in conversation, the right fork at dinner, and show off the right open and eager attitudes so the Westons would let her stay. Although she wanted them to think of her as family, just to *stay* would be an acceptable consolation prize.

But now they've abandoned you, proving they don't think of you as family at all.

She hugged the pillow harder, drawing it between her knees. "Why would they leave me with Clarissa when everyone knows she hates me?"

It was a question that haunted her last thoughts before sleep and captured her first thoughts every morning. Yes, it was true that Genevieve and Morgan, and even the earl—

19

who'd told her to call him Uncle Jack—were nice to her. But she couldn't stop feeling as inconsequential to them as one of the servants.

Which left Clarissa and her daughter Beth.

I hate them both.

Tilda didn't like that thought, so threw off the covers, tossed the pillow aside and got up. Hate was too harsh a word for what Tilda felt about Beth. There was nothing about Beth to hate. She was sweet and helpful and friendly. The only reason Tilda disliked her was the disparity in their level of acceptance at the Manor. Beth had also been a visitor in this house, yet she had quickly gained the coveted "daughter" designation. Not by doing anything special. Just by being Beth.

It wasn't fair, and there was nothing Tilda could do about it. And so, she got dressed and went to see the twins in the nursery.

At least *they* loved her unconditionally.

In the early morning moments between sleep and awakening, Genevieve Weston remembered.

They left me.

Yet even in her tenuous state Genevieve was savvy enough to know "left" was too small a word. Morgan's family—her family—hadn't *left* her, they'd trusted her to carry on while they were gone.

Her mother's voice sounded in her head. *Are you up to it, Genevieve? I doubt it. You never listened to anything I tried to teach you. And now they've left you as the mistress of the Manor? Whatever were they thinking?*

The responsibility hung over her like a storm cloud.

She thought about snuggling against her husband for support, yet she feared any hint of intimacy might spur him to want more from her, and she wasn't ready for that. Would she ever be ready for that again? She forgave herself for her thoughts. It had only been two months since the twins were born. If only Morgan had allowed her a bedroom of her own. After all, that *was* the traditional arrangement.

Yes, I'll admit the twins were a coup for you, Daughter, but just because you gave Morgan an heir doesn't mean you can become complacent. You married into a titled family because of my hard work. Don't you dare do anything to jeopardize —

"Good morning."

Morgan extended an arm towards her, trying to lure her to his side. She stood her ground. "I'm worried."

He rubbed his eyes and pushed himself to sitting. "It's too early to worry."

Genevieve helped him arrange his pillows, and then her own so they could sit against the headboard. "I didn't sleep well last night."

"Because?"

"Because your grandmother and aunt left me alone to be the lady of the house."

"You *will* be countess someday."

"But I'm not the countess now. How do they know I can do the job without them?" *Why would they assume such a thing?*

"They have seen how quickly you've adapted to life at Summerfield this last year."

"That's the rub. I've endured *so* many changes. From New York to Summerfield, becoming the wife of the heir to an earldom, *and* the mother of twins. That's a heaping helping for anyone. Much less —"

"Don't say it."

"Say what?"

"Much less you." He pulled her under his arm. She couldn't fight against it, so rested her head against his shoulder and heard the beating of his heart. "It's true you came here as a naïve ingénue, but you have risen to every challenge. Victoriously."

That's not what Mother would say. "You overstate."

"I do not. Do you know what Grandmother told me when they began discussing the idea of traveling to India?"

"No."

"She said that the three of us were the main reason they could even consider the trip."

"Three?"

"You, me, and Papa. She called us 'the triumphant trio.'"

Genevieve smiled. "I *can* imagine her saying such a thing." She took advantage of the moment to sit up and move away from him. "I've heard stories about the years when your grandmother was the Countess of Summerfield. She was the essence of capability and duty."

"I can't imagine her any other way. But there's no reason for you to feel overwhelmed."

"Aunt Ruth was. Before your father came along as the true earl, she was the countess and was fully intimidated by the task of following in your grandmother's footsteps. So much so that she hid away in her room, a recluse."

"True again."

She took a cleansing breath. "Then what makes them think I can take up the mantle in their absence?"

"Because you're you."

She let out a huff. "You have to say that. I'm your wife."

"I guarantee I do *not* have to say any such thing." He faced her. "God brought you to Summerfield — to me — to save us. To bind us together in a way that will allow our family to last another 250 years. There's no one else to do it."

"There's Clarissa."

He scoffed. "Clarissa cares only for Clarissa."

"And Beth."

"I *will* give Clarissa credit for dear Beth. Clarissa has surprised us all in her ability to love that girl."

"I love her too."

"As do I. But to your other point, Summerfield would never thrive under Clarissa's care. Or George's, for he only cares for horses. You and I are Summerfield's future."

She admired his ability to make her feel capable, even if she felt anything but. "You will make a great earl someday."

"That is my goal — with you by my side."

Genevieve released her worry with a sigh. "I do love you."

"And I adore you. So…no more worries."
"I will do my best."
"Another attribute."

Genevieve slipped into the empty bedroom at the far end of the hallway. She moved to the chair by the window and took up the Bible she kept nearby.

She turned to the Psalms, seeking comfort and wisdom. And found it.

"I will instruct thee and teach thee in the way which thou shalt go: I will guide thee with mine eye."

As often happened in her quiet time before the busyness of the day began, God gave her a verse to encourage and enlighten. She bowed her head. "Once again, thank you, Father. And please do instruct and guide me. I need You."

She closed the Bible and her eyes, leaned her head against the chair back, and embraced His words in the silence.

Genevieve enjoyed this daily ritual—she needed it. Not just for her faith, but for her well-being. As an only child she wasn't used to being in a house full of people. Growing up she'd often complained about wanting a sibling or a friend to help her pass the days of her childhood, but as she grew older she found pleasure in her own company.

And God's.

Genevieve was never truly alone.

I will guide you with Mine eye.

God would watch over her. It was a relief, as she knew she needed a lot of watching.

In the early morning moments between sleep and awakening, Lila Weston Kidd remembered.

They left me.

Yet even in her tenuous state Lila was savvy enough to know "left" was too small a word. Her family hadn't *left* her, they'd trusted her to carry on while they were gone.

Not in their home at Summerfield Manor, but in her husband's familial home in nearby Crompton Hall. Her home.

Lila's first challenge would come this very day.

As she dressed and went to breakfast, her stomach tied itself into nervous knots. Joseph's aunt and cousin were arriving today for an extended visit. As the mistress of the Hall it was her responsibility to make sure everything was perfect.

At breakfast, her father-in-law stressed the point over his final sip of coffee. "You and Joseph will be the viscountess and viscount after I'm gone. It's time to fully play those parts for my sister's sake."

"We will, Father," Joseph said.

Ian's eyebrow rose. "Will you? Sometimes I don't believe you two are up to the task."

His doubt made Lila fumble her fork. She had no idea how to respond.

He wasn't through. " Remember what the Bible says: 'I know thy works, that thou art neither cold nor hot: I would thou wert cold or hot. Because thou art lukewarm, and neither cold nor hot, I will spue thee out of my mouth.' The two of you are too lukewarm."

"That's harsh," Joseph said.

"Perhaps, but I speak the truth." He stood up from the table and left them.

"I'm sorry he was so brusque, my darling," Joseph said.

"There's no need to be," Lila said. "He does speak the truth."

"We are trying our best."

"Are we?"

He leaned towards her across the table and lowered his voice so the footman wouldn't hear. "I know you're nervous about having overnight guests."

She shook her head, not wanting him to discount his father's admonition so quickly. "The details will be handled. But towards your father's words...you and I are alike, Joseph. We are content being at home in each other's company."

"I agree. And now we have little Henrietta turning our duet into a happy trio. I don't see our love of home and family as something to be criticized."

He was missing the point. "Sometimes I wonder if we are too much alike. Is our contentment a lukewarm existence when it should be hot? Or even cold? For those two temperatures require effort. Being hot or cold requires courage. Lukewarm is the result of just letting something...be. Being lukewarm is the coward's way out."

Joseph leaned back in his chair, clearly stunned by her words. "It appears to be two against one."

"That isn't my intent. But when truth is spoken isn't it our responsibility to ponder it?"

He shook his head and set his napkin on the table. "I think these are thoughts for another time."

Delaying the resolution of uncomfortable issues was her husband's way. But perhaps this morning he was right. Lila had enough on her plate.

Dowd entered the dining room. "Mrs. Weston is here, ma'am."

"A tad early," Joseph said.

"Genevieve can come any time of day—and besides, I invited her." She turned to Dowd. "I'll meet her in the morning room." Lila rose from her chair and moved to kiss Joseph on the head. "It will be all right, dearest. Today your father will be proud, for I promise there will be nothing lukewarm about the day."

She hurried to the morning room, eager to greet her sister-in-law. "Genevieve," she said, kissing her cheek. "I'm so glad you agreed to save me."

Genevieve removed her gloves. "I hardly think you need saving. It's Joseph's aunt and cousin coming to visit. Not the queen."

Lila retrieved a list she'd made the day before. "I'm having trouble with the menus."

"You've had dinner parties before."

"A few. But we have never had overnight guests who require all the other meals too. And how exactly are we supposed to entertain them all day, every day, for however long they're staying?"

"They haven't stated how long they'll be here?"

"No," Lila sank onto a chair and indicated Genevieve should sit nearby. "Joseph and I have been married nearly two years but have never met Lady Silvey. She and her son have been traveling in Europe."

"Where is Lord Silvey?"

"He died three years ago—so the son is now the baron. I think the father's death was the reason for the extended trip, an effort to remain busy during their time of grief."

"If they've been traveling so long, they must like to be away from home. Which might mean…"

"It might mean they will be with us for a lengthy visit." She set the menu on her lap. "I'm at a loss. And because Joseph's mother died soon after he was born, there has been no mistress of Crompton Hall for decades. I have no model to use as a guide."

"Who handled the entertaining before your marriage?"

"I believe the housekeeper did the honors during the few instances where entertainment was necessary."

"Then Mrs. Crank should be able to help you now."

Lila glanced towards the door and lowered her voice. "She still intimidates me."

"You find her as cranky as her name?"

Lila did an imitation of the woman: she crossed her arms, frowned, glared under dipped brows, and made her voice bellow with disgust. "Really, Mrs. Kidd. That is not how *we* do things at the Hall!"

"She shouldn't talk to you like that."

"I know."

"You should sack her. You deserve a housekeeper who will work with you, not against you."

Lila sighed. "I'm not adept at confrontation."

"Is anyone?"

"Mrs. Crank is." They shared a laugh. Then Lila asked, "How are the twins?"

"Thriving, thanks to Nanny Colleen, Tilda, and Beth. How is Etta?"

"Nanny Mabel is wonderful with her. But with the arrival of guests I worry that I won't be able to spend as much time with her as I am used to."

"Make the time. Happy children are the goal, rather than children who are forced to sit quietly with a teacup on their lap." Genevieve shuddered.

"That's how you were raised?"

"Prim and proper. A thousand rules and bits of motherly advice that I still hear echoing in my head. All in all, my childhood was quite joyless."

Lila could imagine it so. When Genevieve's mother had brought her to Summerfield she had been obsessed with propriety and manners. And ambition. Mention of Mrs. Farrow caused Lila to ask, "How is your mother faring?"

"I believe she's quite happy with her new husband—and ecstatic that she is now a baroness." Genevieve leaned close. "Although I do think she is incensed that I will eventually be a countess and outrank her."

"How do you feel about her discomfort?"

"I delight in it."

Lila loved talking about their children and families, but she had menus to conquer. "At least tomorrow night's dinner is smaller now due to half of our family leaving for India."

Genevieve sighed. "I admit the Manor is almost too quiet."

"With Clarissa there? Surely you jest."

"I saw her at breakfast, but she seems a little lost."

"Clarissa revels in dramatic times." Lila considered keeping her next thought to herself, then shared it anyway. "If I could get by without asking her to dinner tomorrow night, I would. Even though we are now cousins, she still resents me."

"I know."

Lila felt an eyebrow rise.

"I'm sorry. Perhaps I should have contradicted you."

Perhaps. "Clarissa seems to be perpetually balancing a chip on her shoulder when it comes to Joseph and I."

"She does enjoy playing a part to its fullest. Although in this case I'm not certain which part she is playing."

"That of jilted lover, for certain," Lila said.

"Even though she and Joseph were never . . ."

"They were betrothed through a parental agreement. There was no love involved. On either side."

"But she likes to pretend otherwise."

"Of course. And she will never even pretend to be happy for us. In her eyes, I stole him away from her."

"Which you did not."

"Joseph and I love each other. He never loved her. Their engagement was a farce."

"For her to hold onto bitterness for years makes little sense."

Lila sighed. "It gives her something to do. I truly believe Clarissa is at her happiest when she has something to complain about." She immediately felt guilty for saying such a thing. "I'm sorry. That was rude."

"Though true."

"Really?"

Genevieve smoothed the lace on her skirt. "I'm not sure what she does with her days. She doesn't help around the Manor yet disparages most everything others do. Did you know that Tilda and I are now teaching Beth to read and do her numbers because Clarissa declared she didn't have the time? To Tilda's credit, she recently took over the lessons on her own."

"Clarissa needs purpose," Lila said. "She needs a husband, someone to get her mind off of *our* marriage."

"Unfortunately, titled suitors prefer more conventional ladies without such a questionable past."

Lila shook the thought away. She could do little to solve Clarissa's problems. She had problems of her own. "*I* must concentrate on *my* immediate future. I was thinking of serving duck..."

Lila heard the carriage approach and hurried towards the foyer of Crompton Hall.

Dowd met her there, assuming his duties at the door.

Lila's stomach was doubly knotted with the desire to make a good impression and the fear she would do otherwise.

She looked behind her, hoping for Joseph and her father-in-law to join her and ease the first meeting.

But they were nowhere to be found. The housekeeper appeared, and Lila asked, "His lordship? And my husband?"

"They have been alerted, Mrs. Kidd."

Within seconds, Dowd opened the door. A middle-aged woman conquered the threshold and the room, causing the lavender ostrich feather on her hat to flutter and bend.

Their guest keyed in on Lila, immediately taking her hands captive and kissing her cheeks. "My dear, my dear. We finally meet!"

Lila was pleasantly surprised by her warmth. "I am so glad you could come for a visit. Joseph has told me so much about you."

"Believe but half of it." Then she grinned. "Oh, posh. Believe all of it until I tell you which half is true."

Lila liked her immediately. But as Dowd closed the door, she asked, "Where is your son?"

"Damon had business in London—monkey business if you ask my opinion—but he will arrive in a day or two."

Lila heard the sound of Joseph's boot-steps and saw him enter the foyer with a smile. He took his aunt's hand and kissed her cheek. "Welcome, Auntie."

"Where is my brother?" she asked.

Lord Newley strode in, buttoning his waistcoat. "Here I am. I considered donning body armor for your onslaught, but decided to be courageous and come as I was. Welcome, Sister." He glanced towards the door. "Where is Damon?"

"He'll arrive in a tardy fashion — as is his preference."

Lila remembered her manners as lady of the house. "Would you like to see your room and freshen up?"

"I am as fresh as I'll ever be." She removed her hat, gloves, and coat, handing them to Dowd. "I know it's early, but a cup of tea would be grand. Tea, and the baby. I so long to hold little Henrietta in my arms."

Lila, Dowd, and Mrs. Crank exchanged a few nods, and Lila led her family into the drawing room where they sat on either side of the fireplace. She was relieved when her father-in-law began the conversation.

"How was the Continent?"

"I nearly lost Damon in Paris."

"Lost?"

She smiled. "Let me amend that. I nearly lost Damon *to* Paris. He quite fell in love with the whole of it. And *it* loved him. Too much."

"How so?" Joseph crossed his legs, spotted a smudge of dirt on the toe of his boot, and wiped it fresh with his thumb.

She flipped the question away. "You remember your cousin. Wild and reckless but able to charm his way through every soup and stew he stirs up."

The men of the house had shared Damon-stories with Lila. "Rogue" seemed a good description of his character. Because of that, Lila wasn't disappointed his arrival was delayed. She appreciated the chance to get to know his mother first.

Lila went to address her, then suddenly realized she wasn't sure of the protocol. Best to deal with that issue immediately. "What should I call you?" she asked. "Lady Silvey?"

The woman smiled. "Let me share an amusing story, dear Lila. My forename is Sylvia. But when I married my husband who was a baron, I became Lady Silvey. So my name potentially is Sylvia Silvey."

Lila stifled a giggle.

"It's quite unfortunate. Luckily, our society does not allow my first name and my title to be uttered in the same breath." She leaned close to Lila. "No Sylvia Silvey allowed. So call me Sylvia."

Lila was glad to dispense with their titles.

"And you? What shall I call you?" Sylvia asked. "For you have an intricate name history too, do you not?"

"I do. I was born Lila Hayward, a shopkeeper's daughter. When my father was found to be the earl, I was suddenly Lady Lila. Then I married Joseph, the son of a viscount—"

"Which only earns *me* an 'honourable' designation, rather than 'lord,'" Joseph said.

Lila gave him a smile. "An honourable designation which you justly deserve, my darling. You are the most honourable man I know." She turned to their guest. "So now I am Mrs. Kidd."

"Actually," Joseph said, "Since she is the daughter of an earl, she can continue to be called 'lady': Lady Kidd."

"I tried that on for a short while, but now I prefer to be known as Mrs. Kidd." Lila didn't like to draw attention to the fact her father was of higher rank than her father-in-law.

Lord Newley interjected. "After I am gone and Joseph becomes the viscount, you will be Lady Newley."

Which led her back to her answer. "Call me Lila."

Sylvia slapped her hands upon her legs. "Oh, the intricacies of the peerage. Now that that is settled..."

They all looked to the doorway where Nanny held Etta. The baby grinned at Lila, who gladly took her upon her lap.

"Well look at you," Sylvia said. "Sitting up so tall."

"She just mastered that feat," Lila said. "She was six-months old yesterday."

Sylvia took possession of the baby, holding her under the arms, letting Etta stand on her lap. Etta immediately reached for her earrings.

Lila stopped the baby's hand before she could cause harm. "Hair, earrings, and spectacles are fair game for little hands."

The earring forgotten, Etta put a hand on Sylvia's mouth.

"Bub, bub, bub," Sylvia said.

Etta beamed. As did Sylvia.

31

"You're fast friends already."

Etta's legs buckled and she sat on Sylvia's lap, facing her, one pudgy leg on either side. She played with the mother-of-pearl buttons on Sylvia's dress. "I always wished for a girl that I could dress in lace and silky pretties. That's hard to do with a boy."

"Thank goodness," Joseph said.

The tea arrived. Between cups, saucers, biscuits, and baby, a fine time was had by all.

Thank goodness.

Chapter Two

"Thank you, Dixon."

Genevieve took the letter from the silver salver, and immediately recognized the ornate cursive of her mother. She broke the seal.

My dearest daughter,

Horace and I are off to Switzerland and plan on staying with the Count of some Swiss something-or-other before heading off to Pisa where my delectable baron has a villa. I must say I do like being a baroness. If only Mrs. Vanderbilt and Mrs. Astor could see me now! They'd drool in their demitasse cups.

But before we're off on our travels, I wanted to address your concern about being left alone in Summerfield.

Embrace it! Now is your chance. Without Ruth and Adelaide fuddling around, you can take your rightful place as mistress of the Manor. They've always been polite enough — in their ever-so-proper English way — but now is the time to take advantage of this opportunity. Make yourself indispensable to the earl. Do the required work, but also flatter him and make him glad that his son married an American, all the while remembering that it is they who benefited most from the match. Don't let them forget that our money saved them.

I taught you everything you need to know. Now is the time to remember it, Daughter. Don't you dare forget what I've taught you. You have a tendency to be easily addled and forget. Now is not the time to be a weak girl. Step up! Upset the apple cart, if you must, Genevieve.

Make them know that you are — and will always be — a Farrow.

How is Lord Newley?

Your loving,
Mamma

Genevieve stifled a groan. She should never have shared her concern about being left behind. As far as her mother's advice? It was rubbish, or at least the motivation behind it deserved the dust bin. The conniving manipulation Mamma espoused once again made Genevieve glad she'd left Summerfield. To attempt to do a good job under the eagle-eye of her mother would have tainted a worthy goal and would have added to Genevieve's stress ten-fold.

Make that one-hundred-fold.

She glanced at the inquiry about Lord Newley. It was the only interesting part of the letter, for it indicated her mother's sustained interest in the man she probably could have married if she hadn't been such a deceitful, scheming woman. It had been for the best that Newley turned his back on Dorcas Farrow — for his own sake. And Lila and Joseph's. And Crompton Hall's.

Genevieve rose from her desk and strode to the fireplace. There was only one response to this letter. She tore it in two...

There was a knock on the door. "Mrs. Weston?"

"Good morning, Tilda. How may I help you?"

"Nanny wants to take the twins for a walk and I was going to go along — unless you need me for something else."

"Thank you for asking, but by all means, join them." She tore the halves into fourths, and tried to tear them even smaller.

"What are you doing?"

Genevieve displayed the remnants of the letter. "I am responding to a letter from my mother."

Tilda smiled. "It wasn't a good letter?"

"I'm sure she thought it was superior as letters go. Full of motherly advice and direction."

"Which you don't want to take?"

Which I already suffer in my thoughts. She extended the scraps to Tilda. "Care to join me in a burning?"

Tilda took a share and together they threw the letter into the fire and watched it burn. As her mother's words turned to ashes, Genevieve took a cleansing breath.

"I didn't know that would be so pleasurable."

"So, her advice didn't help you?"

"Not this time." She felt the need to explain. "My mother taught me many things, and I would not be at Summerfield if it weren't for her. But I have been living under her wing and scrutiny far too long." It felt good to say it aloud.

"So it's time you jumped out of the nest?"

Genevieve liked that image, and drew in a deep breath to hold onto her courage. "I...yes. I think it is time I flew on my own. Very good, Tilda. Well said." She turned back to her desk, then paused. "Perhaps I will join you in that walk. I'm feeling the need for fresh air."

After the walk with Genevieve and the twins, Tilda decided she was due some alone-time before she and Beth had a reading lesson.

She quietly slipped from the corridor into her favorite room—the library. It was darkened by walnut paneling on all six sides, and smelled of leather, dust, and knowledge. She felt she was entering a cozy haven where the world couldn't touch her, where she could touch *other* worlds within the covers of the hundreds of books that lined the walls.

She perused the shelves for a new novel by her favorite author, Miss Thackeray. She happily chose *Bluebeard's Keys and Other Stories.* Actually she'd read her first Thackeray book—*Old Kensington*—back in Aldershot when she was thirteen. That year Papa had hired a governess. Miss Green was a delight. Tilda still remembered a line Miss Green often quoted from the Kensington book: "Happiness and sorrow overflow into other cups besides our own." How interesting that the quote was still valid.

Miss Green had taught Tilda the countries of the world using an atlas with colored pictures, taught her how to figure percentages, and ignited her joy of reading. One of her few possessions was a copy of *Old Kensington*—a gift from Miss Green. When she'd discovered more of Miss Thackeray's books in the Summerfield library Tilda had squealed loud enough that a footman had stepped into the room and asked after the noise.

Tilda adored Miss Green, who had been far different from any of the other women Papa had hired to watch after her. She was young and pretty, and didn't smell of snuff or brandy. Miss Green had shown Tilda how to arrange her hair in a pretty fashion, and had even taught her how to sew on buttons and add lace to a cuff or collar. They'd shared happy times talking about life, the world, and their dreams.

She was the mother Tilda never knew, and Tilda had loved her as she'd loved no one else. Even better, Miss Green had loved Tilda.

But then her governess had met a lieutenant she loved more. The saddest day in Tilda's life was not the death of her father, but watching Miss Green and her new husband ride away in a carriage.

Remembering the sadness now, she shook her head violently, forbidding the memory further entry.

Back to the books. As far as Tilda knew, she was the only one who read any of the books here. When she'd first met George he'd given her a copy of *The Merry Adventures of Robin Hood* which had spurred her to read the rest of that series. Yet she much preferred the love stories of Miss Thackeray, Jane Austen and Elizabeth Gaskell.

Now with George gone, Tilda had the library to herself. She felt a stab of regret and sadness, but as she chose a volume she let another emotion enter.

Joy.

She'd never been in a place that seemed so entirely hers, so entirely perfect. Except for that minute detail of true ownership, these were her books. These stories, art books, atlases, and tomes about the Crusades, English kings, and women in love were for her enjoyment.

"You're mine," she whispered.

The books did not argue with her.

"Read the verse again, Beth."

Beth held the Bible in her lap as Tilda looked on. Laboriously, she read the words, getting stuck on "laden."

"Ladden?"

"Laden. Only one 'd' means it's a long-a. Read the entire verse without stopping."

"'Come unto me, all ye that labour and are heavy laden, and I will give you rest.'" Beth blinked, then took a deep breath as if she'd finished a race. "I did it."

"You did it."

Beth stroked the page. "To think that I didn't even know my ABCs until you and Genevieve taught me."

One more accomplishment to make Tilda invaluable to the family.

"You're making good progress. And now you know your numbers too. Do you want to practice addition?"

"I think I'm ready for bigger numbers."

"Two-digits?"

"Is that the next step?"

"It is." Tilda took up a slate and began the lesson.

Clarissa stood in her bedroom, her hands on her torso. "Loosen it, Dottie. I didn't notice before, but you've laced it too tight."

"Sorry, Miss Weston."

Dottie unbuttoned the back of Clarissa's dress and helped Clarissa pull her arms free. Clarissa stepped out of the dress, then waited while Dottie untied the bustle, unhooked the petticoats, and finally allowed access to the corset-laces.

Beth sat at the dressing table nearby, playing with her mother's jewelry. "That is a lot of bother to fix a few tight laces," she said.

"If I can't breathe during dinner tonight I might faint. And wouldn't that be a nice bit of gossip for Lila to spread through the village."

Dottie yanked on the laces to loosen them. "Is this better, miss?"

Clarissa breathed in and out, in and out. "Better. Tie it up. But since we're this far undone, I think I'd rather wear the blue shantung."

As Dottie fetched the dress, Clarissa shooed Beth off the bench, sat, and began to change her jewelry to match the blue dress.

"Your hair is coming down in back," Beth said.

"Fix it, please."

Beth gathered a few hairpins and got to it. "You don't seem excited about going to dinner at Crompton Hall."

"Why should I be?"

"You seem...irritated."

"About what?"

"I assume the usual."

Clarissa sighed, hating that there was a 'usual' peeve about Lila and Joseph. "I wish they didn't bother me so."

"Not they," Beth corrected. "Her."

Clarissa fingered her earrings, not wanting to meet her reflection — or Beth's — in the mirror. "Lila is just so...so..."

"Happy?"

Clarissa snickered. "That *is* the gist of it."

"How dare she?"

"Exactly."

"But that's not all there is." Beth squeezed her shoulder, making Clarissa look up.

"You're too savvy for your age."

"Living on the streets of London taught me how to read people. Reading their intentions wrong could get a body hurt."

Dottie came out of Clarissa's wardrobe closet with the blue dinner dress draped over her arm.

Clarissa didn't want the maid to overhear any more than she already had. "Would you fetch me a cup of tea, Dottie?" She looked to Beth. "Would you like a cup?"

"None for me," Beth said.

Dottie lay the dress on the bed and left.

As soon as she was gone, Beth asked, "I'm glad Mrs. Kidd has Etta to make her so happy. Aren't you?"

"Yes, yes. She has Etta and I have you. In that, we're even."

"So it's a competition?"

Clarissa was shocked. "Of course it's a competition."

"But if it isn't a matter of her having a husband and a child, then what upsets you about her?"

Let me count the ways. "She's gone from shopkeeper's daughter to the wife of Joseph, Lord Newley's heir."

"That happened three years ago."

"Yes."

"As her father rose up...are you still upset your parents were demoted? And you?"

"That *was* a bother, but it's not anymore. Not really."

"So what is it?"

Clarissa was ashamed at her pettiness, yet couldn't pretend it didn't exist. "It's quite simple, really. Lila has taken over Genevieve."

When Beth didn't respond, Clarissa explained. "Watch them when they're together, acting like they're the jammiest bits of jam in the pot."

"You're jealous."

"You asked to know, so yes. I'm jealous. First I have Tilda barge into this house and worm her way into my mother's affections, then Genevieve marries Morgan and becomes the family darling, and now Lila inserts herself as Genevieve's best friend."

"They have babies in common."

"It's all very logical, but it annoys me that my family is no longer my own." Clarissa heard the clock on the mantel strike the hour. "That's enough of a discussion of my failings and flaws. Help me get dressed."

Lila sat at her dressing table, letting her maid finish her hair.

Although Lila had been anxious about the first dinner in Lady Silvey's honor — Sylvia's honor — after spending the afternoon with her, all worries were erased. Sylvia was a complex combination of a world-traveler, the belle of any ball, and the elder sister Lila never had. Lila was eager to know every facet of her delightful personality.

"There, Mrs. Kidd." Fanny held up a hand-mirror so Lila could check the back upsweep.

"Very nice. Now I must check the dining room."

Fanny collected the hair things. "I do like Lady Silvey's maid. She's traveled all over Europe and has seen so many amazing sites."

Lila felt a wave of regret. "I'm sorry Mr. Kidd and I aren't the traveling sort." *We even stayed at home for our honeymoon.*

Fanny shook her head vehemently. "Oh, no, ma'am. I'm not complaining, just mentioning."

Lila set aside the issue and went downstairs.

The dining room was resplendent with the pristine white Caldron china with the gold rim and gleaming Waterford crystal. There had been more elaborate settings to choose from, but after much thought Lila had decided to go with something classic rather than overly ornate and fussy.

She adjusted a yellow aster that was hanging too low in the centerpiece.

"The essence of autumn."

Sylvia stood in the doorway of the dining room. Her gown was a gold Dupioni silk with fringed edging. It was suitable for an audience with Queen Victoria. Lila felt horribly underdressed in her Melrose linen with a bit of lace at the neckline, and immediately began second-guessing her choice of china. What had she been thinking? Sylvia had traveled the world. She would be used to the highest standard of entertaining.

Sylvia stepped forward, circling her closed fan near Lila's eyes. "There will be none of that."

Lila was caught off guard. "What are you talking about?"

"Doubt. Self-judgment." She held her wrists towards Lila. "Help me unclasp these bracelets."

Lila did as she was told, and Sylvia set the jewelry on the edge of the buffet. She removed her long gloves and a massive necklace of diamonds and emeralds. As Lila watched, Sylvia opened a drawer of the buffet and deposited her jewelry and gloves.

"There," she said. "That's better."

"You looked lovely. You look lovely, but—"

"I looked utterly over-dressed." She leaned close, lowering her voice. "I'm afraid I was trying to impress. A bad habit, but one that is often necessary in the dining rooms of the Continent." She stroked her forearms. "I do prefer a little less than too much. I apologize for the misstep, my dear."

It had all happened so fast, Lila was at a loss. "You didn't have to do that. You looked stunning."

"Thank you for the compliment. Unfortunately, once a woman is of a certain age, the need for compliments far out-measures the reality."

Lila was touched. "I have never met anyone like you, Sylvia."

"I'll take *that* as a compliment."

"It was meant as such."

They stood by the table, studying it. Finally, Sylvia said, "We're expecting nine? Perhaps you'd list the guests for me? I'm horrible with names."

Lila led her across the foyer into the drawing room where they shared the settee. "My father, Jack Weston will be coming."

"The earl. Your father is no longer married?"

"He is not." Lila stifled a sudden thought: *And neither are you.*

"What of his wife, you mother?"

"She died three years ago."

Sylvia nodded. "I'm so sorry. Continue your list."

"My cousin Clarissa is coming with her adopted daughter, Beth."

"I sense the absence of a husband?"

"There never was one, I'm afraid." She paused a moment, wishing to be kind. "Clarissa spent some time in London where she performed on the stage."

"Oh. An actress?"

There was disdain in her voice, but Lila chose to ignore it. "When she came home, she brought along a little orphan girl. Beth is a darling, and I admire Clarissa for taking her in."

"What does the family think of the arrangement?"

Lila felt her defenses rise. "We approve." *It's the only unselfish thing Clarissa has ever done.*

Sylvia put a hand on her arm. "Then I approve too. Continue your list."

"My nana is coming, Mary Hayward is her name."

"I do enjoy nanas… you are close?"

"Very. She runs the mercantile. I miss not being there with her."

"Ah. That's right. You and your father used to be shopkeepers."

"And my brother, Morgan—who will be here too, along with his wife and my dear friend, Genevieve." She straightened a knife. "Dinners like this are a far cry from the simple family dinners we had in our quarters behind the shop."

"Who is coming that is not family?"

Lila thought over the list. "I suppose technically, the only non-family member is Tilda, the Weston's ward."

"Ward?"

"Tilda is the orphaned goddaughter of the dowager's husband."

Sylvia looked in the air a moment, following the connection. "How kind of them to take her in."

"That is their way. My Aunt Ruth was especially kind to her."

"Is Ruth coming?"

"No. Unfortunately, the dowager and her husband recently left for a visit to India, taking Ruth, her husband, and their son with them."

"My, my," Sylvia said. "They virtually cleared out the place, leaving poor Tilda. The girl must feel practically abandoned."

Lila had never thought of that. "I'm sure my brother and Genevieve are making her feel at home. Genevieve is American."

"Have they been married long?"

"A year. They have twins."

"What a joy. Do you suppose we British will ever let her lose the 'American' label?"

Lila laughed. "Perhaps when she has grandchildren."

"I wouldn't count on it." Sylvia touched her ring finger — which was empty because of the gloves.

"I'm sorry I never met your husband. I'm sure you miss him horribly."

"Yes. And no. Our relationship was complicated."

Lila cocked her head. "Your honesty is refreshing."

Sylvia shrugged. "Dishonesty and hedging the truth are too much work. I realize some may take offense, but I've determined that I don't require the friendship of those who do."

Since Lila was curious, and since they were alone... "Tell me about him. About the two of you."

She clasped her hands in her lap. "We were in love. And then we weren't."

"Oh."

"It wasn't as disappointing as it sounds. We had many good years, some lesser years, and some years where apathy reigned." Sylvia raised a finger to make a point. "But we never hated each other. I thank God for that."

Lila hesitated, then shared her thought. "It makes me sad to hear such a thing."

Sylvia touched her hand. "Oh don't be sad, Lila. As I said, we had many good years. One learns to adapt to the hand one is played. But honestly, I am happier as a widow than I ever was as a wife."

"That sounds utterly tragic." Lila froze, immediately regretting her words. "I apologize for my rudeness."

Sylvia squeezed her hand. "Never apologize to me, Lila. I want us to be bosom friends. And with that bond comes honesty and no minced words. Life is too short. Agreed?"

Lila wasn't sure what to think. She'd never had a full confidante.

"You weren't close to your mother, were you?" Sylvia asked.

Lila laughed. "You are far too good at reading me."

"And?"

"No, we weren't close."

"Why not?"

"I was a disappointment to her."

Sylvia gasped. "I don't believe you. You are a charming woman, with a beautiful family."

"Mother died before father discovered he was the rightful Earl of Summerfield. Before Joseph and I married."

Sylvia pondered this a moment. "She would have been the Countess of Summerfield."

"She would have embraced the title and brandished its authority freely and often. She also would have held it against Ruth. Mother felt no friendship towards Ruth."

"Why?"

"It was an old grievance involving young love. Before my father rose up, Frederick and Ruth were the earl and countess. So if Mother had lived to take the title…"

"Ruth would have suffered more than she actually did."

"Mother would have made sure of it."

Sylvia nodded. "Sometimes death prevents more heartache than it creates."

Lila had never thought of it like that, but she was right. "Sometimes I wish Mother knew about Joseph and Etta." Her thoughts clouded. "Yet she'd probably still find me at fault in some way."

Sylvia put an arm around her shoulders. "You can't make a sour pickle sweet."

Lila laughed. "*You* are sweet. I'm so glad you're here."

They heard carriages, exchanged a glance, and stood as one. "I'll tell you the secret of a successful hostess, Lila."

"Please."

"Take a deep breath, pinch your cheeks, and blame any faux pas on the weather."

"What?"

"Never mind, dear. All will be well."

Tilda was proud of herself for knowing which fork and knife to use, but was glad Beth faltered a bit, picking up her meat knife to butter her bread. It was rewarding to know more than someone else—even if that someone was just Beth.

Tilda had dined at Crompton Hall a few times, but never with anyone near as entertaining as Lady Silvey. The woman shared story after story about her travels in Europe, and thought nothing about telling the story of the time when an entire plate of oysters on the half-shell ended up in her lap.

Also entertaining, was witnessing her special interest in the earl—which was returned. The only flirting Tilda had seen was the not-so-innocent kind between soldiers and women in the pubs in Aldershot. But the flirting tonight…it would be nice if the earl found a wife.

Tilda didn't participate in the conversation too much, afraid she'd say something dim or daft. But she did enjoy watching the grown-ups interact.

It was very clear that all the Summerfield ladies liked Lady Silvey immensely. Apparently, her ladyship had seen Clarissa when she was on the stage in some play.

"I cannot believe you were one of the 'rapturous maidens,'" Lady Silvey said. "The flowing costumes were very Grecian."

"And very comfortable."

Lady Silvey put a hand to her ribs. "Oh, to be free of constraints."

"I agree with you," Genevieve said. "I do believe women's fashion is designed by men, for no woman would choose corsets."

"They are far too tortuous," Lila said.

"Now, now," the earl said. "I hardly think this is proper dinner table talk."

Morgan laughed. "Perhaps you ladies should come up with alternatives to your torture. We could sell them in the mercantile."

"And scandalize the county," Genevieve said.

"The county would probably love a good scandal," Lady Silvey said.

The earl shook his head. "We've already given them a fair share."

Tilda looked at her plate. Was he referring to *her* and the terrible blackmail by her chaperones last year? Or her trying to gain George's affection? Or her borrowing Clarissa's clothes and looking through her jewels? Or the time Tilda had been caught by a maid as she took one of the necklaces back to her room, which led to Tilda stuffing the necklace under the maid's bed, which had cost the servant her job...

Tilda's list of sins and missteps was long.

Luckily, Clarissa returned to the subject of the theatre. She beamed when she spoke of it, even though Tilda had heard that things hadn't been easy for her. "In the play, I should have performed the lead role—Patience—but was never given the chance."

"Our loss," Lady Silvey said.

"Joseph and I saw the play too," Lila said.

46

Joseph cut his carrots. "If I remember correctly you were performing under the name Clara West."

"I was." She smiled a mischievous smile. "I was living incognito."

"What does that mean?" Beth asked.

"I was pretending to be someone else."

"How adventurous," Lady Silvey said.

"Yes. But also very difficult." Clarissa smiled at Beth. "Difficult or not, I was glad for the experience, for the highlight of my time in London was gaining a daughter."

"Lila told me. How commendable." For the first time, Lady Silvey addressed Tilda. "And you are the goddaughter of...?"

"Colonel Grady," Tilda said. She cleared her throat. "He and my father served together in Her Majesties', and when Papa died, I came here." She looked at Clarissa, then away. "The elder Mrs. Weston was like a mother to me."

The earl winked at her. "You are a welcome addition to our family, Tilda."

"Hmm," Clarissa said.

Tilda drew in a breath, glad Clarissa didn't say more. She didn't need to.

As soon as the carriages were through the gates of Crompton Hall Genevieve said, "You were rude, Clarissa. You should apologize to Tilda as soon as we get home."

"Whatever for?"

"The 'hmm.'"

"The what?"

"You know very well what you meant by your comment—small though it was. You hurt her feelings."

"*If* she has any."

"Clarissa!" Morgan's voice caused her to jump. "We don't understand why you hold this grudge against the girl. She's been with us a year. She's part of the family."

"Not my family."

Beth's voice was small. "You did hurt her, Mum. That's why she went home in the other carriage with Uncle Jack."

"See?" Genevieve said. "This vendetta against her must stop."

"Gracious. Can't a person make an offhand noise without people —?"

Morgan reached across the space between them and grabbed her hand — and none too gently. "'Ye who is without sin cast the first stone.'"

"Meaning?"

"Perhaps we shouldn't have welcomed *you* back from London and all the lies you told during your time away."

Clarissa felt a stitch in her stomach. "I would have survived."

Morgan tossed her hand into her lap. "You act like a child, Cousin."

"I'm as old as you."

"Then act like it. If your mother and father were here, they would scold you mightily for being petulant and unwilling to share your family with a girl in need."

Clarissa noticed Beth cowering in the corner. This conversation was going too far, venturing into wounds that Clarissa wished to remain closed. She smiled at her daughter, who returned a tentative smile of her own. For Beth's sake she would apologize.

"I'm sorry for hurting Tilda. I'll try to be better."

"You need to tell her that," Genevieve said.

Now *that* was going too far. "She'll be fine."

"Yes, she will," Morgan said. "As soon as you say you're sorry."

They rode the rest of the way in silence. The thought of apologizing to Tilda irked Clarissa far more than it should have. She knew her feelings against the girl were overblown, and realized her grudge was petty. The truth — as illogical as it was — was that Clarissa just didn't like Tilda. If nothing else, this evening proved she needed to do a better job of hiding it.

When they reached the Manor and left the carriage, Clarissa was scorched by the searing eyes of Morgan and Genevieve. *Yes, yes, all right already.* She caught up with Tilda as the girl entered the house.

"Tilda?"

Tilda turned around and Clarissa was shocked to spot a glimmer of pain and apprehension in her eyes. "Yes?"

"I...I apologize for hurting your feelings at dinner."

Tilda's eyes brightened.

Clarissa was going to call that enough, but Genevieve's nod hinted she had to say more.

"You *are* welcome here."

"Thank you." Tilda rushed forward and gave Clarissa a peck on the cheek before running inside.

"See? That wasn't so hard, was it?" Genevieve said.

Clarissa strode past her. "I suppose not."

But as she headed upstairs Clarissa felt the burden of knowing she'd lied.

Tilda burst into her bedroom, shut the door, and leaned against it. *She apologized! She said I belong in the family!*

She heard some voices in the hallway, and put her ear to the door. Maybe they'd say other nice things about her.

She heard Genevieve and Clarissa.

"Don't press me, Genevieve," Clarissa said. "I apologized. That's the extent of my largesse."

What's 'largesse?'

"It wouldn't have to be. She's a nice girl. We're all the family she has."

"Mmm."

"Stop it, Clarissa."

Their voices trailed off.

Tilda sank to the floor. So much for family.

Lila knocked gently on the door to Sylvia's room. When her maid opened the door, Lila feared she'd caught Sylvia already in bed. "I apologize for the late hour, but I thought Lady Silvey should have her jewels—"

Sylvia appeared in the doorway, dressed in a lace-trimmed dressing gown. "Ah. I nearly forgot about those."

"I didn't want Dowd or one of the footmen to find them and imagine all kinds of intrigue."

Sylvia let the maid take the jewelry and the gloves.

"Again, thank you for helping me carry out the dinner. As the guest of honor you went above and beyond."

"You're welcome. Just know that the dinner was a success. I very much like the Westons."

"I feel I must apologize for Clarissa's attitude towards Tilda."

"No love lost there."

"From Clarissa's end. I find the girl quite charming. She's ever so good with the twins, and Etta when we visit."

"Then I commend her and will ignore Clarissa's ungracious 'hmm.'"

They said their goodnights. For it had been that. A very good night.

Chapter Three

Lila's eyes shot open. It took her a moment to transition from sleep to awake.

A thunderclap made the house vibrate and the crystals on the wall sconces titter. Rain pelted the window panes like fingernails tapping against the glass.

She liked rain storms, but missed being on the top floor where she could hear the rain on the roof. Back in her family's living quarters above the mercantile, she'd often cuddled with a pillow when a storm came through, letting its music lull her back to sleep.

She would try that again. But first she reached out and touched Joseph's back. He slept through everything. It was just as —

A scream!

Lila bolted upright.

Another scream!

She shook Joseph to wakefulness. "Joseph! Wake up! Someone is screaming!"

Joseph raised himself up on his arms and wiped the sleep from his eyes. "What?"

"Screams!"

They heard people running on the floor above them.

They jumped out of bed. Joseph pulled on a pair of pants as Lila grabbed her dressing gown.

There was a frantic knocking on their door. "Sir! Ma'am! There's a fire!"

They ran into the hallway and Dowd pointed towards the back stairs. "Lightning hit the roof. I felt it."

Lila's immediate thought was for Henrietta in the nursery — which was on the floor above. "Where is Etta and Nanny?"

Dowd's face turned white. "I've been getting the servants out and...I don't know."

Joseph raced past him with Lila close behind. At the top of the back stairs was a hallway leading to the servants' bedrooms, and to the left, the nursery. Lila heard the crackling of flames in the ceiling overhead. She smelled smoke and could feel the heat.

Joseph ran towards the nursery door, put a hand to it for but a moment, and opened it. Smoke billowed out like a black monster trying to grab them.

"Etta!" Lila yelled from the very core of her being.

"Stay here!" Joseph put the sleeve of his nightshirt over his nose and went inside.

But Lila couldn't stay there. She hurried to the doorway and saw him move towards the crib. She could see the form of Nanny there, getting Etta. "Go!" he told the woman. "I'll get her."

Coughing, Nanny stumbled towards the door. Lila reached inside the room to guide her out.

But steps away from the door a beam fell upon Nanny, knocking her down.

Lila ran to her, but Joseph rushed towards Lila, carrying Etta. He pushed the baby into her arms. "Take her! I'll help Nanny!"

Lila retreated to the hallway. Etta's eyes were open. She coughed and cried. She was alive!

Sylvia appeared at her side, pulling Lila down the corridor. "Come away."

"No!" Lila said. She couldn't leave Joseph and Nanny. "Take her!"

There was no time for Sylvia to protest. She took Etta to safety as Lila returned to the room.

But then there was another awful rumbling and cracking. Lila looked up.

"Joseph!"

Another fiery rafter fell.

Joseph was flattened next to Nanny. But unlike Nanny he was still moving. He batted at the flames consuming the rafter as he tried to push himself free.

Lila rushed into the room.

"No!" Joseph yelled. "Get back."

Lord, save them!

"Help!" Lila screamed. "Please come help!"

Ian and Dowd reached the landing and rushed towards the nursery.

In concert, they shoved the rafter off Joseph with their feet. Then they dragged him out of the room, not stopping until they reached the stairs where footmen carried him down, one holding him under the arms, the other holding his legs. Lila could see he was burned on his hands. Did he have broken bones? How could he not?

Ian called after then, "Take him outside!"

But it wasn't over. "Nanny's still in there!" Lila screamed, pointing to the nursery.

The two men returned to the room. The smoke in the hallway stung Lila's eyes and made her cough.

"Go on!" Ian said, looking back at her. "See to Joseph."

Lila nodded and ran down the stairs to find him. She coughed violently, her lungs trying desperately to repel the deadly smoke.

She got outside just as they were placing Joseph on the sopping grass under a huge tree. The rain pelted Lila as she ran to him. It was a welcome relief from the heat and smoke.

Lila fell to his side, her eyes locked on her husband. She called to the men. "Dr. Peter? Has anyone gone for Dr. Peter?"

Mrs. Crank hurried forward. "I did, Mrs. Kidd. I sent Billy on a horse to fetch him."

Lila removed her dressing gown and wadded it up as a pillow beneath her husband's head. She used the sleeve of her night dress to wipe the wet soot from his face. "Darling. Please, Joseph. Wake up."

She was aware that the full household of Crompton Hall was outside, huddled together, watching the red flames consume the roof.

The house was of little consequence compared to Joseph. She couldn't tell if anything was broken, but his hands were red and raw with burns. She had no idea how to care for them. *Father, thank you for getting him out, now help —*

Getting *him* out. Where was Etta?

Frantically, Lila looked around, and thankfully spotted Sylvia holding the baby nearby, shielding her with a blanket, bouncing up and down, soothing her. That meant Etta was all right.

But Nanny?

Lila scanned the front of the house twice before she saw Ian and Dowd carrying Nanny out the door. "What a relief."

They lay Nanny on the ground and other servants knelt beside her.

Suddenly, a high-pitched wail pierced the chaos. Then another.

The wails could only mean one thing.

No! Nanny can't be dead!

Ian came towards her, his chest heaving. His distraught face confirmed her fear. "She's gone, Lila. She never regained consciousness."

"She was trying to save Etta."

"Is the baby all right?"

"Sylvia has her."

Ian rubbed his face roughly. "I can't believe this is happening. Nanny…she was loyal to the end." Then he knelt beside Lila and put a hand on her shoulder. "How is my boy?"

"He hasn't opened his eyes. And his hands…" She gestured towards them, but didn't dare touch their rawness. "I pray Dr. Peter gets here soon." She glanced at Ian. "Please sit with him. I'll be right back."

He nodded and removed his coat, handing it to her. Only then did Lila realize she was in her nightdress and it was plastered to her body by the rain. She donned the coat and left father to comfort his son.

She ran to Etta and took the baby in her arms, holding her close, finding comfort and giving it. "Oh, my dear girl. Thank God you're all right."

Etta began to cry and Lila did her best to soothe her, cupping her hand over her daughter's face, protecting her from the rain. "There, there. It's all right now. You're safe."

Sylvia touched Etta's head. "She's fine. No burns. But Nanny…" She nodded over her shoulder.

There was a group of women around Nanny's body, crying and consoling each other. Yet what consolation was there? A good woman was dead.

They heard horses. Dr. Peter dismounted before his horse came to a stop. Lila thrust her daughter into Sylvia's care once again, and pointed towards Joseph. "Over there."

Dr. Peter ran faster than Lila, kneeling at Joseph's side. He put an ear to Joseph's chest. "He's breathing. His heart is beating."

Thank you, dear Lord!

Peter delicately examined Joseph's hands. Then he checked his limbs and felt his ribs. "There doesn't seem to be anything broken."

Lila was shocked by the news. "A beam fell on him."

Peter nodded. "He needs to have his burns looked at— inside somewhere."

Ian had already thought of this and pointed to a wagon coming close. "We can transport him to the stables, to the coachman's quarters."

They carefully lifted Joseph into the back of the wagon. Peter and Ian jumped in, and Ian pulled Lila up to join them.

"Etta!" Lila held out her arms, desperately needing her daughter to go with them.

Sylvia ran forward and handed over the baby. "My prayers are with you."

Lila nodded her thanks as Peter removed his cloak. They each took a corner, creating a tent, protecting Joseph and Etta from the driving rain.

Only when they were underway, did Lila look back at the fire and the destruction of their home. The flames were nearly quenched by the rain, but smoke hung in the air and she could see the charred destruction of the roof and upper floor.

"Blessed rain," Ian said.

Lila nodded, but needed God to grant one more blessing.

Genevieve awoke to a pounding on their bedroom door.

Morgan sat upright in bed. "Yes?"

Dixon came in, wearing a robe. "Pardon, but a rider has just arrived from Crompton Hall. It's been hit by lightning. It's on fire."

Morgan sprang out of bed. "You alerted my father?"

"He told me to gather the male servants to assist."

"I'm coming." Morgan got dressed.

Genevieve readied his boots. "What can I do?"

He put a palm to his forehead. "Pray."

"Of course. I will." She kissed him goodbye and immediately fell to her knees to pray for safety.

But then she thought of other things to do. She rang the bell for her maid, and began to get dressed.

Lila sat beside her husband, who was safely tucked into the coachman's bed. His hands were bound with bandages, making him look like he was wearing boxing gloves. He had not regained consciousness. She bowed her head and prayed more fervently than she had ever prayed.

She glanced at the folded blanket that had been placed on the floor in the corner, where Etta lay sleeping. Her family was together. And safe. *Thank you, Father.*

Lila heard voices in the next room, but they were of no concern. Others could handle whatever came next. Her place was by Joseph's side.

There was a soft knock on the door and Ian entered. Lila put a finger to her lips and nodded towards Etta.

With a nod he asked, "Has he awakened?"

"No." She felt compelled to ask after the others. "Were there other injuries—besides Nanny?"

"None. We were lucky."

Nanny wasn't so lucky.

"The fire is out," he said. "We'll assess the full damage in the morning. It looks bad, but doesn't seem to be a total loss."

"The total loss is Nanny's," she said.

"I know. It's a tragedy."

Genevieve appeared in the doorway. "Lila." She gazed upon Joseph. "I'm so sorry."

Then she heard her brother's voice. "Morgan's here?"

Genevieve nodded. "He's been here with Jack and the others, helping with the fire. I've come to take you to Summerfield. Most of the staff too, though a few have offered to stay at the Hall and watch over things."

The logistics of the crisis fell upon Lila's weary mind. The rooms for the servants were gone. They needed housing and care. "Thank you for thinking when I could not."

Sylvia appeared behind Genevieve, wearing a blanket around her shoulders. "I'll get the baby." She gently retrieved the sleeping Etta.

Genevieve helped Lila to stand. "We've got you. Don't worry about a thing."

Easier said than done.

Tilda and Beth peered over the stair railing to the foyer of Summerfield Manor which was abuzz with their new guests. Genevieve came in first, supporting Mrs. Kidd who was in her nightdress, wearing a man's coat.

"She looks done in," Tilda said.

Then Mr. Kidd was brought in, carried by Morgan, Lord Newley, and two servants.

The housekeeper rushed past the girls. "Bring him up here. We have a room ready."

With difficulty the men carried Mr. Kidd up the winding stairs. He didn't open his eyes, and his hands were bandaged. They took him to a room at the end of the hallway.

Genevieve and Mrs. Kidd reached the top of the stairs. "Beth, go tell your mother we need—"

Clarissa came towards them. "What do you need?"

"Lila needs a change of clothes, and a fire in her room— the room next to Joseph's."

The way she phrased it—a fire in her room—seemed badly worded.

They all turned towards the foyer when they heard a baby whimpering.

Lady Silvey was carrying Etta. Most of the woman's hair was tucked in a nightcap that tilted precariously, with damp locks hanging forlornly to her shoulders Beneath a blanket she wore what *was* a white dressing gown, now stained with soot and mud.

Tilda ran down the stairs, "I'll take Etta." She took the baby in her arms and brought her upstairs.

Genevieve returned from Lila's room, kissed the baby's head, then helped Lady Silvey up the last few stairs. "We have a room ready for you, Sylvia."

Mrs. Camden stood nearby, a robe over her nightgown, writing on a paper. Beth went to her.

"Mrs. Camden?"

"Yes, Beth?"

"I'll double up with my mum if you need an extra room."

The housekeeper touched Beth's cheek. "That would be nice of you, Beth. We need every bedroom we can get."

I should have offered. Tilda was just about to do so when Genevieve told her to take Etta up to the nursery.

A chance missed. And yet...

She kissed the baby on the forehead. "Don't worry about anything, Etta. Tilda is here."

"You needn't of given up your room, Beth," Clarissa said. "Not that I mind your company, but you deserve to keep your room." She looked towards the hallway beyond her bedroom door. "This endless procession of unexpected guests is distressing."

"Their distress is larger than ours, Mum. They just lost everything."

"But all these strangers…it's disturbing just the same."

Clarissa pulled the covers back on the bed they would have to share. There were five pillows — plenty for both of them — yet Clarissa liked to make herself a moat. Would a four-pillow moat be comfy enough?

"I can sleep on the settee," Beth said.

"Don't be ridiculous. Climb in."

A three-pillow moat was created.

Lila stood in her assigned room and stared at the bed. She wanted to sleep, needed to sleep, needed to be comforted. She wanted to snuggle against Joseph, with his arm holding her safe, his heart beating strongly in her ear.

But Joseph couldn't snuggle anyone. And Lila couldn't be comforted.

But Etta could.

Lila slipped out of her room, hearing voices down the hallway as the servants of Crompton Hall were settled into their respective lodgings. She hurried away from their voices and went to the nursery. She put her ear against the door, listening for her baby's cry.

All was silent.

I should leave.

Not yet. She couldn't leave until she saw with her own eyes that Etta was well. She quietly opened the door and peered in. The twins were in their cribs, the moonlight revealing their peace, as well as signaling that the storm outside had passed.

Where was Etta?

Lila heard a familiar whimper and looked for the source. There, on the floor near the window was her daughter, lying on a makeshift bed of quilts and coverlets padding the floor. And there beside her was Tilda, sleeping on her side, a protective hand assuring Etta she was safe and loved.

Lila closed the door, thanking God for people who cared. She returned to her bedroom. It was her turn to sleep.

She stared at the nightdress Clarissa had draped on the bed. Everyone had offered to help her undress, or bathe, but Lila had sent Fanny to get settled into her own room, and had also sent Genevieve away.

Prematurely.

For now, having seen Etta was safe, she found she couldn't move. The act of taking off what she had on and donning clean clothes seemed as insurmountable as being asked to run up and down the staircase a dozen times.

Yet everything *was* under control. Etta was in Tilda's care, Ian and Sylvia were probably asleep in their appointed rooms. And even Joseph was being cared for by Dr. Peter who had offered to sit with him through the rest of the shortened night.

Her thoughts turned to Nanny. Dear, sweet, joyous Nanny Mabel, who'd kept such good care of Etta from her birth to this very night. Nanny had died trying to save the baby she loved.

As Joseph almost died.

Lila shivered, then shook her head violently. She looked down at her soot-encrusted nightdress and the dried mud on her feet.

Memories flashed. The fire. The smoke. The chaos and screaming. Nanny at the crib. Joseph thrusting Etta into her arms as a beam fell on Nanny, and then on him. Nanny's body in the grass. And the wailing, the awful wailing...

Lila slipped to the floor and curled on her side, letting the dreadful reality take her captive.

Chapter Four

"Mrs. Kidd!"

Lila opened her eyes to find Fanny kneeling on the floor beside her.

Kneeling on the floor?

Lila tried to sit up but her muscles argued against the movement. Fanny helped her to stand.

"Why were you sleeping on the floor, ma'am?"

Memories of last night assailed her: screams, smoke, fire, Nanny and—

"Joseph! I need to see Joseph!"

With a gentle but firm hand, Fanny steadied her and prevented her from leaving the room. "Dr. Peter is with him, ma'am. I think it would be best if you got dressed first."

Lila realized she was still wearing her muddied nightdress. She glanced at the bed and spotted the clean gown Clarissa had brought for her to wear. She felt Fanny needed some explanation. "I didn't have the energy to change."

"I'm so sorry, ma'am. I knew I should have stayed with you."

"It's not your fault. I sent you away." She pressed a hand to her forehead, forcing herself to fully be in the moment and think logically. "Help me get dressed so I can see my husband."

Clarissa sat at her dressing table, waiting for her maid to finish her hair. The girl seemed distracted.

"If your work is boring you, Dottie, you may go elsewhere."

"No, of course not, Miss Weston. I'm sorry. It's just —"

"Just what?" Clarissa turned around on the bench. "What's going on?" Dottie's best quality was her willingness to tell Clarissa Manor gossip.

Dottie bit her lip, making her look younger than her eighteen years. "There's just so much commotion with the extra people here."

"No one likes it."

"I'm not complaining. I think it's nice your family took everyone in."

"Ah yes. We Westons are a dependable lot." *To a fault.*

Dottie made a turn-around motion with her hand and Clarissa faced the mirror again, letting Dottie finish her hair. "I do feel dreadful about Mr. Kidd's burns."

"How is he?"

"I don't know, miss. But Dr. Peter stayed the night with him. Actually, it's Mrs. Kidd who causes the most worry."

Lila? "Why is that?"

She glanced towards the door, a sign she was going to share some sensitive information. "This morning Mrs. Kidd's maid found her sleeping on the floor of her room, still wearing the filthy nightdress she had on when they brought her here."

"But I brought her a fresh one. I laid it on her bed."

"Apparently it was still there when Fanny found her. Everyone's feeling real sorry for her."

Clarissa scoffed. *As intended, I'm sure.*

"Miss?"

"Are you finished with my hair?"

Dottie set the brush down. "I am. If you need me I'll be helping Miss Tilda get dressed."

Having to share her maid was another sore subject.

How ironic that Clarissa only disliked two women in the entire world and now both were living at the Manor.

God certainly knew how to annoy her.

Lila rapped gently on the door to the bedroom where they'd brought Joseph. As she entered she was stunned to see him sitting up in bed with Dr. Peter and his wife Molly at his side.

She ran to him. "You're awake!"

"I am," he said, though his voice was hoarse.

"His vocal cords are scorched from the smoke and heat." The doctor pointed a finger at Joseph. "And he has been told to whisper — and that a very little — until they heal."

Joseph nodded. Then he held up his bandaged hands. "Freshly mummified."

Lila turned to the doctor. "How is he doing?"

"Besides the burns he has a very bruised shoulder from the beam falling on him. But he will recover."

"I will come every day and change the dressing," Molly said.

"I'd appreciate that," Lila said.

Lila wanted to take his hands in hers and kiss them, but dared not. "Thank God you are all right."

"Etta?" Joseph whispered.

"She is fine. Tilda has set herself up as Etta's own personal nanny since…"

"I told him about Nanny Mabel," Dr. Peter said.

"I tried to save her," Joseph whispered.

"Yes, you did. You were very brave."

Joseph's valet arrived, carrying the clothes he'd been wearing. They looked freshly cleaned.

"You're not getting dressed," Lila said. "Surely you need to stay in bed."

"The house," Joseph whispered. "Have to see."

Lila looked to the doctor, wanting an ally. "Doesn't he need to rest?"

"He does. If he wishes to get dressed and go downstairs, I will allow that, but I will not allow you to ride to Crompton Hall."

"Damage…"

"I know there's damage," Dr. Peter said. "But the other men can deal with it for a few days."

Joseph began to cough.

"See, dearest?" Lila helped him take a drink of water. "Your lungs are rebelling because you inhaled so much smoke. We need you well. The house will wait."

He nodded, then pointed at her. "You go."

She put a hand to her chest. "Me?"

He nodded. "Be my eyes."

"Yes, of course. I will accompany the men. I don't want you to worry about anything." *I will do the worrying for both of us.*

Lila saw Peter and Molly out, then returned to his side.

He held up his hands. "Can't do much."

"I know it's frustrating right now. But let me be your hands."

He put a bandaged hand over his heart. "You are my heart."

She held back tears. "As you are mine. You are alive. Etta is alive. We have much to be thankful for."

He nodded and looked upward. "Thank God."

"Every minute of every day."

Papa put a hand on Lila's knee as the carriage took them to Crompton Hall. "I must admit, I was surprised you wanted to go with us."

"Joseph asked me to." She couldn't tell if he approved or disapproved. "I won't be in the way."

"I didn't mean that."

On the opposite seat her father-in-law adjusted the cuff of his shirt under his coat. "We men *can* handle it, my dear."

Morgan laughed. "Don't try to fight her, Newley. When my sister is determined to do something, it's best to stay out of her way."

She was glad for his support. "Joseph wants me to be his eyes and ears."

"As if I can't be?" his father asked. But then he raised a hand. "Forgive my testiness. I'm not arguing. You and Joseph are two halves to a whole. And it's your home too, Lila."

Lila enjoyed a surge of pride. It was wonderful to be included in this bastion of male capability. She had no idea what they would find at Crompton Hall, yet knew that somehow, some way, all would be handled — and she would be a part of it.

The discussion ended as they turned into the drive and had their first look at the damage. The roof over half of Crompton Hall was blackened or missing, exposing the bedroom floor. A few chimneys were missing entirely or had taken on grotesque shapes. The floor with the servants' rooms and the attic were gone. The nursery was a wall-less shell.

"It's a miracle anyone made it out alive," she said. Her thoughts returned to dear Nanny Mabel. Her jolly nature and loving care of Etta would be sorely missed. "I should make arrangements for Mabel's funeral."

"I spoke with Pastor Lyons last night. It will be in two days' time."

"Thank you for doing that," Lila said.

With a nod Ian turned his attention to the Hall. He pointed. "The entrance and front rooms look damaged, but still somewhat intact."

"From the outside," Papa said.

There was no need for more speculation, as they arrived and went inside to see for themselves. As Ian suggested, the main rooms of the ground floor were only partially damaged by fire and rain because the roof above them still held. The spaces were dear to her, not so much for the entertaining that occurred there, but because of the family evenings spent in the drawing room with Joseph reading aloud by the fire, Ian enjoying his pipe, and Etta cuddling with Lila before Nanny took her up to bed.

Lila set her memories aside. Joseph had wanted her to be his eyes and ears. She needed to stay focused.

As the group ventured to the upper story on a stairway that was partially burned, they saw that the bedrooms were a total loss, with downed beams and other parts of the roof fallen on furniture. Broken furniture. Although the fire was out, much of the burnt wood still hissed, as if the fire didn't want to let go until its work was fully finished.

Lila shoved aside her despair over the massive loss and lifted her skirts to step through the debris. She picked up a pair of silk shoes, sooty and soggy, yet otherwise unscathed. "I believe some items could be salvaged."

"You may never get the stink out of them," Papa said.

"We need to try."

Mrs. Crank came into the room and nodded. "Your lordships. Mrs. Kidd. I overheard your wishes to salvage what we can. We have already started." She nodded to Lila. "I have your jewel box safely set aside."

"Thank you." Lila cared for the sentimental element of the jewels far more than their value. She'd brought no jewelry into the marriage, but had been gifted all of her late mother-in-law's pretty items, many with origins spanning the centuries.

There were voices below, and Morgan went to see who had arrived. "Timothy!"

Her dear friend was just the person they needed to see.

Timothy came upstairs. "Your lordships. Mrs. Kidd. I'm so sorry for your loss."

"Thank you, Timothy."

"I've come to offer my services in the rebuilding," he said. "And I will not be alone. My father and many of the men of Summerfield will be here soon to help."

"We are grateful to all of you," Ian said.

"Perhaps we should gather outside and bring some order to it," Papa suggested.

"I will go help Mrs. Crank with the salvaging," Lila said.

It was a start.

Genevieve sat at the desk in her morning room and studied the extensive list she'd made of things to do—must-dos—to deal with the influx of five more guests and twenty-eight additional servants into the Manor household.

She checked the list of twenty-five bedrooms and their occupants, old and new. Five bedrooms were taken by her own family—actually four, since Beth had offered to move in with Clarissa. Four more were newly assigned to Joseph, Lila, Ian, and Sylvia. Etta was up in the nursery. Their four maids and valets took guest rooms close by, with Crompton Hall's butler, housekeeper, and cook taking another three. Six servants had been accommodated on the servants' floor, but that still left fifteen to be housed in the remaining ten guestrooms. They would have to double-up.

"Beds we have," she said to the room. "But food…"

As if summoned by her thought, there was a knock on the door and Mrs. McDeer entered. "You wanted to see me, Mrs. Weston?"

"I did. How are you faring in the kitchen?"

"Not well, ma'am. With thirty-three additional mouths to feed…truth is, I don't have that amount of food at hand. When the Manor has guests, I get notice so I can properly prepare."

"I know. I can't imagine that all the Manor bedrooms have ever been filled."

"Never in my forty-two years here."

"Have you sent someone to the mercantile to check on their stock of food items?"

"Just this morning. Mrs. Hayward gave me what she could. She sent a wagon to London for more supplies, but that won't help me get through lunch and dinner."

"Have you asked their cook if there is anything useful at Crompton that wasn't damaged by the fire?"

"I have. And she's gone to see what they can bring back."

"That's the best we can do for now. Cook simply with an eye towards economy. I trust your choices and judgment."

"I appreciate that, ma'am." Mrs. McDeer smiled. "This isn't what you bargained for, is it? You being left alone to handle *this*?"

"No one could be ready for this," she said. "Carry on."

Rooms. Food. Genevieve checked those items off her list and looked at the third. *Clothing.* That would be addressed at her next meeting.

She heard voices in the hall, set her list aside, and stood to greet those she had invited. The ladies entered in a gaggle: Lady Silvey, Beth, Tilda, and Clarissa.

"Thank you for joining me, ladies," Genevieve said as soon as all were seated. "As the men undertake the rebuilding of Crompton Hall—"

"Where is Lila?" Sylvia asked.

"She went with the men."

"She what?" Clarissa asked.

"Joseph asked her to go in his stead as he is supposed to rest for a few days."

Sylvia adjusted her bracelet. "I will believe that when I see it. I've never known a man who is able to rest when there is work to be done—other than my lazy husband, of course."

Genevieve was shocked she would admit such a thing.

"He wasn't a hard worker?" Tilda asked.

"Oh he worked very hard on things that interested him, such as gambling, womanizing, and drinking."

"Sylvia, if you please. Young ears," Genevieve said, with a look to Beth and Tilda.

"It's all right," Tilda said. "My father was the same sort."

Sylvia put a hand on her knee. "I am so sorry, dear. I didn't know."

Tilda shrugged.

"To get back on point," Genevieve said. "The men will deal with the building, Mrs. Camden has dealt with the lodging, and Mrs. McDeer, the meals. But we need to deal with the clothing. Much was lost." She looked at Clarissa. "You and Lila are the same size, so will you lend her what she needs until new items are ordered?"

Clarissa's face darkened before she nodded. "If I must."

Genevieve chose to ignore her attitude. "Sylvia, I would be happy to lend you items, as we too are close in size."

"I am very appreciative."

"Jack and Morgan will share what they can with Ian and Joseph. But that leaves the servants," Genevieve said.

"And Etta," Tilda said. "She's six-months-old and the twins are but two. Their clothes don't fit her. And we need more nappies and wool covers."

"A good observation," Genevieve said. "Which is why I have called you here. We women need to sew clothing for the servants and for little Etta."

"Sew?" Clarissa said. "I don't sew."

"I don't either," Sylvia said. "Do you, Genevieve?"

"I do. My family earned their fortune through the sale of sewing machines and my father made sure I knew the ins and outs of its usage. When I moved to Summerfield I had my personal machine shipped here. I've even sewn a few simple dresses this past year, plus layettes for the twins."

Clarissa made a face. "I've never understood why you sew. It's not like you need to sew for the economy of it."

"I need to sew for the creativity of it," Genevieve said. *So there.*

"Is the machine hard to use?" Beth asked.

"Not hard, but it does take some practice."

"The mercantile has fabric," Tilda said.

Genevieve nodded. "And I've been collecting sewing patterns for years, and get dress ideas from *Weldon's Ladies Journal* and *The Delineator*. Actually, Butterick Pattern Company has a store in London. Nana can order from them, plus order more fabric and sewing notions." She pointed towards the front of the house. "I have asked Dixon to set up my machine in the music room, and we can use the large table in the dining room to cut out the garments."

"My maid, Sadie, is good with a needle," Lady Silvey said.

"As is my Jane," Genevieve said.

Beth raised her hand. "I want to learn."

"That is commendable." She had three who were willing and one who was not. Genevieve knew she needed to corral the latter before she lost her completely. She clapped her hands together. "I appreciate your enthusiasm, Beth. But first, why don't you and Tilda go to the mercantile and pick up what supplies they have. I have a note you can give to Nana, telling her what we need now, and from London. Meanwhile, I will give Lady Sylvia and Clarissa their first lesson on the sewing machine."

"I think I'd be better at designing rather than sewing, " Clarissa said.

"We'll need help from all sides. Come now, ladies, let's make some clothes."

Tilda and Beth walked to the village on their supply errand. Tilda kicked a pebble, then Beth had a turn, back and forth down the long Manor drive and onto the road.

"I heard you slept with the babies?" Beth asked.

"Slept with Etta. On the floor. Poor thing. She doesn't understand what's going on. I think she misses Nanny Mabel."

"We had two babies, and now three. It's good we're here to help."

"I have to do something to earn my keep." She glanced at Beth. "Don't you feel that way?"

"I do. That's why I help Mum get dressed and do errands for Mrs. McDeer and Mrs. Camden."

Tilda missed the pebble with a swing of her foot, so had to try again. "At least you *have* a mother."

"You have Aunt Ruth."

"Had Aunt Ruth."

"I'm sorry she left you behind."

"Why should you be? The lot of them leaving doesn't affect you." She stopped walking, picked up the pebble, and threw it across the road into the grass. "Speaking of *them*…George and I are the same age. We're friends. Why would they take him and not me?"

Beth hesitated, which meant…

"You know why, don't you? Tell me."

Beth started walking. "We need to fetch the supplies and get back. They're waiting on us."

Tilda took her arm, stopping her. "Why wasn't I invited along? Beth, please. I have no one in the entire house to talk to anymore. I'm all alone."

"They wanted to separate you and George *because* you are the same age. You're both sixteen, of an age when…you know."

Tilda stomped a foot on the ground. "I knew it! I ruined everything."

"How?"

"When I first came here I was stupid and manipulative and set my sights on George in a boy-and-girl sort of way."

"I didn't know that."

"You weren't here yet. Uncle Grady stopped me from making a total fool of myself, but damage was done."

"But you and George seem close. You were always out riding together. Playing cards together."

"We are close. He forgave me and we enjoyed each other's company."

"Perhaps they want to prevent you from getting too close."

Tilda began to walk again in silence. A few minutes later she spoke. "Deep down I knew the reason, and actually, I agree with them. I am not well-born. I am not a suitable match for George Weston, the nephew of an earl." Beth opened her mouth to say something, but Tilda stopped her, "There's nothing you can say to make it better."

"Then take heart in knowing it's the same for me. I won't marry well. Even Mum won't, because she went off to be an actress — and because she took me in."

"She doesn't seem concerned about it."

"She isn't, but I am."

"You want her to marry?"

"I'm thirteen. I won't be around forever."

"Are you planning to leave Summerfield?"

71

"No, no. Not like that. I simply mean someday I will be grown and will naturally leave. I don't want her to be alone. Now, she's in her prime. I want her to be able to set up her future with a proper husband who's worthy of her."

"Your mother hates me."

"She hates too many people."

Tilda stopped again. "Who else?"

"I shouldn't say."

"You have to say."

Beth nodded to a farmer as he drove by in his wagon. "She doesn't like Mr. and Mrs. Kidd much. And I'm not sure she cares for Genevieve much either."

"How awful for her. For them."

"I think they deal with it better than she does. It stirs her up."

"Then I feel sorry for her," Tilda said. *But not too sorry.*

"I do too."

"Is there anything any of us can do to make her like us?"

Beth looked to the sky, then said, "No."

Tilda shooed a fly away from her face. "All this time I thought if I was nice enough or said or did just the right things she might like me. To know it doesn't matter is...sad."

"I know."

"But it's also rather freeing." Tilda cocked her head. "Blimey. I guess it's one less thing to worry about."

"I suppose that's a good way to think of it."

Tilda paused at the door to the mercantile. "What choice do I have?"

Beth was wise enough not to answer.

They entered the shop. "Beth, Tilda," Mrs. Hayward said. "Good day to you. How can we help you?"

Getting help with supplies was far easier than getting help with people like Clarissa.

Dixon entered the music room and lifted his brows in a look of disdain. The room was in disarray, for the ladies had commandeered a game table for the sewing machine and moved chairs around so Sylvia, Clarissa, and Genevieve could sit around it.

"Yes, Dixon?" Genevieve asked.

"Lord Silvey has arrived."

Sylvia popped up from her chair. "Damon!"

"Send him in, Dixon."

The ladies stood to greet him, smoothing their dresses and touching their hair.

Sylvia's son conquered the room with his stride. Genevieve was immediately taken with his confidence and good looks. His black hair was tousled yet somehow looked perfectly kempt at the same time. He was taller than any of the other men in Summerfield, which added to his dashing entrance.

He scanned the ladies' faces, then opened his arms to his mother. "Mamma!" He captured her with his embrace.

"Damon, my dear boy. You've finally come."

He let her go, taking a step back. "I would have been here earlier today but I find that the estate to which I was traveling is no longer livable, and so I was sent here." He looked at Clarissa, then Genevieve, then Clarissa again. "Which of you very fine ladies is the mistress of this very fine house?"

Genevieve stepped forward. "I am, Lord Silvey."

Sylvia hurried to make the introductions. "Genevieve, this is my son, Damon. Damon, this is Mrs. Weston, the daughter-in-law of the earl."

He gave her a smart bow, then once again turned his eyes on Clarissa. "And you are?"

"Clarissa," she said.

"Miss Weston," his mother corrected.

Another bow. "With the same last name I'd easily assume you are sisters, yet with one blond-beauty and one raven, I might be mistaken."

"We are cousins-in-law," Clarissa explained. She gave him a coy look. "Although it *is* true that Genevieve is fair and I am not."

He chuckled. "I shall have to test that."

Genevieve was shocked. She'd never seen Clarissa flirt, though she should not have been surprised at her talent.

Damon pulled his eyes from Clarissa's and scanned the room. "Well then. What have we here? Another type of music coming out of the music room?"

"It's a sewing machine," Sylvia said, drawing him over. "Because of the fire at the Hall the servants are in need of clothes, so Mrs. Weston had the idea of creating them ourselves."

He glanced at the machine with little interest. "You, sew, Mamma?"

"I can be taught." She put a hand on the crank. "I am rather enjoying it."

"Toil on then." He left the sewing machine as if bored, and sat at the piano. He played a skilled arpeggio from low to high. "Hmm. Nice tone."

"How grand that you play, Lord Silvey," Genevieve said. "I only possess a minimal talent."

He offered her a passing glance and turned his gaze to Clarissa. "And you, Miss Weston? Do you have a minimal talent?"

"I guarantee you, Lord Silvey, my talent is far from minimal."

They shared a suggestive grin—which was horribly awkward.

"Do play us something, Son," his mother said.

He thought a moment, then donned an impish grin. He sang the song looking directly at Clarissa. "'Wherever I'm going, and all the day long, at home and abroad, or alone in a throng. I find that my passion's so lively and strong, that your name when I'm silent still runs in my song. Sing Ballynamony ho, ro—'"

"That is not the type of song I was suggesting, dear boy."

"I know what you were suggesting, Mamma." He transitioned into a Mozart piece. "Better?"

"Much."

Clarissa stroked the edge of the pianoforte. "Actually, I find classical music much too...classic for my taste."

He banged his hands upon a dozen keys at once. "Then I shall ban it from my repertoire."

Genevieve was stunned. It was as though the music room was no longer her own. And as far as the sewing lesson?

She nodded to Sylvia, hoping for her help. "You are much welcome here, Lord Silvey—"

"Damon. All who hold me in high esteem me call me Damon. I won't tell you what I'm called by the ones who hold me otherwise." He winked at Clarissa.

He had such a way with words—of twisting them. "You are much welcome here, Damon."

At that moment Joseph entered the room, surprising them all. Genevieve rushed to his side. "Joseph, you are up and about."

"I am," he whispered, pointing to his throat. "Scorched."

"Ah," Genevieve said. "I pray your voice recovers soon."

"And your hands." Sylvia stepped up. "Damon, Joseph was injured in the fire."

With a glance to Joseph's injuries, Damon said, "Did you try to bat it out yourself, Cousin? From what I've seen you were sorely unsuccessful." He grinned. "Sorely? Get it? Ha!"

"Damon!"

"No piano playing for you!" Damon waggled his fingers.

"Never could play." Joseph put his bandaged hands behind his back.

Since there was no time to dissect Damon's rudeness and questionable sense of humor, Genevieve stepped forward to reclaim the room. "Would you like to see your room, Damon?"

"There *are* no rooms," Clarissa said.

"Oh dear," Genevieve said. "I'm afraid we *are* full at the inn. It seems I made assignments for four of you from the Hall, but forgot—" She was devastated for not thinking of Damon's arrival.

Joseph raised a hand. "Now that I am on the mend, Lila can move in with me."

"How novel," Damon said. "A husband and wife in the same bedroom?" His smile was full of mischief.

Although it was obviously *done* – as Genevieve and Morgan also shared a room – it was never spoken about in polite company.

But then again, there was nothing polite about Lord Silvey.

Clarissa motioned towards the door. "I will show you the way. Follow me."

"Anywhere, dear lady." With a nod, he left them. The room shuddered back into place.

"I'm so sorry," Sylvia said. "Damon is often a whirlwind."

More of a spinning vortex.

"He meant no offense, Joseph. You know of his brash manner."

"I do." He offered a nod. "Ladies." After he left, the room was empty but for Sylvia and Genevieve.

"Now then," Sylvia said. "Let us get back to the lesson."

Genevieve would have liked to discuss Damon's odd character a bit more, but obviously Sylvia did not. "We're down to one volunteer," she said. "Just you."

Sylvia glanced towards the door. "I would like to say that Clarissa will return, but I am guessing not."

"She and your son did seem to have an instant affinity towards one another."

"Damon has never had trouble attracting women."

"Is he a lady's man?" *A philanderer?*

Sylvia returned to her place at the sewing machine. "Not anymore."

"So he was?"

She fidgeted with the scrap of fabric in the machine "He has changed his ways."

Genevieve wanted to ask '*How do you know?*' but chose to give the man the benefit of the doubt.

For now.

"And this will be your room," Clarissa said, as they entered Lila's bedroom.

Damon strode in and pointed to two dresses hanging on the outside of the armoire door. "Mrs. Kidd has good taste."

"Actually, those are mine. She lost her clothes in the fire."

He fingered the sleeve of a green batiste. "I should have known the good taste was yours."

"Why? You know nothing about me."

He flipped the sleeve away. "A point I plan to rectify." Damon sat upon the bed, bouncing once or twice. He waited for her reaction.

Clarissa wasn't sure how to react. There was no doubting he was a charming man with a quick wit—two attributes that piqued her interest. Yet there was something a bit *much* about him, something that could completely overwhelm. Unknown was whether such power would prompt joy or danger.

"Come," she said. "There's more of the house to see."

Upon returning to Summerfield Manor, Lila gave Dixon her hat, and began to go upstairs. Thinking better of it, she turned and asked, "Do you know if my husband is sleeping?"

"I don't believe so, Mrs. Kidd. I saw him in the music room with the ladies, and then I believe he was going to the nursery to see your daughter."

"He's up and about?"

"Very much so, ma'am."

Lila hurried to the nursery. The door was open, but before entering she gazed upon Joseph and their child. He sat on the floor with Etta as the baby sat and gnawed on the corner of a blanket. When she began to topple over, he held

77

out a bandaged hand to stop her fall, but winced when she made contact.

"I'll get her, Mr. Kidd," Nanny Colleen said.

Lila saw a look of frustration on her husband's face, and immediately showed herself. "Well, well. Look at you, Joseph. Out of bed and playing with Etta."

"Out of bed, yes," he whispered. "But not playing well."

Lila took Etta in her arms. The little girl grinned and grabbed Lila's nose. "Hello, sweet girl."

Joseph stood, using a forearm as leverage. "I'm much relieved she is no worse for our calamity."

"And you? You're supposed to rest. And talk little."

"I will whisper, but I must talk. I rested to the point of madness. How did you find Crompton? Fill me in."

Etta began to fidget and whine. "It's time for a bottle," Nanny said. "Let me take her."

Lila relinquished Etta to Nanny, giving her a kiss and a wave. As she and Joseph walked down the corridor of bedrooms, they heard laughter. A door opened and one of their housemaids came out. Seeing them, she stopped in the doorway. Another maid could be seen in the room.

"Martha?" Lila said. "What's going on here?"

She bobbed a curtsy and put a hand to the open neckline of her dress. She began to quickly button it properly. "Sorry, Mrs. Kidd. Mary and I were just trying on the dresses we're borrowing." She pulled at the waist of her skirt. "Mine's too big."

It most certainly was. The logistics of clothing their staff from Crompton Hall threatened to overwhelm. "Beggars can't be choosers," Lila said. "It's very generous of the Summerfield staff to share with you."

Joseph spoke in a near whisper. "New uniforms are being sewn as we speak."

"They are?" Lila asked.

He put a hand to his throat. "Genevieve is in the music room with a sewing machine."

"When did this happen?"

"While you were gone."

Lila addressed the maids. "Be appreciative, please — of the borrowed clothes *and* the fine accommodations."

Martha nodded. "Oh, we are, Mrs. Kidd. It's quite a luxury staying in such a fancy room with so many pretty things."

Lila felt a stab of apprehension. "How many guestrooms are the staff using?"

Martha looked to Mary, then said, "Fifteen or sixteen I think."

"That many?"

"We's two of the lucky ones," Martha said. "Six are staying on the servants' floor, but me and Mary got one of the posh rooms."

"Then mind you take care of it," Lila said.

The maid nodded. "Mrs. Crank and Mr. Dowd told us that we're all responsible for keeping our own rooms clean."

"A commendable assignment." Lila thought of another issue. "How do you use the rest of your time?"

Martha and Mary exchanged a look, and Mary giggled. "We're enjoying the free time, I guess."

Lila stepped away with Joseph, but her thoughts swam. "How many came over?"

"Twenty-eight servants, and five of us. Six with Silvey."

"It's too much, Joseph. We're too much. Too many."

"Where else would you have them go?"

"Crompton is not a complete loss. Let's go to my room and I'll tell you what I saw," Lila said.

Joseph shook his head. "Your room is no longer your room."

"Since when?"

He chuckled. "Come into *our* room and I'll tell you about Summerfield, and you can tell me about Crompton."

Lila wasn't sure which was the more daunting task.

Chapter Five

Clarissa opened one eye and saw Beth standing in the moonlight, buttoning her dress.

It was still night. Wasn't it? The dark autumn mornings made it seem earlier than it was.

Beth sat on the window seat and put on her shoes. She dropped one.

"You're up."

"Go back to sleep, Mum."

"Is it morning?"

"Not for you. Not yet."

"Good." Clarissa turned over and nuzzled her cheek into a pillow.

Genevieve couldn't sleep — a common malady since the twins were born. Although it was an hour before their usual waking, she slipped out of bed and donned a dress she could get on without help — sans corset. Blasted thing. She'd gotten used to being free of its encumbrance during the last months of her pregnancy and rather hated the necessity of returning to that element of torture. Yet, the truth was, she needed its benefits. She'd gained an enormous amount of weight carrying the twins, and her body doggedly refused to return to any semblance of her pre-baby figure.

Her mother's voice accompanied her own inner chiding. *Really, Genevieve. The birthing is accomplished. It is imperative you regain your figure quickly. To do otherwise shows a disgraceful lack of willpower.*

It was embarrassing to wear her pregnancy dresses after the pregnancy had ended, but she had no choice. Perhaps she should sew herself some new dresses that fit her new shape.

But that was a worry for another day. Today had worries enough of its own. She pinned up her hair in a quick manner. It would have to do. Besides, there were few people up this early to judge her hairstyle.

She left the bedroom, carefully turning the knob until the door was properly closed. She felt a wave of satisfaction that it was accomplished without even a click.

Then she went downstairs and entered the kitchen.

"Beth?" Genevieve asked upon seeing her.

"'Morning, Mrs. Weston."

"What are you doing down here so early?"

"She's being a dear girl and is helping me make morning rolls," Mrs. McDeer said. "We're needing double what we usually do."

Which spoke to the central worry of Genevieve's unrest. "Is Mrs. Camden up yet?"

The cook glanced at the clock. "Should be any minute."

Mrs. Camden came in the kitchen, tucking her blouse into her skirt. She pulled up short when she saw Genevieve and Beth. "Goodness. Good morning to you both."

"And to you," Genevieve said.

"I'm helping make rolls," Beth said.

"I see that."

"We appreciate her help immensely," Mrs. McDeer added with a smile to Beth.

Mrs. Camden turned to Genevieve. "Can I be of assistance, Mrs. Weston?"

"I'm hoping we can assist each other. May we talk?"

"Of course. Come into my sitting room. Would you like tea?"

"No thank you." Genevieve had never been in the housekeeper's living quarters off the basement corridor, but found the small parlor quite cozy and inviting. She was offered a seat on a settee while Mrs. Camden sat at a small desk.

"Well then, Mrs. Weston. What is on your mind?"

"Thirty-three extra guests. Thirty-four with Lord Silvey."

Mrs. Camden sighed deeply. "Indeed."

"At least we have bedrooms enough."

"That we do. And Mrs. McDeer and I have discussed the meals."

"I'm sure you have it well-managed. And the ladies and I are sewing some new clothes for the servants."

"Mr. Dixon told me. That's very kind of you."

"We shall see."

"Perhaps some of the maids could help with the sewing — at least with the cutting and handwork?"

"You've anticipated my need. Thank you."

She began to rise, and Genevieve motioned her to sitting again. "There's something else."

"Yes, ma'am?"

"I think we need to find tasks that would occupy the Crompton servants. As it stands they have little to do beyond keeping their own rooms clean, and—"

She nodded knowingly. "Idle hands…"

"Mr. Weston said the male servants can return to Crompton to help with the building."

"If the Hall is anything like Summerfield Manor, their footmen might take issue. They can be a snobbish lot and generally abhor any assignment that might dirty their hands."

"We all have to pitch in."

She sighed again. "Agreed. We will give them no choice."

"And the female house servants could be of use with cleaning. Mrs. Kidd said numerous items were salvaged but are in need of a good clean or repair. And Mrs. McDeer could use more kitchen and scullery help."

"Again, agreed."

"Will you and Mr. Dixon coordinate with Mrs. Crank and Mr. Dowd?"

"We will. I've also thought about assigning Prissy to help Nanny Colleen with Etta. Prissy's a good girl and has been with us many years."

"That would be very helpful." Genevieve stood and took a deep breath. "I feel better now. Thank you for your help, Mrs. Camden."

"Be assured we will get through this, Mrs. Weston. It's all under control."

"As much as it can be."

Mrs. Camden's response was a very noncommittal shrug.

When Genevieve returned to the bedroom, Morgan opened his eyes.

"You're dressed?"

"Of a sort."

"Where have you been?"

"I met with Mrs. Camden and we crafted a plan to assign tasks for the servants from the Hall."

He hung his legs over the side of the bed. "It is strange having—"

They heard a thump and heavy footsteps sounding from the floor above them.

He sighed and covered his ears with a pillow. "We purposely arranged for empty servant-rooms above our bedroom."

"Until now." She didn't have time for his complaint, for it could not be rectified any time soon. "Now if you please, get up and move to your dressing room. I need to call Jane and get dressed myself."

"But you are dressed."

"Not dressed appropriately enough to preside as the mistress of the Manor."

He got out of bed and stretched with a moan and groan. "You do have the greatest burden, dear one. I can rely on Papa, but since there is no countess…"

"It falls on me."

He moved close and touched her hair. "I can think of no one to better handle the lot of it."

He kissed her cheek and left just as Jane arrived to help Genevieve dress the role of mistress of Summerfield Manor.

As soon as the breakfast dishes were cleared from the dining room table, Genevieve asked the footmen to move the chairs against the wall.

"That's better," she said. "Full access for cutting."

Sylvia studied a pair of scissors as if she'd never held one before. She opened and closed them, as if fascinated. "You actually trust us to cut fabric with these?"

Lila laughed. "It's not surgery." Thank goodness.

Sylvia eyed the fabric Genevieve was smoothing across the table. "But once it's cut, it's cut. It's so…final."

"That it is," Genevieve said, making sure the selvage edges of the fabric were together and the fold was smooth. "But again, it's just fabric. If mistakes are made, we will get more. Our skills *will* improve with practice."

Lila nodded. "When we had the mercantile, Mother and I used to hand-sew our own clothes. So I know the basics and am eager to learn how to use the machine."

"I appreciate your skill," Genevieve said. She smiled when Tilda and Beth came in. "More help. How splendid!"

"But where is your mother, Beth?" Lila asked.

"She's off with Lord Silvey."

Sylvia flipped a hand in the air. "Actually, I was surprised to see Damon at breakfast at all. During our travels I was lucky to see him for luncheon." She opened and closed the scissors twice in the air. "I am glad Clarissa has taken him under her wing."

"I think she's happy for the diversion," Lila said. "And the chance to not be…elsewhere." *Around me and Tilda.*

"What?"

"Never mind," Lila said.

Sylvia shrugged. "Although Clarissa didn't seem too interested in our project, she will probably find Damon to be project enough." She chuckled.

It was disconcerting that a mother would speak of her son's character in such an nonchalant manner, as though his shortcomings were amusing. Although Lila hadn't had time to form her own opinions, Damon was being painted as impulsive and selfish. Not the proper companion for any woman — even Clarissa. Especially Clarissa, who shared those traits.

Four maids stepped into the doorway. Genevieve stood to greet them. "Dottie, Jane, come in. Fanny and Sadie, is it?"

Sylvia captured her maid's arm. "Yes, indeed, this is my dear Sadie. I told her all about the sewing and she wants to learn."

Lila smiled at her maid. "I'm glad to see you here, Fanny."

"We want to learn too, Mrs. Weston," Jane said, nodding at Dottie.

Genevieve clasped her hands beneath her chin. "Oh, ladies. My cup runneth over!"

After their sewing lesson, Tilda and Beth were sent off on yet another trip to the mercantile for supplies. They resumed their pebble-kicking game from last time.

"There's too many of us in the Manor," Tilda said.

"Too many and not enough space," Beth said, taking her turn with the pebble.

"It was annoying to have to clear our sewing from the dining table so they could set it for lunch."

"There's no other large table in the Manor," Beth said. "'Cepting the servant's table where *they* eat. Or the kitchen table where Mrs. McDeer cooks."

They walked into the village square just as Mrs. Keening came out of the bakery, fanning herself with her shawl. Her cheeks were blotchy red.

"Hello, girls."

"Hello, Mrs. Keening. Are you all right?"

"The ovens heat the entire bakery. It doesn't seem to affect my husband, but I have these moments when I have to seek the cool air outside or expire. Care for a fresh roll?"

"Always," Tilda said.

"Go inside and say I said it was all right."

The girls got their warm rolls, then joined her on the bench outside the bakery.

"You make the tastiest rolls," Tilda said.

"Better than Mrs. McDeer."

"Glad to hear it. Speaking of…I hear you have a houseful at the Manor."

"We do," Beth said.

"Servants and guests, alike?" she asked.

"Thirty-three additional, I believe," Tilda said.

"Thirty-four," Beth said. "You need to count Lord Silvey."

Mrs. Keening leaned forward to see the girls' faces. "Is he the dapper gent who came through here with hair as black as his horse?"

"I don't know anything about his horse, but yes, that describes him," Tilda said.

"A lord, you say?"

"A baron," Beth said.

"My my. Upper and lower guests. What are you doing with all those extra bodies?"

"We're sewing for them," Beth said.

"What?"

"Everyone at Crompton Hall lost their clothes in the fire. The family can borrow from the Westons, but the servants need uniforms and —"

"Aye," the woman said. "Mrs. Hayward and Rose were telling me they're having to order more sewing supplies — and an actual sewing machine?"

Beth nodded. "We're all learning how to sew. Mrs. Weston already has a machine and is teaching us."

"Mrs. Kidd knows a bit of it," said Mrs. Keening. "At least she did back when she was just Lila Hayward."

"We've taken over the dining room with our cutting, but it's a bother to set it aside for meals."

"Today we had nine ladies working at once."

"Or trying to work."

Mrs. Keening sprang to her feet. "Stay right here."

She went in the bakery and came out with a key. Then she walked next door to an empty store front and unlocked the door. "Take a look at your new sewing gallery."

The main room was virtually empty. It was large, with sunlight streaming through the windows. "What did it used to be?" Tilda asked.

"Ages ago it was a candle shop, but when kerosene lamps took over it was an office for the village newspaper."

"We had a newspaper?" Beth asked.

"For a time. But then there wasn't enough news to print—and our village grapevine does quite well without putting it to paper. Most recently it was a butcher shop, but the mister and I made them move because the stink of it was hurting our business at the bakery."

"So now it's without a tenant?" Tilda walked around the space.

"It is. You interested?"

"You own it?" Beth asked.

"Bought it with hopes of expanding, but we're getting too old for that much change and to-do." She strolled to the windows. "Nice light for sewing. We'd give the Westons a good price."

Tilda could barely contain herself and could tell that Beth was of the same mind. "Don't let anyone else take it, Mrs. Keening," she said. "I'll go back right now and talk to them about it."

"I'll hold it for a while, but it's first come, first serve."

Tilda couldn't remember anyone being in the building in the year she'd been at Summerfield, but didn't argue.

They bid Mrs. Keening goodbye and walked across the square to the mercantile. "I think it's perfect," Tilda said.

"Me too. Do you think Genevieve will agree?"

"I hope so." In spite of her doubts as to the demand for the space, Tilda felt the clock ticking. "Let's hurry with our errand and get back to the Manor to talk with the ladies."

Genevieve's thoughts spun 'round like the bobbin in the sewing machine. "A storefront. In Summerfield?"

"With space to work all in one room," Sylvia said.

"I know the space," Lila said. "It was a newspaper and then a butcher shop."

"That's what Mrs. Keening told us," Tilda said.

Genevieve looked around the music room which was littered with scraps and supplies. "I'm sure Mr. Dixon and Mrs. Camden would be delighted if we moved our mess elsewhere."

"How much is the rent?" Lila asked.

"Uh...I didn't ask," Tilda said. "But she said she'd give a good price."

"I'll negotiate," Lila said. "I've known Mrs. Keening all my life. She and my mother were gossip-partners."

Sylvia chuckled. "I know the kind. Is there any furniture in the store?"

"A few tables and odd chairs, but not enough," Beth said.

"Timothy and his father could build us some," Lila said. "They don't have to be fancy, just functional."

"And we could get them made to be just the right size for the space." Genevieve said.

Sylvia arched her back. "Perhaps a cutting table could be raised a few inches so we don't have to slump over?"

"A capital idea!"

Lila headed for the door. "I'll stop at the Timothy's carpentry shop and ask about some tables."

"But Timothy is at Crompton, working on the rebuilding."

"Maybe one of their apprentices could handle it—as you say, we only need functional tables, not masterpieces."

"Can I go too?" Beth said.

Genevieve took Beth's face in her hands. "Of course you can, dear girl, for you came up with the idea."

"With Tilda. Tilda thought of it too."

"Then good for Tilda too."

Tilda felt her heart race. It wasn't Beth's idea, it was hers! "Can I go with you too, Mrs. Kidd?"

Genevieve shook her head. "Nanny was asking for help with the children. Could you go check with her, please?"

Tilda felt the project slip away from her grasp.

Surprisingly, Beth came to her rescue. "Please let her come along."

"Very well then," Genevieve said.

Tilda mouthed a thank you to Beth. It was about time things went her way.

The handshake was accomplished. The deal was done.

Lila and the two girls stood in the storefront that would soon become their sewing shop.

Lila looked around the large room, imagining the large cutting table, and busy women at small tables, sewing on machines or doing the finishing work by hand. Chatting and laughing, feeling good and doing good.

"It's perfect," she said softly.

"I think so too," Beth said.

"And me three," Tilda said. She pointed to the windows. "They need washing, and the floor and cobwebs need a good brooming. Could I borrow a broom from Mrs. Keening?"

Lila was surprised she was offering to do the work. "We can send a few of the maids down from the Manor."

Tilda brushed off a window sill. "I'd rather do it myself. It's our project. Our shop." Her voice resounded with pride.

Lila held out her hands and the three females made a circle. "This *is* our project, a project that's meant to be."

"Why do you say that?" Beth asked.

"Look how everything has fallen into place. There was a need, Genevieve saw an answer to that need, and you two girls found a way to more fully meet that need."

"God did it," Beth said.

"Yes, He did." It was the perfect time to consecrate the shop. She bowed her head. "Dear God, thank you for the opportunity to help others through our work. And thank you for this marvelous space that will allow many more women to be involved. Show us what you want us to do with our efforts. Amen."

"And help us get some really nice tables and chairs," Beth added.

"And help me not get bit by mice or spiders as I tidy the place," Tilda said.

"Amen, again," Lila said. They were such good girls. "Tilda, do you really want to clean?"

"I do."

"Then go to the mercantile and tell my grandmother what you need: a broom, a pail, sponges, rags..."

She ran out the door. "I've got it. Don't worry."

"I wouldn't think of it," Lila said. "She's excited about this, isn't she?"

"We both are," Beth said. "We're both wanting to be useful...to prove we belong at the Manor."

The statement was bothersome. "Don't you feel you belong?"

She shrugged. "Sometimes."

Lila leaned down to Beth's eye level and brushed a stray hair away from her pretty face. "You always belong, Beth. At the Manor, in Summerfield, in the family, and certainly as part of this project." She flicked the tip of Beth's nose. "Understood?"

"Yes'm."

Lila stood upright. "Let's you and I go see about some tables."

"And chairs," Beth said.

Clarissa stood in the middle of the square with Damon and spread her arms as she turned in a circle. "And here is Summerfield."

He gave it a cursory glance. "Mmm."

She remembered her own "mmm" during dinner at the Kidds', the "mmm" that had caused her so much trouble. Hearing Damon's reaction to the town that was her home made her understand the other's reaction to her own "mmm" regarding Tilda.

"I'm sorry," she said. "'Mmm' is totally unacceptable."

His left eyebrow rose. "It's a very nice *little* village." He gestured towards a bench. "Shall we?"

She sat and nodded at passersby who seemed interested in her presence—but mostly Damon's. It was rare enough that a man as handsome and debonair as Damon strolled into Summerfield, but rare indeed that he was in her company. That any man was in her company. *Take that, gossipers!*

He pointed to the far edge of the square. "Isn't that Mrs. Kidd and your Beth?"

Clarissa stood. "It is." She strode after them and Damon followed. Theirs was no aimless stroll. Lila and Beth had a definite destination in mind.

She saw them go into the carpentry shop. What would they want with Timothy?

Timothy was *her* friend. It didn't matter that years ago he'd been keen on Lila. Timothy and Clarissa had the stronger bond. They had become fast friends when he'd helped her find Beth in London and bring her to Summerfield.

She walked faster.

"What's the rush?" Damon asked, hurrying to keep up.

Clarissa didn't answer, but stepped into the shop just a few seconds behind Lila and Beth, in time to hear Timothy call out, "Bethy!"

He held out his arms to Beth, and she ran to fill them. It warmed Clarissa's heart to see the affection they shared.

Timothy looked up and his eyes took in Lila, then Clarissa, and then Damon.

"My, my, I don't think the shop has ever had this many visitors."

Lila turned around and looked surprised. "Clarissa. Lord Silvey. What are you doing here?"

"I return the question." *Why are you here with* my *daughter?*

Beth took Clarissa's hand and pulled her to the window. "See that shop to the right of the bakery, Mum? Mrs. Kidd has just rented it."

"For what?"

"As a place for us to spread out and sew. Tilda's at the mercantile getting cleaning supplies and..." She turned to Timothy. "We came here to get some tables and chairs made."

Lila nodded. "That is our business here, Timothy. We need one very long, raised cutting table and perhaps four smaller tables for the actual sewing, and either chairs or benches enough for ...?" She looked to Beth. "I'm not sure how many will end up working there."

Count me out.

Beth listed through the people who apparently had showed up to sew this morning. "Nine," she finally said.

"At least nine," Lila said.

Timothy ran a rough hand across his face. "We're rather busy with the rebuilding of your house, Mrs. Kidd."

"You can't have everything, Lila," Clarissa said.

"Though," Timothy said, "perhaps it's still possible. My father's health doesn't allow him to go to Crompton to help, but he'd probably love to work on your tables."

"And chairs," Beth added.

"And chairs." He put a hand on her head, then said, "You've grown a good three inches this year."

"I'm thirteen now."

"Too old for me to call you Bethy?"

She shook her head adamantly, "Never too old for that."

"Let us go," Damon said to Clarissa. "I'm sure there's some other exciting venture to show me in Summerfield."

She felt her face grow hot. "Nice to see you, Timothy."

"As always, Miss Weston."

Miss Weston. This past year she'd been negligent in keeping up their friendship. She wasn't quite sure why.

Damon held open the door. "Clarissa? Shall we?"

As soon as Clarissa and Damon left, Timothy looked to Lila, "Who is he?"

"I'm sorry. I should have introduced you. Where are my manners?"

He shook his head. "I care little for manners. Who is he?"

Beth answered. "He is Lord Silvey. He's the son of Lady Silvey who was visiting Crompton, but he came late and found it burned, so came to Summerfield, and now he's staying there. With us."

"All correct statements," Lila said. *But there's something else about him that troubles me. I don't understand it, but I sense it.*

Timothy must have sensed it too, because he said, "Bethy, go back in the workshop and say hello to my father. He'd love to have a chat with you."

As soon as they were alone, he got to it, "What is he to Clarissa?"

Lila was surprised by the direct question. What should it matter to Timothy? "Since the men are busy with Crompton, and the women are starting this new sewing project, there was no one to entertain Lord Silvey when he arrived."

"Except Clarissa."

"She's good at entertaining people." She decided to add, "And not that interested in sewing."

Timothy looked towards the windows where they could see Clarissa taking Damon's arm as they paused in the square. "What sort of man is he?"

Such a blunt question.

"I don't really know, other than to say he's charming and well-traveled. He and his mother just got back from a tour of the Continent."

"Oh."

"Why the interest in Lord Silvey?"

Timothy busied himself with straightening a sketch of an armoire that was nailed to the wall. "I just want her to be happy."

Lila hesitated to say the next, but did so anyway. "I don't think there's a romantic connection between them, if that's what you want to know."

He seemed to relax. "Good."

"Good?"

"I mean, I'm sure he's a nice enough gent, but I ..." Timothy stumbled over his words, and looked towards the back. "It's just that we found Bethy together and I admire Clarissa for taking her in. I've heard how that ruined her chances at finding a proper match, and I..." He looked down. "Never mind. It's none of my business."

Her curiosity was piqued. Lila put a hand on his arm and waited until he looked at her. "But you'd like it to be your business?"

His breathing had turned heavy. "It doesn't matter what I want. Clarissa is polished walnut. I'm knotty pine."

They heard laughter from the back. "And Beth?"

He looked towards the laughter a few moments before answering. "I thought she might have been a dovetail that could join us together."

His face was so forlorn, as though Damon's presence had destroyed his hope. "As I said, Timothy, they are not romantically involved. He's just visiting."

He took a deep breath and let it out. "It's not as though she and I have stayed close.

"There have been many adjustments this past year with both Beth and Tilda staying at the Manor, along with the birth of the twins, and —"

His smile made his worries fall away. "And your child too. How is Henrietta?"

"She is mastering the art of sitting on her own."

"Soon she'll be crawling."

"And walking."

"Riding. You still have Raider, don't you?"

"I do. Though I don't go riding as much as I'd like to."

"Why not?"

It was a good question with no good answer. "I should make the time."

"If you ever need the company of a friend, don't hesitate to ask."

"Thank you."

"Now then, let's go rescue Bethy from my father's stories."

While Damon played softly on the piano, Clarissa strolled around the music room amid the scraps of fabric, half-made garments, and sewing paraphernalia.

He stopped playing. "Does the mess bother you?"

She let a skirt fall back to its place, draped over a chair. "Why should it? It's of no consequence to me."

"But *they* are of great consequence to you."

"Not at all."

"You've been quiet all day. The family barely got two words from you at dinner."

"They had plenty to talk about without me, going on and on about their stupid sewing shop."

"Which bothers you."

She was going to say "not at all" again, but decided she'd better not. "If it will get their mess out of the house, I'm all for it."

"The mess that bothers you 'not at all.'" He grinned.

She moved towards the piano, needing distraction. "Play for me."

"Not yet. For I would like you to tell me who bothered you the most today in the village: Mrs. Kidd or Timothy? Or seeing them together? Or perhaps seeing them with Beth?"

All of the above. "Stop it."

"Stop what?"

"You are far too observant."

"You offer much to observe."

She sat on the bench beside him. "Let's play a duet."

"But I'd like to discuss my observations."

She glanced at him. "Not if you wish for me to stay in the room."

He sighed dramatically. "Coward."

She'd rather be called a coward than any of the other names that would come to mind if he fully grasped how much the encounter in Summerfield had vexed her.

She pulled out music for a duet. "One, two, three…"

They played the song expertly and sang the lyrics, with Damon creating a harmony to Clarissa's melody. She let the music carry her away from any stressful musings. Music was an elixir, with Damon's harmony and accompaniment melding with Clarissa's notes to make the sound full and complete.

As he makes me full and complete?

She suddenly stopped playing, unable to coordinate her eyes, hands, voice, and thoughts.

"Why did you stop?"

She turned her head to look at him, his face just inches away.

He kissed her. Then she kissed him.

They pulled away and studied each other.

"Our voices blend," she said.

"*We* blend."

They kissed some more, just to make sure.

Clarissa slipped into her bedroom, trying her best not to wake Beth.

To no avail.

"You're late," Beth said, sitting up in bed.

"I didn't mean to wake you."

"Why are you late?"

Clarissa sat at the dressing table and removed her shoes. "Since you're awake, come help me undress so I don't have to call Dottie."

Beth set the shoes aside and began unbuttoning the back of her mother's bodice. "You didn't answer me. Why are you late?"

"I don't have to go to bed at the same time as a thirteen-year-old."

"I know that, it's just that you were so quiet at dinner. What's wrong?"

Clarissa sprang to her feet and began dancing around the room. She was in love!

Yet she couldn't tell Beth. Not yet.

"What's got into you?"

She stopped and grinned. "Nothing at all, dear girl." She kissed Beth, then said, "To bed now. Tomorrow is another glorious day."

But Beth wasn't so easily appeased. "What happened to make you so happy?"

She might as well say it. Clarissa removed her corset and flung it across the room. "A man, Beth. Can you believe it? A man!"

"Lord Silvey?"

She sat at the dressing table and began to undo her hair. Instead of answering her daughter, Clarissa happily sang the song she'd shared with Damon.

Beth interrupted. "I'm not sure about him, Mum. He's charming, but I met people like him in London. There is something about Lord Silvey that's dodgy. It's like finding bread on the street, only to look to its back side and see mold."

Clarissa laughed. "Moldy men. How funny."

"That's not what I meant."

"Oh fiddle. You said you wanted me to find someone. And now I have."

"You've only known him a few days."

"Length of acquaintance does not always matter. There is an affinity, Beth. We...blend." She was contented with the word. "Be happy for me. Please."

Beth hesitated. "I'll try."

Chapter Six

Lila stood at the window to their bedroom, wishing she was home.

But there was no home.

Joseph approached from behind and awkwardly wrapped his arms around her. "Penny for your thoughts?"

"I want to be home."

"So do I."

She turned to face him. "Is there something wrong with us preferring to be home?"

He moved to touch her cheek, yet pulled his hand away before it made contact. "It would be wrong if we didn't wish to be home."

Lila nodded. "The Westons have been so generous and thoughtful. I was surprised they came to Nanny Mabel's funeral."

"They are supportive in every way."

She nodded again.

"Come now. You wish to say more."

She fueled her thoughts with a breath. "Clarissa hates that we are intruding on her space, and hates me borrowing her clothes."

"I know."

"You've seen it?"

"Sensed it. At least she's not being blatant about it."

"I think I'd rather suffer a blatant cut than her polite disapproval."

"Be brave. We have never had her approval, and probably never will. Remember, we have done nothing wrong."

"Except be happy."

He smiled. "How dare we?"

Lila turned to the other issue on her mind. "Genevieve is so welcoming, so kind, and so gifted at being the mistress of the Manor. And I'm…"

"Don't say you're not. Your dinner for Sylvia was an enormous success. Surely, you have no regrets."

"None. About that. But I do regret that the responsibilities that are expected of me aren't…well, they don't fit with…"

"What you enjoy doing?"

She let out a breath. "That's it exactly. But there's more to it than simply tasks I enjoy or don't enjoy. It's as if my heart is in the village but I am stuck at the Manor."

"So you were happier as a shop girl?"

She hesitated, not wishing to hurt him. "I enjoy talking to people, helping them, being friends with them."

"So Father and I aren't enough for you?"

She plucked a thread from his lapel. "It's not that. I love you both. I love my life."

"Parts of it."

It was hard to put into words. "It's just that I feel my life was more fulfilling and helpful to others when I was a merchant's daughter rather than when I am a viscount's daughter-in-law." She hurried to add. "Please don't take offense. I love you both immensely."

"I know you do. But it sounds as if you prefer people over position."

She jumped on his words. "That's it! You've said in four words what lays heavy on my heart."

He stepped to her side and gazed out the window. "Unfortunately with the rebuilding of the Hall, there is little opportunity to change our lives—more than they've already been changed by the fire."

She took his arm and leaned her cheek against it. "Please don't think I'm unhappy." She glanced at his hands. "I'm very happy, and very, very grateful that you and Etta are alive and safe."

Joseph looked down. "I wish I could have saved Nanny." It was not the first time he'd expressed that wish.

The clock on the mantel chimed half-past nine, forcing them to leave their discussion. "Do you have a meeting with the men?"

"I do." Joseph headed towards the door. "What are you going to do this morning?"

She hid her smile. "You will see."

Lila, Genevieve, and Sylvia stood in the doorway of the earl's study and waited for the men to notice them.

"Newley is there now," Jack said, "checking on the final debris removal." He saw the women and looked up from his desk. Joseph and Morgan sat nearby, and also turned around to look at them.

"Hello, darling," Joseph said to Lila. "Genevieve. Sylvia."

Morgan gave Genevieve a wink—for she'd told him about her plan.

The earl stood. "Ladies? What can we do for you?"

Since the earl was Lila's father, she'd been assigned to speak for all of them. "Papa, we wanted to ask a favor—of all three of you men."

"Sit with us," he said.

They'd agreed on this point too. "We don't wish to take much of your time," Lila said.

"But you do want a favor," Joseph said.

Lila exchanged a glance with Genevieve. Subtlety wasn't working, so Genevieve took over. "It's been two weeks. Our sewing workshop is up and running and we would like to have a grand opening for the village."

"*For* the village?" the earl asked. "I thought you were replacing burned uniforms."

"We were," Sylvia said.

"At first," Genevieve said. "But once we settled into the new space we got the idea of opening it up to anyone who would like to sew. A communal workshop."

"Do you think there *are* women who want to sew?" he asked.

"We do. They've just never been given the means or the opportunity to learn how to use a machine."

"So what can we do for you?" Joseph asked.

"We thought it would be especially meaningful if the three of you presided over the opening." Genevieve searched every face. Morgan seemed confused, for she hadn't mentioned this point to him.

The men looked at each other, as if assessing their answer without any discussion.

"I don't think so," the earl said.

"I agree," Morgan said.

"And I," Joseph said.

Genevieve couldn't believe it. "Why won't you do this? It will only take a short—"

"It's not a matter of time," Jack said. "It's because it is your project."

"We have had nothing to do with it," Joseph said.

"You ladies birthed the idea and determined every detail," Morgan said. "And Lila, you negotiated the rent and ordered the tables."

"Tilda and Beth have helped too," Genevieve said.

"I'm sure they have," Jack said. "Which solidifies our decision not to intrude on your moment of glory."

"My, my," Sylvia said with a smile to Jack. "Men who are willing to share the glory? I'm not sure what to think of such an extraordinary display of manhood."

Jack blushed. He looked to his desk, then back at Sylvia with a smile. "We will share a bit of the credit—when it is well-deserved."

"So you're only minimally extraordinary?" she teased.

"Fully. I assure you." He winked at her.

Winked at her? There was some obvious flirtation going on between them. Genevieve would have to ask Sylvia about it later.

"Be it known," Joseph said with a smile to his wife, "we are very proud of you."

"You have proved to be amazing women," Morgan added.

Jack nodded. "Actually, I've been meaning to commend all of you for other reasons." He looked at Sylvia. "To you, Lady Silvey, goes the award as the most adaptable houseguest in the county."

"Only the county?"

He grinned. "We appreciate your attitude and how you've jumped into the fray to help."

"I am extraordinarily good at jumping." She offered a small bow.

More flirting?

Jack continued. "Genevieve, I appreciate what you've done since your mother left to get married. And then, with the India contingent leaving...you have proven yourself a natural at being the mistress of the Manor."

Genevieve was touched. "Thank you. I am trying."

"You are succeeding." But Jack wasn't through. "And you, daughter. To lose your home and have to move out and deal with all you have lost..."

Lila found Genevieve's hand. "What I've gained."

"See, gentlemen? Witness the remarkable women in our lives." He began to applaud, and the other men stood and joined in.

It was embarrassing. "Enough of this," Genevieve said.

Suddenly, Clarissa appeared in the doorway. "I heard applause. To my knowledge I am the only one in this household who receives applause."

"Until now, Clarissa," Jack said. "Genevieve, Lila, and Sylvia are ready to fully open the sewing workshop in the village."

Genevieve saw a quick veil of irritation drop over Clarissa's face. But then she offered her own fleeting applause. "Bravo."

"Are you involved in the workshop, Clarissa?" Morgan asked. He knew very well she was not, for he had listened to Genevieve's complaints.

"I'm afraid I have little aptitude for the small talents of life."

Small talents? "The small talent of sewing helps others. What does your larger talent do in that regard?" Genevieve asked.

It was ironic that at the moment Clarissa had a full audience, she was without words.

She turned on her heel. "Damon and I are going out for a ride. Ta-ta."

"Well said, Genevieve," Jack said after she'd left them.

The men chuckled, then turned back to their work. As the women left, Lila grinned, "I agree. Well said."

Their words of praise were as good as any standing ovation.

After interrupting the men in her uncle's study, Clarissa met Damon in the foyer to go riding. But at the front door she hesitated. "Go ahead to the stables, Damon. I will be with you shortly. I forgot something."

"Nonsense," he said. "I'll wait for you."

"There's no need."

He adjusted his hat in the foyer mirror. "Tis no problem. I will wait."

"Suit yourself." She went upstairs to her room, closed the door, and leaned against it. She hadn't forgotten anything, but needed a moment to be alone.

Although she'd pretended otherwise, the applause the other women had received from the men grated on her. Sewing *was* a small talent—especially compared to the talent she'd shown on stage, the talent that had often earned standing ovations.

They weren't standing for you. You were in the chorus. They were standing for the lead players.

She pressed her fingers to her forehead, willing the distinction away and forcing her to face the issue at hand.

Was she upset because of their accomplishments or for her own lack of involvement?

"I don't want to *sew*." She spat the last word as though it was foul.

Then you can't be concerned about their workshop, or any of the accolades it brings.

Her thoughts flit back to the applause. Obviously it loomed at the center of the issue.

And then she knew the core of it. "The family has never given me applause."

Her family hadn't known about her time on the stage until it was over. When she'd returned home — with Beth — they had welcomed her back, but their reception had been tainted by an underlying layer of disapproval and judgment. They loved Clarissa but did not support her choices. Yet as time passed, they seemed to accept and love Beth more freely than they accepted and loved Clarissa.

She shook her head violently. "This is ridiculous. Stop it, Clarissa. It does no good."

Suddenly, there was a knock on the door she was leaning against, making her start. She stepped away and took a breath. "Yes?"

"Olly olly oxen free."

It was Damon.

"Are you all right?"

With her acting ability she should have been able to pull off a lie, but on impulse, she opened the door and said, "No, I am not."

He cocked his head. "May I come in?"

Although it was totally improper to have him in her bedroom, she stepped aside so he could enter. She closed the door behind him.

"What's wrong?"

How to word it... "The women are setting themselves against me."

"How so?"

She'd used the wrong phrase. "Never mind. I exaggerate. Let's go."

He put a hand on her arm, stopping her. "There is no never mind to it. We're not leaving until you explain."

She sighed dramatically. "I feel left out."

He sniggered. "Of their sewing bee?"

"It's not the sewing so much."

"You don't like them banding together without you?"

Her shrug made him try another tact.

"You don't like their success?"

"They're not successful. It hasn't even opened yet."

He put a hand to his chest. "Surely, it's not because they've left you alone to entertain me?"

Was he serious or jesting?

He pulled her close. "*I* can be very entertaining."

She pushed him away. "I enjoy spending time with you, Damon, but let's not get cocky about it." With that, she turned on her heel to leave.

He took her arm and pulled her back. "You said you forgot something?"

She could tell by the glint in his eyes what *he* wanted. Expected.

Clarissa knew that withholding affection could often be a powerful tool. "I can do without."

Then she left the room and received a good dose of satisfaction when he followed.

Bravo.

Genevieve made the choice for the three of them to walk to the village for the grand opening. "I hope you don't mind," she said. "But my nerves require movement to dissipate."

"I enjoy the walk," Lila said.

"As do I," Sylvia said. "And don't be nervous. It's a grand thing that the men gave us their blessing."

"And applause."

"And kind words." Genevieve linked her arm through Lila's. "Your father is very kind to praise us as he did."

"He's a kind man."

"A charming man," Sylvia added.

Genevieve stopped walking in order to face her. "You two have a certain rapport between you."

"I noticed that too," Lila said. "Which means...?"

Sylvia put her hands to her flushed cheeks. "We've tried very hard not to let the rest of you know, but—"

"Know what?"

"Know that we find each other...amiable."

Genevieve laughed. "Amiable? What an old-fashioned term."

"A bland term," Lila said.

"A totally unacceptable term."

Sylvia wrapped the ribbon from her hat around a finger, looking very much the coy maiden. "Perhaps that is a bit understated."

"Tell us!"

Sylvia let the ribbon go. It coiled in a ringlet that touched the lace on her bodice. "We have spent some very agreeable moments together."

"Alone?"

"As much as we can be alone in a house full to overflowing."

"More than moments?" Lila asked.

"A few strolls through the garden. A few conversations in his study and in the music room."

"Did you seek him out or did he seek you?" It was an important distinction.

"He sought me out at first, but now we seek each other. Whenever we can."

Genevieve and Lila both sighed then laughed at their synchronicity.

Sylvia's face grew serious. "Do you approve? Jack was afraid you wouldn't—which is why we have taken great pains to be discreet."

Lila pulled Sylvia into an embrace. "Of course we approve. Papa has been alone long enough."

"So you...you wouldn't object if I became your step-mother?"

"It has come to that already?" Genevieve asked.

"Not yet, but I expect it may."

Lila stood between them, linked arms, and began to walk. "I'm not sure I will ever be able to call you 'mother.'"

"Sylvia will do."

"Does your brother know?" Genevieve asked.

"Ian came upon us once..." She smiled slyly. "As we were kissing."

"Kissing?" Lila scrunched up her face.

"We are not ancient, you know."

"I know it's not proper to ask, but how old are you?" Lila asked.

"I could be coy and state that a woman never reveals her age, but since you will be my daughter... I am forty-nine."

"But Papa is only forty-eight."

"I've always wanted to be the older woman." Then she added, "But not that old. Not *too* old."

Genevieve laughed. "I am not sure you will ever be *too* old."

"Jack will keep me young."

"And you, him," Lila said.

As they approached the village Genevieve felt a new spring in her step. "Your joyful news has made my nerves evaporate. Well done!"

It was time.

Genevieve stood outside the new sewing workshop with the door closed, and a small but eager crowd gathered around her. During the last two weeks the whole of Summerfield had been curious to see what Mrs. Weston and Mrs. Kidd were doing in the empty storefront on the square. Sewing? With a machine? Now two machines, for the one Genevieve had ordered had been delivered yesterday.

She had worried about not having the men present to add ceremony to the occasion. Yet it was rather nice to be able to do the honors themselves, though perhaps a big unveiling was overdoing the event a bit.

Now that she had their attention…

"Ladies and gentlemen, thank you for coming today. I'll let Mrs. Kidd begin the remarks."

Lila cleared her throat. "As you all know, the tragic fire at Crompton Hall left its servants without proper attire. What started as a small project has grown and expanded into this venture. Inside are tables and benches made by the Billings' carpentry shop that have transformed an empty space into the first of its kind, a sewing workshop." She nodded to Genevieve.

"When I first came to Summerfield I had my sewing machine sent over, and just today, another has been added." She motioned for two housemaids to come close. "Look at the outfits we have made using these machines."

Some of the women stepped forward to examine the seams and the top stitching.

"Smaller stitches than I ever make," one said.

"Faster too," Genevieve added. "For these two skirts, blouses, and aprons, were created in two days."

There was an outcry of "Two days?" and "That's not possible."

Lila drew her grandmother and Rose forward. "Mrs. Hayward and Rose have been ordering in sewing patterns, fabrics, thread, and other sewing necessities."

"All on sale for ten-percent off this week," Rose said.

A woman raised her hand. "But I don't know how to use a fancy machine like that."

Genevieve and Lila exchanged a look. This next was a new development. "We will offer free lessons to anyone who wishes to learn."

Five women raised their hands.

"My Ted needs a new shirt."

"My baby is growing right out of her clothes."

"I haven't had a new skirt in years."

109

Genevieve's heart warmed at their interest—it was more than they expected. Would they be able to handle the demand?

There was no time for second thoughts.

"Let's see inside," someone said.

Genevieve put her hand on the doorknob. "I present to you the Summerfield Sewing Workshop." She opened the door and led the people inside.

Tilda and Beth were prepared, offering a tour of the facilities. Sylvia was ready at one of the sewing machines, giving a brief demonstration.

The maids came in to allow for more inspection of their garments, and Mrs. Hayward stood by the large cutting table with a sample of the mercantile's wares.

Genevieve and Lila positioned themselves by the window, answering questions and receiving accolades. It was pleasantly overwhelming.

When they had a free moment, Lila leaned over to Genevieve, "Did you ever expect this?"

"Not at all."

"We *did* ask God to show us what He wanted us to do with the work we do here."

Genevieve laughed. "As the men let us have the glory, I give it back to the Almighty. I do hope we can keep up."

Clarissa and Damon rode through Summerfield on their way to a special picnic spot Damon had hinted about.

What had been a quiet little village the day before, now teemed with activity—all centered on the storefront beside the bakery.

Through the window they could see ladies and children inside.

"Is that my mother?" Damon asked, nodding towards the store.

It was. Lady Silvey, Lila, Genevieve, Tilda, and even Beth. Clarissa tried unsuccessfully to squelch a wave of jealousy. "Help me down."

Damon dismounted, then lifted her to the ground. She strode into the building.

"Mum!" Beth rushed forward, wrapping her arms around Clarissa.

"What is going on?" she asked.

"It's the Summerfield Sewing Workshop. You missed the grand opening. Look at all the people. Isn't it wonderful?"

Actually... "But what are they all doing here? I thought you were sewing uniforms for the servants."

"We were, and we are, but Mrs. Weston and Mrs. Kidd got the idea to open it to the ladies of Summerfield so they can learn to sew their own clothes."

"Like a business?"

"Not quite. We're not getting money for it. But they *will* be buying fabric and patterns at the mercantile."

Which is owned by the earl and Morgan.

Damon slipped his riding crop under his arm. "How entrepreneurial. How...American."

"Mrs. Weston is from America," Beth said. "Her father earned his fortune selling sewing machines."

Speaking of...Genevieve came to greet them. "I'm so glad you came. What do you think of our endeavor?"

"Do you really believe you can teach these ladies to sew?" Clarissa asked.

Damon's mother approached. "They taught me, and I guarantee I had no knowledge whatsoever of seam allowances and selvages, and only knew 'darts' as a game played in a pub."

"You've been in a pub, Mother?" Damon asked.

"Don't be a snob, Damon. Remember that delightful pub in Munich?"

"Yes, yes." He took Clarissa's arm. "Shall we go?"

"Why don't you stay and help?" Genevieve asked.

"I would be of little help."

111

"And we have plans." Damon tipped his hat and led her out. He walked the horses to a stepping stone, and helped Clarissa mount her sidesaddle. As they rode out of the village he caught her eye, "Aren't you glad I came along and saved you from being involved in such nonsense?"

She used her crop and trotted ahead.

The place Damon chose for their picnic was not new to Clarissa, but she let him believe it was.

He had come prepared. He spread a cloth on the ground and removed a bevy of food and drink from his saddlebags. There were sandwiches, apples, and two slices of last night's chocolate cake.

"When did you plan all this?" she asked, as she adjusted the slices of ham and cheese on the bread.

"Last night. I have Mrs. McDeer fully under my spell. The cake was her addition."

"Who don't you have under your spell?"

He took a bite of sandwich, then lay on his side, leaning on an elbow. "Are you jealous?"

"Of Mrs. McDeer? No."

"Of the other women who have come under my spell?"

She hated feeling her cheeks grow warm.

"Surely, you've had your own romantic conquests in London," he said. "After all, you were on the stage. You lived on your own."

She threw an apple at him, and it bounced off his chest. "Why do people assume such a thing?"

"Because it's usually true."

"It is not true. A woman can retain her honor while using her talents on the stage and living an independent life." She paused, not sure she should say the following aloud. "Though it was difficult."

"Very well, then. I commend your virtuous victories."

"Don't mock me."

"What would you like me to do with you?"

She would have thrown the other apple if it had been within reach. She took a bite of her sandwich, trying to gain the courage to ask her own question. "So…what kind of experiences did you have while traveling through Europe with your mother?"

"That is a veiled question."

"I thought it quite straightforward."

His eyebrows rose, then fell. "Mother is a jolly sport."

"Because…?"

"She allowed me *my* independence."

"So you didn't travel together?"

"We did, but once we settled in a city we were usually there a month or more so we had time to see the sites together, but otherwise we found our own…entertainment."

She sighed. "How can you make every word sound steeped in scandal?"

He leaned closer. "Because it was."

"I don't believe you."

"Good. Because you shouldn't."

It was her turn to raise an eyebrow. "So…you exaggerate?"

"Perhaps. A little."

Good.

"It makes for better stories, don't you agree?"

"You haven't shared full stories with me, only snippets."

"Snippets then. It makes for better snippets." He collected the stray apple and took a bite out of it. "So what do you truly think of me? Have my purposeful misleadings led you astray?"

"Astray from what?"

"From the fact that I am a rather boring fellow who enjoyed seeing Europe with my mother."

She laughed. "No matter what is truth and what is story, you can never be called boring."

He made a by-your-leave gesture with his hand. "Thank you, Miss Weston."

She felt better about him, yet needed to press the issue a bit more. "So...you didn't charm the single ladies of Europe?"

"A few." He sat upright and leaned towards her, whispering in her ear. "But none as delightful or beautiful as you."

"How many is a few?"

He nibbled her ear lobe, then kissed her cheek, and her mouth... They fell upon the grass, making Clarissa forget the question.

Lila stood at the counter of the mercantile, making a list of sewing items to order.

"Nana, I think we need some bolts of cottons, perhaps with a small print, something ladies would like as their Sunday dress."

"We do have this one," Nana said as she unfurled the end of a bolt that showed blue flowers on a gray background.

Just then, a customer came in with a baby slung across her chest, a little boy, and a girl who was on the edge of her bloom. It took Lila a moment to recognize her.

"Mrs. Bramm," she said. "And is this pretty girl Mary?"

Mrs. Bramm fingered her collar and bobbed a curtsy. "My, my. Mrs. Kidd. I didn't expect to see you in here. You don't work here no more, do you?"

"No, I don't."

"Course not," Mrs. Bramm said to herself. "What with you and your family rising up, then you marrying..." She shook the murmurings away. "It's nice to see you."

Nana showed the little boy a box of blocks to amuse him while his mother shopped. "It's nice to see you too, Mrs. Bramm. What is your baby's name?" Lila was unable to see whether it was a boy or girl with only the side of its head and a small arm showing.

"His name's Daniel. Three-months-old today. And that there is Frank."

"I remember you when you were Daniel's age."

The boy paid her little attention, so Lila turned to the girl. "How old are you now, Mary?"

"Twelve." The girl didn't make eye contact, but focused on the flowered fabric.

"It's a pretty piece, isn't it?" Lila said.

"Stop touching the fabric," her mother said. "Yer hands ain't clean. And we didn't come for anything so fancy." She turned to Nana. "Mrs. Hayward, we needs flour and some nails to fix the boards in the..." She looked to the floor. "The necessary building."

While Nana filled the order, Lila did a little observing. The dress Mary wore was getting too tight, the hand-sewn seams near to bursting, and the sleeves and length inches too short. She was becoming a woman and would need a dress with more shape in both the hips and bosom. Lila purposely stood beside the girl to gauge her height. She was slim, so a standard pattern would fit her...

"Do you like blue?" Lila asked.

"Yes, ma'am. It's my favorite." She reached to touch the fabric again, as though it was a magnet drawing her fingers close. But at the last minute, she remembered her mother's chiding and pulled her hand back.

"It's been a while since you've had a new dress?"

"A while."

"Mary. Frank. Come now."

"Nice seeing you, Mrs. Bramm," Lila said. "Mary."

The girl's gaze lingered a moment as she walked out to the square.

Lila unrolled the bolt. "Three yards should make a dress, don't you think?"

"You want a dress made out of this?" Nana asked.

"It's not for me, it's for Mary."

"They don't have the money for it. They're two months behind on their tab as it is."

"I'm not going to charge them. It will be my gift."

Nana took Lila's chin in her hand. "There you go again, being my precious gem." Then she nodded towards the shelf. "There is some pretty lace over there for the collar and cuffs."

The wife of Summerfield's estate manager sat at the sewing machine as Genevieve looked on. "It will take some practice to control the treadle, Mrs. Collins, but you're already doing better."

"I'll get it," the woman said. "Mr. Collins would appreciate me making the children the clothing they need, faster than by hand. There's always so much to do with four little ones."

The four little ones were climbing on a table and bench in the far side of the room. Beth and Tilda were doing their best to keep them happy, but Genevieve knew Mrs. Collins' time was short.

When the two-year-old bit the three-year-old and was whapped in the mouth by the four-year-old, who was yelled at by the five-year-old, the time was up.

"Oh dear," Mrs. Collins said. "I wish I could stay longer. My life is lived in five-minute pieces. If only the four of them would coordinate the same five-minutes."

After she left with her brood, it was the first time the workshop had been quiet all morning.

The women all took a breath at the same time—which made them laugh.

"The workshop is a success," Sylvia said.

"Three ladies said they would be back later," Beth said.

"And Mrs. Collins would have stayed longer if not for her children acting up."

Tilda looked at the spot where the children had been playing. "They would have been better behaved if we had some toys here."

"Why wasn't the older one at school?" Sylvia asked.

"There is no school," Genevieve said. "The teacher we had moved to London, so the school is currently disbanded."

"Summerfield doesn't have a school? That's dreadful."

"We're trying to get another teacher hired, but it's hard to compete with the offerings of London."

Tilda raised a hand. "I could teach them."

"That's a wonderful offer," Genevieve said, "but I'm afraid you need to be quite knowledgeable to be a teacher."

Beth stepped up. "Tilda's good at teaching reading and numbers. She's teaching me right now."

"Taking up where you left off," Tilda said with a nod to Genevieve. "Beth is doing quite well."

"Which proves Tilda can teach," Beth said.

Genevieve didn't want to totally discourage their enthusiasm, but there were standards. "Let me think about it."

Tilda's shoulders slumped with disappointment. "Until then, we *could* make a place here at the workshop to entertain the children while their mums learn to sew."

"We could have toys and books," Beth said.

"And I could even teach some of them their ABCs or get them to draw."

Tilda did have drawing talent. Genevieve's thoughts spun with the new idea. She moved to the side of the room where the Collins' children had been playing. "Perhaps if we moved this table towards the window, we could create a little corner—"

"A children's corner!" Tilda said.

"Well done, Tilda," Sylvia said.

At that moment, Lila came in the workshop, carrying a fold of blue-flowered fabric. "We have a dress to sew, ladies!"

"And we have a new idea for you, Lila."

Chapter Seven

Genevieve wrapped her shawl tighter around her shoulders as she walked into the village. The sun was just coming up, casting long shadows across the square. No one was about, though she did see a light on in the bakery.

It was not surprising. No one but the servants were up at the Manor either. And right now, Lila, Sylvia, Clarissa, Tilda, and Beth were cozy in their covers with little thought to the projects left to do at the workshop.

Genevieve used her key and stepped in. It seemed colder inside than out. She lit the sconces on the walls and made quick work of a fire in the heating stove in the corner.

"There," she said, feeling rather proud of herself. "I may be the wife of the heir, but no one can say I'm helpless."

She moved to the neat stacks of dresses-in-progress, and chose the one for Mary Bramm. Between Lila and Genevieve they had determined the probable size of the girl and cut out the fabric. Lila had started to sew the seams, but hadn't pinned them first, so the edges weren't even. Genevieve hadn't said anything, but she was not going to give the girl a gift that was badly made.

She sat near a lamp and ripped out the faulty seams.

And fumed while she worked.

Fumed about the inequitable way the sewing tasks were accomplished. Sylvia and Lila helped, but as novices they needed constant overseeing. Tilda and Beth also pitched in when the shop was free of children who needed tending. But they could not be counted on for a steady contribution to the stack of sewing that threatened to drown them.

The workshop was definitely a success. Since the grand opening a week ago, they'd had a constant stream of ladies wanting lessons. The large table had been used to cut out at least eight dresses and skirts, and those pieces now sat stacked by the window, waiting to be sewn. And this wasn't counting the rest of the servants' uniforms and clothes for Etta left to sew. The mountain of chores dogged Genevieve's sleep and had brought her here this early morning to finish Mary's dress.

Once the faulty sewing was ripped out, she took up the pins and carefully matched the seams for sewing. The treadle took on the rhythm of her grumbles, *If I don't do it no one will, if I don't do it no one will...*

Genevieve heard the door open and turned towards it, ready to commend whoever had come to help her.

But it was Mrs. Keening. "I saw you come in, Mrs. Weston. I have to gets up early, but you?"

"There are things to do."

"Ain't there always." She touched the calico of a dress for the butcher's wife. "This is pretty."

"You should stop at the mercantile and pick a piece for yourself. Mrs. Hayward has brought in a nice shipment of pretty fabrics."

"I can't sew more than a button."

Genevieve wanted to get back to work, but knew now was the time to promote their offerings. "We can teach you. Perhaps in the afternoon when you're not busy?"

The woman stroked the fabric. "I suppose Mr. Keening could run the place a while—if he don't burn it down."

"When you have a free moment today, go talk to Mrs. Hayward."

"I may do that." She looked down at her terribly dingy dress that probably had been a pretty caramel color a few decades earlier but now resembled the sunbaked stone around the communal water well.

"With the ginger in your hair a green or turquoise would be pretty on you."

She put a hand to her hair, which had already come loose during her morning baking. "You think so?"

"I do. And I know some fabric of that color arrived yesterday."

"A new dress. Crikey." She suddenly lifted her nose and took a whiff. "Ack. Ralph's burning the bread. I needs to go."

"I look forward to seeing you." Genevieve turned back to the machine, and began a new rhythm. "'She riseth also while it is yet night, she riseth also—'"

She stopped sewing as she realized she'd just repeated a Bible verse.

Her Bible! Where was her Bible?

Her mind flit through the goings-on of the past few weeks. She hadn't had her quiet time with God ever since Summerfield Manor had been overrun with guests.

"My Bible is probably still in the guestroom—the guestroom that is now occupied by servants!"

She stood, ready to retrieve it immediately.

But then she sat down. She had work to do here.

The Bible could wait.

"Lila, if you please?" Lord Newley said to her after breakfast.

"Of course."

As he led her to the earl's study, her thoughts swam. Had she done something to offend him? Was there a crisis with him or Joseph or Crompton Hall? She got along well with Ian, but they would never share the warmth and camaraderie that Genevieve shared with *her* father-in-law, the earl. Ian was not a warm man, but rather was consistently temperate, with the possibility of clouds.

She was a bit relieved when he didn't take a seat behind Papa's desk, but simply entered and stood.

"Yes?" she asked.

"I see you have been involved with the ladies' sewing project."

"Yes, I have. We've been able to provide new uniforms for a good number of our servants."

"Very commendable." He studied the toe of his boot for a moment before looking at her. "But I need you to focus on the Hall, Lila. The rebuilding of the structure is progressing slowly, but steadily, with Joseph and myself able to make most of the larger decisions. But when it comes to the interior, to the choices regarding the décor and furnishings, draperies and finishes… I need you to make those decisions. Once made, you will need to go to London."

"London." The thought of going to the city made her heartbeat tremble.

"It's not like I'm asking you to go to Moscow. It's just London. You've been there before." His eyebrow rose. "You are familiar with London, yes?"

"I used to occasionally visit Nana and Grandfather there. And Joseph and I were there. Once."

"Once." He shook his head. "I have explained to Joseph that you two need to be more social. We all have a responsibility to participate in the London season for the good of the family name."

"I am sorry for that." A dark veil fell over her joy for marrying a man who was as much of a homebody as herself. Alone, they were perfection. But in regard to society? They were misfits.

"You do feel comfortable enough to go?"

"I can do it. I *will* do it. But where should I go to purchase the things we'll need? I have no idea where to buy items worthy of the Hall."

He looked past her a moment. "It needs to be done, Lila. I must be able to depend on you. *Can* I depend on you?"

Not really. "I'll do my best."

Genevieve snipped the last thread from Mary's dress. She stood to take a proper look at it just as the door opened and the ladies filed in.

"Well now. Here you are," Sylvia said. "We didn't see you at breakfast and no one knew where you were."

"Mrs. McDeer made scones with raisins," Beth said. "They were yummy."

"You had three," Tilda said.

Lila collected their bonnets and shawls and hung them on hooks. Only then did she fully look at Genevieve.

"Mary's dress! You finished it!"

I resewed every seam.

They came close to give the dress its due. "I do like that narrow lace on the neck and cuffs," Sylvia said. "Quite appropriate for a young lady."

"But not too fancy," Lila said. "When I chose the fabric, I was going to get yard-good lace for a collar, but Nana said no. Not for a dress that would be worn much, and would be Mary's one-good dress."

"If she's twelve she'll probably grow out of it before she wears it out," Sylvia said.

Tilda held up a bundle she'd been carrying. "I brought some paper and pencils for the children today. I thought we'd draw."

"It's so good of you to share your talent, Tilda," Lila said.

And then they dispersed, each to their own venture, leaving Genevieve holding the dress she had created in the early morning hours. She wanted to clap her hands, demand their attention, and force them to recognize her sacrifice.

But then a customer came in and all hopes for a dramatic moment of validation and praise faded like the fabric on Mrs. Keening's dress.

"Afternoon, Nana."

Nana stopped what she was doing and came over to give Lila a hug. "Would you like to see the new fabrics that were delivered?"

"Of course." They moved to a counter where new bolts were displayed. "I especially like this turquoise one."

"That's the one Mrs. Keening chose when she came in an hour ago," Nana said. "She said it looked pleasing with her coloring."

"Since when does she pay attention to coloring and fabrics?"

"The same question could be asked of many of the women in town. Suddenly given options, they've discovered a newborn sense of fashion."

Lila laughed, then looked around the store. "I do miss this place."

"It's still here."

"But I'm not."

"Ah, the curse of being a proper lady."

"I have the life most women could only dream about."

Nana gazed at her over her glasses. "But...?"

Lila glanced at the front door, not wanting to start the discussion if a customer was imminent.

"I don't miss living in Crompton Hall."

"It's a little hard to live there now..."

"Even if it were fully renewed. Even if the fire had never happened. I much prefer to spend time in the village, here with you, than in those echoing rooms, twiddling my thumbs."

"You twiddle much?"

"Too much. There's not enough to do. Even if I wish to be involved in my family's business, as a woman it's not my proper place. And I can't take on the chores of the servants, for they need their employment."

"You have Etta."

"I do. But, Nanny Mabel said it wasn't appropriate for me to spend too much time with her."

"Is there too much time with a child?"

Lila shrugged and got to the point. "If it wouldn't be too improper, I would love to work here, in the store." She pointed to the table of featured goods that greeted customers upon entering. "Remember when I made a display of blackberry preserves using a basket of fresh berries to draw the eye?"

"You mother worried that customers would eat the berries without paying."

"Which they did," Lila conceded. "But they also bought the preserves."

"I remember another display you did with toothpaste pots and brushes."

Lila's memories sailed back three years. "I remember how Mother wanted to order expensive silver-handled, badger-bristle toothbrushes, but Papa wouldn't let her because customers preferred the economy of boar-bristle with bone handles."

"I remember that. Your mother's tastes were always more sumptuous than sensible."

Lila tidied a row of combs. "I miss her. Sometimes."

"Of course you do. But take comfort in knowing she'd be proud of you, Jack, and Morgan."

"She'd be a grandmother times three."

"She'd be the Countess of Summerfield."

The irony that Lila's status-seeking mother had died before the secret revealed their proper titles and position continued to dog her. And yet… "I'm not sure the county could have handled Fidelia Weston as their countess."

Nana chuckled. "She would have kept the pot stirred, that's for certain."

It came down to two facts. "I like being with people, Nana. Not as a mistress, but here in the village, among friends I grew up with. Instead, I've just been given the assignment to decorate the Hall, get furniture ordered, and shop in London… I don't enjoy those things at all, nor do I have an aptitude for them."

Their discussion was interrupted by Mrs. Bramm coming in the store with her children. Upon seeing Mary, Lila remembered the finished dress.

"Mary, stay here!"

"What?" Mrs. Bramm asked. "What do you need with Mary, Mrs. Kidd?"

"Just stay here until I get back."

Lila rushed across the street to the workshop. She retrieved Mary's dress that was laid nicely on a table.

Genevieve looked up from her lesson with Mrs. Crown. "Where are you taking that?"

"Mary's at the mercantile. I want to give it to her."

"But I—"

"I need to hurry before she leaves."

In the square, Lila folded the dress carefully, held it behind her back, and rushed into the mercantile.

"Mary? Remember that blue fabric you liked a week or so ago?"

"Yes…"

Lila brought the dress forward and held it by its shoulder-seams. "Voila! For you."

Mary's mouth gaped open, and she looked to Lila, then her mother, then Lila again. "Me?"

"We made it at the workshop. For you. As a gift."

"We can't take such gifts," Mrs. Bramm said. "It's too much."

Lila thought quickly. "Many of us are just learning how to sew, and working on Mary's dress allowed us much-needed practice. By wearing it, she does us a favor by advertising the workshop."

Mary's eyes widened with hope. "Please, Ma?"

"Well…I suppose. To help out the ladies."

Mary held the dress at arm's length, staring at it, as if fearful it would evaporate.

"Come in the back and try it on," Lila suggested.

She led the girl to the living quarters and waited outside her old bedroom while the girl made the change. *Please, God. Let it fit!*

The bedroom door opened and Mary stood before her, beaming. "It fits!" Lila said.

"It does." Mary ran a hand along a sleeve and touched the lace edging. "It's the most prettiest dress I've ever seen." When she looked at Lila her eyes were filled with tears. "I can't thank you enough, Mrs. Kidd." She stepped forward to awkwardly give Lila an embrace. She quickly stepped back, as if only then realizing it wasn't proper.

Lila took her hand. "You are very welcome. Enjoy it."

"Oh, I will. I needs to show Ma."

The sound of her feet running down the stairs brought back memories of Morgan's footfalls. And her own. Her family had been so happy here.

Lila followed her down.

"Gracious sakes," Mrs. Bramm said. "You look like a young lady."

"She is a young lady," Lila said, amazed that Mrs. Bramm seemed surprised that her daughter was on the way to fully-grown.

As soon as they left, Nana put an arm around Lila's shoulders. "Well done, dear girl."

It was. Very well done indeed.

There was a spring in her step as Lila returned to the workshop. Genevieve would be so happy about Mary's reaction—and the fine fit.

But when Lila entered the shop, Genevieve wasn't there.

"Where's Genevieve?" she asked the room.

Sylvia looked up from her sewing. "She left."

"Where did she go?"

"I don't know. She was helping Mrs. Crown and suddenly, she excused herself and left."

Tilda pointed to her bonnet and shawl. "She can't have gone far. She didn't take her things."

Lila's good news would have to wait.

How dare she! I made that dress!

Genevieve stormed down the road leading from the village to the Manor. Her lungs and legs burned from the fast pace, yet her emotions would not allow her to give them rest.

Lila had betrayed her.

Genevieve had been caught off guard when Lila rushed into the shop and snatched Mary's dress away.

I should have gone after her. I should have gone with *her into the mercantile. I should have been there when Mary received the gift. It was* my *gift.*

It was Lila's idea.

She shook the traitorous thought away. She'd had to resew most of Lila's work on the dress. If Genevieve hadn't come into the workshop early, the dress wouldn't have been completed today at all.

Her mother's voice sounded in her head: *Demand your due. You must stand up for yourself, Daughter, for no one else will.*

Genevieve turned around, taking a few steps back towards the village.

Then she turned again, to continue her path towards the Manor.

She made fists, feeling the bite of fingernails in her palms. *What should I do?*

A calico kitten stepped out of the grasses that lined the road and peered up at her.

Genevieve started to pick it up, then remembered how her mother had called all pets "dirty animals." The little thing didn't look dirty.

She picked it up, cuddling it under her chin. "Where did you come from?" She scanned the fields on either side, looking for movement in the grasses, for its mama or siblings. "Where's your family?"

The kitten began to purr and rumble against her chest. It looked old enough to be weaned, but it still wasn't fully grown.

A farmer approached with a small flock of sheep. When he saw Genevieve he stopped and offered a small bow. "Mrs. Weston."

"Mr. Kirby."

He nodded to the cat. "I see you've found a friend."

"I believe she has found me. Do you know who she belongs to?"

"Probably from the litter the Daughtry's had a few months ago." He paused to use his pole to keep a lamb in line. "If you wants to keep her, I'm sure they wouldn't mind. They have plenty enough."

"Thank you. I think I will."

He and his flock moved past and Genevieve was left standing on the road, alone.

But not alone. Not any longer.

She looked towards heaven. "Thank you for calming me."

Then she turned back to town.

As she entered the workshop, she gained every eye.

Beth ran forward. "A kitty!"

Tilda followed, and soon every female in the shop was taking their turn holding the cat.

"Where did you find her?"

"On the road. She stepped out of the grass."

"Can we keep her?"

Genevieve had thought of this. "I think we'll leave it up to her. Beth, go get a few crusts of bread from Mrs. Keening and ask to borrow a bowl for some water."

"It sounds like she's moving in," Sylvia said.

"As I stated, it will be her choice. We often keep the door open so she's free to come and go. If she comes back she is very welcome."

"What her name?" Lila asked.

Genevieve had thought of that too. "Pax."

"That's an odd name," Tilda said. "Does it mean something?"

She looked at Lila. "It does. It means 'peace.'"

Very appropriate, all in all.

"I don't see why we have to go to Crompton Hall," Damon said, as he and Clarissa rode side-by-side. "It's full of busyness, noise, debris, and workers. Unless, of course, the latter is your reason for the visit."

"Workers?" Clarissa asked.

"Some women like to be seen, to be appreciated. Are you that sort of woman?"

"Every woman is that sort of woman." In truth, she had no interest in the workers. Well…maybe just one.

"So what is the reason for our jaunt?"

"Curiosity."

"You are interested in beams and bricks?"

"I am interested in the design of it. There has not been any new building in the county for decades. Every manor and hall is centuries old. I cannot help that I am curious."

"I'm guessing your curiosity has much to do with who owns the Hall."

She pretended otherwise. "The sooner the construction is completed, the sooner Summerfield Manor is ours again." Wishing to put an end to the subject, she chose one of her own. "Plus, I wish to go to Crompton Hall because it's something to *do*."

"Are you getting bored with me?"

"Not bored with you—your person—but bored with our activities. Aren't you overly done with cards, singing, strolling, and riding?"

"Never," he said with a wink. "For what else is there?"

When Damon had first arrived, Clarissa had taken on the task of his entertainment with full fervor—mostly because it relieved her of being involved with that sewing silliness. But as the weeks passed, she'd found that Damon was far too willing to *be* entertained and not willing enough *to* entertain. Yes, he was witty and she was very fond of him—almost too fond. But he generally left the choice of amusement to her, and she was plum out of ideas.

It would have helped if there were friends and neighbors who would socialize with her. But upon Clarissa's return from London with Beth, they'd shunned her. It hadn't bothered her—much—until now, when their company would provide a blessed diversion.

"So, what shall we do this evening?" he asked her.

With Damon confirming his flaw, Clarissa spurred her horse into a run, leaving Damon choking in its dust.

Damon had been correct. Clarissa's presence at Crompton Hall drew every male set of eyes—which was quite enjoyable.

She rode at the outer edge of workers, searching for Timothy. She preferred not to ask after him, but if she must—

Her eyes found him across what used to be the rose garden, giving instruction to two men. He glanced up, saw her, and raised a finger, asking for a minute.

"There's Timothy," she said to Damon. "Help me down."

By the time Damon had lifted her from her sidesaddle to the ground, Timothy had finished his business and was walking towards her.

"Good afternoon, Timothy."

"Miss Weston. Lord Silvey. Have you come for a tour?"

"Is a tour to be had?"

"A partial one. Some areas are still too unstable to approach, but come, I'll show you what we've done so far."

He showed them where damage to the public areas had been reframed, the stairs repaired, and the bedrooms well on their way to their original configuration.

Clarissa stopped at the bedroom that had been hers when she'd first returned from her London foray. She'd hidden out at the Hall until she was ready to face her family. Her memories touched upon her days and nights here, which suddenly led to an idea.

"Are you putting in separate bath rooms and water closets?"

"Well…no. We're replacing what was, not adding different rooms."

"But now is your chance to modernize with indoor plumbing. I'd give anything if the Manor had those luxuries, but Father and Uncle Jack say the cost is prohibitive. But here… Why hasn't anyone thought of that, Timothy?"

He beamed. "Because no one has the vision you do, Miss Weston. It's a grand idea. But it does complicate things."

She flipped his comment away with a hand. "What's a few complications for another two hundred years of use?"

"There are no such skilled workers in Summerfield. Plumbers? Is that what they're called?"

Clarissa swept a hand to encompass the dozens of workers. "So all these men are from Summerfield?"

"Not at all. And finding additional men throughout the county and beyond has already caused delays."

"Then a few more well-chosen delays won't matter."

Damon entered the conversation. "Didn't you say you were eager to get the Manor back—"

She stopped his words with a look. "I think it's imperative that measures are taken to make Crompton Hall an example of modernized manor architecture."

Timothy laughed. "I never took you for a visionary."

"Nor did I," Damon said.

In truth, she was just as surprised as they were, but pretended otherwise. "Your astonishment regarding my extraordinary attributes only proves that people don't know me as well as they think they do."

Timothy smiled. "I appreciate your ideas. I'll talk to Lord Newley about them."

She began to second-guess her involvement. This was Lila and Joseph's home. What was she doing, making it better? "It is of no concern to me if the changes are made or not made. It was just a suggestion."

"A good one. An insightful one."

She turned away before he could see her blush. "Let's go, Damon. We've taken Timothy away from his work long enough."

After reading a bedtime story to the twins and enduring yet another evening with Damon and Clarissa singing at the piano, Genevieve fell into bed.

Morgan got in beside her. "You're tired."

"Overly so. Why do some days seem to have forty hours instead of twenty-four?"

"The day has been dragging?"

"Not at all. It merely seemed never-ending because I was so busy."

"You were up too early. No more going to the workshop at dawn. No one knew where you were."

"I must do what needs to be done."

"Others can help."

Which brought up the memory of Lila taking credit for Mary's dress. Should she bring it up? The image of Pax intervened.

"I found a kitten today."

"Here?"

"On the road. Her name is Pax and she's our pet at the workshop. Everyone has adopted her."

"I didn't know you liked cats."

"I didn't either. My parents never allowed any. But I find her … calming."

"Hence her name?"

She nodded her cheek against the pillow and sent another thank you to God.

My Bible!

She sat erect in bed.

"What's wrong?"

"My Bible has been in the blue guestroom ever since the Kidds moved in."

"You're only just noticing it?"

She sank back to her pillow. "Don't make me feel worse than I do."

"You can get it in the morning."

"Help me remember," she asked, as she lay her head on her long-awaited pillow.

Chapter Eight

As soon as the breakfast dishes were cleared away, Lila went into the dining room. She needed a table, and didn't want to intrude on the desk in Genevieve's morning room.

Faced with a table and sixteen chairs, Lila began to sit at the one that was the most accessible — Papa's chair at the head of the table — but she hesitated. She couldn't imagine anyone objecting to her use of the room. But to make sure no offense could possibly be taken, she took a seat at the chair she sat in for meals, facing the door.

Her props were few: some paper and a pencil. But her thoughts were many. After being challenged by Lord Newley to step up and act like the mistress of Crompton Hall, she needed to focus on the needs of the property.

She adjusted the stack of paper so the corners were even, then checked the nib of the pencil — being disappointed that it was sharp. *It* was ready to begin. Was she?

Where to begin? *Lord, help me do this.*

She leafed through the papers. Ian had provided her with an inventory of the furniture that had escaped the fire. She perused the list, but immediately felt her heartbeat quicken. Was "mahogany sideboard" the sideboard that was in the dining room, or the sideboard that stood in the corridor leading to Ian's study? And there were twelve "wardrobes" listed. Which to which bedroom?

Four silver candelabra. One silver footed soup tureen. Two silver epergnes...

"What's an epergne?"

"It's a multi-armed centerpiece with little dishes where you can put flowers, nuts, or candy." Clarissa swept into the room. "What are you doing in here? Why aren't you off…sewing something?"

Lila ignored the disdain in her last question. "I have been asked to oversee the refurbishing of the décor and furnishings at Crompton Hall."

Her eyes brightened. "Now *there* is an enjoyable task."

"Enjoyable?"

"You don't think so?"

Lila sighed deeply. "Not at all. I know next to nothing about design. Beautifying Etta's nursery was task enough."

"Does Newley wish for the Hall to be the same? Or will he allow changes?"

"I don't know. It hasn't been touched since his wife died."

"Which was when Joseph was born."

"So, it's probably due for some change." Lila admitted.

"It was a rather dark, somber place."

Lila was relieved at her assessment. "I always thought so too. I meant to take on the job, but never got to it—nor felt I was up to the undertaking."

"There is your problem, Lila. You think of it as a chore."

"Without the proper creativity and talent, I see it as nothing less."

Clarissa pointed at the list. "What is that?"

Lila gladly handed it to her across the table. "It's a list of the furniture and decorations that remain."

Clarissa glanced over the pages. "It's much too vague."

"That's what I thought. I have no idea which sideboard or wardrobe is which."

Clarissa handed it back to her. "It needs to be redone with more detail, and arranged according to room."

"Thank you. That's a good idea." Unwittingly, she expelled another sigh.

"What now?"

"Even if I knew what went where, I have no inkling of what to do next. And Ian wants me to go shopping in London and—"

"Shopping?"

"I know I should be excited about the prospect, but I have no notion of where to go."

"Has he given provided a budget?"

"None. Although I am certain he would appreciate frugality."

"Frugality and a fine estate do not mesh. And stop acting like he's asked you to clean the stables. He's asked you — directed you — to shop. In London. In fabulous London."

A sudden idea presented itself in the air between them. "Would you be interested in shopping for me?" Lila asked.

Clarissa's eyes brightened in a way Lila hadn't seen in months. "If I was responsible for the shopping, I would want to be the one who designs the rooms from the onset."

A weight fell from Lila's shoulders and landed on the floor with a thud. "Done!"

Clarissa blinked. "You'd let me take over the design?"

"Let you? Would you please take over the entire enterprise? You have impeccable taste. You are familiar with other manor houses. You know what is required."

Clarissa looked at the inventory pages, yet Lila could tell her mind was elsewhere. "I spoke with Timothy about making some real changes in the hall."

"Such as?"

"Adding bath rooms and water closets."

Lila couldn't have been more shocked if she'd mentioned solid gold door knobs and a reflecting pool. "What did he say?"

"He was going to talk to Newley about it."

"A real bathroom with a bathtub and sink."

"And water closet. Running water."

"It's hard to fathom."

"Now is the time to do it — perhaps the only time to do it. Where is Lord Newley now?"

"I believe he's at the hall with Papa and Joseph."

"Perfect." She turned to leave, then spun back again. "To be clear, I do have your permission."

"Permission, and more. You have my blessing, and my complete and utter gratitude."

Clarissa smiled. "You're welcome."

Lila sat a moment in the silence. What had just happened? Then she remembered her prayer, asking God for help.

She leaned her head back and grinned at the heavens. "Thank you!"

She gathered her pencil and the blank pages, stood and moved her chair in line with those on either side.

She was free!

To prove it, she exited the room, handed a surprised footman the supplies, and walked out the front door.

And then, though she was a grown woman and the mistress of a fine manor, she raised the hem of her skirt and ran to the village.

Lila burst into the mercantile, winded and perspiring.

Nana put a hand to her chest. "You frightened me!"

"Sorry." She put her hands on her hips, taking deep breaths.

"Is something wrong?" Rose asked.

"Not at all." Lila took a folded fan off a shelf, feeling soothed by the cool air. Her lungs calmed, allowing her to say more. "I have been set free!"

"I didn't know you were bound," Rose said.

Lila explained about the assignment from her father-in-law, and how Clarissa had saved the day.

"That's very nice of her to take over the project," Rose said.

Nana chuckled. "From what I know of Clarissa, it's no burden for her to shop."

"But it's more than shopping," Lila said. "She has to plan every detail of every room. Including the new baths."

"It's hard to comprehend running hot and cold water," Rose said.

"A luxury we will never have in the village," Nana said.

"Maybe someday."

She flipped a hand. "Tis no never mind to me. A body doesn't miss what a body doesn't know."

Lila looked around the mercantile. "The other day I was thinking that we should create a display of the new fabrics up front, perhaps adding ribbons, lace, thread, and even a pattern or two."

"Don't you need to get to the workshop?"

"They'll do fine without me." She gathered the prettiest fabrics.

It felt wonderful to be back where she belonged.

Genevieve looked up from her sewing. "Where is Lila?"

Sylvia was helping Mrs. Keening cut out her dress. "My brother gave her an assignment regarding the furnishing and decorating of the Hall."

"I do hope that work won't replace her work here. We need her."

"Begging your pardon, ladies," Mrs. Keening said, "but I saw Lila run into the mercantile a good hour ago."

"She must be visiting her grandmother," Sylvia said.

Mrs. Keening moved to the window. "I think it's more than that. Look."

They watched as Lila created a display in the mercantile's window.

"She doesn't have time for that," Genevieve said. "Mrs. Ross is due any minute." She glanced at Tilda and Beth. "She's bringing her four children. Are you ready for them?"

Tilda nodded. "I brought some more drawing paper today. I thought we could do some leaf rubbings."

"And I brought some books with pictures of birds in them."

Everyone but Lila was doing their part. This was not acceptable. Genevieve had a mind to go over there and tell her that—and would have, if her student, Mrs. Conklin, hadn't spoken up.

"Mrs. Weston? Can we finish this, please? My Dwayne will be coming in from the field and will need his lunch."

"Of course."

Lila was spared a piece of Genevieve's mind. For now.

Genevieve was glad for Mrs. Conklin's husband. With her needing to leave to get him lunch, she knew she would soon be able to go to the mercantile and confront Lila.

But just as Mrs. Conklin left, a new customer came in.

"G'day to you, Mrs. Weston."

"Good day to you…" She couldn't remember her name.

"Mrs. Pearson."

"Mrs. Pearson. Yes." Genevieve looked towards Sylvia and Tilda, hoping they could take care of the new customer. But Sylvia was helping Mrs. Ross, and Tilda and Beth had their hands full with the Ross children.

She drew in a breath and managed a smile. "How can we help you today?"

Mrs. Pearson was carrying a soft bundle and motioned towards the table. "May I?"

"Of course."

She untied the string around the bundle, and peeled back the outer fabric. Inside was a piece of lovely ivory batiste dotted with peach flowers.

"Ooh," Genevieve said, touching it.

"That's what I've always thought."

"Always…?"

"It was a wedding gift, or rather it was given to me by an aunt to make meself a wedding dress. But Herbert and me ran off to get married, and I . . ." She shrugged. "I's had it ever since."

"And now you'd like to sew it up?"

"We's coming up on a twenty-year anniversary, and I was thinkin' it might be nice to have something pretty to wear."

"Absolutely," Genevieve said. "After twenty years, you deserve it."

"So…what now? I heard through the grapevine 'bout this place, but haven't thought to stop in till I remembered this piece. How does all this work?"

Genevieve explained about the lessons. Then, she got an idea that would combine helping Mrs. Pearson as well as give herself a heady dose of satisfaction.

"What a pretty display, Mrs. Kidd," Mrs. Pearson said.

Lila adjusted the draping of the fabric that she'd placed on top of a crate. "Thank you." She looked to Genevieve. "How do you like it?"

"Very nice. But we could use your help at *our* shop."

Lila glanced in that direction. "I'm sorry, I didn't know you were busy."

"*We* are very busy."

Genevieve was upset with her? Lila wasn't sure what to say.

"We need your help, Lila. You promised, yet you've been more tardy than present."

Oh my. To be chastised in front of a customer was bad form.

Nana intervened. "How may we help you, Mrs. Weston? Mrs. Pearson?"

Mrs. Pearson showed off the lovely piece of fabric and shared the story behind it.

"We have two new patterns in our stock," Nana said.

Lila was glad for the distraction. Anything to avoid the daggers Genevieve was hurling from her gaze.

Was Lila in the wrong? She was helping the cause by creating a display that would promote sewing. Surely Genevieve could see that.

Mrs. Pearson purchased her sewing supplies and had the amount applied to her tab.

Nana came close and whispered. "Genevieve is upset. You need to mend things."

"I didn't mean to make her angry. I was just doing—"

"Something you wanted to do, rather than what you'd promised her you would do?"

Probably.

As Mrs. Pearson and Genevieve left the store, Genevieve said, "Coming, Mrs. Kidd?"

Did she have a choice?

Clarissa loved being surrounded by men of influence. Men she respected. Having their full attention for what she was about to *say* instead of them being attentive because of her looks, was especially gratifying.

They studied the simple drawings she'd sketched, the ones that revealed where the new walls should be erected.

Lord Newley pointed at the water closet for the public floor that would take out a corner of the music room. "Are you sure this is necessary? Making the music room smaller..."

"When was the last time you fully used that room?" she asked.

He looked at Joseph, who shrugged.

"Exactly. If I'm not mistaken, neither of you men, nor Lila, plays the pianoforte. Correct?"

"Correct."

"So making an unused room smaller in exchange for a room that will aid in the comfort of every guest and every resident of the hall is a wise trade-off. And the baths off the bedrooms are a luxury worthy of the finest houses in all England, if not beyond."

He glanced at her and smiled. "No need for the flattery, Clarissa. I do see the benefits. Yet, the skilled workers that would be needed..."

Timothy spoke up. "I can find the proper workers in London. I've already made inquiries."

Newley's eyebrows rose. "You have?"

Uncle Jack added, "You two are in on this together?"

Clarissa took responsibility. "I came up with the idea last time I was here. Timothy was a willing listener and assured me it was possible."

"Could be possible," Timothy said.

Don't back out on me now.

Newley looked at Damon. "Your family estate doesn't have full plumbing, does it?"

"If only it did." He yanked on his cuffs. "As far as such luxuries on the Continent, I can assure you, those countries are far behind England in even thinking about such renovations."

Newley's face brightened. "Being ahead of the Continent would be an added perk."

"And bring added satisfaction," Joseph said.

"I envy you the possibilities," Uncle Jack said. "To make such changes at Summerfield Manor would cost vastly more than for you to make them here, when the Hall is down to the bare bones."

He drew in a breath. "Then it's settled. Yes. We'll do it."

"Bravo!" Clarissa said with a clap.

He offered her a bow and a clap of his own. "Bravo to you, Miss Weston. I laud your insight and creativity."

"You are very welcome. Now, about the shopping in London…"

Genevieve complained about her very long day as the maid fixed her hair for dinner.

"You're working too hard, ma'am," Jane said.

"Only as hard as is needed."

In the mirror she saw Jane shake her head. "I've heard a proverb that says a man's work is from sun to sun, but a woman's work is never done."

"Very apt," Genevieve said.

Proverb.

Her Bible! She jerked. "Are you through?"

"Almost."

As soon as Jane finished, Genevieve hurried out of her room, and down the hall to the bedroom where she used to have her morning quiet time with God.

She heard voices and came upon two servants arguing outside the bedroom's door.

"But it's my turn to have the nice room," one said.

"First come, first served."

"That's not fair. I—"

Upon seeing her, they stepped away from each other and bowed. "Mrs. Weston."

She pointed to the bedroom. "You are staying here?"

"Yes, ma'am."

"There is something inside which I need to retrieve."

He began to step away from the door, then hesitated. "May I get it for you?"

"I would rather get it myself." When he didn't give way, she added, "I assume that is agreeable?"

His expression revealed his nerves. "Of course, but..."

"But?"

"It's kind of a...a mish-mosh."

She didn't wait for more excuses but opened the door. The room was a jumbled mess with clothes strewn about, dirty dishes scattered on tables, and a very fragrant chamber pot near the bed.

"I'm sorry, ma'am. I'm afraid I've let it go."

The other servant peered in and stifled a laugh. "Let it go, mate? It's long gone."

Genevieve agreed with his contempt. "If you do not get this room spotless before I come back with Mrs. Camden and Mrs. Crank, *you* will be let go."

"Yes, ma'am."

"And you," she nodded to the other servant. "This is now your room. Get your things."

"Yes, ma'am. Thank you."

Genevieve was about to leave, when she remembered the purpose for her visit. She retrieved her Bible and strode out the door. "Remember, gentleman, cleanliness is next to godliness."

Genevieve sat next to the window in her room, and was just about to open her Bible when there was a knock on her door.

"Yes?"

Mrs. Camden and Mrs. Crank entered. "You needed something, Mrs. Weston?"

She slapped the Bible shut and stood. "I just witnessed a pigsty within the walls of Summerfield Manor."

"What?"

She explained about the servants and their messy room. "I believe he said it was a bit of a mish-mosh. I don't know the British definition of that dubious term, but it was totally unacceptable. I thought the visiting servants had been told to keep their rooms tidy."

"They were, ma'am," Mrs. Camden said.

"I am so sorry, ma'am," Mrs. Crank said.

She pressed her fingertips against her eyes and sighed. "I do not have time to do my work and yours. Is that understood?"

The two women nodded, apologized, and left the room.

Genevieve closed her eyes, but before she could properly rest, the mantel clock struck seven.

Dinner was served.

Genevieve was at dinner, at least physically. But mentally and emotionally she found herself trapped in the events of her day. Each annoyance, each slight, each moment of tension were stirred like the ingredients in the soup that was set before her.

And were just as steaming.

"I had the most delightful time today at the mercantile," Lila said. "I created a new display of fabrics in the window."

"I saw it," Sylvia said. "You have an artistic talent for composition." She looked to Tilda. "As do you, young lady. Teaching the children at the workshop how to draw is a brilliant idea. Have you always been an artist?"

"I'm not an artist, but I've always liked to draw."

"You should see the sketches she made of the entire family last year," Jack said. "She's quite good."

"I'd like to see them sometime."

"How did you spend your day, Papa?" Lila asked.

He winked at Sylvia. "Lady Silvey and I went riding."

"He showed me the countryside. I especially enjoyed the ruins of that ancient church."

Jack's second wink offered romantic implications, causing Morgan to say, "You and I should take a look, Genevieve."

She felt her cheeks redden and suddenly suspected that everyone at the table knew that she and Morgan had not been intimate since the twins were born.

Thankfully, Clarissa turned the discussion towards herself. "I had a very productive day at Crompton Hall." She nodded at Lila. "Since I am now in charge, I—"

"In charge?" Ian said.

"Of the décor, yes, Lord Newley. I believe the designation suits. You and Joseph are in charge of the building, and I, of the décor."

"What are your plans?" Sylvia asked.

Clarissa began a discourse that threatened to go on and on and on, *ad infinitum*, with the men commenting back and forth. They were proud about this, enthused about that. They oozed happiness and satisfaction.

Genevieve's nerves tingled and danced with irritation and frustration.

"What's made *me* happy," Lila said, "is being able to spend my time at the mercantile. I so enjoy helping Nana and Rose, as well as making displays for the store."

With a surge of emotion Genevieve pushed her chair back and stood. "I'm so glad you are enjoying yourself, Lila. And you, Clarissa. And even you, Sylvia. Yet, all of you made a commitment to *me*, to spend time in the workshop. You each have abandoned me to do the work all by myself!"

"I was there for part of the day," Sylvia said.

"As was I," Lila said.

"After I went to the mercantile and ordered you back."

"You did not order me. I chose to come."

"Reluctantly."

Clarissa dabbed a napkin to her mouth, looking far too unconcerned for Genevieve's taste. "I suppose if you want the renovation of Crompton Hall to be delayed, I could join you and sew a hem on some maid's uniform."

"Not some maid, twenty-eight maids. And clothes for *your* daughter, Lila." She pointed towards the upper floors. "I have had to handle the logistics of having thirty-four guests move into this house—thirty-four guests who need lodging, food, and direction."

Joseph fumbled his spoon, and Lila leaned in to help. "We know how hard this has been for you, Genevieve," she said.

"We appreciate your gracious hospitality," Joseph added.

Morgan stood and began to go to her, but she couldn't bear the thought of his condescending touch. Although her feelings were valid, she knew the others would swat them aside and rationalize their own actions.

Before Morgan could reach her, she tossed her napkin on her chair and calmly walked out of the room.

Morgan followed, and caught up with her in the hall. "Genevieve, you need to go back and apologize."

She spun to face him. "I will do no such thing. Everything I said was true."

"Truth should not always be spoken aloud."

"Maybe it *should* be, more often."

He studied her face, then said softly, "Discretion needs to be one of the attributes of a countess."

His words and his gaze caused the fight to abandon her. Not only had she embarrassed her family, she'd failed at a higher level. The weight of the Weston's trust—that she could handle things well in their absence — added to her burden. *You have shamed me too,* added her mother's voice.

She ached from her outburst, but also from her intense need to be left alone.

"Go back to dinner," she told Morgan.

"Not without you."

The notion of facing everyone she'd just offended filled her with dread. Returning to the dining room was impossible. Morgan might as well ask her to jump to the moon.

The need to escape overwhelmed and churned within her. Genevieve felt something give way inside, as though the string that bound the attributes of propriety, manners, and common sense had snapped. She filled her lungs with air that immediately demanded release. "Go. Back. To. Dinner!" she shouted.

The look of horror on Morgan's face forced her to run out the front door, away from all her tormentors and accusers.

Away from her total failure and humiliation.

Lila jumped when she heard Genevieve's shouted words. Then everyone in the dining room froze, their faces pulled with shock and concern.

"Well that was pleasant," Clarissa said.

Damon snickered.

"Enough," Papa said.

They all looked to the door of the dining room when Morgan entered. He didn't say anything but calmly returned to his chair. He nodded to the footmen, "Serve the next course, if you please."

That was it? They would just move on?

Lila looked at the doorway, wanting to run after her friend. Genevieve was angry with her as much — if not more — than anyone else.

She stood. "I'm going after her."

"No!" Morgan said. Then he lowered his voice. "Leave her to herself. I forbid anyone from going after her. When the time is right, I will go." Again, he nodded at the footmen. "Continue."

The busyness of the dinner service usurped any discussion about what had transpired. As soon as the footmen left the room with the soup bowls, Morgan spoke.

"I apologize for Genevieve's outburst. She's obviously very anxious and strained."

"Of course she is," Ian said. "We have placed a terrible burden upon this household."

Papa waved his concern away. "Yes, it is true that the fire necessitated all of us to adapt. But I'm also sure it's not easy on all of you to be uprooted."

Lila nodded. "Everyone's hospitality is beyond compare, Papa. I am so sorry I was selfish and thought of my own preference of working at the mercantile." She looked at the other women. "We *did* agree to learn how to sew, and Genevieve has graciously given us lessons."

"I told her I'm not a seamstress," Clarissa said. "She knew that from the start."

"Perhaps you could have learned anyway," Morgan said.

"I will make an attempt to spend more time at the workshop," Sylvia said, with a nod to Papa.

Lila agreed.

"And I will try to be more involved with handling our servants while they are here," Ian said. "I will speak with Mrs. Crank this evening and decide on what should be done."

The discussion ended as the next course was served.

On her way to the workshop, Genevieve kept looking behind, expecting to spot someone rushing after her.

She had mixed feelings when no one came.

Did they care so little for her angst that they chose to leave her alone?

Or were they angry at her? They should have been angry. Genevieve was angry at herself, not for her comments to the group, but for her complete loss of decorum in shouting at Morgan. She had never yelled at anyone like that in her life — not even at her mother, who had sorely tested her on occasions too numerous to count.

Yet she also felt relief. For above all other needs, right now she needed to be left alone. Her thoughts were so jumbled and conflicted she knew solitude was the only way to calm them.

The village square was empty as she walked to the workshop, in much the same state it was when she'd come that morning.

She welcomed the chance to slip into the building unseen. Once inside, she did not light a sconce against the darkness, but was content with the moonlight.

She leaned against the door and caught her breath, waiting for her heartbeat to stabilize.

"Meuw…"

Pax rubbed against her skirts, arching her back.

Genevieve nuzzled her against her neck. "Hello, sweet kitty. You are just what I need." Within minutes, Genevieve's body calmed.

But not her thoughts.

What had been gained by her outburst? What would change?

Perhaps nothing. She had to be prepared for that.

She jumped when she heard a soft knock on the door. *They came after me.* She wasn't sure whether she wished to speak to them or not.

"Genevieve? It's Nana."

She *did* want to speak to Nana. "Come in."

"I thought I saw you," Nana said. "But why don't you light some lamps?"

"I don't want anyone to know I'm here."

"Why?"

Genevieve sat down and gave her attention to Pax, not wanting Nana to see her face.

Nana was not one to be put off so easily and pulled a chair close. "Why are you hiding away?"

Genevieve chuckled. "You are far too perceptive."

"I've lived long enough to know when a woman is seeking solace from an argument."

"More than an argument. A battle."

"Between you and Morgan?"

"Between me and everyone."

"Were they mean to you?"

"I was mean to them. I verbally attacked them, all of them."

Pax walked across Genevieve's lap to Nana's, lying across her legs as Nana pet her. "Was the attack warranted?"

Genevieve was surprised by her question. "Is an attack on one's family ever warranted?"

"It's often necessary."

"So it was acceptable that I made a scene?"

Nana scratched between Pax's ears and the kitten purred. "Why don't you tell me what happened and I'll let you know."

Genevieve fully confessed to the evening's outburst, but also shared her frustrations, and her fears for her marriage. Nana did not interrupt, but listened intently, nodding occasionally.

"So," Genevieve said, laying her arms open, ready to accept Nana's judgment. "There are my faults, frailties, and follies."

Nana was silent, making Genevieve fear she had shocked her too mightily.

Nana set Pax on the floor. "Firstly, tact is not one of your strong suits."

"I will agree to that—though in my defense, I have never, ever acted like this before tonight."

"And yet," Nana said, raising a finger, "I do believe you were justified in your grievances. They made a commitment to help, then abandoned you."

"They did!"

"But," Nana continued, "not everyone has the same gift." She held out an arm. "My arm has a different function than my leg. My heart serves a different purpose than my mind. So it is with the people around us. We have all been given different functions, with unique gifts that we are compelled and propelled to use. Lila's gift is being a saleswoman, displaying goods, helping people in the shop."

"But I was teaching her how to sew."

"Was she good at it?"

"Well, no. I had to rip apart every seam on the dress for Mary Bramm."

"I'm not discounting the need for good workmanship, but if the heart is not in the work, then the quality will suffer."

"Sylvia and Clarissa abandoned me too."

Nana's eyebrow raised. "Lady Silvey is in love with my son."

"You know about them?"

"I have eyes." Her smile was full of satisfaction. "I am very happy for them. Jack deserves a good woman as a wife."

"Wasn't Fidelia a good woman?"

To her credit, Nana hesitated. "She was a difficult woman who refused to find happiness where she'd been planted. Because of that, she made everyone around her miserable."

"Lila mentioned that your lives were less stressful after she died. She felt guilty for feeling that way, but—"

"She spoke the truth. A family cannot thrive in the midst of an angry bee and not suffer from her stings."

Suddenly, Genevieve took the analogy upon herself. "Lately, I've been an angry bee."

Nana put a hand on hers. "One outburst will be forgiven, especially considering the extenuating circumstances. Not to mention being the mother of twins within the first year of your marriage. Your first anniversary is approaching, is it not?"

Her failings as a wife forced her to look down. "I haven't been very attentive to Morgan since the twins were born."

"That's understandable."

She looked up. "It is?"

"Your body has been through a trauma—happy though it was. Is Morgan being unreasonable or demanding?"

"Not at all. He's very sweet. But I know he wants to resume…but I just can't yet. Emotionally." She couldn't believe she was having this discussion with Morgan's grandmother—or anyone, for that matter. Marital relations were never, ever discussed. Yet it was very freeing to do so. "Plus, I don't feel very pretty." She put a hand to her midsection. "I'm…fat."

"Gracious sakes, you *are* hard on yourself, aren't you? It's said that it takes nine months to have a child, and nine months to recover from having a child." She picked up Pax again. "Though if you could have fed the twins yourself, that would have helped in the recovery."

"Ladies do not feed their own children. You know that. Lila didn't feed Etta."

"I'm not condemning either of you for the choice, for you had none. It's just a fact that doing so helps the figure recover. But don't fear. Your weight will come off. And even if it doesn't…" She offered a sly smile. "Most men like a little something extra to hold onto."

"I've got more than a little extra, but thank you for the encouragement."

"Give yourself time, dear. Give everyone time to adjust to their new situations. And forgive them their failings."

"As I need to be forgiven."

"As we all need to be forgiven."

Genevieve leaned over and gave Nana a hug. "Thank you for being here for me, and for your wise words. I never knew my grandparents, so…"

"I am happy to fill the role."

Just then, the door opened and Morgan entered. "Here you are. Nana? Why are you here?"

"We're just having a little chat. Take her home, Morgan. Your wife has had a hard evening."

With a kiss to each of their cheeks, Nana left.

"Are you all right?" Morgan said.

She rushed into his arms. "I'm so sorry. I shouldn't have yelled at you. I shouldn't have confronted people that way."

"No, you shouldn't have." He stroked her hair. "But all is forgiven. And all have accepted their parts in the problem — except Clarissa. But none of us expect her to acquiesce."

She chuckled.

"Lila wanted to come after you but I told her not to."

Genevieve felt a tug to her heart. "I'm sorry for hurting her. And the others. I have many fences to mend."

"They all can wait until tomorrow."

She was glad for the delay. "Let's go home. I'm quite exhausted."

"I'll tuck you into bed myself." He took her hand. "Tonight you can get a deep and rejuvenating sleep."

Genevieve was thankful he didn't ask for more. Despite her conversation with Nana, she wasn't ready.

Lila stood in the darkened drawing room, peering outside. Genevieve hadn't returned and it had been over an hour. *Please let her be all right. Guide me towards mending our friendship.*

"What are you doing?" Papa asked from the doorway.

"Looking for Genevieve. Aren't you worried?"

He shook his head. "Morgan went after her. We expect she's at the workshop."

She rushed towards the front door. "Then I'll go too."

Papa put a hand on her arm. "No, Lila. Let him go alone. He's her husband."

"And I'm her best friend. I want to make things right between us. We used to be close. I've ruined that."

"You haven't ruined anything. She's just going through a sticky patch right now. She'll come out of it." He put an arm around her shoulders. "Weren't you going to play cards tonight?"

"I don't feel like playing."

"It will be a good distraction."

"What are you going to do this evening?"

He grinned. "I thought I'd take Sylvia for a stroll under the stars."

"I like her, Papa. Very much."

"Good. For I like her too."

"I bid five," Clarissa said.

"Six," Lila said, with a wink to her partner, Newley.

"Stop that!" Clarissa said. "No signals."

"It wasn't a signal."

Ian winked back.

"I can wink too," Damon said. "But my wink may mean something different than yours."

Clarissa was used to his suggestive comments. She held her cards close to her chest. "Damon, it's your bid."

"Pass."

"My lovely daughter-in-law can have it for six."

"Bravo, wife," Joseph said, looking over her shoulder.

"I don't think this three against two is fair," Clarissa said to him.

He held up his bandaged hands. "If I could hold the cards I would play."

"Clubs is trump," Lila said.

Clarissa had no clubs. "I would have gone in hearts. Did you have hearts, Damon?"

"I always have hearts for you, my dear."

The game of Pitch continued — an American game Genevieve had taught them, though she'd bowed out of tonight's game. Just as well. They didn't need more of her drama. Clarissa had business to attend to across the cards.

"I've sketched some possible wall placements for the baths," she said. "If all of you would like to have a look."

"I would love to see them," Lila said. "Running water near the bedrooms. I can't imagine."

Clarissa played the final card for the hand, losing the three to the Kidds.

"We won!" Lila said.

"The hand. You won the hand," Damon said.

"It's your deal," Clarissa said. "I'll get the sketches."

"I'm eager to see them," Newley said.

She'd anticipated their interest and had the papers close by. She set them on top of the cards and led them through her ideas. Lila and Joseph were very receptive, which spurred her to expand to talk about design and color choices.

Damon shoved his chair back and stood. "So much for cards."

"I apologize," Lila said. "We could go through this another time."

"Actually, we can't," Clarissa said. "The framers need direction as soon as possible."

Damon rolled his eyes. "And *you* have to direct them?"

"It's what I have been tasked to do." She looked at Joseph and Newley. "Correct?"

"Correct. We had a meeting on site this morning. Clarissa's ideas have been approved. Timothy is awaiting the details."

Damon rose and executed the extravagant bow of a cavalier. "I hereby bow to milady's profound expertise and superior proficiency. Or is it your superior expertise and profound proficiency?"

"Damon, stop it."

"Stop what?"

"Being sarcastic."

"What sarcasm can be found in you taking the reins of the refurbishing a grand estate when you've never previously arranged so much as a vase on a mantel."

"That's uncalled for," Joseph said. "We trust Clarissa's taste."

"And I need her help to do what I cannot," Lila said.

"Or will not?" Damon asked.

With a warning look to his nephew, Newley took up the sketches and handed them to Clarissa. "Thank you for showing us. You have our permission to proceed."

Joseph extended his arm to Lila. "Would you like to retire, my dear?"

"Of course." The three Kidds left.

"What's got into you?" Clarissa asked Damon. "Why do you spout such rubbish? You ruined the evening."

Damon gathered the cards. "So you enjoy playing cards with your nemeses?"

"There was a purpose in the game. I needed their approval of the drawings."

"Then why not just ask them without ruining the game?"

She grabbed the cards from him, sat in her place, and began to deal. "Sit. By all means, let's play cards."

"Re-deal for solitaire, my dear." He walked out.

Clarissa tossed the cards on the table, then swiped her hands through the lot of them until the table was clear.

There. I won.

Lila got under the covers. "I heard Morgan and Genevieve come back to the house together," she told Joseph.

"I did too."

"I wanted to talk to her. Apologize."

"Not tonight."

"That's what Papa said."

"You have a wise father."

She adjusted her braid across one shoulder. "In spite of what Genevieve said, I do enjoy making the displays again. It's like old times."

"Times that are over," Joseph said.

"What?"

He got in beside her and she helped him adjust the covers. "You are not a shopkeeper's daughter anymore, Lila."

"But I enjoy it immensely. And I'm good at it."

"That may be, but—"

"With Clarissa taking over the decisions regarding the Hall, I have the time."

"I don't think my father is pleased about that."

"He's not?"

"He assigned you the task, not Clarissa."

"But she has an aptitude for it. She loves shopping and making creative decisions. I was overwhelmed and didn't even know where to start."

"Then have her help you, not take over."

"My help would have delayed the project. As we heard from Genevieve, it's imperative we move home as soon as possible."

"I did feel badly for her, but also embarrassed. To make such a scene…"

"I'll make amends in the morning—at the workshop." She sat up beside him. "Is your father angry at me?"

"Not angry. Perhaps disappointed."

"Clarissa will do a good job. Isn't that the main point?"

"The main point is that you, as mistress of the Hall, do the work of the mistress of the Hall."

She fell upon her pillow, deflated. "And here I thought I was doing something virtuous, recognizing each of our talents and using them to their best cause. I felt wonderful about my choice. I actually ran to the mercantile after being rid of the—" She stopped her words.

"Rid of the responsibility?"

Yes. But no. "Should I tell Clarissa to stop?"

"It's too late now. Did you know it was her idea to add the plumbing rooms?"

"I did. And I never would have thought of that. So her assignment to the task is a good one, is it not?"

He turned his back to her. "I'd like Father to be proud of you rather than Clarissa."

The breath went out of her. What had she done?

Chapter Nine

As per Morgan's hopes, Genevieve slept hard and long. When she awakened, he was already gone. She summoned Jane to help her dress. Her stomach growled. She'd not eaten dinner last night.

She longed for—but dreaded—breakfast. After the previous evening's outburst, she was not looking forward to seeing everyone. If the world was perfect she would apologize, they would accept, and life would go on. Would the problems between them be solved? Time would tell.

Ready to begin the day, she hesitated with her hand on the doorknob.

"It will be all right, ma'am," Jane said.

Genevieve hated that the servants knew of her outburst. Yet, how could they not?

She opened the door. It was time to appease the victims of her folly.

As she neared the top of the stairs, she heard talk and laughter rising up from the foyer below. Morgan and…

Molly?

She stepped behind a column so they couldn't see her. Their voices were too low to hear their words. Only their laughter rang loud and clear.

Why was Molly in the house? Molly, who'd been engaged to Morgan once upon a time. Molly, who'd continued to hold a place in his heart even after Genevieve had arrived from America to marry him.

But Morgan chose you. And Molly married Dr. Peter.

She shoved such logic aside, preferring to focus on the distressing fact they were enjoying each other's company.

Lila, Beth, and Tilda filled their breakfast plates from chafing dishes of eggs, ham, breakfast rolls, and stewed tomatoes. Morgan stepped into the dining room behind them.

"You are all later than usual," Joseph said.

"I had a chat with Molly," Morgan said.

Joseph held up his fresh bandages. "She says I soon will be free of all this."

"Bravo." Lila took a seat next to her husband. "We are late because we were playing with the babies. Etta is a master-sitter."

"She only toppled once — on purpose," Beth said. "Max and May were getting fussy. May had a poopy."

"Beth!" Clarissa said. "The word."

"What word should I use?"

The adults exchanged looks. It was a good question.

"You don't speak of it," Clarissa said.

"Well, that's silly. Not speaking of it doesn't change the fact she messed her nappy."

"Beth!"

"Sorry."

Tilda giggled.

Ian spread jam on his roll. "I am on your side, Beth. It is what it is."

Just then, Genevieve entered and silence fell upon the room.

"Did you sleep well, darling?" Morgan asked. "I tried not to wake you."

"I am fully refreshed." She stood in the doorway a moment. "I want to apologize for my outburst last night. Please forgive me."

"You are forgiven," Papa said. "And I assure you, changes will be made to lighten your load." He gave Lila a pointed look.

Lila nodded. She smiled at Genevieve, hoping to gain her gaze. But to no avail.

"Eat heartily," Morgan said, nodding to the serving dishes. "A good breakfast is a good beginning to the day."

"I'm not terribly hungry." Genevieve took a napkin and filled it with two rolls. "If you'll excuse me. I need to get to the workshop."

"Someone still has a buzzing bee in her bonnet," Clarissa said.

"She *is* working overly hard," Morgan said.

"Then tell her to stop."

"I have. She won't listen."

"Where did you find her last night?" Lila asked.

"At the workshop. Talking with Nana."

Lila tried to suppress a wave of jealousy. Nana was *her* Nana, and only Genevieve's by marriage. She cut into a tomato. "Today I will make amends and sew long and hard."

Clarissa waited for her teacup to be refilled. "No matter what Genevieve says, I will *not* spend my day sewing."

"You never have sewn with us."

"I have had other things to do with Damon visiting. "

Which begged a question. "Damon and Sylvia often sleep late," Lila pointed out. "As do you. Why are you awake today?"

"Alas, my life has forever changed. Now I must rise with the rest of you because I have work to do." She drank her tea, stood, and glared at Lila. "Keep in mind that if I were sewing at Genevieve's beloved workshop, I would not have time to do *your* work for Crompton Hall. Perhaps you and Genevieve need to agree on my assignment. Do you want me sewing a painfully simple dress for a farmer's wife, or completely redecorating and redesigning a grand hall?"

Papa intervened. "That is uncalled for, Clarissa."

She shrugged. "I don't appreciate being accused of laziness."

"No one accused you of laziness," Lila said. "Not at all."

"No one did, Clarissa," Ian said.

She put her napkin on her chair. "If you'll excuse me, *I* have work to do."

Lila sat in stunned amazement, with her fork held in mid-air. She set it on the plate, her appetite gone.

"Once again, I am glad I was not born a female," Joseph said.

"What is that supposed to mean?"

"You get upset about the smallest things."

"None of our issues are small things."

His shrug incensed her. "Would you prefer we take to fisticuffs or a duel as men are wont to do?" Lila asked.

"There have been no duels in England for thirty years."

"That you know of." It was a moot point, and Lila rose to leave. She had other concerns besides continuing an argument about men and women. She needed to get to the workshop as soon as possible. Yet... she preferred *not* to face Genevieve alone.

"Tilda? Beth? Are you ready to go?"

"I am," Tilda said.

Beth shoveled some eggs into her mouth, took up her roll, and joined them.

Lila hoped there was safety in numbers.

As the women left the dining room, Lila heard Morgan say, "Women."

"Always a drama," Papa said.

Lila wished she had some defense, but in this morning's case, they were right.

Tilda wished someone would say something. Walking to the village with Beth was usually fun—Tilda was up eight to two with the pebble-kicking game—but today, with Lila along...

She obviously sensed the unease. "I am sorry for pulling you away from breakfast before you were through."

"I was done," Tilda said.

"I had enough," Beth said. "Mrs. McDeer said she's going to send chicken to the workshop for our lunch today. I hope she sends pears. I love pears."

The conversation fell silent again.

Until Tilda said, "I'm sorry Clarissa and Genevieve were rude to you, Lila."

Beth nodded. "Mum gets offended easily. She doesn't mean it. Not really."

"I think she does," Lila said.

"Me too," Tilda said.

Beth swiped a fly away from her face. "She *is* trying to think different, be different. But it's hard for her."

Tilda tossed her hands in the air. "It's hard for me too. I'm always walking on eggshells around her, afraid she'll throw a wobbler. I wish I didn't think about it so much."

Lila put an arm around Tilda's shoulders.

Beth looked ready to cry. "I'm so sorry she's mean to both of you. I've told her not to be mean."

Lila drew her into the embrace. "It's not your fault, Beth. And it's not our fault either."

"It's Mum's fault."

Unfortunately there was nothing to argue, and nothing they could do about it.

Their job today was to appease another woman with a chip on her shoulder.

Lila hated that her heart beat faster as they approached the workshop, but not knowing the reception she'd get from Genevieve eliminated any hope of calm and nonchalance.

Added to the tension from breakfast was the fact that Lila hadn't sewn anything since working on Mary Bramm's dress. Perhaps Genevieve had a right to be peeved.

More than anything, Lila grieved the loss of their close confidence. She considered Genevieve her closest friend, but since the fire and the workshop and the mercantile issues...things had changed between them.

So today, Lila was determined to be the kindest friend, and the finest and most industrious seamstress she could be. Unfortunately, she was well aware of her limitations in the latter respect.

Beth and Tilda entered first and broke the silence by picking up Pax and cuddling her.

"How nice that Pax is still hanging around," Lila said.

"A point you would know if you'd been here more often."

Sigh. "What would you like me to work on?"

"Hmmph."

"Genevieve...I'm here to work."

"Finally."

Lila's nerves turned to anger. "I apologize for my time at the mercantile. I made the display of sewing items to increase the interest in the workshop."

"Hmm."

"I also had work to do for Crompton Hall."

Genevieve peered at her over her lashes. "Which you have handily pawned off to Clarissa."

"She offered to do it!"

"How nice it must be to have others do your work."

Lila fought the impulse to leave by taking a deep breath. For the sake of their friendship and the family, they needed to make peace.

"Genevieve, you are being unfair, but I admit I may have been lax in giving the workshop the time it deserves."

"The time you committed to when we started."

Why are you rehashing all this again? Didn't you say enough last night? "I am here now and will be here all day. Show me what to do."

Genevieve was silent a moment, her chest heaving. Lila appreciated her effort to contain another retort.

Lila stepped to the cutting table. "Whose dress is this? I do like the fabric."

Genevieve stood beside her and shared the details.

It was a start.

"No, Lila," Genevieve said. "I've told you many times to pin before you sew. I am tired of ripping out your work."

"When have you ripped out my work?"

"Mary's dress had to be completely re-sewn."

Lila's mouth gaped open. "Why didn't you tell me?"

"Because you weren't here." She pointed to the seam. "Pin. Then sew."

Genevieve stepped away from the machine, and was tempted to send Lila to the mercantile to do her silly displays. Of all the women in the village who were learning how to sew, Lila was the least talented.

Or maybe you're extra hard on her. You need to remember she's your best friend.

"Come and eat lunch, you two," Tilda said.

"The pears look yummy," Beth said.

"And Pax is sniffing at the chicken."

Interruptions didn't help the work get done. "Finish the seam and then we'll eat." Lila did so and showed it to Genevieve. "Better."

They sat around the cutting table and Beth handed out their lunches. "There's an extra one."

"Where is Sylvia?" Genevieve asked. "I assumed she'd be here."

"She's gone riding with my father," Lila said. "Didn't she tell you?"

"Of course not. Why should *I* need to know?" She took a bite out of a pear, causing juice to run down her chin. "Napkin!"

Beth handed her one. Genevieve knew she should say thank-you, but couldn't get the words out.

What's wrong with me? Why am I still so testy?

And then Genevieve realized the partial reason for her mood when Molly came into the shop. Seeing Molly twice in the span of a few hours pressed upon her nerves.

"Afternoon, ladies," she said.

Lila stood to greet her. "How can we help you today, Molly?"

"When I was talking to Morgan this morning, he mentioned your workshop. I've heard others around the village talking about it, so I decided it was time to come see for myself."

"Why were you talking to Morgan?" Genevieve asked.

Molly looked confused. "I... when I come to change Mr. Kidd's bandages, I enjoy getting up to date on the family news."

Genevieve couldn't get her mind past the fact that Molly and Morgan had spoken more than once, bandage-duty or no bandage-duty.

"Would you like to learn to sew?" Lila asked.

Molly looked at the sewing machines. "I would. I used to do alterations on Mrs. Weston's gowns when she was the countess, but they were minor, and the sewing was always hand-done." She put a hand to her midsection. "Plus, it seems I've lost some weight working with Peter, so I think it's time for a new dress."

She's flaunting her slim figure when she can obviously see that I am still battling the weight of carrying the twins.

Genevieve set the balance of her lunch aside. "When are you going to have children?" She was appalled to hear her words said aloud, for there had been no transition to the subject except in her own mind.

Molly reddened. "We had hoped to have a child by now, but..."

Lila touched her arm. "God is never late and never early. It will happen. You two will make wonderful parents."

"I hope so."

Lila directed her to a sewing machine. "The process here is that we find a pattern you like, some fabric and then..."

Genevieve grabbed her pear and stood, "I'm going for a walk."

Molly and Lila watched Genevieve exit.

"I upset her. I shouldn't have come," Molly said. "I know I am not her favorite person."

"It's not you," Lila said. "She's been on edge for a few days."

"Is something wrong?"

"Nothing that can't be fixed." *I hope.*

Molly nodded, but her eyes lingered on the door. "Perhaps I shouldn't have talked to Morgan, but I assumed she was over being jealous of our past relationship. Surely she knows how much he adores her. He and I are just friends."

"I'm sure she knows in here," Lila said, pointing to her head, "but perhaps not in here." She pointed to her heart.

Molly stood. "If you don't think it's a good idea I sew a dress here..."

"It's a fine idea. *She'll* be fine. Let's go to the mercantile and choose your supplies."

Lila looked out the window of the mercantile and sighed.

"What's that for?" Nana asked.

Lila hadn't realized she'd put the full breadth of her emotions into the one sigh. "Dread, I guess."

"My, my. Dread is a powerful word."

Too powerful. I'm overreacting.

"Never mind."

Nana came to stand beside her, peering out the window. "I don't see any dragons or crazed criminals in the square—unless you count old Mr. Gibbs, who likes to snitch a good share of berries when I have a basket sitting outside."

Lila turned her back on the object of her stress. "I need to go back to the workshop and sew."

Nana gasped and her hands flew to her face. "Oh no! Not that!"

Lila sighed a different kind of sigh. "I know that it's silly to dread going back there. I do enjoy sewing. Somewhat. Sometimes. But I'd rather be here."

"And I'd rather be in London, waltzing with the Prince of Wales." She draped her arm around Lila's shoulders. "For this season of time you've made a commitment to the workshop. You can tackle the tasks with joy or bitterness. It's your choice."

Put so succinctly, Lila *had* no choice. "I know you're right."

"Of course I am."

Lila remembered something. "You spoke with Genevieve last night?"

"I did."

"What did she say?"

"Under the rules of the Nana-rulebook I cannot divulge private conversations."

"I just want to understand her. We used to be so close and now I feel her drifting away."

Nana put an arm around her. "The Genevieve you know is still there. At the moment, duty is an extra cloak she's having to wear—a heavy one."

"I will try to help her. I truly will."

"I know you will. You have a big heart and a loving spirit. Now walk across the square and get back to work. The mercantile isn't going anywhere."

She kissed Nana's cheek. "How did you get to be so wise?"

"Living through lots and lots of mistakes."

Lila chuckled. "If that's the case, I'm well on my way to being a very wise woman."

Lila returned to the workshop and was surprised to find it empty but for Tilda pinning up the hem on a dress.

"Where is everyone?"

"Genevieve hasn't come back yet, Beth took the lunch dishes back to the Manor, and Lady Silvey has never come in."

There was only one person she was concerned about. Genevieve had left when Molly came in. Surely she didn't still hold a grudge against Molly after all this time. . Morgan had chosen Genevieve. Molly had chosen Peter. Both women were happily married.

Weren't they?

Enough about that. What would please Genevieve the most would be finding Lila and Tilda hard at work.

She looked at the dress Tilda was pinning. "Do you like sewing?"

The girl shrugged. "It's a good skill to have, so I'm glad for that." She glanced towards the children's corner. "But what I really like about being here is teaching the children. It makes me feel...filled up."

"You're very good at it. And a very good artist too. Did you always like to draw and want to be a teacher?"

"I've never thought about it. Though I *have* always enjoyed learning. There was a woman Papa hired to look after me who had a way of making learning fun. She made me love reading. And she taught me how to draw."

"How wonderful. What was her name?"

"Miss Green."

Lila saw a wistful look cross Tilda's face. "What happened to her?"

"She got married and moved away." She stopped pinning. "I miss her."

"You're very lucky to have had her in your life. Everyone needs an encourager. You had Miss Green and I have Nana."

"She's very nice. She always gives Beth and me a peppermint when we come in."

"That sounds like her."

"Have you always been close?"

"Not at all. While growing up Nana and my grandfather lived in London and we would rarely visit. We became close after he died, when Nana came to live with us." She considered not explaining more, then decided Tilda might benefit from the knowledge. "Actually, if grandfather hadn't died, if Nana hadn't moved here, the big secret would never have come out. Papa would still be running the mercantile, I wouldn't be married to Joseph, and Uncle Frederick would be the earl and Aunt Ruth, the countess."

"And Morgan wouldn't be the heir."

"Which means Genevieve wouldn't have come to Summerfield from America."

Tilda's eyes were wide. "Crikey. That's a lot to come out of one man's death."

"I prefer to think of it as God setting things in place for His plan to fall into place."

"So you think everything that *is* that wouldn't have been, is God's doing?"

"I do." She put a hand to her midsection. "I feel it. I know it."

"So am I a part of that plan too?"

"Do you feel like you are?"

Tilda stopped pinning. "Sometimes. But most of the time not. Ruth was so nice to me that I felt like I'd come home, but then she left me alone with Clarissa, who hates me."

Lila considered this a moment. Then she said, "Perhaps putting you in this situation is God's way of making you stronger, or of setting you on a new path."

"I don't feel very strong."

"Strong yet. Give yourself time." Lila looked at the sewing machine, which was calling her into service. "Isn't it odd that sewing doesn't seem to be a gift either one of us possess, yet here we are, sewing."

"If it's not God's plan, I'm very willing to let it go."

"Me too. But until then…"

Back to work.

Clarissa studied the framing of one of the new bath rooms at Crompton Hall. She measured the width of the existing bedroom, hating that it was made smaller by the addition, but knowing the benefits far out-weighed the loss.

She consulted her notes. She'd deemed this room the Green Room to differentiate it from Newley's Room and Joseph's Room—which she'd been told was also Lila's room. Really? Husbands and wives didn't usually share a room—her own parents didn't. That both Joseph and Lila, and Genevieve and Morgan chose to do so felt like a slap in Clarissa's face. A we-are-happy-and-in-love affront to her spinsterhood.

A workman stepped forward. "Will you come and check the position of the other bath walls, Miss Weston?"

"Of course."

She left the Green Room, only to find Damon sitting in the hall on a crate stamped NAILS.

"Are you through yet?"

The worker discreetly moved on without her.

"Don't be absurd. I told you I would be here at least half the day."

"They know what to do."

"They do—because I told them. But they are also wise enough to check with me before they finalize the placement of the walls. It's much easier to move a wall two inches now than after it's nailed in place."

"Clarissa the engineer."

"Clarissa the designer."

He laughed. "With training from...?"

"From the fact I have impeccable taste, a penchant for organization, and a desire to create something magnificent."

He leaned close. "Even if it benefits Joseph and Lila?"

"Even then." She really needed to move on. "Why can't you be happy for me? I'm finally good at something in Summerfield."

"Good at doing other people's work?"

"Lila still has a voice in it. She liked my sketches."

"Yes indeed. They all liked your sketches." He stood. "Seeings as I have little taste, a penchant for pleasure, and a desire to spend the day doing something other than waiting for you to be finished *designing*, I believe I will take my leave."

"You're going back to the Manor?"

"Or somewhere." He walked away from her, down the hallway. "Ta ta."

The notion to call after him came. And went. Maybe it would be good for him to entertain himself.

She looked at the other end of the corridor and saw the workman, waiting for her.

"I'm coming."

As evening fell on Summerfield Manor Tilda took the book she'd finished back to the library. But before she could go inside, she heard voices.

Angry voices. Clarissa and Damon.

She turned around to leave, then changed her mind, stepping behind a potted fern in the corridor.

"If you don't want me here, I'll be happy to leave," Damon said.

"Of course I want you here. Don't be peevish."

"Peevish? I assure you I am more than peeved."

"Then don't be a twit. Is that a better term?"

"What's got into you, Clarissa? When I first arrived we had a grand time together."

Tilda heard a short expulsion of air, as though he'd pulled her close.

His voice softened. "Very grand."

There was the sound of irregular breathing.

"Stop. Now."

"Why?"

"Just listen to me," Clarissa said. "I have a proposition for you."

"Now *that* sounds grand."

"I need to go to London to shop for the Hall. Would you like to go with me?"

"Just us two? Off in London? Of course."

There was a moment of silence between them.

"Not just us. I would bring Beth too. It would give you two a chance to get to know each other better."

"I know her well enough."

"Damon...if we marry you will be her father. I want you to be close."

"But wouldn't it be nice, just the two of us?" The tone of his voice was heavy with implications.

"Save that for the honeymoon. This is a working trip."

"Meaning you will be distracted and I will find no pleasure in it at all."

"Meaning I have a list of things to accomplish. But *not* meaning that we can't fit in some enjoyable moments."

Tilda heard the sound of kissing. She didn't understand what Clarissa saw in him. Or vice versa. Could two people who were utterly selfish become unselfish together?

It was doubtful.

Suddenly, she heard footsteps and realized they were leaving the room. In her hurry to step away from her hiding place, she bobbled the fern and it fell off the pedestal with a crash.

Just as suddenly, Damon was there.

Tilda began to pick up the pieces.

Clarissa joined them. "Look at what you've done, you clumsy girl."

"I'll clean it up."

"Yes, you will."

"I'll help her," Damon said.

"Very well. We'll talk again soon, my dear. I would like to leave for London tomorrow morning as I have arranged a one-o'clock meeting with a furniture designer."

She walked away as Damon knelt beside Tilda, as if to help her.

But he didn't help her. Instead, he grabbed her arm roughly. "Get an earful, little girl?"

She tried to shake his grip away, but he held tight, hurting her. "I was just passing by." She thought of her book. "I need to get a book to read."

"I didn't think dim girls like you knew how to read."

She finally yanked her arm free of him. "I read a lot. More than you, I'm guessing. Have you read *Pride & Prejudice* or *Robin Hood* or *The Three Musketeers?*"

"No amount of book-learning will change the fact you are a girl who grew up in pubs getting friendly with your father's soldier friends." He took her chin between his fingers and pinched hard. "I bet those friends taught you a few things, didn't they?"

She batted his hand aside. "Stay away from me, or I'll tell —"

"Tell who? Clarissa, who wants you gone? Or maybe the earl, who probably hasn't thought about you for more than a minute since you helped the Whites blackmail him? You are only here because of the good graces of Ruth. Oh wait. She's not here anymore. Hmm."

"I didn't help the Whites. They used me."

"Whatever." He stood and ground the toe of his boot into the dirt on the floor. "Just so we know where we stand."

As he walked down the corridor, Dixon came around the corner, and gave him a nod. "Your lordship. I heard something break?"

Damon motioned towards the mess. "It seems dear Tilda has accidentally toppled a fern." He caught Tilda's eyes, "See, Tilda? I told you they'd forgive you. For *this.*"

Genevieve slipped into the nursery, hoping to play with Max and May.

She was quickly stopped by Nanny, who put a finger to her lips. "Shh. Sorry, Mrs. Weston. They just nodded off."

Genevieve stood there a moment, unsure what to do. She hadn't seen the twins all day, and now to not see them, not hold them until the morning?

Nanny stood her ground, and Genevieve had no choice but to step out.

But then the tears came.

She leaned against the wall of the corridor and let them come. It had been a horrible day. She'd started the day catching Morgan and Molly having a jolly in the foyer. Then Lila had been late to work, and Sylvia had not come in at all. And Molly had shown up and flaunted her svelte figure, wanting to sew a new dress to make herself look even more enticing.

Genevieve put her hands on her hips, reminded yet again that she was not the pretty young girl who'd crossed an ocean to come to Summerfield. Logic—and Nana—told her it was normal to retain some of the weight from her pregnancy, but Molly's beauty made her wish for her old figure sooner, rather than later.

Morgan hasn't complained. And Lila doesn't have her full figure back either since Etta's birth. You're too hard on yourself. Nana said so.

She swiped the tears away and took a deep breath, attempting to regain her composure. Yes, it had been a difficult day, but it was over. It was time to go to bed, snuggle against Morgan's shoulder, and sleep.

With that thought buoying her spirits, she went to their bedroom, expecting to see him getting into bed.

But Morgan wasn't there. She tried to remember the conversation at dinner. The men had been discussing something, but she'd had too much on her mind to add their problems to her own. They were probably making arrangements for tomorrow's work.

She called for Jane. When her maid arrived, Genevieve asked, "Have you seen Mr. Weston?"

"I have not, ma'am."

"Never mind." Genevieve got ready for bed, expecting Morgan to arrive at any time.

But he didn't.

She sent Jane away and adjusted the pillows and covers. *Soon. He'll be here soon.*

But as a half-hour turned to an hour, her mind ran wild. *Morgan isn't talking business with the men, he's somewhere with Molly!*

She ran to the window that looked out upon the gardens. She remembered Morgan saying that he and Molly used to meet under the arbor for their secret rendezvous.

Were they there now?

Genevieve put on slippers and her dressing gown and held it tightly around herself. She crept into the dark hallway, then down the stairs to the front door. She was glad no servants were about.

She had just opened the door, when—

"Genevieve? What are you doing?"

Her heart beat in her throat. She turned to face Morgan. "I couldn't sleep without you beside me, so I thought I'd get some fresh air in the garden."

"In the rain?"

It was raining? She looked outside.

It was raining.

"I guess I didn't notice."

"I guess you need to get back in bed." He drew her under his arm and led her upstairs. "I'm sorry I wasn't there. Papa and I got to talking and lost track of time."

So he wasn't with Molly. This time.

Chapter Ten

Clarissa adjusted a pin in her traveling hat. "You packed the jewelry for my blue evening dress?"

"I did, miss," Dottie said. "And the plumed headpiece."

"And Beth's mauve dress?"

"Yes, miss." Dottie pointed to the other trunk. "Beth's clothes are in there and yours are in the larger trunk."

"Very good." Clarissa glanced at the door. "Where *is* she? We need to depart within the half-hour to make it to my appointment on time."

"I'll get someone to carry down your luggage and check on Beth for you, miss."

"Thank you."

As Dottie left the bedroom, Beth entered. She was wearing the same dress she wore to breakfast.

"Where's your traveling suit? Get dressed. Quickly now."

Beth sank onto a chair. "I'm not going."

"Not...? Why?"

"I don't feel well." She put a hand to her stomach.

Clarissa removed a glove and felt her forehead. "You don't feel feverish."

"It must be something I ate."

"We've eaten the same food. Is anyone else ill?"

"I don't think so." She took off her shoes. "I'm going back to bed."

"But you can't. We need to leave. I have meetings. And I was planning to take you to the theatre one night. You can't miss that."

"You go, Mum. I'll be all right. There are plenty of people here to take care of me."

Clarissa was torn between two responsibilities. One, only she could attend to, and the other…

Dottie came in with two men to take the trunks.

There was no time to argue. "Just take the large one," Clarissa told them. "Miss Beth is staying behind. She's not feeling well."

"You can't go, miss?" Dottie said.

Beth shook her head. "I need to go back to bed."

As soon as the men left, Dottie helped Beth into her nightgown and into bed. Clarissa tucked her in, stroking her daughter's hair, peering into her eyes. "I feel horrible leaving you behind. Are you certain you don't want me to stay? Because I will."

"Go. I'll be all right."

"I'll make sure of it, Miss Weston," Dottie said.

Damon appeared in the doorway. "Are you two ready?"

"Beth's not going. She doesn't feel well."

Damon came to her bedside. "I'm sorry to hear that. Is there anything I can do?"

Beth shook her head adamantly and pulled the covers under her chin.

"All right then. You have a nice rest and I'll bring you a special gift. How's that sound?"

Beth gave a single nod. She seemed distressed. Which led Clarissa to say, "I'm staying. My place is here with you."

"No!" Beth sat up in bed. "You need to…please go. Crompton Hall is depending on you."

Clarissa sighed. "Unfortunately, you are right."

Damon strode towards the door. "Come now, Clarissa. We need to be off."

Clarissa put a hand on Beth's hair. "I'll miss you."

"We'll go another time."

"We will. I promise." With a kiss to Beth's forehead, they left.

Soon, she and Damon were in the carriage heading to London.

He took her hand. "Don't worry about Beth. She'll be fine."

"I know. It's just that I imagined this would be a special time for the three of us."

He pulled her hand to his lips. "Now, just the two of us. That's not totally disagreeable, is it?"

Clarissa smiled at him. "No, it's not."

On the way to the workshop, Tilda kicked a pebble, but the game wasn't as much fun without Beth.

She heard a carriage coming down the drive and turned to wave. She saw Clarissa and Damon inside, but was disappointed Beth didn't wave goodbye.

Lucky girl.

She envied Beth going to London. Tilda had never shopped in fancy stores, and would have loved to tag along and help Clarissa spend the Kidds' money. She'd heard Clarissa say they were going to the theatre too. The only theatrics Tilda had ever seen were various women at the pub where her father and his cronies hung out. They'd sing suggestive songs to raucous applause and whistles. One time when Tilda was ten, they'd made *her* sing a song, but had laughed uproariously, teasing her because she didn't know what the words meant. She'd been so mad she'd never sang for them again. How dare they make fun of her? *They'd* taught her the song.

Tilda picked a wildflower on the side of the road and spun it under her nose. It had little scent, so she threw it into the grasses.

Soon life would smell very sweet for Beth. Tilda would have bet a quid—if she had one—that Clarissa and Damon would get married. Which meant Beth would have a mother and a father.

I've never had two parents, and now have none.

But it was more than Beth getting parents that bothered Tilda. A marriage would solidify Beth's position in the Manor and in the Weston family—leaving Tilda high and dry, the only resident in Summerfield Manor who was not a relation. It came to this: being the colonel's goddaughter meant little — especially when he was out of the country.

Let it go. There's nothing you can do to change it.

As she entered the village and headed towards the workshop, Tilda didn't really begrudge Beth her good fortune. She just wished for some of her own.

***

I'd like Father to be proud of you rather than Clarissa.

Lila was haunted by Joseph's words. Although she was ever so glad Clarissa had taken over the duties at the Hall, she pondered whether the personal cost was too high. She wanted her father-in-law to think well of her, to trust her, to approve of her.

Which is why she sought him out after Clarissa and Damon left for London.

"Would you care for a walk, Ian?" she asked him. "Perhaps in the garden?"

His left eyebrow rose — for it *was* an unusual request — but he agreed and they took to the garden path.

"Well then, Lila. Although I enjoy a stroll with my favorite daughter-in-law, it does make me curious. Is everything all right?"

"I'm not sure," she said. "I... I feel I may have disappointed you."

"How so?"

"In delegating responsibilities to Clarissa, in not being the kind of mistress of the Hall you wife was."

He stopped walking and faced her. "Anabelle?"

She nodded. "I want to do her memory justice. I want to make you proud and I'm sorry if I—"

He lifted a hand, stopping her words. Yet he didn't speak right away, but looked past her, over her shoulder.

"Will you tell me about her?" Lila asked. "I know so little other than seeing how beautiful she was in the painting in the drawing room. And Joseph can't tell me much because he never knew her."

Ian broke out of his reverie and pointed to the arbor up ahead. "Let us sit."

They walked through the blooms of purple clematis and sat on the bench. He leaned on his walking stick. "Anabelle was an amazing woman: delightful, vivacious, and charming. She was very cheerful and empathetic, always looking for ways to help others. She lived by the heart rather than the head."

Lila imagined her as a grand hostess. "I'm sure she reveled in society events."

"She loathed them."

Lila did a double-take. "Really?"

He nodded. "When we'd go to London for the season, she declined most of the invitations and only reluctantly gave parties at the Hall. She would rather spend time with me than a houseful of friends."

"She was a homebody?"

"She was. It was hard for me to get her to travel, even to Lon—" He stopped his own words and looked at Lila, the glow of revelation on his face "She was very much like you."

Lila felt a shiver course up her arms. "She was?"

He nodded, his face aglow as though he was fully embracing the thought. "She was happiest close to home. And like you, her life revolved around God, family, and doing good for others."

"I'm touched by your kind words. Thank you."

He stood, needing to pace. After a few passes he stopped in front of her. "I was wrong, Lila. I held you to a standard that never existed. Anabelle would have jumped at the chance to delegate the design tasks and shopping to someone like Clarissa. When she was charged with bringing the hall out of the 1820's, she balked and was overwhelmed."

"I understand that feeling."

"She was miserable."

"As was I. I was daunted."

He returned to the seat beside her. "She was with-child at the time, and simply wanted to focus on the birth of her first-born. Seeing her stress, I told her to wait until after the birth to worry about furniture and draperies." He looked to the ground. "And then she died. She held Joseph in her arms a few minutes, then left us forever."

Lila's throat tightened. "I can't imagine your sorrow."

"The sun went out of my life."

Lila put a hand on his arm, letting her touch speak for her.

With a shudder he drew in a breath and let it out, as if expelling the memories with the air. "I confess that I took little joy in Joseph for the first years of his life. I let nannies take care of him while I let myself be consumed with work. And grief."

"You found a way to get through it."

"A flawed way, but a way. Sylvia offered to come live with us, but she was newly married and had her own responsibilities with the baron." He gazed in the direction of the Hall. "After Anabelle died, I left everything as it was."

"To keep things as they were when she lived there?"

He shrugged. "And because *I* was too overwhelmed with the project."

"It appears neither one of us women were traditional manor-house mistresses."

He offered a small smile. "No, you are not."

"We both care about friends and family more than chandeliers, china patterns, and having dinner parties just because it's expected."

"You choose people over pomp and position."

Her smile widened. "That's virtually what Joseph said."

"So are we right?"

"Very much so." She had a thought. "Perhaps knowing when it's best to delegate certain tasks to those more capable is the sign of a wise woman?"

He laughed. "Well presented, Lila. Perhaps you'd like to pursue a seat in Parliament?"

"If it's all right with you, I would prefer to pursue a way to help the people of Summerfield."

"Working at the mercantile?"

"Part of the time. But in other ways too."

"At the workshop?"

She chuckled. "After learning a bit about sewing, I realize *that* is also a task best delegated to others."

He pulled her arm through his. "You seem to be a woman who knows who she is."

"You give me too much credit. But I am a woman who wishes to know such a thing. With my whole being I long to be the woman God wants me to be."

He smiled at her, his hazel eyes kind. "It appears you are well on your way, and that makes me very proud. Be yourself, Lila. That is who God—and I—wish for you to be."

Lila leaned her head against his shoulder. The disposition of the man she'd always thought of as temperate, with the possibility of clouds, had let the sun break through.

Lila sat next to Nana on the bench outside the mercantile. The sun that had warmed her walk with Ian in the garden, continued to warm her now as she recounted it. "And then he told me to be who God wants me to be." Lila took a much-needed breath.

"A wise man." Nana took hold of her chin. "How many times have I told you the same? You are a rare gem, sparkling—"

"In the sun. I know."

"I hope you know."

Lila took Nana's hand and kissed it. "What would I do without your encouragement?"

"Flounder horribly."

Their laughter was cut short when Mr. and Mrs. Wilton approached the store, the husband supporting his wife with a hand at her waist, and another under her forearm.

Lila's heart broke at the sight of them. They'd just lost their fourth baby. Each one had died before they were a month old.

Nana rushed towards her. "You dear woman. Come sit a minute. Lila? Go fetch Mrs. Wilton some tea. The water's still warm."

"No thank you, Mrs. Hayward," the woman said — though she did take a seat on a bench. "I'm just feeling a bit flimsy today."

"Of course you are. And you have every right to feel that way. I know exactly how you feel."

Lila hadn't thought about it for a long time, but what Nana said was true. "Nana lost three babies," Lila said.

"You did?"

"I did."

"But then you had his lordship."

Not exactly. Lila exchanged a look with Nana.

"I didn't bear him," Nana said, "but God did bring him to me. He was the child I so desperately needed. In His amazing way God provided both the dowager and I the son we needed."

When Mrs. Wilton looked confused her husband leaned in, "Remember, Lizzie? The Weston boy wandered off in the woods and Mrs. Hayward took him in as her own."

Recognition flooded her face. "I remember now." She looked at Nana. "I'd be fair happy if I found such a boy. Or girl. We don't much care which." She began to cry again.

"The tea, Lila?"

Lila went to fetch it, but knew that tea would not ease Mrs. Wilton's pain.

As she sewed, the voice of Genevieve's father consumed her thoughts: *Good business involves helping others while making money.*

The workshop *was* helping others. But there was no money in it. There were no dollars involved. Or pounds. Or pence. The Summerfield Sewing Workshop was not a money-making establishment.

Which—in spite of her father's words—was all right. Genevieve wasn't working for money, but satisfaction. At her first inception there was never talk of charging for any of their services. The workshop was an offering to Summerfield. Wasn't that one of the duties of her position? To help the village? To give of herself?

But at what cost *to* herself? To her family? She was worn out and wrung dry, and missed seeing her children and Morgan throughout the day.

"Like this?" Mrs. Keening showed Genevieve the hem of her dress.

"Yes, that's right. You're doing fine work there."

It was not idle flattery. The baker had done a very nice job of it, though Genevieve had given her considerable help with the sleeve set-in. Yet since that *was* one of the more difficult steps of sewing, she didn't mind. The next dress Mrs. Keening sewed would be easier.

Genevieve was relieved it was a slow morning. Lila and Sylvia were there, sewing on buttons—a task worthy of their sewing talents. Tilda was talking with Molly about how long to make the sleeves of her new dress.

Molly's presence, coupled with Genevieve's unquenched desire to see her children, gave her an idea. "Tilda, would you go back to the house and fetch the twins?"

"Bring them here?"

"I don't see why not. Other women bring their children here, why can't I?"

"Why can't *we*?" Lila said. "It's a marvelous idea. Bring Etta too, please. With Beth gone you'll have to ask Nanny or Prissy to come along. But I'm sure they'd be happy for the outing."

When Tilda left, Molly was consigned to Genevieve's care. It was a small sacrifice in order to spend more time with her children.

Tilda walked towards the nursery and passed Dottie carrying a tray of tea and crackers. The maid stopped outside Clarissa and Beth's room, ready to knock.

"Dottie? Who is that for?"

"Beth."

"Beth went to London."

"No she didn't. She's sick. She stayed behind."

This didn't make sense. The trip had been a large part of the conversation at breakfast.

Tilda nodded towards the door. "Can I see her?"

"I think she'd like that."

They found Beth in her nightgown, sitting on the window seat, reading a book.

"You should be in bed, miss," Dottie said. She set the tray before her. "Mrs. Camden had me bring this up for you."

"Thank you, Dottie," Beth said. "And tell her thank you."

Dottie turned down the covers and plumped the pillows as though enticing Beth to bed. "Can I get you anything else?"

"No. I'm fine."

As soon as Dottie left, Tilda said, "You don't look sick."

"Because I'm not."

Not? "Then why didn't you go to London?"

Beth closed her book and put her bare feet on the floor. "Damon said I shouldn't go. Couldn't go."

"Why would he say that?"

"Because he wants my mother all to himself."

"But *she* wanted you to go. Weren't you packed?"

"Yes to both." She looked to the floor and shuddered.

Tilda had experienced such shudders before, a byproduct of growing up around soldiers who did not hold her in high esteem. "What did he do to you?"

Beth didn't answer immediately, which made things worse.

"Beth..."

She moved away, as if needing space to explain. "This morning after breakfast he cornered me in the alcove. He pushed me against the wall." She raised an arm straight out. "He put an arm on the wall so I couldn't get away."

"And then?"

"He said to stop getting between them. I was a nuisance. I was preventing Mum from being happy. He told me to stop being so selfish."

Tilda scoffed. "You? Selfish? He's the selfish one. From what I've seen he barely lets your mother out of his sight."

"Until she started spending more time at Crompton Hall. He doesn't like that."

"Why doesn't he go with her?"

"Mum is working very hard. I don't think Damon knows how to work."

Tilda shoved aside the tiniest flash of satisfaction that Beth's happy-family scenario was in jeopardy. But this was serious. Damon had shown himself to be a cad. "Did he tell you to pretend to be sick?"

She nodded and mimicked a man's voice. "'You're not going, you annoying brat. You're going to suddenly get sick and stay behind. You're going to insist your mother goes without you, and you will never, ever tell her about this conversation. Or else.'"

"Or else what?"

Beth put a hand to her own chin. "He grabbed my face hard. His eyes were blazing. I...I don't want to find out what he meant by it."

Tilda tried to get her thoughts to settle. "Do you think your mother is safe with him?"

"Physically, probably. Emotionally, no." She returned to the window seat, leaned her back against the side wall, and tucked her feet under her nightgown. "When Damon came I was happy for my mum. I know I'm one of the reasons she hasn't had a beau. Lady Silvey is nice. I thought he was too."

Tilda mimicked Beth's position at the other end of the window seat. "I'm sorry it's turned out so bad."

Beth shrugged. "I'm not worried about Mum in London. She can handle herself. I'm worried he'll make her fall in love with him and propose." She looked down. "That he'll somehow make her agree to get rid of me."

"She'd never do that. She loves you."

"But what if she grows to love him more? I don't want to go back to the streets."

"The family would never allow that."

Beth's breathing was heavy. "If...if it ever came to that, would you run off to London with me?"

What an odd thought. Yet Tilda said, "Of course I will." She was surprised to find that she meant it. "Maybe you should tell someone about his threat."

Beth shook her head adamantly. "Not with him and his mother living here. She's Lord Newley's sister. He's his nephew. A baron. Why would they believe me?"

"I suppose. And in the bigger picture, what would your accusation really matter?" Tilda realized the words were harsh. "Not that they don't care about you, but..."

"I agree."

They both looked out the window. It was strange to think that just a few hours earlier, Tilda had walked to the village totally absorbed with jealousy, begrudging Beth her happy future. Now, though she should be happy with this turn of events, she found little joy in it.

Then Beth said, "Why aren't you at the workshop?"

"Genevieve and Lila sent me back to get the children."

"To bring them to the shop?"

"We've been taking care of other people's children there. Why not theirs?"

Beth popped off the seat. "I'll come too."

"Will they let you?"

"Who is they? The men are all busy. The women are at the workshop. No one will care. Help me get dressed."

It was a parade to the workshop. Tilda carried Etta, Nanny Colleen carried Max, and Beth carried May. To keep the children amused the women sang "Mary had a Little Lamb", bouncing the babies to the rhythm.

The group received the attention of the old men who spent their days in the square, and received applause for the song.

Lila came out of the workshop, clapping. "That was wonderful, ladies." She took Etta in her arms. "Hello, sweet baby. Have you come to see Mama and Aunt Genevieve?"

They all went inside, where Genevieve and Sylvia hugged and played with the twins. Seeing the love between the women and children made an empty place in Tilda ache. But just a bit. She'd never known her mother, so the pain was less than for one who had known such love and lost it.

"Look at these darlings," Sylvia said. "What a lovely bit of sunshine to the day." She turned to Beth and paused. "Beth. You're here. I thought you went to London with Damon and Clarissa."

"You *are* here," Lila said. "What happened?"

Beth and Tilda exchanged a look. "I wasn't feeling well, so I told them to go on without me. But I'm better now."

"I'm sorry you were feeling poorly," Lila said. "I'm sure if Clarissa wasn't on a mission, she would have stayed behind. I know you were both looking forward to it."

"We were," Beth said. "But I'm not sad about it. Not too much."

Sylvia captured Max's hand before he could grab her eyeglasses. "I am sure my son is happy having Clarissa all to himself." She caught herself. "Beth, I mean no offense."

"I'm sure you are right," Beth said.

Sylvia handed Max off to Nanny. "I do think there are wedding bells in the future, don't you, ladies?"

"Has Damon proposed?" Genevieve asked. There was a tone to her voice that implied she hoped he hadn't.

"Not that I know of. But I know my son. That *is* his intent."

"How do you think Clarissa will answer?" Lila said.

Sylvia looked shocked at the question. "In the affirmative. Why would she turn him down?"

None of the ladies responded. Perhaps it was best.

What would they do if they knew the truth about Damon? What *was* the truth about Damon?

"Bye-bye," Lila said as Etta was taken back to the house.

Genevieve gave her own wave before returning to the workshop. "It was marvelous having them here for a while."

"It was a very good idea," Lila said. "Thank you for thinking of it."

Genevieve looked across the empty workroom. It was nice to have a lull. Even Sylvia had gone, which presented the chance to discuss...

"What do you think about Clarissa and Damon as a couple?"

Lila picked up fabric scraps and put them in a basket. "I want to be happy for her."

"But you aren't."

"Are you?"

Genevieve stoked the fire so she could heat up the iron to press open some seams. "As you said, I want to be."

"Simply put, there is something about him that doesn't ring true."

"Yet Sylvia is such a delightful woman: honest, forthright, and kind."

"A mother's attributes do not necessarily extend to a grown son," Lila said.

"Yet they did travel the Continent together for an extended period. If he were an unsavory sort, wouldn't she know?"

"And if so, wouldn't she tell us? Warn us?"

"She encourages their match." Genevieve licked her finger and tested the bottom of the iron. Finding it hot enough to use, she quickly moved it to the cloth-covered board they used for pressing.

"Her encouragement surprises me a bit," Lila said, as she re-rolled a spool of blue ribbon. "For Clarissa's past is not a secret."

"Perhaps Sylvia doesn't approve of Clarissa as much as she approves of the Weston family. Our name. And even our income."

"Surely as a baron Damon has income?"

Odd how no one had thought of this. "I assume so. They obviously had the funds to travel. Such travel does not come cheap."

Lila stopped all movement and looked towards the Manor. "Will he make a good father to Beth?"

The question caused Genevieve to stop her ironing. "I don't know. He's charming..."

"But is he loving? Patient? Thoughtful?"

Genevieve thought of the Damon she knew. Those words did not come to mind. She returned to, "He's charming."

Lila shook her head. "Charm fades."

"And now Clarissa is in London with him—alone."

"God help her," Lila said. "Please God. Help her."

After her meeting with the furniture designer, Clarissa checked another item off her list. It had been a very productive, yet exhausting day.

More productive because Damon had left her alone to take her meetings and attend to the shopping. He'd offered to check-in at the hotel for the both of them, so when the day was finished, their rooms would be waiting.

Clarissa had endured a few sideways glances and contemptuous attitudes from the men she had met with. It wasn't proper for her to traverse London without a male companion or at least a maid. Yet she ignored their disdain, presenting her needs succinctly with a smile and wit that quickly won over each clerk and salesman.

She and Damon had arranged to meet for dinner. Clarissa found herself famished. As Damon finished his second bottle of wine, Clarissa enjoyed a bread pudding that filled the last crevasse of her hunger.

He nodded towards her bowl. "Didn't your mother tell you that it was uncouth for a woman to display a healthy appetite? For food, that is."

She ignored his sensual innuendo. "I refuse to let you make me feel guilty for enjoying my meal. I worked hard today."

"Meaning you don't work hard back at the Manor?"

She knew his comment could be taken with offense, but refused to let it faze her. "No, I don't generally work at the Manor. Until the Crompton Hall project, I quite wasted most of my days. Yet now I find that I quite enjoy the challenge."

He sat back and sipped his wine, studying her. "A fine lady who enjoys work. Hmm. You're an anomaly."

"Genevieve and Lila are working hard. As is your mother."

"A gaggle of ladies at work."

Now, she *did* take offense. "You might try it sometime."

"A gaggle of ladies?"

"Work."

"And why would I want to do that?"

"You're being facetious."

"No, I'm not."

It was Clarissa's turn to study him. "I've never asked before, but since we are getting down to the nitty-gritty…did your father leave you enough of a fortune to sustain this life of leisure you prefer?"

"I am a baron. I have a barony. I have an estate — though not nearly as grand as Summerfield Manor or Crompton Hall. But I am set. For life." He set down his glass and took her hand. "All I need now is a baroness."

Clarissa was shocked at his admission, though knew she shouldn't have been. "Are you proposing marriage?"

"I believe I am."

"Oh."

He sat back, taking his hand with him. "Oh? I offer you the world and you say 'oh?'"

She regretted her tepid answer, yet found she could not retract it. "I did not expect a proposal this evening."

"And I did not expect to give one."

"Then perhaps...we move too fast."

He found her hand again and traced a thumb over her fingers. "Perhaps not fast enough."

Clarissa retrieved her hand and pushed the pudding bowl away. "I am tired and of no mind to discuss the future. What I need now is sleep."

He nodded once then called for the check. "I am not easily swayed, Clarissa. I will not let this die."

In the carriage on the way to the hotel, Clarissa's mind flooded with thoughts as her body demanded sleep. *If* she could sleep. For Damon had proposed.

They entered the hotel and walked to the lift. She held out a hand to him. "If I could have my room key, please."

"Our room key."

"What?"

"Our room key. I only procured one room."

Clarissa stepped away from the lift and let others pass. She lowered her voice and tried to keep her countenance calm as her emotions rose. "I insist on two rooms, Damon. I thought you knew that."

"I knew no such thing. Without Beth along we are free to be adults, to act as a couple in love."

"Love is one thing, sharing a room is another. I cannot believe you presumed—"

"I cannot believe you didn't."

She raised her chin, done with the discussion. "Please get me my own room."

He hesitated.

"Now, please."

"Very well. But I hereby express my disappointment and surprise. As a woman who lived on her own for two years, I didn't take you for a tease or a prude."

With that, he marched to the front desk.

Clarissa felt an impulse to walk out of the hotel and find a room elsewhere, but exhaustion stopped her. He'd made a mistake. Perhaps she had been wrong not to make things clear.

Just get through the night. By morning everything will have blown over.

Damon returned, dangling a key. Clarissa took possession and they rode the lift in silence. Her room was on a lower floor than his.

She exited. "Good night, Damon."

When he didn't respond, the lift operator looked at him. "Third floor please," Damon said.

The door closed between them.

So be it.

It wasn't easy getting undressed without Beth's help. If only Beth hadn't gotten sick at the last minute, Clarissa would have asked Dottie to come along. Even during those years on her own she'd had a maid to help her.

Until Agnes stole from me and ran away.

Just in time for Beth to come into her life.

Which ignited an odd thought. Beth was not her maid. Was Beth a handy girl to have around or a true daughter?

Clarissa shook her head violently. A year ago she had not traveled back to London to fetch Beth to be her maid. She'd sought her out because she cared for the girl and wanted to give her a good life.

"Will life with Damon be a good life?"

The room rang with the question. Although Clarissa knew a proposal had been possible, to be assailed with it this evening was a total surprise. She regretted her very noncommittal "oh" yet knew even now, she would not be able to offer him a *yes*.

Actually, in his eyes, the room fiasco might have negated the proposal. Was that a tragedy or a blessing?

Clarissa turned out the lamp and got in bed. She'd looked forward to sharing a room with Beth, showing Beth the finer side of London, having Beth help her make decisions about furnishings. She'd been excited about taking Beth to nice restaurants, surprising her with her own shopping spree at Harrods.

Beth never asked for anything. She was the purest, most giving person Clarissa had ever known.

Damon asked for everything, and there were signs that purity and generosity were more absent than present.

Of course, she could make the same statement about herself.

"But I'm a better person now," Clarissa whispered.

Because of Beth.

Clarissa sighed with the immensity of her situation. She'd been offered the chance to be a baroness. A few years ago there would have been little to no hesitancy in her answer. If being a baroness gained her fine clothes, a grand house, and the chance to travel the world, she'd accept.

But now things were different. She was different. But was she different enough to say no to the chance?

If she told Damon no, would there ever be a proposal from another man? Or would she go through life alone?

Not alone. She would always have Beth.

"And Beth will always have me."

That thought, above all others, rang the most true. She repeated it again with more strength and conviction. "Beth will always have me."

It felt right.

It was right.

Clarissa turned on her side, adjusted her pillow, and fell into the deep sleep of a woman who knew her own mind.

Tilda was just getting into bed when she heard a knock on her door. "Come in."

It was Beth. In her nightgown.

"Is something wrong?"

She came in and shrugged. "I was used to having my own room, but since sharing with Mum, and now having her gone..."

Tilda folded down the covers on the far side of her bed. "Climb in."

Beth quickly got settled. "Thank you. I feel better now."

Tilda turned out the light.

But Beth wasn't done talking. "Do you think Mum and Damon are... are sharing...?"

"No! I know that's what he wants. But it isn't proper."

"I don't think he cares about what's proper."

"Obviously."

After a moment, Beth took Tilda's hand. "God, please take care of my mum. Keep her safe."

"And free of *him*."

Amen.

Chapter Eleven

It was unnerving for Clarissa to wake up in a London hotel and have no idea if she was on her own or if Damon was going to be a part of her day. It was even more unnerving to know that she wasn't certain which scenario she preferred.

She sat at the dressing table and attempted to do her hair. She swept it up in the way she'd watched Dottie do a hundred times, but when she looked at the back of it, the curl-under was crooked. She tried again. And again.

Then there was the issue of her clothes, which buttoned up the back. How would she ever get dressed without a maid?

Last night she'd been careful and had unhooked her corset in front instead of the usual way of undoing the laces in back. So she *could* get that back on. And luckily, the dress she'd worn yesterday also opened in front, so she put it back on. Yet with the restraints of her corset, she could barely bend over and lace up her shoes. She sat upright, bested. "This is ridiculous."

But the fact was, she couldn't wear the same dress. If no one else noticed, Damon would, and he'd ask why, and she'd have to admit her lack of planning in not bringing Dottie along, and then he'd point out that if they were sharing a room, *he* would have been able to help her—and he could help her now, and...

For the sake of her pride and propriety, none of that could happen.

She called for a bell-boy.

Soon there was a knock on her door, and she went to answer it in her stocking-feet.

"Yes, miss?" the bellboy asked.

"Would you please send up a maid to help me dress?"

"Of course, miss."

"Quickly, please."

"Yes, miss."

Until then, Clarissa gathered her notes. She still had some shopping to do, with the theatre tonight.

If Damon stayed.

If he didn't, she would skip the entertainment. The truth was, she was eager to get through her business and return home to check on Beth. Yes, she knew her to be in good hands, but she would feel better if she could see for herself.

There was a knock on the door. "Come in."

Clarissa expected to see a maid, not Damon.

"Good morning," he said, standing in the doorway.

"Yes, it is."

"May I come in?"

"If you leave the door open, yes."

He strolled inside, his eyes taking in the whole of her. "Haven't I seen that dress...?"

"It's the only thing I could get on by myself. I need help with today's ensemble, so—"

His smile was full of mischief. "I'd be glad to help."

"Thank you, but they're sending a maid."

"My loss." Then he changed the subject. "Did you sleep well?"

"Like a baby. You?"

"Like a man filled with guilt."

He'd gotten her attention. "Guilt?"

He took her hands in his. "I'm sorry for catching you off guard last night, both in the proposal and the room situation. I went too far, and for that, I apologize."

She was sincerely surprised and pleased. "Contrition suits you."

"Does forgiveness suit you?"

She touched his cheek. "It does. I accept your apology and offer my own."

"For what?"

She couldn't think of anything specific, but knew her thoughts had not been in his favor and her mood contentious. "I apologize that my response caused a rift between us."

He kissed her forehead. "I want no rifts. None."

"Agreed," she said. It felt good to make amends—and it certainly would make the rest of the trip easier.

"Miss?"

A maid stood at the doorway. "Come in."

Damon kissed her hand, and left. "I will meet you in the lobby and we'll go to breakfast."

That sounded divine.

"Timothy!" Lila waved at him as she crossed the village square.

"Mrs. Kidd. How nice to see you."

"Call me Lila, Timothy," she said when she reached him. "I'm always Lila to you."

He pointed towards the Hall. "Have you been to Crompton recently to see the progress?"

"I have not. But I hear glowing reports from Joseph. We both thank you for stepping up to oversee such a large project."

"It's stretching my expertise."

"You are rising to the occasion."

He opened his mouth to speak, shut it, then opened it again. "Clarissa is in London?"

"Shopping for the Hall. I'm afraid I was overwhelmed and delegated my responsibilities into her able hands."

He nodded once. She could see there was more he wanted to say. She helped him out. "Lord Silvey accompanied her."

"Oh."

"Beth was supposed to go along, but became ill at the last minute."

His face showed his concern. "Is Bethy all right?"

"She is. The illness quickly faded."

He nodded, then looked up. "But that means Clarissa and Lord Silvey are alone."

Lila felt badly for him. "They are. But if it makes you feel better I'm sure they're having a horrible time."

His smile was bittersweet. "I have no right to care, or to even know her business."

"But you do."

"I do."

"You care for Clarissa," Lila said.

He looked at her through blond lashes. "I do. I always will."

"She cares about you too, Timothy."

"We are...good friends."

Lila knew he wished it was something more.

Did Clarissa know how much he cared? If she did, would it change things between her and Damon?

"I should get back to work," Timothy said. "It was nice seeing—"

"You should tell her."

"Tell her what?"

"Tell Clarissa you love her."

She expected him to deny it, or be flustered by her blatant statement. She did not expect him to say...

"I would like to, but the time never seems right."

The earth rotated a bit on its axis with the notion of Clarissa and Timothy being a couple rather than Clarissa and Damon. Lila found she liked the idea. It felt right and good.

She touched his arm briefly. "Timothy, if you feel this way, you need to let her know."

"It wouldn't be proper."

"Would it be proper for you to spend your entire life with your love pent up inside? I've learned that we often regret what we don't say as much as what we do."

"She doesn't love me."

I'm not sure Clarissa knows what love looks like. "We have no knowledge regarding her feelings. Clarissa is a complex woman."

He chuckled. "I know."

"At times she wears her heart on her sleeve and at other times she keeps her true feelings hidden — perhaps even from herself."

"Beyond our feelings…I am just a carpenter. She is the niece of an earl."

Lila hated that title trumped love, but it was a valid consideration. "We both know that Clarissa cares little for such restrictions."

"Actually, I hold that as my only hope. That somehow, someday…"

His feelings were that strong? Lila felt a clock ticking. It did not bode well for Timothy that Clarissa was in London with Damon. Not that they were doing anything elicit — in spite of Clarissa's bold choices, Lila knew she had strong boundaries — but their time together could only strengthen their bond.

To the point of marriage?

"I will help you, Timothy."

He let out a breath. "Help me win Clarissa's love?"

"If you'd like me to."

He hesitated. "I don't wish to win anything. Love is not a game. But I do long for direction, for opportunities. I've been praying that God will guide me. If He wishes for us to be together, then we will be together."

"Your faith commends you even more in my eyes."

"But in hers?"

Lila knew little about Clarissa's faith, for she held her relationship with the Almighty close.

Lila prayed the Almighty would hold Clarissa even closer.

Genevieve looked out the window of the workshop. Timothy and Lila were chatting. She knew they were old friends and used to go riding together.

She used to go riding with you, too. Why have you built this wall between you?

Before she could consider an answer she spotted Morgan walking towards the mercantile, probably to visit Nana.

But then he was distracted as he heard his name called out. He smiled at the speaker, and Genevieve was alarmed to see Molly walking towards him.

Stay away from my husband!

She watched them chat and laugh, much in the same way they'd done in the foyer of the Manor. Suddenly, Morgan pulled Molly into an embrace — a quick embrace — but an embrace nonetheless.

If this is what they do in public, what do they do in private? Was her own busyness providing the couple a chance to rekindle their love?

When Lila approached the door, Genevieve stepped away from the window and took a deep breath to calm herself.

"How is Timothy?" Genevieve asked her. "And the rebuilding?"

"Both are fine."

Although she'd answered quick enough, Genevieve saw her hesitate. "You wish to say more?"

Lila shook her head. "What would you like me to work on today?"

Just then, Molly came in — burst in, rather. Her face was beaming. "Good morning, ladies."

"You look happy today," Lila said.

"I am happy. And yet I also have bad news."

"What's that?"

"I no longer wish to make the dress I originally chose to make."

"Why not?"

"Because soon it will be too tight." She grinned and put her hands across her abdomen.

"What are you saying?" Lila asked.

"I am with child!"

Lila and Sylvia rushed to congratulate her.

Genevieve's first thought betrayed her fear. *Whose child?*

Lila noticed her reticence. "Genevieve?"

She forced the horrid thought away. "Congratulations, Molly. What a nice…surprise for you."

"It is a surprise. We were beginning to fear it would never happen."

Genevieve's thoughts ran wild. *It hasn't happened with Peter. But now that you're with Morgan, Morgan who gave me twins. Now you're with child?*

"Genevieve?" Lila said. "Is something bothering you?"

Genevieve forced herself to smile. "Perhaps you will have twins."

She held everyone's gaze a few moments, then Molly said, "I will not bother God by praying for such an abundant blessing. One healthy child will be enough."

More than enough.

Tilda and Beth walked down the road, each one holding the hand of a little boy. The boys' older sisters skipped ahead. They were taking the Miller children—aged 4, 5, 6, and 7—to the meadow to draw while their mother learned to sew.

"Stop it, Stephen," Tilda said, as her boy tried to swat his brother. She changed him to the outside hand, foiling further swats. She noticed Beth looking straight ahead, clearly not in the moment. "Is something bothering you?"

Beth drew in a breath. "I'm afraid."

"Of what?"

Beth nodded towards the children. "Let's get them settled. Then we can talk."

They turned into the meadow and the children were set free to run. "Stop at the big oak," Tilda called after them.

Surprisingly they did, each calling "I won!" as they tagged the tree.

Tilda got them seated in a circle, gave each one a tablet of paper, and spread some colored pencils around.

"I want a yellow one!"

"You can't have it, it's mine."

Tilda stood between the sisters. "You will all share nicely or no one gets to draw."

"What should we draw?"

She pointed at the oldest and made her way around to each child. "I want you to draw Stephen, you draw Samuel, you draw Mary and you draw Lucy."

Stephen, the youngest crossed his arms with a pouted lip. "I want to draw a boat."

"Fine. You draw a boat."

"You've never seen a boat."

"I want to draw a boat."

Tilda calmed them with her hands. "You each have your assignments. Do your very best to make your picture look like your sibling."

"Or a boat," Stephen said.

With a stern point of her finger she said, "And share the pencils." Then she led Beth to the far side of the oak tree. "Quickly. Before they mutiny. What are you afraid of?"

"Damon. They're coming home tomorrow."

"You shouldn't be afraid of him. You did as he asked. You pretended you were sick. You stayed home."

"He got rid of me so he could have my mum all to himself. What's to prevent him from trying to do it again?"

"Say no to him. Your mother will be home. She can protect you — if you tell her what he's done."

"What if she doesn't want to protect me? What if she chooses him over me?"

"She would never do that. She loves you."

"She probably loves him more. A man wins over a daughter every time."

"I don't know about that."

"I do. My mother left *me* behind."

"For a man?"

"I don't know. I was a baby."

"Then don't say such a thing. Didn't your father ever tell you why she left?"

"She didn't want a baby. She didn't want me."

"It has nothing to do with you, it sounds like she didn't want to be a mother to anyone. Ever. That's not your fault."

Beth shrugged. "What if Damon makes Mum choose?"

"He wouldn't dare." Though it did seem possible.

Beth spun a leaf between her fingers. "I don't want to be in the way."

"You're not. She chose you. On purpose."

"Miss Tilda?" A summons came from the tree. "Samuel won't let me have the green pencil."

Duty called.

At the end of the day Genevieve started up the drive of Summerfield Manor. Coming towards her was Dr. Peter.

Just the man she wanted to see.

He removed his hat. "Mrs. Weston."

"Doctor. How is your patient doing?"

"Mr. Kidd's hands are healing nicely. And his dexterity is good."

"I am glad to hear it."

"Good evening then," he said.

But she wasn't through. "I hear congratulations are in order."

He cocked his head.

"The child?"

"Oh. Yes. It's quite a miracle. I wasn't sure we…well, we thank God for giving us this gift."

"Speaking of gifts, I'd best go see my two darlings. Good evening."

As they went their separate ways, Genevieve's suspicions grew with each step. As Molly had done, Peter implied that a pregnancy was near impossible. Yet Molly was pregnant.

With Morgan's child. You know it's true.

The intensity of her thoughts forced her to stop walking, as if thought and movement could not share the same moment.

She had no proof other than seeing them together: laughing, talking, and clearly enjoying each other's company.

It's not as though I've been good company these past weeks. Morgan and I have barely exchanged ten words.

She heard the sounds of a carriage coming through the gates behind her and stepped aside.

The open chaise pulled beside her and stopped. "Would you like a ride the rest of the way?" Jack asked — with Sylvia by his side.

"No, thank you. I'll continue my walk."

"You work too hard," Sylvia said.

And you work too little. "We could have used your help this afternoon."

Sylvia linked her arm through the earl's. "Blame Jack. He wanted to show me the place where he and Morgan used to fish."

"You like to fish?" Genevieve asked.

"Goodness no. But I like the company and the stories. Jack, tell Genevieve about the time Fidelia fell into the stream."

"Not now, Sylvia." His cheeks had reddened. "Are you certain you don't want a ride?"

"I'm certain."

"We'll see you at dinner then."

They pulled away and Genevieve averted her eyes to escape the dust in their wake.

Up ahead, she could hear their happy exchange as they left the chaise and entered the house.

Jack and Sylvia. Damon and Clarissa. Joseph and Lila. Three happy couples living under the same roof. Couples in love.

Then there was Genevieve and Morgan. They'd been happy once. Genevieve still loved him. But since the twins were born something had changed between them.

It's not the twins fault, it's yours.

All signs pointed to Morgan giving up on her moods and her busyness, and finding happiness in the arms of Molly. Cheerful, lovely, slender Molly.

Genevieve didn't feel cheerful. Or lovely. Certainly not slender.

Suddenly, what had been the end of a normal day turned upon itself and Genevieve felt all her energy flow out of her, as if a crack had breached her being. Summerfield Manor might as well be a hundred miles away. The trek from here to there seemed insurmountable.

And so, she gave up.

Genevieve sank to her knees, letting the lure of the ground fully take her. She rolled onto her side, her outstretched arm protecting her cheek from the rough gravel.

I'm on the ground. I'm lying on the ground.

She watched as an ant climbed over the rocks, up and down, determined and indomitable.

Since she held neither of those qualities, Genevieve closed her eyes and tried to think of nothing.

Voices. Shouting.

They sounded from a land far away, a land unconnected to the place where Genevieve had gone.

Go get Dr. Peter!

Did you see her fall?

Genevieve? Are you all right?

Of course she was all right. In her world she was stretched out in a boat, a parasol shading her eyes but allowing her body to be warmed by the sun. Birds chirped nearby. A soft breeze caressed her skin, making the water rock the boat like a cradle, back and forth, back and forth...

But then she felt herself being lifted from the boat. She endured some jostling as she was carried to the shore.

No! Please put me back where you found me.

She opened her eyes and saw a door frame above her. Then the coffered ceiling of the foyer. She closed her eyes against the sight.

I don't want to be inside. Take me back to the lake!

"Put her down here," someone said.

She was laid upon a cushion that was tightly packed, obviously not meant for comfort.

The drawing room. It has to be the drawing room.

Although she knew she could open her eyes to confirm the notion, she kept them closed, trying to hold onto her wonderful dream.

Someone held her hand and stroked her face. *That's nice. Are you here in the boat with me? Is there room?*

"In here!"

The hands pulled away and another hand took her wrist. There was silence. Blessed silence.

Someone opened her eyes without her permission. *Stop that! Let me be!*

More voices talked around her. Getting louder, arguing.

Finally, she'd had enough. She opened her eyes. "Stop it! Be quiet!" She began to sit up and too many hands tried to help. She swatted them away. "Leave me alone!" She let her feet find the floor. Only then did she fully leave her tranquil refuge and return to reality.

Wretched reality.

The voices quieted and she suffered their worried looks.

"I'm fine. Leave me be." She began to stand, but dizziness forced her back to the settee.

Morgan sat beside her, one arm around her shoulders, the other taking her hand. "What happened?"

I had enough. Enough of you, enough of this house, enough of my doubts and failures and —

"Let's get her to your room," Jack said.

"I'm fine," she began to say. Then she changed her mind. If she were in her room, they'd leave her alone. *That* is what she wanted most. "Yes," she said. "Get me to our room."

As they helped her climb the stairs, she remembered the diligent ant, climbing up and over the obstacles in his way. It felt odd to admire an ant.

Genevieve snuggled her cheek into the pillow and moaned with pleasure. Sleep, blessed sleep. If she was lucky she'd dream about her boat on the lake.

She vaguely heard a door open and wished the intruder away. She kept her eyes closed and pretended to be asleep.

The smell of soup nearly enticed her to end her farce. Nearly.

She heard Morgan say, "Sit up, my darling. You need to eat something."

She would love to, and not just soup. She was hungry for the mutton that was on the menu tonight, and turnips, and fresh bread laden with creamy butter. Followed by Mrs. McDeer's famous chocolate buttermilk cake.

Genevieve felt herself smile at the thought of it, the very taste of it. Then she remembered slender Molly.

The only way she would win her husband back was to regain her figure. And that meant not eating.

She had a choice to make. Ignore the tray and risk having him leave it to entice her to eat. Or acknowledge his presence and tell him to take it away.

The temptation would be too much. So Genevieve stirred, waving her hand in its direction. "Take it away."

"You need to eat, darling."

"Take it away!"

"You're not thinking clearly."

"No. I'm not. But I have no wish to eat. Take it away or I'll toss the lot of it on the floor."

He shook his head, clearly disappointed and confused.

It couldn't be helped.

Morgan took the tray and she heard the door shut behind him. Unfortunately, the aroma of the soup lingered.

I'm back.

Walking into the Savoy Theatre was like stepping into the past. Yet the Clarissa who walked through the front entrance on the arm of a baron was far different than the Clarissa who had used the stage entrance and spent time putting on makeup and getting in costume. The disparity made her shiver.

"Are you cold?" Damon asked.

She shook her head, dispelling the ancient memories.

As they made their way through the crowd to their seats, she was warmed by the recent memories of the day. Damon had been true to his apology and had been the essence of manners and gracious attention. He'd even accompanied her on her shopping expedition, not complaining once. She wasn't sure why he'd changed from testy to charming, but was glad for it. His transformation almost made her regret the two hotel rooms.

Almost, but not completely.

Damon looked around the theatre. "This is quite agreeable. Yet, it is a far cry from Royal Albert Hall or the Opéra de Paris."

"Don't be a snob. It's not a burlesque hall either."

"I'll take your word on that."

The orchestra began the overture. Clarissa's stomach pulled with anticipation, oddly more nervous watching than she had ever felt performing.

The curtain opened and the play began. She scanned the faces of the actresses, looking for her friends. *There's Martha, Bernice, and Frieda. Daphne has a speaking part. Good for her.*

The lead actress made her entrance and Clarissa felt a different kind of stitch in her stomach. She'd longed to be a star, to capture an audience and make them so enraptured they were fully transported into the story. She'd longed to impress people, inspire them, and perhaps even enrich their lives in some small way. Being able to elicit that kind of response would have been extremely satisfying.

Damon broke the moment by taking her hand. She may not have enraptured an audience, but she enraptured him. And she hoped she inspired and enriched Beth's life. Both were changed by her presence—as she was changed by them.

But the satisfaction…was her life in Summerfield satisfying enough to fill her up the way acting had?

Remember, Clarissa. You never were the lead. You were in the chorus. You never were a star.

She'd been an actress who had garnered little respect from anyone, blending into the background. Was she a star now? A leading lady in her own life?

During her time on stage, she'd lived alone and had been fully independent, making her own decisions.

And how did that play out?

The reality of being fully responsible meant she'd often been hungry and cold. She could only afford a small flat in a neighborhood she shared with law-breakers, ladies of the evening, and vagrants.

Beth was a vagrant, living on the stairs of my building. If I hadn't saved her, she would still be there. Or worse.

Upon this thought lay the source of her satisfaction. Now she was a mother and owned the possibility of being a wife.

She glanced at Damon's profile as he watched the play. He was as handsome as any man she had ever known, and twice as charming.

A few years ago, during her final social season in London with her family, she'd enjoyed a string of men hanging on her every word. She'd received their notes professing undying affection. They'd kissed her hands, offered lingering looks, and had exchanged romantic whispers behind her fan. Those were jolly times. Clarissa had played the part of the ingénue well—though without much sincerity. The chase of romance seemed far more satisfying than the catch.

This non-committal stance was the reason her parents had arranged a match for her with Joseph Kidd. If *she* didn't do her duty by choosing a suitable mate, they would do it for her. Losing Joseph to Lila had been a slap to her ego, even if she knew it was for the best.

She was too much for him, he too little for her.

What would her parents think of Damon? They could bear no objection. He was a baron, and the nephew of their dear friend, Newley. She'd considered writing to them in India, but had chosen not to. If the romance came to nothing, it was best they didn't have yet another failure to hold against her. If it was successful…

Damon took his hand from hers in order to applaud at the end of a song. Clarissa added her own applause, though she had no memory of the music.

Perhaps her disinterest was a sign she'd moved beyond what could have been. The theatre was a season of her life, one she did not wholly regret, for it had brought her Beth.

The present season was bursting with promise. She fully enjoyed working on Crompton Hall and knew she was up to the task. And she fully enjoyed her time spent with Damon.

Her future was bright.

Once again, the audience applauded.

She smiled and accepted the accolades as her own. Yes, indeed. Bravo, Clarissa Weston, bravo.

Chapter Twelve

"Take the tray away, Jane."

Genevieve turned her back to the breakfast tray, even though the smell of sausage and eggs enticed. She knew if she began to eat, she wouldn't be able to stop. Best not eat at all. It was imperative she become trim again as soon as possible, before Molly told Morgan that he was the father of her baby.

Jane set the tray on a table. "I'll leave it here, ma'am. For when you feel up to it."

And torture me with its proximity? Genevieve sat up in bed and pointed to the door. "I said take it away!"

"Yes, ma'am. Right away." Jane left the room just as Morgan came in.

"Good morning, dear one. Was the food not to your liking? I can have Mrs. McDeer make something else for you."

She hugged a pillow. "I'm not hungry."

"You didn't eat last night either. You have to be hungry."

"Well, I'm not."

He sat on the side of the bed and stroked some hair away from her face. "I'm glad you slept in. You've been working far too hard, with your days far too long. Take the day to rest and recuperate."

It sounded like a lovely idea—though impossible. "If I don't go in, nothing will get done."

"So a few dresses are delayed? Your health and well-being are more important than a few dresses."

She sat up, causing his hand to fall away. "Don't minimize the importance of my work! The ladies are

211

enthusiastic. We have four new dressmakers in the village, women who would never have learned to sew if not for me."

"And the other ladies who help you."

She found her pillow. "I assure you, their participation is minimal."

He stood. "It will be even more minimal if you don't acknowledge their contribution. Sylvia and Lila both promised to help more. I thought they were doing so."

"Their attempts are negligible and without enthusiasm."

"Perhaps sewing is not something they enjoy."

She tossed the pillow aside. "Then why did they offer to help? Why tease me with their participation and encouragement only to abandon me?"

He shook head. "It must be hard to get comfortable with that chip on your shoulder."

Obviously, the sympathy she'd garnered last night was gone. "I am merely speaking the truth."

"As you see it."

"It is *my* truth."

"Which you are setting forth as the only truth. Other people have opinions, Gen. And preferences. Perhaps it's time you acknowledge that."

Preferences. He prefers Molly.

She heard voices in the hall. Was that Molly's voice? Was she coming to see Morgan so early?

"Why is Molly here?"

"To help Dr. Peter remove Joseph's bandages."

"I didn't realize his hands were healed."

"There are many things you don't realize. Namely, that other people have busy lives too. They are trying to deal with their own difficult situations. And other people work very hard—a point you seem to ignore."

She didn't let his reprimand settle. The thought of Molly in the house incensed her. "Did you know Molly is with-child?"

"I did. She told me yesterday in the village."

Genevieve remembered seeing them in conversation—and sharing an embrace. "She and Peter didn't think they could have children."

"Time usually takes care of such concerns."

Or those concerns can be erased by finding another man.

He studied her and a crease etched between his eyes. "What are you wanting to say?"

Maybe it was best to just have it out. "Peter isn't capable of fathering a child. You are." As soon as she heard the awful words, she wished she could take them back. To think it was one thing, but to say it aloud...

Morgan stood in stunned disbelief. Then he stepped away from her. "You are accusing me and Molly of...?"

"I keep seeing you together, laughing and talking."

"We are friends—close friends. Old friends. Friends who laugh and have conversations."

Genevieve tried to think of the other evidence, but found the pot empty. "Call it women's intuition."

"Don't blame your accusations on all women. Call it what it is: one particular woman's penchant for reading something into nothing." He pressed a hand to his forehead. "And when, pray tell, are we supposed to have...been together?"

"I came to bed the other night and you weren't here."

He hesitated, thinking. "The night it was raining and I found you going for a walk?" His eyes lit up. "You were going out to find us—to catch us?"

She felt ridiculous. "You said you used to meet at the arbor."

"Years ago, when I was a shopkeeper and she was Ruth's maid. And even though we met out there, we never...how primal do you think we are? No matter what our position in life, we are both honorable people, mindful of right and wrong."

The notion of them romping in the garden *was* ridiculous. Then why had it seemed so possible? Probable?

"I thought you knew me better than that, Genevieve. I thought I knew you. But apparently we don't know each other at all." He walked to the door, then stopped and pointed at her. "I forbid you from getting out of bed today and will inform the entire household that you are to remain in this room."

"I am being held against my will?"

"You are being held as a safeguard against your illogical, impulsive, and destructive will. I will not have you spilling your accusations to others. Nor will this household tolerate another indulgent outburst or dramatic fainting spell. I tell you this, wife: your days of making a spectacle are through."

"Morgan…" She hated that he thought so little of her. She hadn't been feigning her angst. It was very real.

He stood with one hand on the door knob, his head down. "Your accusation that I am the father of Molly's baby scores my very soul."

"I'm sorry. I—"

He fully faced her. "As the mistress of Summerfield Manor you should hold yourself to higher standards. Ruth, Grandmother, and the rest who went to India, trusted you to uphold those standards. You have failed them. And me. So until you can pull yourself together and fully be the woman I love, you will remain in seclusion. I will not let you inflict any more damage on your reputation—or the family's. It's for your own good." He opened the door and Genevieve caught the glimpse of a servant hurrying past. "Ring for Jane if you need something. Enjoy your day."

Silence engulfed her. He hadn't just left the room, he'd left *her*. He'd degraded her, scolded her, and shamed her.

But had he told the truth?

Is he right? Am I wrong?

The only thing she knew for certain was that she was *not* going to be held prisoner in her own room.

She whipped the covers off, got out of bed, and rang the bell for Jane. While she waited, she shoveled in two large bites of eggs, and devoured a sausage.

She was just drinking her coffee when Jane entered.

"Yes, ma'am?"

Genevieve set the cup down. "Help me get dressed."

Jane's breathing turned heavy. She did not move.

"Jane? I told you to help me get dressed."

The maid shook her head. "I'm sorry, ma'am. But I've been ordered not to let you leave your room."

Morgan had certainly made quick work of that directive. She softened her tone. "I am feeling quite better. So please help me dress so I can—"

Jane shook her head, then bobbed a curtsy. "I'm sorry, ma'am. I cannot do that. If you need anything brought *to* you, I'd be happy to—"

Genevieve picked up the breakfast plate and flung it at her. Food flew everywhere, and the plate landed at Jane's feet. "Leave!"

Jane fled.

Genevieve stared after her. "Oh, dear Lord, what have I done?"

She retrieved the plate, fell to her knees, and began to clean up her mess—until sobs overtook her. She bent forward until her forehead touched the floor. "Lord, help me!"

Her thoughts and emotions were as scrambled as the eggs. How could she undo what was done?

Slowly her tears abated and she sat upright. She took a few breaths, calming herself.

But then, in a fit of motion, she stuffed the discarded food in her mouth.

Every last morsel.

"Try moving your fingers," Dr. Peter told Joseph.

He bent them slowly, as though fearful the new skin would tear. But he *did* bend them.

"You did it!" Lila said.

"I did it." Joseph glowed. "The hand doesn't look very pretty, but it works."

Peter gently took Joseph's hands in his and turned them over, with Molly looking on. "The scar tissue will fade, but may never fully go away."

"I can accept that," Joseph said. He wiggled his fingers. "I can work again!"

"You can," Peter said as Molly gathered up the old bandages. "However, I would advise you to wear gloves if you are in unclean conditions, such as over at the Hall."

Molly threw the bandages in the fire. "Perhaps he should wear gloves that are a little large?"

"That's a capital idea," Peter said. "See if one of the men has some gloves that will give your hands some extra room." He nodded at his wife. "That was a good idea, Molly."

"Thank you."

Peter packed up his doctor's bag. "Did Molly tell you our good news?"

"I told Mrs. Kidd," Molly said.

"But no one told me," Joseph said. "What is your news?"

Peter motioned Molly close, then said, "We are expecting our first child."

Joseph extended his hand to shake Peter's, hesitated, then did so again. "How wonderful that my first handshake is to celebrate such happy news." They shook hands. "Speaking of children, what I need right now is to hold my daughter and touch her cheek. Lila, would you care to join me?"

"I'd be delighted."

The ladies walked through the village square. Lila was torn. To their left was the workshop and the promise of a day spent sewing. To the right was the mercantile and its more satisfying promise. She planned to rearrange a portion of the store to make room for more dress patterns, notions, trims, and cloth.

She shook her head. Not today. Since Genevieve's collapse none of them dared deviate from workshop business.

Sylvia offered a dramatic sigh. "I feel like I'm walking a very thin line, as though I need to tread carefully and be a talented seamstress right this minute so I can ease Genevieve's burden."

"If we fail, we all topple." Lila unlocked the door.

Pax came to greet them and Tilda scooped her up and she immediately began purring. "We can only do our best," Tilda said. "Whatever our *best* might be."

Beth nodded. Then she dragged her fingers through a bowl of buttons. "I'll sew on buttons if you need me to. But I'm still not very good at creating a thread shank."

"I'll teach you," Tilda said. "Unless a lot of children come in."

"Then you'll both be free of it," Sylvia said. "If only…"

Their attitude told a forlorn story. Lila faced them with her hands on her hips. "Listen to the lot of us. Acting as though working here is punishment. No wonder Genevieve came to her wit's end."

"I don't dislike sewing," Sylvia said, then offered a grin. "But can I help it if I'd rather spend time with a certain handsome earl?"

"I'm glad you and Papa enjoy each other's company," Lila said. "But…are the two of you conspiring to neglect your respective duties today?"

Sylvia stabbed some stray pins into a cushion. "Perhaps." She shoved the cushion aside. "I don't appreciate being reprimanded. Especially since you don't want to be here either."

Lila put a hand to her brow. "I'm sorry. We *are* in this together."

Tilda held Pax under her chin. "I'm used to doing work I don't want to do. I used to clean houses. I didn't like that one bit."

She made a good point. "But you did it."

"I did it."

Lila drew in a breath and pushed away the selfish thoughts. "Let us rally, ladies. For Genevieve's sake."

Their renewed focus was just in time, as Mrs. Smythe and her two boys stepped in, wanting to finish her dress.

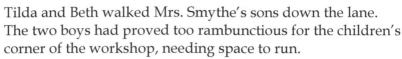

Tilda and Beth walked Mrs. Smythe's sons down the lane. The two boys had proved too rambunctious for the children's corner of the workshop, needing space to run.

"Let go!" the six-year-old said, trying to yank his hand free of Tilda's.

"Race ya!" said the seven-year-old.

The girls had no choice but to let them loose. The boys raced up the road, veering to a side road.

"Don't go far!" Tilda called.

The boys didn't listen, forcing the girls to run after them.

"Where does this lane lead?" Tilda asked.

"I'm not sure," Beth said.

They heard the boys laughing and turned a bend and saw them playing on a swing next to an empty building. A tilted sign above the door proclaimed: Summerfield School.

With the boys happily occupied, Tilda and Beth peered in the windows. It was not a large space, but had a chalkboard up front, a small table and chair for the teacher, and some long benches and tables facing the front.

"It's sad to see it empty like this," Beth said.

"Genevieve mentioned the teacher moved away. I offered to teach."

"What did she say?"

"She said I wasn't qualified."

"But you're a good teacher. The children like you. They listen to you. *I* listened to you. I can read now because of you."

Tilda moved to the front door and they stepped inside. It smelled of stale air and dust.

Beth ran a hand over a table. "It could do with a good cleaning."

Tilda ignored the dirt and even the mouse that skittered along the baseboard. Her thoughts filled every corner, swirling from floor to ceiling, making *her* swirl with her arms outstretched.

"What are you doing?"

"I am going to teach here. I am going to open the school again."

"But Genevieve said you couldn't. You weren't qualified."

"Surely an eager teacher is better than no teacher."

"What about the workshop? We want you there. We need you there."

It was a problem. But Tilda couldn't let it stop her. "Could you take care of the children who come in the shop on your own?"

"I suppose. But I like doing it with you. I'm not sure I want to do it alone."

"What if you were here with me, in the school, helping me teach?"

"We can't be two places at one time."

If only they could.

Suddenly, the boys burst into the school. "What's this place?"

"It's a school," Tilda said. "Haven't either of you been here before?"

They didn't answer but each claimed a table and bench. "What's this?" the older one asked, holding up a slate.

Images of slates, chalk, books, paper, and pencils flooded Tilda's mind. "It's a slate for doing your schoolwork. There should be some chalk…"

The younger boy scrambled under his table. "Here's a piece."

"I want a piece too."

"There's one, over there."

Beth handed the younger boy a slate. "Now you each have one."

"What now?"

The question loomed large, but Tilda didn't hesitate. She went to the front of the room and found her own piece of chalk. She wrote three letters on the board. A. B. C. "What is this letter called?"

"I dunno."

"I dunno either."

How many Summerfield children didn't know their alphabet? Or their numbers? The task was daunting.

"This is an A, the first letter of the alphabet. And this is a B, and this, a C. I'd like you each to write the letters on your slates as neatly as you can."

The boys set their slates on the tables and concentrated on their work. The older one was through first. "Done! I won!"

"It's not a race. Let me see."

Although the letters were wobbly, it was a very good start.

Lila hadn't had time to think about the mercantile. After Mrs. Smythe finished her dress, Molly stopped in to work on hers. And then Mrs. Keening came in to finish the hem on her dress.

Being such a busy day, they could have used Genevieve's help. Lila wondered how she was recovering, especially since Morgan had spread the word that she was to remain confined to bed. Lila would visit her later.

"There!" Mrs. Keening held the dress by its shoulders then pressed it against her body, admiring her reflection in the full-length mirror. "My, my, look at me."

Lila laughed. "You look lovely."

"With all the new dresses in town, we need to have a fashion parade to show them off."

Lila clapped her hands. "That's a marvelous idea!" She looked to Sylvia, Molly, and the girls. "What do you think?"

"I think I want to sew more swiftly so I can be a part of it," Molly said.

"I'll help you," Beth said.

Lila borrowed a pencil from Tilda and began to make a list. "How many women have finished a dress?"

The list grew to eight women—plenty enough for a parade.

"We could dress Etta in one of her new dresses too," Tilda said.

"Even the servants could model their fresh, new uniforms," Beth said.

Lila added to her list. "If this doesn't make Genevieve happy, I don't know what will."

***

"This is ridiculous."

Genevieve smoothed the bed covers over her lap. Although she liked the idea of sleeping late and lounging with nothing to do, choosing those activities was far different from being forced into them by her husband's directive.

With every minute that passed, her sense of panic grew. Today was going to be a busy day at the workshop. Both Mrs. Smythe and Mrs. Keening were coming in.

No one but Genevieve knew how to make a proper hem that did not pucker. Worse than not being there to help was the knowledge that in her absence the other ladies would do the work — and do the work badly — resulting in extra work for Genevieve when she returned.

If she ever returned.

She threw off the covers and strode to the window. The gardeners were pruning dead blooms. She saw Jack and Morgan conferring over the hoofs of some horse. Everyone was working. Productive.

Except her.

Enough. She tugged at the bell pull to call Jane.

Her maid came in. "Yes, Mrs. Weston?"

"I wish to get dressed."

Jane shook her head. "As I said earlier, Mr. Weston left express orders that you were not to leave, that you needed to rest."

Genevieve thought fast. "Who said anything about leaving? I simply wish to get dressed. I cannot lie abed another minute. Now help me."

Once the task was accomplished she was ready to make her escape.

Jane glanced at the breakfast tray. "I'm so glad you ate. Would you like some luncheon? Mrs. McDeer could make you some soup."

"No, thank you." Despite eating breakfast, Genevieve was famished. She'd succumbed to eating while in a weak moment. She would not repeat the offense.

Right now she just wanted to be free.

Genevieve waited a full minute after Jane left, then carefully turned the doorknob of her bedroom and checked the hallway. Two servants from Crompton Hall were chatting at the far end, their backs to her. With dozens of people in the Manor, there might not be a moment when someone wasn't about.

She had to take a chance.

She slipped out of her room and turned towards the front stairs. The sweeping staircase was more exposed than the back stairs, yet it was used by far fewer people.

She strained an ear, listening for conversations below. No one was close. With a surge of courage, she quickly ran down the stairs. She couldn't risk the front door, for Jack and Morgan were just outside. She made a sharp left and slipped into the corridor containing the library and earl's study.

She heard voices at the far end of the hall, and quickly tiptoed towards her destination, her personal haven — the morning room.

Genevieve went inside and closed the door quietly. Only then did she let herself breathe.

Breathing in, she realized that even though she'd reached this goal, it was an interim goal. It was not freedom.

She moved to the French doors that led to the garden. Yes, there were workmen there, but surely her husband's directive had not reached everyone.

She had to risk it. She opened the doors and stepped into the sunshine. Although she wanted to run through the flower gardens to make her way to the village, she dared not draw so much attention. Best to walk with dignity and authority.

She stepped onto the path.

"Mrs. Weston?"

Mrs. Camden stood at the edge of the garden, a basket of cut flowers on her arm.

"Mrs. Camden. It's a wonderful day, is it not?"

She stepped closer. "You are not to be out of your room, ma'am."

"I have spent too much time there already. I feel quite refreshed and—"

"It's your husband's orders, ma'am. I'm afraid I can't let you sneak out like this."

"Sneak? I was not sneaking."

Mrs. Camden gave her the look she deserved. "You do not usually exit the Manor by way of your morning room."

Genevieve expelled an exasperated sigh. "I am going mad up in my room. I truly am refreshed and feel much better."

"I am glad to hear it, but I need you to return there. I will fetch your husband and he will come visit you. Only he can rescind his order."

The way it was presented incensed her. "I am not a prisoner in my own house! It's insulting."

Mrs. Camden's voice softened. "I don't know the whys of it, ma'am, but I have to follow orders. Please go back to your room. I'm sure it can all be worked out between you."

Between us? So everyone knows we argued and that this is a marital matter?

Her embarrassment made her agree. She saved what little bit of pride she had left by saying, "Tell Mr. Weston I wish to see him immediately."

"I believe he's just gone off to Crompton Hall, ma'am."

"Then tell him when he returns."

The carriage came to a stop and Clarissa waited for the coachman to open the door for her. "Home, sweet home," she said.

Damon took her hand and kissed it. "I'm not sure I want to return to reality so soon, my darling."

She smiled at him, yet didn't agree. As soon as the door opened, she strode into the house and towards the stairs. "Dixon, how is Beth feeling?"

"She's quite recovered, Miss Weston. But I'm afraid she's not here."

Clarissa stopped on the bottom stair. "Where is she?"

"I believe she is at the sewing workshop, miss. With the other ladies—all but Mrs. Weston."

She removed her cloak and handed it to him. "Where is Mrs. Weston?"

"She is in her room. Resting."

"From what?"

He looked past her, then down. Something had happened.

"Dixon, tell me what's going on. Beth was sick but now isn't, and Genevieve was well, but now isn't?"

"I'm sure Mrs. Weston would appreciate a visit from you."

Clarissa sighed. She was very glad that Beth was well, but had a hundred things to do. Visiting Genevieve was not one of them. But best to get it done with.

Damon came inside and called after her. "How is Beth?"

"*She* is fine. But Genevieve... I'll see you in a bit."

She saw Dottie in the hallway and handed over her hat. "My things will need unpacking."

"Yes, Miss Weston."

Clarissa smoothed her hair and knocked on Genevieve's door. When she entered she'd expected to see her ill in bed, not sitting on the window-seat, fully clothed.

"You're back from London," Genevieve said.

"So I am. I was told you were ill."

Her shrug elicited more interest than any list of ailments. Clarissa sat on the other end of the seat. "Tell me what's happened. It must have been monumental to keep you from the workshop."

Genevieve shook her head. "It's nothing. I'm fine."

"You are not fine. And it is something." Clarissa sighed and began again. "I know we aren't close, but I can see something is terribly wrong. Tell me, Genevieve. Perhaps I can help."

Genevieve hesitated, but with a nod slowly started her explanation. With each sentence her words gained momentum. Clarissa could relate to her mention of being weary and overworked, yet when she veered into a rambling discourse about herself and Morgan, and Molly being pregnant with Morgan's baby...

Clarissa raised a hand between them, stopping her words. "What *are* you talking about?"

Genevieve drew in a full breath, as though needing to be refueled. "I know I'm wrong, but it didn't seem wrong at the time I confronted him, and—"

"You said all this to Morgan?"

Her face paled. "I did."

"Without proof—much less without any common sense?"

"It seemed plausible. I caught them talking and laughing."

"A grievous offense."

Genevieve stared out the window. "Morgan and I haven't been... close since the twins were born, so I thought he would find..." She shrugged.

Clarissa was shocked that Genevieve was confiding about such personal matters. With her. It reinforced the severity of the issue.

She wasn't versed in the timing of intimacy after giving birth, but since the twins were three months old, it did seem that time enough had passed.

The first question that came to mind was a blunt one. "Is he not interested in you?"

Genevieve bit her lip and looked at her midsection. "I'm fat."

Clarissa tried unsuccessfully to stifle a laugh.

"Don't laugh at me! I can't get into any of my old clothes. I don't feel attractive. Surely he is disgusted with me."

"If he's said anything to you about your appearance I will wallop him. What *has* he said?"

"Well... nothing."

"Has he tried to be affectionate?"

"Well, yes. But—"

"You turned him down?"

"Well, yes. But—"

She was being ridiculous. "Stop it, Genevieve. You're acting like a silly ninny. Morgan loves you. He chose you over Molly ages ago."

"Only because our marriage was arranged and the estate needed my family's money."

Clarissa let her mouth drop. "Are you really that insecure? Do you not see how he looks at you throughout the day? Do you not sense his adoration?"

Genevieve stared straight ahead, her features distraught. "Really?"

"Open your eyes, woman."

"I...oh dear. I've been so foolish. Unreasonable. Blind."

"Yes. Yes. Yes. All three." Clarissa stood to leave, but Genevieve stopped her with a hand.

"How was your trip to London? With Damon?"

"Very productive."

"Did you finish your business for the Hall?"

"I did."

"And...otherwise?"

Clarissa put a hand to her chest and played the part of the offended ingénue. "I do not know what you're implying." She smiled wickedly. "Rest assured, I did not succumb to the full temptation that is Lord Silvey."

"I'm glad."

Clarissa was surprised by her comment. "You approve of my resistance to temptation in general, or the specific lure of Damon?"

Genevieve didn't answer.

"He *did* propose."

She perked up. "How did you respond?"

The memory flooded back. "I believe I said, 'oh.'"

"Oh?"

"Sometimes there is no better response."

"So you haven't agreed?"

What an annoying question. "Didn't I just say that I—"

"Yes, yes. I'm sorry to press the issue."

"What do *you* think I should say?"

Genevieve smoothed her skirt. "Well. We don't know him like you do. He *is* a very charming man. He seems to make you happy."

"Correct on both accounts."

"But does he...to use the phrase you just used regarding Morgan... do you sense his adoration?"

Clarissa *had* used that word in reference to Morgan. Yet it didn't seem to be a word that could ever be associated with Damon. How troubling. Did that mean she shouldn't marry him?

It was a subject for another day. She stood. "I am weary from the trip. Will I see you at dinner?"

"If I can."

"Can?"

"If I am allowed to dine with the family."

"You're being ridiculous."

She shrugged.

"Who holds this decision about whether or not you can dine with us?"

"Morgan. He ordered me to remain in my room all day."

"He ordered?"

She nodded.

"He doesn't have the right to order you to do anything." She headed for the door. "I'm going to have a talk with my cousin and give him what-for."

Genevieve rushed after her. "Please, Clarissa. No. It will just make things worse."

The plaintive look on her face made Clarissa cringe. No husband should wield such power over his wife. It made her think less of both of them—and the institution of marriage.

"I will be down for dinner," Genevieve said.

"*If* Morgan allows it?"

"It's complicated."

She'd had enough. "I'll leave you to your captivity."

And they called her dramatic?

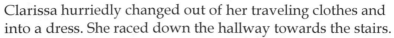

Clarissa hurriedly changed out of her traveling clothes and into a dress. She raced down the hallway towards the stairs.

Damon came out of his room. "Where are you going in such a rush?"

"Beth is at the workshop. I need to see her."

"I'll go with you."

His shirt was untucked and he wore no tie. He wasn't ready to go anywhere. And honestly, after her discussion with Genevieve, and Morgan's rash treatment of her, she was in no mood to be around any man. "It's all right. I will see you at dinner."

She rushed off before he could stop her. As she exited the house, Dixon asked. "Would you like me to order up the pony cart for you, Miss Weston?"

She didn't have time to wait. "No need. I'll walk."

As soon as Clarissa passed the first curve in the driveway, she traded her walk for a run. She hadn't done such a thing since she was a girl, yet the anticipation of seeing Beth filled her with joy as surely as the autumn air filled her lungs. After experiencing the noise, commotion, and crowds of London, the serenity of the countryside was a balm.

Once she reached the village, she slowed to a more dignified walk. She passed a trio of women on the edge of the square, their heads together, no doubt sharing some juicy bit of gossip.

She hoped it wasn't about her and Damon, off in London together. She could imagine them pouncing on such news, embellishing it to suit their need for the salacious.

But then she heard two names that stopped her in her tracks: Mr. Weston and Molly.

She paused to catch her breath, peering at the women until they stopped talking to look at her. One of them bobbed a curtsy. "Good afternoon, Miss Weston. How are you today?"

They weren't getting by so easily. She approached them confidently. "It is nice to see you ladies. I've been in London a few days—but I'm sure you know that."

"We did hear it, miss. Lord Silvey went with you?"

"He did. He was a great help in conducting business for Crompton Hall's restoration."

They looked disappointed. She considered adding a bit of veiled innuendo to the mix, but decided to concentrate on the names she had overheard. "I couldn't help but overhear you mention Mr. Weston and Molly? Is there some news I don't know about?"

To their credit they blushed. "Molly is expecting."

"I did hear that. How wonderful for her and Dr. Peter."

They exchanged a glance between them, but obviously didn't have the courage to say what was truly on their minds.

"Out with it, ladies. I am weary from the trip and would like to see my daughter. If you have something to say regarding Mr. Weston and Molly I suggest you say it. I insist you state it plain. Now."

They all blinked wildly as if their batted lashes could fend off her demand.

"I'm waiting."

"Well," said Mrs. Miller, the wife of one of their tenant farmers. "We heard tell that perhaps Mr. Weston and Molly... them once being sweet on each other and all, considering the fact that everyone knew she and Dr. Peter wanted children, but it weren't happening..."

Hearing it said aloud was alarming. "So you decided to spread a rumor against two of the village's most upstanding citizens—actually four, if you consider Mrs. Weston and Dr. Peter."

"We just thought—"

"You just thought the worst. Instead of celebrating with Molly and Dr. Peter—celebrating one of God's miracles—you tainted their joy with your own sordid imaginings."

"Tis not our imaginings," Mrs. Miller blurted, dropping her eyes as she continue. "One of Crompton Hall's servants overheard the Westons arguing about it."

Clarissa forced her eyebrows to remain where they were. "I'm not sure which is worse: servant gossip or village gossip. Both are deplorable." She thought of the perfect way to end the conversation. "It appears your actions have broken two commandments: thou shalt not bear false witness against your neighbor and thou shalt not covet anything that belongs to your neighbor."

"We don't covet — "

"You covet their happy marriages. Go home ladies and make yourself right with the Lord."

Clarissa turned on her heel and strode to the workshop. So there.

She walked to the workshop. Upon seeing her, Beth ran into her arms. "You're back!"

"And you're well."

Beth nodded. "I am."

There was something wrong. Clarissa put a finger under her chin. "What aren't you telling me?"

Beth pulled away from their embrace and exchanged a glance with Tilda.

"Tilda?" Clarissa asked. "Do you know what's going on?"

She shook her head.

Which left Beth.

But Beth didn't answer.

A child playing in the corner of the workshop started to cry. "I have to go, Mum. I'm so glad you're back."

Clarissa would get to the bottom of this later.

"Tighter, Jane!"

Genevieve raised her shoulders, trying to make her midsection as narrow as possible. Jane yanked on the corset strings, expelling an occasional "Oomph" and "Whoo."

"That's as much as I dare tighten them, Mrs. Weston," Jane said. "You need to breathe."

Genevieve let her shoulders drop and practiced taking in air. A deep breath was not to be had, but if she only took shallow ones, she would be fine.

"Now, the rose-colored shantung," she told Jane.

"You haven't worn it since the baby," Jane warned. "And it is one of your tightest dresses."

"All the more reason to try it now. I haven't eaten anything since breakfast. Surely that sacrifice is worth something." *Please let it be worth something. Morgan will be home soon. I want to look my prettiest for him.*

Jane dropped the skirt over Genevieve's head, being mindful of her hair. The fabric fell upon the bustle and Jane adjusted the cascading lace ruffles and drapery that circled the dress. The moment of truth would come when it was hooked. Or not hooked.

There was some tugging involved, and Genevieve felt the front of the skirt being pulled taut. But then…

"It's hooked!" Jane said. "It's on the last hook, but it's hooked."

"Now the bodice."

Jane held the bodice so Genevieve could slide her arms inside. The bodice opened in the back and Genevieve prayed those hooks would close.

"Will it fit?" she asked as she felt Jane work the closures.

"Just a moment…there! Yes, it's all fastened!"

"Wonderful!"

Jane faced her and adjusted the lace collar and edging that ran down the front of the bodice and at the cuffs for the three-quarter length sleeves. There was a satin bow that tied just below the waist in front, and Jane worked on it until it lay flat.

"Done! You've done it, Mrs. Weston!"

Genevieve walked to the mirror. She had a definite waist, though her upper body looked a bit strained, like too much meat in a sausage casing. Her face was still plump, her chin becoming a multiple if she didn't hold it just so.

She sighed. "It's no use. I look awful."

"No, you don't, ma'am. You're beautiful."

There was a knock and the door opened. It was Morgan.

Genevieve spun around to face him, making the best of it. "Dearest. You're back."

"And you, dear one, are not in bed."

Genevieve nodded to Jane, cueing her to leave them alone. She strode to Morgan and kissed his cheek. "I am feeling much better now." She spread her arms to showcase her gown. "See? All dressed for dinner."

"You look very lovely."

"Thank you." She drew in a breath, but suddenly felt faint. She grappled for a chair.

"You're still not well. You've done too much, too soon. I'll call for Jane."

"No." Genevieve knew that wasn't it. "*You* can help me." With his help she stood and turned her back towards him. "Under the top ruffle there is a placket with hooks. Please remove my bodice."

"Remove...?"

"My corset is so tight I'm going to faint. Help me get it off!"

Although there was some fumbling, within a few minutes, the bodice and skirt were off, and the laces of the corset loosened. Genevieve took her first full breath of the hour. And then another.

"Jane should be ashamed for lacing you so tightly. You need to breathe."

"That's what she told me. It's not her fault. I insisted." She pointed to the bodice and skirt that lay strewn on the carpet. "I wanted to look pretty for you. You've always liked this dress. But I guess I'm still too fat for it. Perhaps if I don't eat tonight — "

He took her shoulders firmly. "You aren't eating because you think you're fat?"

"I am fat. Look at me. I want to be appealing to you. I want to be trim and pretty again like M — " She put a hand to her mouth. She hadn't meant to be so direct.

"Like Molly?" He looked confused.

She shrugged, then nodded. "Yes, like Molly. I feel like a workhorse being compared to a fine stallion."

He laughed, sitting on the bed for support.

"Don't laugh at me!"

He raised a hand trying to contain himself. "Why not? You're comparing the two of you to horses."

"I couldn't think of anything else."

"By the way, a stallion is a male horse."

She swatted his arm. "You understood what I meant."

He reached forward and put his hands on her hips, drawing her close. He looked up at her. "You, my dear wife, are incomparable to any other woman. I adore you as you were, as you are, and as you will be."

She let happy tears come. "You do?"

He stopped the track of a tear with his thumb. "I do. If you remember those were the same two words we said to each other when we were married."

She smiled. "I do."

He pulled her closer, kissed her, then leaned back until they both fell upon the bed.

An hour later Genevieve stood before the mirror once again and smoothed the skirt of her russet-colored dress. She tested out a breath. "This is much better. I can breathe."

"And eat," Jane said. "I'm so glad you're going down to dinner."

"As am I." She watched as Jane collected the remnants of the too-tight pink ensemble. "Forgive me for acting vain to the point of being ridiculous. I should never have forced you to lace me in so tightly."

Jane nodded. "I want you to feel good about yourself in here, Mrs. Weston." She pointed to her head. "But you also need to feel good in body."

"Wise words. I will remember them."

With a final look to the mirror, Genevieve left for dinner.

Out in the hall, she was immediately greeted by Lila. "Genevieve! Are you feeling better?"

She held in a sly smile. "I am. And I am quite famished. I am coming down to dinner."

Lila slid her arm through hers. "I'm so glad. We missed you at the workshop today."

Missed me doing most of the work. Genevieve scolded herself for the negative thought.

"Actually, we have a surprise for you, one I think you will make you very happy."

"What is it?"

"I'll tell you at dinner."

They walked downstairs arm in arm. "Lila, I want to apologize for treating you so harshly. It was insensitive of me not to realize that the rest of you mightn't embrace the sewing as much as I do. It was like insisting all of you enjoy opera or horse racing, when you might care little for either."

"Actually, I do like to ride a good race once in a while. But, I understand your point. And I am very glad for the knowledge I now have regarding dress construction. I would not have gained that if not for you."

"Me, pushing you."

She shrugged. "Pushing is often necessary."

They entered the dining room and Genevieve was heartened by the welcoming comments of her family who were glad for her health and return to their company.

Morgan kissed her on the cheek. "You look lovely, dear one."

She felt herself blush and hoped no one else saw it.

They were seated, the blessing said, and dinner began. When the last bowl of consommé was set in place, Genevieve said, "I wish to thank all of you for your patience and kind care during my...difficulties. I assure you, I am feeling quite well."

"You are very welcome," Lila said. "We are glad you're feeling better." She shared a glance with Sylvia, Tilda, and Beth. "But now for our surprise. So many of the ladies of the village have completed dresses that we thought it would be a wonderful idea to have a fashion parade through the village. We want to show them off."

"It was Mrs. Keening's idea," Beth said.

Lila removed a piece of paper from her pocket. "We have eight ladies who could be involved, not to mention Etta and some of the servants."

"*Will* be involved," Tilda added. "We already asked the ladies."

"I hope that was all right," Lila said.

"We wanted to surprise you," Beth said.

"So...are you surprised?" Sylvia asked.

Genevieve's throat tightened. "I am. But more than that, I am touched by your efforts. I am very blessed to have such a wonderful family."

"I think a fashion parade sounds like a superb idea," Jack said. "Perhaps you should have a few posters made, to advertise the event."

"You could have refreshments," Morgan said.

Newley set down his spoon. "The Harvest Festival is taking place in two weeks. Why not include the parade as a part of it."

Genevieve clapped her hands. "That's a marvelous idea!" The cloud that had shadowed the past few days dissipated, leaving behind sun and blue skies and hope. She held back tears. "You ladies..." She looked at each of them in turn. "Forgive me for pressuring you into a project that became a burden because of my unrealistic expectations. You have shown me the essence of true friendship. Thank you."

"You're ever so welcome," Lila said.

"I agree," Sylvia said. "In return I ask one thing."

"What's that?" Genevieve asked.

"Although we did well enough at the workshop today, I ask that tomorrow you return. We need you."

"I look forward to it. I—"

"Uh...there may be a problem."

It was the first time Clarissa had spoken.

"What are you talking about?" Joseph asked.

Clarissa set down her spoon and shook her head. "Sorry. I shouldn't have said anything. I shouldn't have dampened your enthusiasm."

"Well, now you have," Jack said. "Explain yourself."

Clarissa looked nervous—a condition that seemed foreign to her. "Perhaps we can discuss this later, when we adults are alone." She glanced at Tilda and Beth.

"I'm sixteen," Tilda said.

"And I want to hear," Beth said.

Genevieve felt her stomach clench—and not for lack of food. "Gracious, Clarissa. You're frightening me."

"And me," Morgan said.

"Does it affect the family?" Jack asked.

"It does."

"Then state it plain. Now."

A deep breath seemed to give Clarissa strength. "Today when I was in the village I overheard some women gossiping."

Jack rolled his eyes. "I truly thought the gossip grapevine would have slowed when Fidelia died, but I know that is not the case. Who was their victim?"

"Genevieve."

She wished she could retreat back in her room. "I know I've exposed my frailties for all to see the past few days, but—"

"And Morgan," Clarissa added. "And... Molly."

Oh no!

Morgan flashed Genevieve a look. "You told others about your unfounded suspicions?"

She put a hand to her chest. "I didn't. I swear."

"She tells the truth," Clarissa said. "A servant overheard you and Morgan arguing. *They* spread the rumor."

"What rumor?" Lila asked.

Genevieve truly felt ill. She didn't want to say the words. But Morgan made her own up to it. "Tell them."

"It wasn't true. I was upset and seeing things—"

"That weren't there."

"Seeing what things?" Newley asked.

Clarissa said the words for her. "The rumor is that Morgan fathered Molly's child."

There was a chorus of "what?" and "why?"

"Why would you think such a thing?" Jack asked.

The list of her motives was too long, with ink too dark and smudged. She didn't want to share the full of it.

Morgan saved her. "Molly and I are close friends, and since she has been at the Manor daily to care for Joseph…"

"I saw them talking and laughing and thought the worse. Especially when Molly complained about her supposed inability to have a child — then suddenly she's having a child…" It made sense. Didn't it?

"Quite the mess," Newley said.

"I'm so sorry."

"The main issue is what to do about it," Jack said.

Damon downed his glass of wine in a single gulp. "Fight fire with fire. Surely there's some other scandal stirring in Summerfield, one we can embellish and spread. Tit for tat."

"That is *not* the way to handle this," Morgan said.

Damon extended his glass towards the footman, who filled it. "Then what would all of you suggest?"

They shared a moment of silence.

Finally, Jack spoke. "As the earl, I will go to town, gather what crowd I can, and make a statement, nipping this in the bud."

"Won't that draw unwanted attention to the issue?" Sylvia asked.

"If left on its own, gossip spreads like a greedy vine, strangling everything in its path. This particular gossip puts our family honor into question."

The shame of it fell upon her shoulders. "I will also speak to them," Genevieve said. "I have to speak. It's my ridiculous suspicions that caused this problem."

" I will go with you," Morgan said.

"Well then," Clarissa said. "Since that's settled, can we please continue with dinner?"

They could. Genevieve had lost her appetite.

As they got ready for bed, Clarissa noticed Beth was unusually quiet. They still hadn't had time to fully talk. "Is something wrong?" she asked. "At the workshop you weren't yourself, and you still aren't fully my Beth."

"You shouldn't have told them about the gossip."

"They would have heard soon enough. I think being warned is better than being surprised." She got in bed and nestled into the mattress. "Oh to have my own bed again. I didn't sleep well in London at all."

Beth retrieved a pillow and started for the door.

"Where are you going?"

"I shared a room with Tilda while you were gone. You need a good night's sleep."

"Don't be silly. I missed you, Beth. And I'm ever so glad you're feeling better."

Beth hesitated, as though she wanted to say something. "I'll leave you be. Sleep well, Mum." She kissed Clarissa on the cheek and left the room.

Clarissa huffed. What was wrong with everyone? She hadn't even had a chance to tell Beth that Damon had proposed.

Which led to the question of whether or not she should accept.

Fortunately, the comfort of the bed and the weariness of her body made her forget the questions until tomorrow.

"Of course you're welcome to sleep here again," Tilda said when Beth showed up to sleep.

They both got in bed.

"Did you tell your mother that you were never really sick?"

"No."

"You should. Damon shouldn't be allowed to get away with that."

"Did you talk to Lila or the earl about your idea of teaching at the school?"

"No."

"You should."

And so things were left for another day. Again.

Chapter Thirteen

Genevieve awakened in the arms of the man she loved — the man who loved *her*.

Morgan stirred and opened his eyes. "Good morning, dear one."

She kissed him, and he, her.

Then she remembered the task of the day and her mood darkened. "I have no idea what to say to the people in Summerfield. I wish everyone could forget my stupid folly."

"As we learned after my mother died, it's best to face the gossip head-on. They don't expect that."

"Will they accept what I say?"

"We shall see." He got out of bed, leaned down to kiss her, then yanked the bell-pull to summon his valet before slipping into his dressing room.

Genevieve turned onto her back and smiled in spite of the task in front of her. She was sorry for her sins, but grateful for her blessings. "Thank you, God. I — "

She sat up in bed and looked towards her Bible that sat next to the chair by the window — the Bible she'd retrieved from the blue guestroom. The Bible she hadn't opened since the Kidds moved in.

She scrambled out of bed, picked it up, held it to her chest, then raised her face to the heavens. "I'm so sorry for ignoring You, Lord. I was so caught up in *doing* things that I didn't take time to spend time with You each day. Forgive me."

She closed her eyes and nodded, knowing He would. For the Lord God was dependable. He hadn't pulled away from her, she'd pulled away from Him.

Not anymore. She sat in the chair and placed a hand on the Bible. "I'm back, Father. I lost control for a while, but now..."

Control. Everything fell apart when *she* tried to control circumstances and people. Would things have played out differently if she'd gone to God with her troubles? If she'd trusted Him to help her?

She knew the answer. A verse came to her, and she looked it up. Romans 8: 28. "'We know that all things work together for good to them that love God, to them who are the called according to his purpose.'"

Genevieve let her mind ponder the wisdom. Current events had just proved the verse to be true. Things had *not* worked together for good because she'd ignored God. But now, her eyes had been opened. She had been called — they had all been called — according to God's plan for their lives.

Not my plan, but Yours.

She thought about her upcoming confession to the citizens of Summerfield. Her apology to Molly and Peter. Her humiliation.

She bowed her head, needing to pray, but couldn't find the right words to express her feelings and her need.

She opened her eyes and spotted verse 26, above the verse she'd just read. "'The Spirit also helpeth our infirmities: for we know not what we should pray for as we ought: but the Spirit itself maketh intercession for us with groanings which cannot be uttered.'"

Genevieve gasped and put a hand to her mouth. "Oh, Father. Thank You. You've given me exactly what I need today. Holy Spirit, pray for me. Beseech the Father for all my needs, for everything I can't put into words."

Genevieve bowed her head and let the Almighty God do His mighty work.

"That will be good enough, Dottie," Clarissa said as her maid fixed her hair. "I have a busy day and simply must get going."

As Clarissa moved to leave, the door opened and Beth entered—in her nightdress.

"You're up," she said.

"I am."

"Did you sleep well?" Beth asked.

"I did. And you?" This was *not* what Clarissa wanted to talk about. Why was there tension between them?

"I simply came to get a dress for today."

"You are welcome to it."

"Don't let me stop you from going wherever you wish to be going," Beth said.

Clarissa nodded at Dottie, and the maid left them to argue in private. "Are you angry at me for something?"

Beth said, "No" though Clarissa noticed her hesitation.

"I'm sorry to leave you behind when we went to London. I missed you."

"Mmm."

It was like a slap. "I *did* miss you, Beth. And I am heartily glad you are well again."

Beth took a dress from the armoire and began to get dressed. Clarissa moved to help her.

"I can do it," Beth said.

Clarissa took a step back. "This is utterly ridiculous. I insist you tell me what's bothering you."

"Did you have a good time with Damon?"

She was jealous? "I did. Though the trip would have been even more enjoyable if you'd been along."

"I doubt Damon would agree with that statement."

Probably not. "He proposed to me."

Beth stopped her buttoning. "How did you answer?"

"I didn't."

"Which means...?"

"Which means I didn't have a definite answer for him."

Beth shrugged and resumed buttoning her bodice. "Do you love him?"

"I...I believe I do."

"That doesn't sound very certain."

Clarissa was getting annoyed. "I hardly think you, a thirteen-year-old *girl,* with no experience in regard to romance, has the right to judge the level of my love."

"It was just a question."

"And I gave you my answer: I believe I do love him. Now, if you'll excuse me, I have to go to Crompton Hall and share the design details of my London trip with the Kidds."

Clarissa didn't wait for Beth's response. She had enough exasperating people in her life. She didn't need Beth adding to her burden.

Clarissa was thrilled the walls of the bathrooms were in place at Crompton Hall. Although *she* was adept at visualizing beyond what was there, it was questionable that Joseph, Lila, and Newley had the same ability.

Newley put his hand upon a wooden stud in a bath wall. "This is such a modern idea, Clarissa. I commend you for going above and beyond what was, and being creative enough to bring the hall into what it *could* be."

"You're very welcome. I enjoy doing it." Clarissa noticed Lila take a sudden interest in a newly created window sill. She couldn't ignore the inner satisfaction of successfully achieving what Lila could not. Clarissa strode to a window seat and set her carpet bag upon it. "Now let me show you illustrations of the porcelain fixtures I have ordered." She took out ink drawings of sinks, claw-footed tubs, and commodes. "I do believe these commodes with the floral embellishments on the bowl are exquisite—as commodes go."

The three of them looked through the pamphlets and illustrations. "What is this?" Newley asked.

"It's called a needle shower."

"That doesn't sound very pleasant," Joseph said.

"I believe it is, for you are washed complete-around."

"Doesn't the water get everywhere?"

"There can be a curtain, but..." She regretted showing them that particular picture. "I decided it was best to stay with the full bathtubs."

"I agree," Newley said. "They, in themselves, will be a luxury unheard of in most great houses."

Clarissa could relate to his competitive nature. "You will certainly be one-up on Summerfield Manor."

"I will admit that is an extra perk," Newley said.

"What about the furnishings?" Lila asked.

"Let me show you what I found." Clarissa was only too happy to share.

It was a noted event when the Earl of Summerfield summoned villagers to the square, one usually reserved for births, deaths, or crises of the crown. Jack had sent word to a few key families—including the ladies who'd gossiped—yet had not told them the reason for the gathering. That done, he let the gossip grapevine be utilized for his own higher purposes.

"Don't be nervous, Genevieve," he said as they rode in the carriage to town.

"You are not the first wife who suspected her husband of a dalliance," Sylvia said, then added, almost to herself. "Sometimes with good reason."

Morgan took her hand in his and rested it on his knee. "Let it be known that *this* husband takes his marriage vows very seriously and will never break them."

Genevieve found truth and sincerity in his eyes, which added to her shame for ever doubting him. *Father, thank you for this man. Forgive me for my accusations. In the village today, help me only say what You would have me say. Help me make it right.*

Genevieve's stomach tightened as they drove into the square. The crowd looked to number over a hundred. One hundred sets of ears. One hundred opinions and judgments.

The carriage stopped and they disembarked. Jack and Morgan were jovial and seemed at ease as they met the people. Sylvia was charming and gracious.

Genevieve did her best, but wished for some of Clarissa's dramatic talent. Her smile felt pasted on, her greetings forced. She felt better when she spotted Nana, Rose, and Mrs. Keening—who all gave her a little wave. That's when she saw Molly and Dr. Peter, walking up to the edge of the crowd. *We should have gone to them first—privately! Were they aware of the gossip?* She scanned Molly's face, seeking pain or anger, but blessedly saw neither.

It was too late for such thoughts. Jack made his way to the center of the square. The rest of the family followed and stood behind him. He raised his arms to quiet the crowd.

"Welcome, one and all. Thank you for taking time out of your busy day to gather here."

"Who died?" one of the men asked.

The people shared a chuckle.

"As far as I know, no one has passed away." Jack turned to look at his family. "Unless there's something going on I don't know about."

"No, sir," Morgan said. "I believe we are all alive and well."

"That's a relief. And as the royal family also seems well, I think we can set aside death as the reason for today's gathering."

"Then why are we here, your lordship?"

"We are here for two reasons."

Two?

"Firstly, I have a confession to make."

"So do I!" said a man.

"Be quiet, Carl. Let the earl talk."

Jack seemed totally at ease. Genevieve knew why. He'd been the owner of the mercantile most of his life. These people who were now under his patronage were also his friends.

Jack smiled at the talkative man. "Carl, are you through?"

"I am, my lord."

"Good." Jack looked over the crowd, as if taking in each and every face. "I have been a part of Summerfield most of my life, and before I discovered my true heritage, my family ran the mercantile."

"We still do," Nana called out.

"Indeed, we still do." He took a fresh breath. "The benefits and blessings of a small town are many: the close ties that span generations, and the willingness to support each other in good times and bad. Unfortunately, there is one aspect of a village that is detrimental to everyone involved."

"Not enough ale?" Carl shouted.

His wife yanked at his arm.

Jack ignored him. "I'm speaking of gossip."

The crowd murmured and Genevieve spotted more than one person look specifically at her.

Jack raised his hands, quieting them. "My family is not without sin. When my wife, Fidelia, was alive, she overly enjoyed the full force of the gossip grapevine. Perhaps I was lax in allowing it, for we all know that gossip tarnishes the peace that shines over Summerfield."

Heads nodded, and the worst gossipers got a strong look or tug on the arm from their spouses.

"I may have been lax then, but as your earl I have determined that such destructive practices need to stop immediately for the sake of peace *and* godly living. For the Lord declared that we should not bear false witness to our neighbors." He looked over the crowd. "And we are *all* neighbors. Citizens. Comrades. And friends."

Genevieve found it easier to look over their heads to the upper window of the butcher's shop at the far end of the square. She braced herself for the accounting of her folly.

Jack continued. "As friends we must follow the teachings of Jesus to love our neighbors as ourselves. And forgive them as we wish to be forgiven."

When he turned to look at Genevieve she thought she would faint.

"Our dear Genevieve has something she wishes to say."

Now? Oh, dear Lord. Please give me the words!

246

She stepped forward and exchanged her gaze of the window for the sight of these villagers. These mostly-kind villagers who had welcomed her —

And then she knew what to say.

"I want to take this chance to thank all of you for graciously welcoming me to Summerfield when I arrived a year ago. I came here as a stranger to the area, but also as a stranger to England itself. I admit I was scared to death. What would I find here? Would I be happy? Would I be up to taking on the responsibilities that awaited me here?"

She felt a calm come over her and let the rest of the words flow. "What I found here was love, acceptance, patience, and...and mercy. For I was — and continue to be — a woman who makes mistakes, who...sins." She let the word patter over the crowd. "As the earl made his confession, I now make mine. I recently allowed my insecurities to turn into suspicions against my husband." Genevieve quickly pondered whether she should speak in generalities or mention Molly by name. She decided it was best to make things clear. She nodded towards Molly. "And towards Molly Evers."

There was a gasp and people turned to look upon Molly — who looked fully confused. "I...I don't know what you're talking about, Mrs. Weston."

Genevieve nodded over the crowd. "There was gossip in Summerfield that I believed you and my husband...that your child..."

Molly put her hands over her abdomen. "No. Never!"

Genevieve raised a hand, calming the voices around her. "I am fully to blame." She began to cry. Morgan handed her a handkerchief which she dabbed at her tears. "I was a foolish woman who let her imagination run afoul." She extended a hand to Morgan and he took it, and pulled it to his lips. "It was my insecurity that ignited this rumor. That others ran with it and perhaps embellished it, does not negate my guilt." She looked into Morgan's eyes. "I caused my husband pain, and cast false aspersions on Molly, who has been a trusted friend of our family for years. I apologize and ask

God to pardon me, and ask Morgan and Molly to forgive me."

"Of course, dear one," Morgan whispered.

Genevieve looked to Molly — everyone looked to Molly. "I...well yes, of course I forgive you."

Genevieve took in the full breath of peace. "Thank you, both of you." Then she took a moment to look over the crowd. "Let us sever the gossip grapevine once and for all. Molly and my Morgan were hurt this time, but next time it could be one of you."

She saw three women chat among themselves, and knew from the names Clarissa had given, that these were the tenders of the vine.

One of the women raised her hand. "We three are guilty too. We spread the rumor." She looked to the others. "We'll do our best not to do it again."

"Old habits..." said an older man nearby.

"I'll stop gossiping if you'll stop spending so much time at the pub, Matthew."

The crowd tittered good-naturedly.

Jack stepped forward and put his arm around Genevieve. "I think you'll agree that the Westons got a gem in our dear Genevieve."

The people began to clap, causing Genevieve to return to the back row. As they clapped outwardly, she clapped inwardly, thanking God for helping her get through her confession. Like the ladies, she would try very hard never to let such a thing happen again.

But Jack wasn't through yet. "Thank you for your gracious reception and open minds. But remember I told you I had two things to speak with you about?"

"What's number two?"

He looked to Sylvia and offered her his hand. She took it and stepped forward. "I would like to formally introduce you to Lady Silvey, who has graciously agreed to be my wife."

A shout erupted and new applause broke out.

Genevieve kissed both of them on the cheeks. "I'm so happy for you!"

"When's the wedding, your lordship?"

"In two weeks. During the Harvest Festival. And you're all invited."

Another whoop.

Jack quieted them to share his final words. "Now let's all get on with our day. We shall see you at the nuptials."

People came forward to congratulate Jack and Sylvia, allowing Genevieve time to speak to Morgan. "Your father is wise to end the gathering with such good news."

"He thought it would work well."

"So you knew about their betrothal?"

"He told Lila and I last night. After all, Sylvia will be our new mother." He gazed upon his father. "I know they'll be happy. Papa deserves to be happy."

"I'm sure he has missed your mother greatly."

Morgan hesitated. "Actually, I don't think he has. None of us have missed her much."

"That's harsh."

"Mother was a difficult woman who enjoyed stirring a serene pond into a tempest. We didn't find much joy in her."

"How sad."

He shrugged. "I see nothing *but* joy in Papa's relationship with Sylvia."

"She had a difficult marriage too."

"It seems God is giving each of them a second chance."

Speaking of second chances…Genevieve spotted Molly and Peter still standing on the edge of the crowd, chatting with a few villagers. "Would you come with me?" She nodded towards the couple.

"I think we should."

Morgan and Genevieve walked through the dispersing crowd towards Molly and Peter. Those talking with the couple stepped aside, giving them as much privacy as a public square afforded.

"Mrs. Weston," Molly said. "Mr. Weston."

"You owe my wife an explanation," Peter said to Genevieve.

"I do. Yet my excuses seem pitiful in relation to the pain I have caused."

The two couples began to walk down the road. Genevieve detailed her insecurities about her looks, her stress about the workshop, and her doubts about her marriage.

"But you're lovely," Molly said. "I hope to look half as fine as you do a few months after our baby is born."

"As I said," Morgan added with a pointed look.

Peter was not so easily appeased. "But to accuse Molly and your husband...tis a stretch."

"It was."

He nodded, then stopped walking. "You'll forgive me for being so blunt, but I say enough, Mrs. Weston. I never want to hear of such suspicions again. Either the two of you love each other, or you don't—I can't speak to that. But what I can speak of is the profound and enduring love I share with my Molly." He took her hand. "I will not permit such a love to be tainted in any way, ever again."

Genevieve was thoroughly chastised, as well as inspired. "I agree. Never again."

Ever again.

Clarissa stood at an upper window at Crompton Hall and watched as the carriage carrying Joseph, Lila, and Newley drove away.

"Did they approve all your design choices?" Timothy asked, as he came in the room.

"They did. Of course they did."

"I'd offer my own compliment but you beat me to it."

She knew he didn't mean it as an insult, just an observation. "*You* are doing a marvelous job overseeing the project, Timothy."

"I am. Of course I am."

They shared a smile. Then, for the first time ever, Clarissa was at a loss for words. And so was Timothy. They stood there in silence, sharing an awkward moment.

Clarissa fought back a surge of panic. Timothy was the one person who allowed her to be herself.

"How was London?" he finally asked.

Ah. At least now she understood the reason for the discomfort. "We had a very productive visit." She nodded to her satchel of illustrations and samples.

"How is Bethy feeling?"

So he knew Beth didn't go along, knew that she and Damon had been alone. Suddenly, Clarissa felt embarrassed—which was absurd. She and Timothy were just friends. He had no hold over her.

"Beth is fully recovered."

"That was a speedy turnaround."

She wasn't certain what he meant by that. "Yes, it was."

He plucked some stray nails from the floor. "I'm sure you would have rather had her with you."

" Of course. I'd planned on showing her the better parts of London."

"So you and Damon—?"

"Timothy. Stop. Why the inquisition?"

His fair cheeks mottled. "Sorry. It's none of my business."

"No, it's not."

"If you wish to spend time with the likes of Lord Silvey, then who am I to suggest otherwise."

Now, she was fully confused. "If I didn't know better, I would think you were jealous."

He opened his mouth to speak, then seemed to make a mental correction, making the words that came out of his mouth his second choice. "I am concerned."

Clarissa raised her eyebrows. "About...?"

"Him."

"You don't know him."

"I know *of* him."

You do? "What have you heard?"

He hesitated, then turned to leave. "Nothing. Forgive me for overstepping my — "

She took his arm to stop his exit. "Timothy. What have you heard about him?"

He studied her face, and she saw compassion and concern in his eyes. "Honestly? Not a thing."

"Then why do you disparage him?"

"Because I sense something about him."

The tossed her hands in the air. "You sense something about him? You sound like a woman."

"I can't express my concern?"

"If you have proof. Facts. Logic to support your views."

"You sound like a man."

She was relieved to have reason to smile. "Let us not have any tension between us. I get enough of that from others."

"From him?"

"Timothy!"

He raked a hand through his tousled hair. "Forgive me for expressing my concern over something that is beyond my business."

Clarissa was glad for the apology, yet oddly mourned it. "Of course you are forgiven. I want you to speak plainly, no matter what the subject. I need you to do that."

"Plainly."

"Why…yes."

"Hmm." He nodded, yet looked past her. With a sigh he turned his gaze upon her and said, "I want you to be happy, Clarissa."

"Thank you."

"But do be careful. Don't let yourself be deceived."

He turned on his heel and left the room, leaving a myriad of doubts in his wake.

Naptime. Tilda and Beth left the twins and Etta in Nanny's care and headed downstairs.

"Do you think we can go to the workshop?" Tilda asked. "Surely the earl's had his talk to the villagers by now."

"I wish they would have let us go with them," Beth said. "It's odd they made us stay away."

It *was* odd. Hopefully, they'd hear about it later. Surely someone in the village would tell them what it was all about.

"Do you want to go with me to the meadow?" Tilda asked. "I'd like to do some drawing."

"And I could practice my reading."

That settled, they stopped in their room to collect their things. Dottie was there, making the bed. "May I help you, miss?"

"We're going outside for a while," Tilda said. She collected her drawing supplies and Beth retrieved her book.

"Have a nice outing."

At the top of the stairs heading to the foyer, the girls paused when they spotted Damon and Dixon below.

"A letter has just arrived for you, my lord."

"Thank you." Damon stood alone in the foyer, opened the letter and read it. "Tears and tarnation!" He stepped into the drawing room.

Their curiosity piqued, the girls hurried downstairs and found him pacing, the letter still holding his interest.

"Good morning, Lord Silvey," Tilda said from the edge of the drawing room. "Bad news?"

"Nothing that concerns you two." He tossed the letter into the fire. "If you'll excuse me." He left the room.

Beth rushed towards the fireplace, grabbed the poker, and pushed the letter off the logs.

"Quick!" Tilda said. "Get it!"

Beth retrieved the partially burned letter and together they looked it over. At the top was the letterhead for a solicitor's office in London. Much of the message was burned away.

Tilda read: ...*named in the divorce of Frau Kostner and* –

Suddenly, Damon came into the room. "Give me that!" He snatched the letter away. "What are you doing, you little brat?"

Beth took a step back. "We wondered what got you so upset."

He took another step forward. "I am not upset and my correspondence is none of your business. Ever."

"It is if you're involved in someone's divorce."

His eyes grew wide and wild. "You don't know what you're talking about."

"I saw it. I read it. Frau something-or-other."

"Frau Kostner," Tilda said. Her stomach clenched, waiting for his reaction.

He turned his gaze towards her. His eyes flamed with anger and she immediately wished she hadn't mentioned it.

Suddenly, he grabbed their upper arms and dragged them into a corner far from the doorway. He shoved them against the wall so hard that Tilda's head ricocheted against it.

"I've had enough of your interfering, acting as though you have any position in this family. You are nothing. Both of you, nothing. Do you understand that? You have no more significance than a foul odor: annoying but of no consequence."

"That's not true," Tilda managed. "She's Clarissa's daughter."

"Clarissa is not your mother. She's a gullible woman who plucked you off the streets out of guilt. I'm surprised she's kept you this long. You know she tends to be capricious. What interests her yesterday, will not interest her tomorrow."

"Wouldn't your words apply to you, as well?" Beth asked.

He slapped her. Hard.

"Stop it!" Tilda stepped between them. "Stop or I'll call his lordship."

"His lordship is in the village. Everyone is gone but me and you two...you two annoyances. In fact, I think I'd prefer to have the house to myself." He paused, pondering a thought. "So, this is what's going to happen. You are going to pack a bag and catch the afternoon train to London."

"We will not!" Tilda said.

"Why should we?" Beth asked.

With a single movement, Damon pulled Tilda close, grabbing her behind, breathing against her face. "If you don't go now, quietly, without alerting anyone, I will come to your room tonight, and every night. How convenient that you are staying together. Two for one."

Tilda pushed him away. "Don't you ever touch me again!"

His grin was evil. "What are you going to do to stop me?"

"We'll tell on you," Beth said.

He stepped away and smoothed his coat. "Tell on me? Lord Silvey? The son of the woman who's going to marry the earl?"

"Marry?"

"Still more evidence of how little you are a part of this family. Yes, marry. My mother will soon be the Countess of Summerfield."

When had this happened? Why hadn't they been told?

"Besides that," he said. "I am the man who is going to marry your mother."

"You will not marry her! She didn't say yes to your proposal."

He smiled wickedly. "She didn't say no, either." He examined his manicure as if it were more important than they. "You silly, naïve girls. Our marriage *will* happen. It is inevitable." He sighed. "After what happened between Clarissa and I in our hotel in London…she'll marry me. I guarantee it."

"You disgust me," Tilda said.

"As intended, you irritating git." He pulled a watch from his pocket. "You have five minutes to pack a bag. Go out the side entrance, run to the station, and catch the two-thirty train." He reached into the inside pocket of his coat and removed his wallet. He pressed some money into their hands. "Spend it wisely. I'm sure you'll find a way to get by after that."

He left them trembling from fear and anger.

"We're not going to leave, are we?" Tilda asked. "For good. He wants us to leave for good."

Beth's eyes flit around the room, obviously deep in thought.

"Answer me, Beth. What should we do?"

Beth nodded, as if agreeing with her own thoughts. "I think we should do as he asked."

"We can't let him win."

Beth pulled Tilda toward the stairs. "I don't plan on it. Let's get our things."

The train pulled away from Summerfield.

"I can't believe no one saw us leave," Tilda said.

Beth looked out the window. "It makes it seem as though we're supposed to go."

"I'm glad I left a note," Tilda said.

"You did?"

"In our room."

"I wish you hadn't done that," Beth said. "I don't want them to know where we are."

"Why not?"

"Because I don't want them to come after us before we've done our business."

"Which is?"

Beth angled her body to talk to Tilda confidentially. "Beemer and Scott, Solicitors."

"The letterhead."

She nodded. "We're going to find out why Damon's been named in a divorce."

"Why would they tell us?"

Beth bit her lip. Obviously she hadn't thought of this. "We have to get them to tell us because if they don't, if we don't get some evidence of Damon's nasty nature, Mum is going to marry him."

The family took their places for dinner.

"Where are the girls? They never miss dinner," Genevieve said.

"Especially since this is a special dinner." Papa reached for Sylvia's hand. "A celebratory dinner."

"Celebratory?" Clarissa draped her napkin in her lap.

"Sylvia and I have an announcement. We are getting married."

"How wonderful for you." When no one else offered their congratulations, Clarissa added, "Do all of you know already?"

"We do," Lila said. "Papa told us last night."

"I told the people of Summerfield today," Jack said.

"I think it's marvelous," Newley said. "To my sister and her new husband!"

They all toasted, but Clarissa couldn't help but feel left out.

Damon leaned close and whispered. "You know, we could add *our* announcement to the mix."

She shook her head no. "It's their special time." But that wasn't the reason she declined.

Dixon stepped forward looking to Jack, "Would you like us to begin serving without Miss Beth and Miss Tilda, your lordship?"

"I think you should. But send someone to check on them please."

Clarissa pushed her chair back. "I'll go. The rest of you, please eat."

She walked upstairs to Tilda's room and knocked, assuming they were in the midst of some game or deep in conversation.

When there was no answer, she opened the door. The room was empty. But then she noticed a piece of clothing sticking out of a drawer. Clarissa opened it to push it in, but found the drawer nearly empty. She opened the armoire the girls shared. She wasn't familiar enough with their dresses to know which were missing, but something was amiss.

Dottie stopped in the doorway. "May I help you, Miss Weston?"

"Have you seen Beth and Tilda?"

"Not since early afternoon."

"What were they doing?"

"They mentioned going outside to draw and read."

"They didn't come in to get dressed for dinner?"

"No, miss."

"Didn't that worry you?"

"I assumed they had other plans."

"With whom?"

She blinked too much. "I don't know. I wasn't worried because no one else seemed worried. Should we worry?"

Clarissa remembered her argument with Beth just that morning. Was Beth upset enough to leave? She pointed to the armoire. "Are any items missing?"

Dottie looked through the dresses. "It looks like Miss Beth's green dress is gone, and Miss Tilda's blue." She moved to the drawers. "Some underthings are missing, and nightgowns." Then she looked in the corner. "Miss Tilda's art supplies have been returned."

"Which means they came back from being outside."

"Yes, miss. It seems so."

Clarissa looked around the room. "Where's the satchel Beth was going to carry for our London trip?"

"Under here, miss." Dottie looked under the bed, then stood. "It's gone. I put it under there the other day when she didn't go with you."

Beth has left? And Tilda too?

Clarissa raced downstairs to the dining room, her fears running wild. "Beth and Tilda, they're both gone! They've packed a bag and left."

"To go where?" Genevieve asked.

"Someone must have seen them leave," Joseph said.

The earl nodded to Dixon. "Go make inquiries with the servants."

"Sit, my dear," Damon said, leading her to a chair.

She shrugged him off. "We need to find them."

"When did they leave?" Newley asked.

"Dottie saw them early afternoon, going outside to draw. She didn't see them after."

"If they packed a bag, they must have had a destination in mind." Sylvia said. "London perhaps?"

"Why would they go to London?"

"Beth was looking forward to her trip there — with you," Genevieve said. "Perhaps she was so disappointed about not going that she decided to go on her own, and asked Tilda to go with her?"

It's all my fault. I shouldn't have gone to London without her. We shouldn't have argued.

"I can't imagine either of them going that far," Morgan said.

"Did they leave a note?"

"I'll go check," Damon said. "You stay here and talk to the servants who might have seen them."

Dixon returned with a gardener, who held his cap in his hands. "Chambers saw something," he said. "Tell them."

"My lords, my ladies. Yes, I saw the girls at two o'clock. They came out the side entrance and walked through the garden heading towards the village."

"Were they carrying luggage?" Clarissa asked.

"Yes, Miss Weston. They each had a carpet bag."

"Why didn't you stop them?"

He looked taken aback, scrunching his cap. "I didn't think nothing of it. I'm sorry."

"No need to be sorry, Chambers," Jack said. "You had no way of knowing. Thank you for your time."

Chambers nodded and left with Dixon.

"Isn't there a two-thirty train?" Sylvia asked.

There was. All signs pointed to the girls going to London.

"I'm going after them." Clarissa headed towards the front door.

Genevieve ran after her. "You can't go alone."

Clarissa turned on her. "If they can go alone, so can I."

Morgan stepped up. "I'll go with you. Dixon, tell them to fetch the carriage as soon as possible, as well as our coats."

Clarissa knew they were right, yet hated the delay. *Please, God. Protect the girls from harm.*

Damon stepped into Tilda's room, his eyes searching for a note, chastising himself for not thinking of this scenario.

And there it was. An envelope sticking out from under the Bible on the bedside table.

He tore it open:

Dear Family,

We are sorry to cause you pain. We are off to London to attend to some important business.

Please do not worry. We will take care of each other.

With much love,
Tilda and Beth

Business? What business?

Damon couldn't take the time to decipher that now. His main concern was not letting the family know where they went.

Having learned a lesson from his previous partial-burning of correspondence, Damon stepped to the fire, tore the note and its envelope into tiny pieces and scattered them into the flame until they existed no more.

Clarissa prayed along with the rhythm of the carriage as she rode to the train station. *Please God, please God. Keep them safe, God, safe, God.*

Morgan sat beside her and touched her leg. "They'll be all right."

"How do you know?"

He sighed. "I don't. I pray they'll be all right. I can't believe they didn't leave a note. Do you know of any reason they would leave like this?"

Clarissa hesitated—but only for a moment. "Beth and I argued this morning."

"Over what—if I may ask?"

"Over Damon."

"Oh."

His response surprised her. "That's a cryptic response."

"I apologize. I meant nothing by it."

"But you did. I believe you meant much by it. Please explain yourself, Cousin."

"I don't wish to hurt you."

"I am beyond worrying about my feelings being hurt. Tell me what's on your mind."

"I don't trust Damon."

"How so?"

Morgan—as others before him—hedged. "It's an instinctive concern, a sense that there's something not... something un-gentlemanly within him."

"Isn't there something un-gentlemanly within all men?"

"If you're asking if there is evil in all men—and women— I will agree with you, but I wasn't talking about that. Most of us do our best to control and contain it."

"Have you seen Damon let it—whatever *it* is—loose?"

"No. I have not."

"Then you judge him unfairly."

"Perhaps." After a pause he asked, "What are Beth's objections to him?"

Clarissa thought back to their morning conversation. "I believe she is jealous of him—of the time we spend together."

"I would think she's reacting to something beyond that, to something more."

"More?"

"If your relationship progresses, he could become her father."

"Does that mean I am supposed to cut off my relationship with Damon, choosing a jealous child over a possible husband?"

"Only you can make that choice."

"I shouldn't have to choose between them."

Morgan shrugged. "Let's find her first. At this point Beth's well-being must be our only concern."

"Yes, Miss Weston, I did sell two tickets to London. One to your daughter and one to Miss Cavendish for the two-thirty train."

"Why did you let them go?"

The ticket master fumbled his pencil. "They're both young ladies. They had the money for the tickets. They were very businesslike in the transaction."

"They weren't upset?" Morgan asked.

"Not really, Mr. Weston. A little nervous perhaps, but nothing more. I'm sorry if — "

"When is the next train leaving?" Clarissa asked.

"Not until morning, miss."

The thought of Beth and Tilda alone in London at night made her danger bells chime.

She stepped away from the ticket booth. "Morgan, take me to London in the carriage."

"I… It's getting dark."

His hesitation peeved her. "It's getting dark here, which means it's dark there. You don't know the bad things that come out at night in London. I do."

Then, Clarissa spotted Timothy on the far platform. He was with another man, transferring some lumber from the side of the track to his wagon. She ran towards him.

"Timothy!"

He looked up from his work. "Clarissa? What's wrong?"

"Beth is missing!" She quickly explained the situation to ̇im. "Will you take me to London to look for them? You ̣ow the way to my old neighborhood."

His eyes grew large. "Why do you think they're going *there?*"

"Please don't argue with me. I need to leave! Now!"

"Then let's go." He spoke to the other fellow, then hurried with Clarissa to the Weston carriage where Morgan was waiting.

"Timothy will take me to London tonight," she told him. "Can we have the carriage?"

"Of course, but…" Morgan shook his head. "If I thought it was wise to go now, I would take you."

"I can't wait." She thought of another reason. "You have responsibilities here, Morgan. I thank you, but I believe this is the best plan."

Morgan hesitated, then got out of the carriage. "May God be with you on your journey, and may the girls be found safe."

Timothy helped Clarissa up to the seat, then climbed in beside her. "Do you wish to stop at the Manor to pack a bag?"

"Drive!"

Lila spotted her brother walking up the drive in the dark. "Morgan's back!"

She ran out the door to meet him. "Where's Clarissa? Did you find the girls?"

The rest of the family poured out of the house with similar questions.

Morgan quieted them. "The girls bought train tickets to London. The next train doesn't leave until tomorrow so Clarissa took the carriage—"

"Clarissa is driving the carriage to London alone?" Papa asked. "You should have—"

"No, Papa. Timothy was at the station and she asked him to go with her."

"Timothy?" Damon asked. "Why didn't she come back here first? I would have gone with her. I want to find Beth as much as any of you."

Do you? Lila was surprised by her thought, yet couldn't contradict the question. "Timothy was the one who helped Clarissa retrieve Beth in the first place. He and Beth are very close."

"As are he and Clarissa," Genevieve added.

All eyes turned towards her. "Well he is. They've been close friends for years."

"I don't like this," Damon said. "It's not proper."

His mother swatted his arm. "As opposed to you and Clarissa spending days alone in London?"

"That was business. She had work to do."

"She has work to do now," Papa said.

Better with Timothy than you, Damon.

Joseph took Lila's arm. "Let's go inside and pray for their safety and for God to help them find each other."

Lila was glad for the prayer. Clarissa and Timothy would need God's help to find the girls in a city of millions.

It wasn't until the horse and carriage settled into a steady rhythm that either of them spoke.

"Thank you for taking me," Clarissa said.

"I am glad to do it."

"Thank you for not asking why they ran away."

"That *was* my next question."

Clarissa found she had to say it out loud — even if it wasn't flattering. "Beth and I argued this morning."

"About what?"

"About Damon."

"Today is Damon's day to be the subject of discussion."

"Why do you say that?"

"You and I also discussed him today."

They had. "How odd that I've talked about Damon more than I actually saw him today."

"Pardon me asking, but why isn't he driving you to London?"

Why indeed?

When she didn't answer, Timothy said, "I'm glad you asked me. I'm honored to be asked. You know how much I love Beth."

She slipped her hand around his arm.

"It's cozy," Beth said as she and Tilda tried to get comfortable in the same narrow bed at the inn.

"It will do." Tilda turned on her side, facing Beth. "At least we found the solicitor's office."

"After asking a thousand people."

"Too bad it was closed. But we'll be there first thing in the morning."

Beth adjusted the thread-bare quilt over her shoulder. "I wonder if anyone is looking for us."

"I told them in the note not to worry."

Beth sat up in bed, causing the covers to fall away. "Do they know why we left?"

"They don't. I simply told them we had business to attend to."

"They'll wonder what business."

"We have to stop Damon, Beth. For all our sakes."

"How bad is it?" Clarissa asked — though she knew just by looking at the wheel they weren't going anywhere.

"If it weren't dark, if we weren't in the middle of nowhere, I'd say we had a chance to fix it in a timely manner. But since it *is* dark, and we are where we are…we'll have to wait until morning."

Clarissa peered at the shadowed countryside. The moon was playing hide and seek. There was a forest on one side of the road, and pastures on the other. An owl hooted nearby.

"I'd argue but I know there is no use in it. My concern isn't for us, but for the girls," she said.

"I've been praying they are safe."

"Thank you for that. I know God hears your prayers."

"Yours too, Clarissa."

She shrugged. "Occasionally."

"Does that correspond with how often you pray? Occasionally?"

"You do keep me on my toes, Mr. Billings." She stepped to the edge of the pasture. "Now, to get through until morning...since you are too much of a gentlemen to mention it, I will be too little of a lady and just say it: let's find a soft spot in the grass to sleep."

"I think that would be wise."

He took her hand and they walked into the pasture. They could see the outline of trees on the horizon. Timothy didn't want to stray far from the carriage so they chose a spot in the open.

He took off his coat and began to lay it on the ground, but she stopped him. "Put it back on. You need to stay warm too." She lay down on the grass, removing a stray rock that would poke, adjusting her skirt and petticoats to cover her legs. He lay down a few feet away.

It was proper. But it was also ridiculous.

She patted the spot beside her. "Come closer."

He moved beside her and stretched out on his back, an arm beneath his head. She did the same, her shoulder touching his. The stars peered down at them. "I fear there are as many people in London as there are stars in the sky."

"We'll find them, Clarissa. I promise."

When she felt tears threaten she turned on her side and lay her head against his shoulder. He wrapped his arm around her, drawing her into the security and warmth of his tender care.

Chapter Fourteen

Clarissa batted at a tickle on her cheek. When it didn't go away, she opened her eyes.

Timothy sat beside her, holding the offending blade of grass. "Good morning."

She rolled from her side to her back and stretched her arms over her head. She didn't stay there long as the grass was heavy with dew. "Help me up."

Her muscles ached and she rubbed a crick in her neck. "Not the most comfortable night's sleep I've ever had."

"I apologize that my arm and chest weren't fluffy enough for you."

"I'm not complaining."

"Yes, you are. But I agree with you. I'm guessing this is the first time you have ever slept on the ground."

"You guess right. And you, Mr. Billings? Is this your first time?"

"Not at all. For I have slept in the occasional field on other trips to London for supplies. But those nights were usually planned for and I had a bedroll."

"And no companion?"

He winked. "No companion. We will have stories to tell when we get home."

She plucked blades of grass off her skirt. "Stories we will *not* tell."

He nodded. "This detail of our trip will remain between you and I."

The shadows of the trees were long, the sun not fully risen. She was awake enough to move past the moment, into the task at hand. The wheel. More importantly, finding Beth and Tilda.

They stepped through the grass to the road and heard the baaing of sheep.

Their owner moved his flock up the road. Timothy approached him and the two men talked, with the man pointing straight ahead.

"Thank you," she heard Timothy tell him. He returned to Clarissa as the sheep moved past. "He says there's a smithy up a mile. He should be able to help. I'll walk ahead and have him come back with me."

"Wouldn't it speed things along if you take the wheel off and bring it to him?"

Timothy's eyebrows rose. "And how pray tell, should I remove the wheel? It's a two-man job."

"Two-person job. Are we not two people? Let me help."

He laughed but didn't argue with her. "Another first to add to your list, Miss Weston."

"A few years ago I didn't even have such a list."

"Did you wish to have such a list?"

"There was no need. I knew how my life would play out and was content in it."

"But now?"

She tucked the lace frill at the end of her sleeves under the cuff. "Tell me what to do."

Tilda and Beth stood outside the attorney's office, eating a roll for their breakfast.

A little boy came up to them, his hand out, begging. Tilda gave him a penny and the rest of her bread.

"That was nice of you," Beth said. "I always liked people like you when I was living on the streets. I depended on nice people like you."

Tilda felt good for the act—and the compliment. Her brow furrowed as she looked down the street, "There are so many children."

Just then a man strode towards them, digging in his vest pocket, as if for a key. Was this Beemer or Scott?

They stepped out of the way as he did indeed, put the key in the lock. Only then did he look at them. "Ladies. May I help you?"

"Yes, sir," Beth said. "At least I hope so, sir."

Tilda pointed to the office shingle that said: *Beemer and Scott, Solicitors.* "Are you one of these?"

He smiled. "I am Beemer. Why don't you come inside?"

They followed him into a paneled office—far less fancy than the earl's study at the Manor, but it did elicit the same feeling of knowledge and wisdom. Mr. Beemer brought over a second chair so the girls could sit side by side. He sat at an enormous roll-top desk stacked so full of papers that there was no possibility for the rolling tambour to be lowered.

"Well then. As you know my name, I would like to know yours."

"I am Tilda Cavendish, and this is Beth Weston. She's the daughter of Miss Clarissa Weston, the Earl of Summerfield's niece."

Mr. Beemer drew a pad of paper to his lap and took some notes. "Miss Clarissa Weston is your mother?"

"I am her adopted daughter."

"I see. And what is your relationship, Miss Cavendish?"

"I am the god-daughter of Colonel Grady Cummings, who is the husband of the Dowager Countess of Summerfield."

His right eyebrow rose. "Well then. What has brought such fine young ladies to my office on this early morning?"

"Divorce," Beth said.

His bushy eyebrows rose. "You are married?"

"No, sir. Neither is my mother. But the man who's been courting her has been named in a divorce."

"A divorce you are representing," Tilda added.

"Indeed. What is his name?"

"Lord Silvey. He's a baron."

He set the paper on the desk and sat back. "Knowing what I know, I understand your concern."

Tilda sat forward. "What has he done?"

"I'm not at liberty to say."

"We have to know," Beth said. "My mum is blind to the type of man Damon really is, but *we* know," she looked to Tilda, "we *know* he is evil."

"Evil is a strong word."

Tilda knew she had to make him understand. "Lord Silvey threatened Beth if she interfered with his marriage to her mother. He ordered the two of us to London so he would be free to finish his seduction."

Beth nodded. "He wants me gone so he can have her all to himself."

"It may seem like that, but—"

Beth shook her head adamantly. "He does not want to be a father to me. He just wants her—even though he doesn't really love her."

Tilda added an important point. "He's told Beth that her mother has second thoughts about adopting her. He says her mother will choose him over Beth."

"Do you believe that to be true?" he asked Beth.

"Well, no. I believe Mum loves me. She gave up the chance to marry well when she adopted me."

"Oh?"

"I used to live on the streets of London. She saved me."

Beemer pondered all this a moment. "That is very commendable of her. Yet she gave up nothing. Since you are already adopted and she already has Lord Silvey's interest… marrying a baron *would* be marrying well."

Tilda feared they'd been whining like little girls wanting their own way. It was time to present a stronger case. "Damon doesn't want Beth around and doesn't love Clarissa. I don't really know what he gets out of the marriage."

"Money?"

The girls looked at each other. "I don't think that's it. He and his mother have recently traveled extensively through Europe. That must mean he has funds."

"And a woman in every city." Mr. Beemer said the words nearly under his breath, but Tilda heard.

"He's done this before?"

Beemer put a hand to his mouth, shaking his head. "I misspoke."

"No, you didn't," Beth said. "Knowing him as we do, it sounds like you spoke the truth. Is that the reason he's named in a divorce? He dallied with a married woman?"

Mr. Beemer sighed extravagantly before saying, "At least one. But the husband of this particular woman didn't take it kindly. He's divorcing his wife."

"Damon broke up a marriage?"

Mr. Beemer stood and moved to the window. "I shouldn't be telling you these details."

"Please, sir," Beth said. "I'm trying to save my mother from pain. I'm trying to save my family."

Tilda decided to add another sin to Damon's burden. "We are here in London because he grabbed my behind and said if we didn't leave Summerfield he would visit our bedroom every night and..."

"Two for one," Beth added.

Mr. Beemer raised a hand, stopping their need to explain further. "Every time I hear of him, he gets more despicable. Please do not let the crass and horrid ways of Lord Silvey color your views of all men. There are many good men in the world who know how to treat a woman with respect and love."

"Thank you, sir," Tilda said. "I'm glad to hear it."

He nodded, as if agreeing to an inner decision. "Although I probably shouldn't do what I'm about to do, for the sake of your mother and for your own safety, I will tell you what I know of him. I'm not saying Lord Silvey is the sole reason for the divorce in question—for the wife was too free with herself with more than Lord Silvey—but in my investigation for the husband I found there are suits awaiting Silvey for other dalliances. As well as gambling debts."

"So he does want the Weston money," Tilda said.

"And perhaps its reputation. I have heard amazing stories of how the earl came into his position, I also have heard many praise his honor and actions. Perhaps Silvey wishes to hide beneath his wings."

They'd wanted the truth and had received it, in full.

"Thank you for your candor, Mr. Beemer," Tilda said. "I'm not sure what we can do to stop him."

"Hold on a moment." He returned to the desk, took out a fresh piece of paper with his letterhead on top, and began to write, pausing to take reference of a paper nearby. At the end he signed his name with a flourish and handed it to Beth. "Read it aloud so Miss Cavendish can hear."

Beth read: "'To whom it may concern, I have been retained by Miss Beth Weston and Miss Tilda Cavendish to see to the protection of their familial concerns regarding The Right Honourable Lord Silvey. Due to numerous legal suits against him—which span many cities and countries—I offer the opinion that it is in the best interest of my clients that Lord Silvey be restrained from having any and all contact with them for their own protection. If you should need further assistance in this matter, please contact me. Sincerely, Bernard Beemer, Esquire.'"

Tilda applauded. "Bravo, Mr. Beemer. That is a marvelous letter."

Beth stared at the page. "It says we are your clients. What do you charge for such a letter?"

He pondered this a moment. "I believe two shillings is a fair price."

Tilda removed the money from her pocket and handed it to him. "Lord Silvey was the one who gave us money to get to London."

Mr. Beemer slipped the coins into a vest pocket. "How appropriate he's paying for the judgment of his sins." He carefully folded the letter and put it in an envelope, sealing it with wax and his stamp.

"It looks very legal."

"It is, ladies. I will stand behind it." He gave them each a business card with his name and address on it. "Call on me any time I am needed. It was a pleasure doing business with you. Do you have enough money to get home?"

"We do, sir. Thank you."

They stood to leave, but at the last minute, Beth rushed to the man and hugged him. "Thank you for saving my mum."

Mr. Beemer's voice broke as he said, "You're very welcome."

As soon as they stepped onto the street, Tilda and Beth took each other's arms and laughed and jumped up and down. "We did it!" Tilda said. She opened her satchel and reverently put the letter and card inside.

"God bless, Mr. Beemer."

"God bless him, indeed! Shall we go to the train station?"

"Shortly," Beth said. "But first I would like to show you where I used to live."

"Isn't that a dodgy part of the city?"

"It is. But I'd like you to see, so you know why it's so important that I stay with the Westons."

Beth was rather turned around in her directions, so they asked a constable the way. "Are you certain you wish to go there, girls?"

"We are," Beth said.

"Be careful then. And be gone before dark."

"Yes, sir."

They walked a long way, but the trek didn't exhaust them as it should have, for they both walked with a spring to their step — the spring of hope and justice to be done.

Tilda noticed the condition of the buildings around them had deteriorated, and the streets grew narrower. The smell of grime and filth intensified.

The people changed too, from the simple but tailored attire of the middle class to the tattered and dirty of the poor.

"You don't need to hold my arm so tightly," Beth said.

"Sorry." Tilda hadn't realized she was doing it. "You lived here?"

"Actually, I lived... there."

She pointed to a building that was as unremarkable as the next. Dark. Foul. With broken windows and trash dancing in its crevices.

Beth walked right up to the door and went inside.

"You're going in?" Tilda asked.

"I am. And so are you. "

They entered a dark foyer with stairs straight ahead, and a hall to the left leading to the doors of flats. Peeling paint marked the walls like the tracks of many tears.

"Which flat was yours?"

"Clarissa lived upstairs, but I lived here." Beth sat down on the stairs.

"I thought when you said you lived on the stairs you were exaggerating."

"Nope." She stroked the stair on either side of her. Then she scooted to one end and lay down, drawing her knees to her chest. "I don't fit anymore."

"No, you don't." Tilda helped Beth to standing. "You don't fit here at all. Let's go home."

With a final look, Beth led them outside and they turned towards the train station. But then she heard shouts. Four children ran up to her. "Beth!"

She knelt and drew them into her arms. "Hello! How have you been? How's your mother?"

The oldest one — a boy of about nine or ten — shook his head. "She died, month before last."

"I'm so sorry." Beth looked back to the building. "So you're living in the flat alone?"

The second oldest—a girl—shook her head. "We's living out here." She pointed down the street. "There's a good place under the steps in the second alley."

Tilda was appalled. "Isn't there someone who can take you in?"

The oldest boy spoke again. "Mrs. Smith said she'd take me, but she didn't want the rest, so I said no. We want to stay together."

"I understand," Beth said. Then she turned to Tilda. "I'd like you to meet Lennie, Laura, Lee, and Lulu Drake. Children, this is Tilda."

They politely nodded, then Laura asked, "Are you back, Beth? We could use a friend."

"No, I'm not back. But sit with us on the steps and tell me about your mother, and the neighborhood."

Tilda saw a street vendor. "I'll be right back." She returned with four cones of chestnuts.

The children devoured them.

"I wish I knew where to look," Clarissa said.

"I think you are wise to start where you and Beth lived." Timothy helped her step around some steaming horse dung.

They'd already had a full day. Although the wheel repair had gone as speedily as could be expected, it had delayed them more than two hours. Then they'd been forced to park the carriage at the edge of the neighborhood, for it was too large to negotiate the narrow streets which were made narrower still by pushcarts.

"Aren't we close?" Timothy asked. "I remember this haberdashery."

"Just around the corner. On the right."

Clarissa felt an odd tug of nostalgia as she approached the building that had been her home for many months. She could still remember the painful pang of hunger and the cold nights when she had slept in layers of clothing to stave off the constant chill.

Yet, they were also months of exciting independence and hope. She'd enjoyed her time on the stage. Partially.

The lesson of realizing her talent was unremarkable had been difficult. She'd longed to earn the adulation of an audience, for adulation's sake. But also to make up for her family's opinion of her, which had always been a bit condescending. They tolerated her dramatic ways, but never dared show true interest at the risk of Clarissa misreading their attention as permission and acceptance.

If there was such a thing as God saying no to her being an actress, He'd done a thorough job of it.

When she gave up the theatre and returned home, no one was more surprised than Clarissa that her family had seemed genuinely glad to see her. They forgave her folly, and even welcomed Beth as one of their own. She'd misjudged them.

Who else had she misjudged?

Genevieve, Tilda, Joseph, Lila...Timothy?

And Damon. Especially Damon.

Her thoughts of him were set aside as they neared her old flat. It was a year older, a year grungier, a year closer to its ultimate death. That Beth might return here filled Clarissa with panic. Beth deserved everything Clarissa and her family could give her—and more. There had never been a purer spirit. Or anyone more capable of—

"Mum!" Beth ran towards her.

Clarissa met her halfway and they collided in a fervent embrace. "You're here! You're safe!"

"I am. We're fine."

We.

With a final kiss to Beth's forehead, Clarissa asked, "Where is Tilda?"

"Right here , Miss Weston." Tilda stood a dozen feet away, timidly raising a hand as if unsure she belonged in the happy reunion.

Clarissa realized in that moment, that she did. Tilda did belong in the family.

She extended an arm towards her. "Come here."

Tilda tentatively let herself be pulled into the embrace. Next, Clarissa motioned for Timothy to make their quartet complete.

"Praise God," Clarissa said. "Praise God."

The ladies sat on the steps of a church as Timothy tore apart a loaf of French bread and sliced a brick of cheese between them.

Tilda studied Clarissa's face. She still couldn't believe that Clarissa had drawn her into a hug and had acted as though she was genuinely glad to see her. She wished she knew why.

The girls had already heard the saga of the carriage wheel and Clarissa's adventure sleeping outdoors all night. Clarissa and Timothy made light of the obvious fact that they'd slept on the grass together. An awkward situation, but nothing was made of it. Clarissa was nearly engaged to Damon.

He was the subject that had oddly been ignored. Yes, Tilda had left a note, and no, the note had not detailed the reason for their journey, but surely Clarissa and Timothy were curious.

As for the latter... why was Timothy here and not Damon? Had there been a falling out that would negate the need for the girls to fully explain their own adventure to see Mr. Beemer?

Finally the questions piled too high for Tilda to ignore them any longer. "Although I told you some of it in my note, don't you want to know why we left Summerfield?"

"Note?" Clarissa asked. "I saw no note."

"Tilda left one in our room, on the bedside table."

"I saw no note," Clarissa repeated. "As for the reason you left? I do want to say I'm sorry for our argument, Beth. I hate that it drove you to leave."

Beth's brow furrowed. "What are you talking about?"

"The argument we had yesterday morning about... the proposal."

Beth shook her head vigorously, making her curls bounce. "Our argument is not the reason we left—though the *subject* of that argument *is* the reason."

"Damon?"

Beth looked to Tilda, who nodded. Yes, now was the time for all of it to come out.

"I'm not sure where to begin," Beth said.

Tilda had an idea, and took Mr. Beemer's letter from her satchel. "Read this."

Clarissa looked at the name printed on the envelope. "Attorneys?"

"Just read it."

She and Timothy broke the seal and held the letter between them, their expressions changing from interest to incredulity. "You need protection? From Damon?"

Tilda nodded. "We do. He slapped Beth."

"Slapped?" Timothy was on his feet. "How dare he? The next time I see him I'm going to—"

Clarissa raised a hand to stop his words. Her eyes were on Beth. "Why did he slap you?"

Beth shook her head. "There's more." She exchanged a look with Tilda. "He...he touched us."

It only took a moment for Clarissa to get the implication. She sprang to her feet. "He touched you?"

Tilda pulled on her skirt until she sat down again. "He implied if we didn't leave Summerfield, he would... he would..."

"Would what?" Timothy asked.

Beth let it out in a rush. "He would come to our rooms every night and…" She let her shrug speak the rest of it.

"The cretin!" Timothy said. "The manky meater. How dare he?"

Clarissa deliberately folded the letter, slipped it into its envelope, and handed it back to Tilda. "Don't lose this."

"I won't."

"I wasn't sick," Beth said. "When I stayed behind for the trip to London, I wasn't sick. Damon told me I couldn't go. He threatened me then too. He wanted you all to himself."

Clarissa breathed heavily, her mouth open, her eyes staring into the air in front of her.

Timothy put a hand on her shoulder. "I'm so sorry, Clarissa." He looked at the girls. "And doubly sorry for you two."

Clarissa snapped out of her shock. "Why didn't you tell me any of this?"

"He warned us not to," Tilda said.

"Plus you were in love with him. You were happy."

Clarissa stood and pulled Beth to standing and into her arms. "I love *you*, Beth. More than anyone in the world, I love you."

Tilda felt tears in her eyes and shared a wistful smile with Timothy.

"We need to thank God for this happy ending." Timothy said, looking at Clarissa.

Clarissa let Beth go, but put an arm around her shoulder. She shook her head. "It's not a happy ending yet, not until we go home and I have it out with Damon."

Tilda raised a hand. "There's something else you should know about him. The reason we sought out Mr. Beemer in the first place." She nodded to Beth. It was her story to tell.

"Sit, Mum."

Clarissa took Timothy's hand and returned to the step. "I don't like the sounds of this."

"You won't like the truth of this," Beth said, as she sat beside her. "Yesterday, Damon got a letter that upset him. Tilda and I saw him throw it in the fire, but we retrieved it and saw a few words of it before he snatched it away."

"The letterhead was of a law office—Beemer and Scott," Tilda said.

"And there were words saying he was named in the divorce of a Frau Kostner."

Clarissa shook her head in disgust. "That usually means there's been an affair."

"With a married woman," he added.

Beth continued. "When Damon ordered us to London, we decided to seek out Mr. Beemer."

"He was very nice and listened to our problem."

"He confirmed what you read in Damon's letter?"

"He never mentioned Frau Kostner by name, but he did imply this isn't the first time."

"Damon also has gambling debts," Tilda added.

Clarissa looked skyward and said with raised fists, "I've been such a fool! I sensed something was off with him, and more than one person expressed doubts about his character, but he always had a way of talking himself out of…" She blinked. "I just remembered something. Damon implied that he had wooed a lot of women throughout Europe."

"So he admitted it?"

"He pretended he was joking."

"He wasn't joking," Timothy said.

"See?" Clarissa said. "Even when he's telling the truth he turns it around to be a lie. I'm not sure he's capable of fully telling the truth."

"He's not an honorable man," Tilda said.

"You deserve an honorable man," Beth said.

Tilda glanced at Timothy—an honorable man. Was there something between them? Could there be?

Clarissa tossed the last of her bread into the street for the pigeons. "Let's go home. Now. I feel the need to right this wrong, immediately."

Right this wrong…

Before Tilda could stop herself, she said "We'd like to bring four other passengers with us."

"Who?"

Tilda looked at Beth, hoping she'd understand.

"Oh!" Beth said. "Do you remember Mrs. Drake, Mum? She lived in the first apartment on the ground floor with her four children?"

"I remember thinking there was no way four children could fit into that apartment without being on top of each other."

"She died," Tilda said.

"I'm sorry to hear that," Clarissa said. "What does that have to do with us?"

"The children are living on the street. We want to take them back to Summerfield. Give them a new life there."

Clarissa drew in a breath. "My, my."

"That's a very kind thought, girls," Timothy said. "But who will take care of them?"

"Mr. and Mrs. Wilton," Beth said.

"They lost four babies," Tilda said. "I heard Mrs. Hayward and Lila talking about it. They're desperate for children to love, and the Drake children are desperate for a family to love them."

"You came up with this idea by yourselves?" Clarissa asked.

Tilda nodded at Beth. "We did."

"We really want to do it," Beth said. "You saved me from the streets, now I want to save them."

Clarissa looked to Timothy. "Can you think of any reason to say no?"

"Not a one," he said. "Where are they now?"

"Probably back near our flat."

"You haven't promised them anything, have you?"

"No," Beth said. "But I know they'll jump at the chance."

"They have no family to take them in," Tilda said. *Please God, let Clarissa say yes.*

"Yes," Clarissa said. "Let's go fetch them, then catch the next train home."

What did I get myself into?

Sitting on the train with Timothy, Tilda, Beth, and four children whose names all oddly started with L, felt like herding sheep. If only Clarissa had a staff to nudge them into place.

The logistics of their act of mercy proved to be numerous, but each had been accomplished.

First, there was the question of the carriage. Timothy offered to drive it home, but Clarissa begged him to arrange for its delivery to Summerfield because she needed him with her on the train.

Secondly, there was the question of funds. She had left Summerfield without a penny in her purse — without even a purse. Timothy had some money with him, but had used it to fix the carriage. They'd had enough for their simple lunch on the church steps, and the girls had enough money for two train tickets home.

Clarissa solved the problem by going to the bank, where she withdrew funds from her family account. It should have been an easy task, but since she was a woman it was made difficult because the bank had no authorization from any of the men in the family. Clarissa's dramatic skills saved the day, as she wiled and guiled the bank president into believing she was who she said she was, the need was great, and her family would condone the withdrawal — for it wasn't much. Just enough to pay for train fare and some food.

And then, there was the issue of alerting Summerfield the children were coming, and explaining their idea about the children staying with the Wiltons. Clarissa sent a telegram to Jack, announcing Beth and Tilda had been found safe, mentioning four orphans, and telling him to ask Lila about the Wiltons. She'd condensed the issue to one word: "Adoption?" She could trust Lila and her father to arrange what was right. At the last she said that the eight of them were returning home and would arrive on the afternoon train.

"I'm making a very large assumption they agree with our plan," she told Timothy. "This could go terribly awry."

"It could, but it won't."

"How can you be certain?"

He pointed to heaven. "God arranged for Tilda to befriend the Wiltons and learn of their pain and longing for children. He arranged for Beth to become reacquainted with the orphaned children who long for parents." He wove the fingers of his hands together. "Two parents, four children, one family."

She let his optimism carry her through the rest of the tasks at hand — which were numerous.

By the time they rounded up the children and made it to the train station, Clarissa was in need of a long nap. Considering her inconstant sleep on the ground the night before, it would have been well-deserved — if it would have been an option.

Which it was not.

As they passed through the station — with each adult holding the hand of a child — Clarissa cringed at the odd looks they received from other passengers. Well-deserved looks, for they *were* a sight. Four well-dressed adults leading four disheveled children with hair that hadn't seen a comb in weeks, who smelled of filth and poverty, and whose clothes were ill-fitting and ragged. Their progress was hampered by the children's awe. They had never seen a train or been in a train station with its massive ceilings and ornate decorations. Their entire world had been shades of dingy gray, with the occasional slice of blue sky overhead. The passengers' clothing, the signage, the luggage, and the crisp uniforms of the conductors, made them gaze and gape. If they hadn't been in danger of missing their train, Clarissa might have halted the entourage to give them time to take it all in.

And she was mistaken about public opinion. For as they were boarding the train an elderly woman smiled at her and said, "What a nice thing you're doing, saving these poor children. God bless you."

Her kind words caused Clarissa's thoughts to turn the corner from what must be done, to what must be felt.

The latter proved to be the most difficult charge. Her feelings presented themselves as a mangled smattering of every feeling she'd ever felt, so chaotic that she couldn't put a finger on any emotion long enough to discern or describe it. Until she could sort it through, she found herself withdrawing, as though she looked down upon the lot of them from a distance, observing but not engaging.

Timothy led the way to their compartment, which they entered directly from the platform. The children immediately plopped onto the two long benches, facing each other.

"'Tis so soft," Laura said, bouncing on the cushion.

Lulu immediately lay down, which caused the rest of them to pile upon her, giggling with delight.

"Sit, children," Clarissa scolded. "You need to make room for all eight of us."

Lennie began counting the occupants. "One, two, four—"

"Three, then four," Tilda corrected.

He started again and got it right.

Timothy stashed their food at the end of a row and took Lulu onto his lap. "We are here. We made it."

Clarissa allowed herself a deep breath. "We did. Somehow we did."

The conductor collected their tickets, then closed the outer door. The children squealed when the train blew its

whistle, and they all rushed to the station-side window.
The train began to move and their balance bobbled.

"It's all right," Beth said. "Wave!"

The children waved at the people on the platform,
then grew silent as their view changed from buildings to
countryside.

"We're going so fast!" Lennie said.

"Thirty miles per hour," Timothy said.

"I ain't never been any miles away from home. Not
even one."

Clarissa wondered how many people in London
could make the same statement. Actually, many in
Summerfield could say the same.

Lee relinquished the view to sit next to Beth. "I'm
hungry."

Bread, pickled herring, cheese, apples, and jars of
milk were distributed. The children ate ravenously,
causing the adults to relinquish their share.

"When was the last time you ate a full meal?" Beth
asked.

"'Don know," Laura said. "We did like the nuts you
bought us."

"We had a potato the other day," Lee said.

"One potato between you?" Tilda asked.

"It was only half to begin with."

Clarissa's heart melted and her weariness left her.
She knew what it was like to be hungry. A year at home
had caused the memory to fade, only to be made
painfully clear by the children's need.

"You'll never be hungry again," she told them. "I
promise."

Whether the Wiltons wanted the children or not, it
was a promise Clarissa was dedicated to keep.

The children slept.

An hour into their journey, after eating and learning some songs with Tilda and Beth, they'd sought the bench, and one by one, put their heads on the lap of their four saviors, and fell asleep.

"Ah," Clarissa whispered. "Blessed silence."

"I don't think they understand what's happening to them," Tilda said.

"I didn't when you brought *me* to Summerfield," Beth said.

"I just hope the Wiltons agree to all this."

"They will," Timothy said.

She smiled. "Always the optimist."

"God's plans will not be foiled."

Tilda smoothed Lulu's hair. "So you think He approves?"

"I know He does."

"Hmm." Clarissa could virtually see Tilda's thoughts churning. "What are you thinking?"

She took a moment to gather her thoughts. "If Damon hadn't been such an awful man and ordered Beth and me to London, we never would have learned the truth about him, and we never would be bringing the children to Summerfield. God worked bad for good."

"Another optimist."

"You can't deny the logic," Tilda said.

"No, I suppose I can't. But it brings up the enormous issue I have to deal with when we get home."

They all nodded. "Do you know what you're going to say to Damon?" Timothy asked.

"It's more a question of what I *won't* say to him. When I think of what could have happened if I'd married the man, his probable abuse of Beth and Tilda, the girls running into harm in London..."

"Ask God to give you the right words," Timothy said.

"I will pray He gives me words that aren't curse words." Out of the blue, some choice words came to her, words that would bring much satisfaction.

"Now, you're smiling," Tilda said.

"I am."

"Why?" Beth asked.

"Because God has just given me the perfect words to share with Lord Silvey."

"They seem to give you much pleasure."

"Oh, they do. They *will*."

Timothy laughed. "Set the words aside and rest. For our day is far from over."

For Damon, it would be a long day indeed.

Chapter Fifteen

Late morning, Genevieve walked the hall of bedrooms with Sylvia, going over their plans for the rest of the day. The doors of the rooms were opened wide and numerous maids were busy making beds and tidying the rooms.

"I wish I could think of something to do to help the situation," Genevieve said. "The girls gone overnight, Clarissa gone after them...I feel so helpless. All night I kept hoping I'd get a knock on the door, telling me they were home safe. I kept praying and praying..."

"As did I. We have to trust that..." Sylvia stopped in front of Damon's room. The door was closed. She spotted the man who'd been acting as Damon's valet and approached him. "Where is my son?"

"He hasn't risen yet, your ladyship."

"It's nearly noon."

"Do you wish me to wake him?"

Sylvia's face clouded. "I will do the honors."

She flung open his bedroom door so it ricocheted off the wall. Genevieve remained in the hall and heard a grunt and moan, "What? Mother, what are you doing?"

"Get out of bed, you lazy man! How can you sleep late when the family is in crisis with Beth and Tilda alone in London?"

"Clarissa's gone after them."

"She has also been gone overnight. Doesn't that bother you?"

Genevieve saw the interest of the servants nearby. She wished she could reach into the room and pull the door shut without Damon seeing her. That being impossible, she waved at the servants to resume their work.

"Clarissa lived on her own in London," Damon said. "I know she can handle the simple task of finding a room."

"Finding a room is not the issue. She's finding two young women amid a million others. Which begs the question: why didn't *you* go with her?"

Genevieve wanted to know the answer too. She heard a rustling and saw Damon walk from the bed into her sightline. He turned and saw her, then came towards her. "If you'll excuse us, Mrs. Weston?" He closed the door in her face.

If the hallway hadn't been populated by so many servants coming and going, Genevieve would have stood by the door to listen. As it was, she was forced to move along.

Genevieve sat at her desk and tried unsuccessfully to concentrate on correspondence. Beyond the constant worry about Tilda and Beth, she was curious about Sylvia's argument with her son. Damon needed a thorough change of attitude. Was Sylvia strong enough to bring it about?

As if on cue, Sylvia knocked on the door jamb of the morning room. "May I come in?"

"Please." Genevieve held her questions at bay.

Sylvia sat in a chair close by, her face drawn. "If my son were a child, I would give him a mighty spanking. Or I'd like to. Alas, I know I wouldn't because I never have been able to discipline him. And his father never cared one way or the other how he behaved. He has been quite molly-coddled." She sighed. "He is the man he is because we let him become that man. And I am sorely sorry for it."

"I appreciate your candid admission," Genevieve said.

"Truth is truth. Spending so much time with him in Europe gave me insight I never would have achieved at home."

She'd opened a door Genevieve had to walk through. "I only know Damon the charmer. What kind of man is he? Truly?"

Sylvia studied the lace on her cuffs, then abandoned it when she found the words. "Truly? He is a dishonorable cad."

Genevieve was taken aback. She'd expected the mention of a few faults, but nothing so devastating. "In what way?"

"In most ways."

Genevieve longed for details. "I'm sorry. I'm sure it's hard seeing him...falter. But can you explain? I'd like to understand him better."

Sylvia snickered. "'Falter' is a kind word for it." She leaned her head back and drew in a slow breath as though she needed air to fuel her thoughts. "After my husband died and Damon became the baron, I thought it would be good for us to travel the Continent together. I thought it would be a way for us to grieve, or celebrate, or simply deal with our new lives."

"It sounds very nice."

"It was—at first. Until Damon realized the perks that came with *being* a baron—being Lord Silvey—instead of simply being the son of a baron." She glanced at Genevieve, then away. "He was highly sought after by women."

Ah. "And *he* sought them?"

"In abundance. At first I withheld my disapproval, hoping he would marry. But then..." Her next words came out in a rush. "He began to spend time with women who were clearly already married."

"Oh dear."

"Many were married to men of great influence who did not take kindly to this dashing rogue having his way with their wives."

"Who can blame them?"

"Venice was especially dicey. We had to leave in the middle of the night or Damon would have been called to a duel."

"I didn't think there were duels anymore."

"The *conte* — the count — in question didn't much care if it was legal or not. So we fled. There were other quick departures in Nice, Munich, and Lucerne, yet some of those were due to Damon's gambling debts."

"From bad to worse."

"I cannot control him. He is like a wild horse running free. Anytime I would try to speak to him — which grew more and more difficult — he would tell me to mind my own business and dash out again, stirring up more trouble."

"For your own sake perhaps you should have left him behind. Especially if he was being willful and ignoring your wishes."

"It was one alternative. I chose a different route."

Sylvia paused, letting Genevieve fill in the silence.

"You came here, to Crompton Hall, to your brother's home."

"*After* cutting off Damon's funds. As the baron he had access, but I stretched my influence as his mother with our bank, and they granted my favor of restricting his income — until he could prove he was capable of being responsible."

"That was very wise."

She shrugged. "I'm rather surprised he showed up here in Summerfield at all, but I was relieved. Perhaps he could change, perhaps he wanted to change."

From what Genevieve had seen, there was little evidence of either.

"I'd hoped Ian could be a father figure to Damon — a good father figure. Plus, I was hopeful for the example of his cousin, Joseph. The two are such honorable men, successful with the estate, happy with Lila and Etta…" She traced the brocade design on her skirt. "I'd hoped they would be of good influence on Damon and he'd settle down and want what they had. I prayed he would grow to be a true and decent nobleman."

Genevieve knew none of that had occurred. "It was a good plan."

"It was. But then there was the fire. Damon never had a chance to be at the hall and spend normal days with them."

"Had you hoped he would fall in love with Clarissa?"

Sylvia hedged. "I knew she was home and had a wild streak like his own — yet hers had been tamed. I thought they would have things in common. That they found such a quick affinity was a pleasant outcome. Even little Beth was an asset, for it would give Damon an immediate family."

Genevieve had never liked the Beth-Damon part of the equation. "What does he think about that?"

"He does not confide in me." She glanced upward and to the right, towards the bedroom where she'd left him. "I hate to admit it, but there is a lacking in him, a lack of compassion, of selflessness." She looked at Genevieve. "Why didn't he accompany Clarissa to London to look for the girls? A gentleman would have insisted. A gentleman who loved the woman would do anything to ease her fears and save her child."

A door had opened to breach a subject. "Then perhaps theirs is not a good match."

"Perhaps not. Actually, I hope they do *not* marry."

"Really?"

Sylvia nodded. "He would not be good for her."

Genevieve couldn't believe what she was hearing. "I agree."

Sylvia looked surprised, but merely nodded again. "Does Clarissa love him?"

"She's interested, but I see some hesitation."

"May it continue. Lord, may it continue." Sylvia drew another breath as if to calm the effort it had taken to divulge her son's failings. She nodded once, as if ending the subject. "Timothy Billings took Clarissa to London?"

"He did. He's a dear friend who helped her bring Beth to Summerfield a year ago."

"Merely a friend?"

Genevieve cocked her head at the notion there could be more between them. "I honestly don't know."

"At least she has alternatives."

Timothy? A suitor? Was their match even possible in the world of titles? *I wasn't titled.*

But I was rich.

Genevieve set the issue of Timothy aside and returned to the other man in question. "Don't you think we should tell her the truth about Damon?" Genevieve asked.

"She probably wouldn't believe us."

Sylvia was right. "She'd probably accuse us of trying to ruin her chance to find love."

"Yet perhaps enduring her anger would be preferable to enduring her pain when she does find out," Sylvia said. "Or her pain after they marry and he makes her miserable. I've experienced a miserable marriage. I wish that on no one. Ever."

Genevieve took Sylvia's hand, then she bowed her head and together they prayed for Damon and Clarissa. Beth and Tilda... Timothy.

And wisdom.

For weeks, most of the women had taken their noonday meal at the workshop, and even the men's midday meals had been haphazard, as the Kidds were usually at Crompton Hall overseeing its progress. Today, with the family troubles on their minds, they all dined at the Manor. All but three. The empty chairs at the table spoke volumes.

Slices of cold meat and cheese were served with bread, along with a compote of fruit. While awaiting his turn, Damon yawned loudly.

"Really, Damon," his mother said.

"My apologies. I have not had time to fully awaken."

Lila hadn't seen him at breakfast, so she assumed he'd slept late. How could he sleep with the girls gone, with their fate uncertain?

"Are you going to London to help with the search, Damon?" Papa asked.

He looked taken aback, as though he'd been asked if he was going to dance a ballet. "I think not. London is such a large city."

"Which is at the crux of the problem," Ian said. "Come now, Nephew. I do believe you are the natural choice to join the search."

Natural perhaps. But obviously unwilling.

A footman entered the dining room with a message on a silver salver. "Your lordship?"

Papa opened the envelope and his expression turned from concern to joy. "The girls have been found! They are safe!"

Everyone applauded with joy — except Damon, who only joined in after his mother gave him a scathing look.

"But there's more. It's best I just read it aloud." He cleared his throat, then began. "'Girls safe. 4 orphans returning with us. Ask Lila speak to Wiltons. Adoption? All eight on afternoon train.'"

"Adoption?" Sylvia asked.

Lila's thoughts sped back to an afternoon at the mercantile. "You all know that the Wiltons recently lost their fourth baby."

"Of course we do," Genevieve said. "It's tragic."

Lila needed to see the words. "Papa, may I read it again, please?" The telegram was handed over and she filled in the gaps. "Apparently they found four orphans in London and are bringing them back with the hopes that the Wiltons will adopt them."

Damon scoffed. "Out of the whole of London, they pick four random orphans? It's absurd."

"It's not absurd and I doubt they are random," Joseph said. "Beth had roots there until Clarissa saved her. I would guess these are children she knew."

"More urchins for Summerfield," Damon said. "Just what we need."

"We," Papa said with special emphasis, "have a responsibility to help those in need."

"We do," Morgan said. "If Clarissa thinks this is a good idea, then we need to trust her."

"And support her," Sylvia said, offering Damon a pointed look.

He opened his mouth to speak, then thought better of it, and merely shrugged.

What is wrong with you? Lila pushed back from the table. "If you'll excuse me, I need to go speak with the Wiltons."

"I'll go with you," Papa said.

She shook her head. "I think having a visit from the Earl of Summerfield might be too much."

"They knew me well when we ran the mercantile."

"I know, Papa, but I think it's best not to overwhelm what will already be an overwhelming moment."

"I'll go with you," Joseph said.

"Perfect. We'll let you know what they say."

"I wish we knew their ages and sizes," Genevieve said. "We could start making them some new clothes."

"There's time enough for that," Morgan said. "They need a home first."

"They need a family first," Lila said.

Lila and Joseph drove to see the Wiltons. The jostling of the carriage added to the jostling of Lila's thoughts.

"Why is your face heavy with worry?" Joseph asked.

She let out a breath and took a new one. "What if they say no?"

"One step at a time," he said. "If they are desperate for children, they will welcome them. They lost four, now they can gain four."

"But will it be a good match?"

He pulled on the reins, letting the carriage come to a stop. "Your worries are logical, but also offensive."

"Offensive? To whom?"

"To God."

She let the admonition sink in. "You're right. This situation is so extraordinary that mere man could not have arranged it. It has to be His doing."

Joseph squeezed her hand and kissed her cheek. "Isn't it grand to be a part of it?"

As they drove up to the Wilton cottage, they found Mr. Wilton on a ladder, picking apples, and Mrs. Wilton gathering fallen fruit from the ground. Both stopped their work and went to greet them.

Lila could only imagine their curiosity and offered them her widest smile as Joseph helped her down from the carriage.

"Good day," Lila began.

The couple nodded their respect, wiping their hands on their clothes. Mrs. Wilton captured a stray stand of hair and hooked it behind her ear.

"Good afternoon, Mr. and Mrs. Kidd," the husband said.

"It's very nice to see you, again, Mrs. Kidd," Mrs. Wilton said.

Her husband gave her a questioning look. Lila rushed to explain, for the explanation would lead to their reason for the visit. "Mrs. Wilton and I saw each other at the mercantile a week ago. We are very sorry for you recent loss."

"Losses," Mr. Wilton said. "I keep asking God why He would take four children from us, but He's not given me any answers."

What a perfect opening. "I think God may have an answer for you today. May we sit?"

They moved to a bench near a well. The women sat side by side, while the men stood across from them. Lila shared a shortened version of the story of London, and the telegram they'd received about bringing four orphans to Summerfield. "Clarissa — Miss Weston — mentioned you two by name..." She was glad she'd thought to bring the telegram with her. She handed it to Mr. Wilton.

He handed it to his wife. "I can't read."

Mrs. Wilton read it aloud, but stopped short of the end, her mouth hanging open. "What's it say next?" her husband asked.

"It says 'Adoption?'"

"Meaning we should adopt them? Accept them as ours? Sight unseen?"

"They're coming in on the afternoon train," Mrs. Wilton said, pointing at the telegram. "Our children are coming in on the afternoon train!"

"Hold on there, Bessie. This is daft. Children don't just appear out of nowhere."

"They do if God wants them to. We've been praying for children, Lloyd. Healthy children. More than that, children to love. A family to love. These children need us to love them." Her voice strengthened. "And we need them to love." She looked at Lila. "I don't even know how to thank you. Yes, we will take them in as our own."

Mr. Wilton sighed and shook his head. "There's no arguing with Bessie — not that I really want to."

Bessie beamed. "You don't?"

"Who am I to argue with? You *and* God Almighty?"

Bessie jumped into his arms. Lila moved to Joseph's side. "This is a very good thing here," she whispered.

Lila and Joseph left the Wiltons to prepare their cottage for the influx of four children—of undetermined age. If only Clarissa had been more specific.

No matter. There was also much to be done in the village, so they stopped at the mercantile and told Nana and Rose the happy news.

"The girls are found safe! Thank you, Lord!" Nana said.

"And four orphans?" Rose said. "That's a complete surprise."

"A happy one." Lila explained about the Wiltons.

"An answer to many prayers," Rose added.

The practical side of the situation took over. "The Wiltons will need bedding and food and clothing for the children."

Rose went to the shelves. "We only have one blanket in stock. If I'd known I would have ordered some."'

"I know what we need to do," Nana said. "Spread the word to the citizens of Summerfield. They will rally up, I know they will."

"What a great idea," Joseph said. "Lila and I can ride through the countryside and spread the word."

"Rose and I will go door to door in the village," Nana said. "Those children will be so blessed."

Lila agreed, though she added, "I think *we* are the ones who will be blessed."

A few hours later Mrs. Keening appeared in the doorway of the mercantile. "Where do you want them?"

"Want what?" Lila asked.

She pointed to the square. "Haven't you ladies been paying attention? Look outside."

There was a growing pile of donations for the new children growing near the water pump. Blankets, two chairs, a rolled up straw mattress, baskets of food...

"Glory be to God," Nana said.

Lila felt her throat grow tight. "We spread the word and hoped, but—"

"And prayed, yes?" Rose asked.

"And prayed."

"Seems God answered in a large way." Nana took Lila and Rose's hands and lifted them up, while bowing her head. "We thank you, Lord, for your abundance!"

Tilda used a comb from her satchel to try and tame Laura's knotted hair—unsuccessfully. Beth was trying to do the same for Lulu while Timothy tied Lee's shoes, and Clarissa supervised Lennie tucking in his shirt.

"There now," Tilda said.

"How does we look?" Laura asked.

You look like four orphans, taken off the streets.

"You look very nice," Tilda said.

"Now *act* nice," Clarissa warned. "Be polite, say 'please' and 'thank you', and do what people tell you."

"Ain't we been good on the train?" Lennie asked.

"All in all, yes," Clarissa said. "I'm quite surprised."

"We're very proud of you," Timothy added.

Tilda liked Timothy's way of saying it better than Clarissa's.

Clarissa gathered them close, putting a hand on the two children at the ends. "You'll be very happy in Summerfield. They're all good people." She glanced at Timothy, then the girls, and Tilda could read the other worry in her mind: *If* the Wiltons agreed to take them in.

Timothy put a hand on Lennie's shoulders. "God brought you here, children. He will watch over you." Lennie peered up at him, his face hopeful. Timothy flicked the tip of his nose and smiled.

Tilda wanted desperately to believe Timothy and was surprised to find she did. There was a sincerity in his nature that made it easy to trust him. Beth had always spoken so highly of him and now Tilda knew that everything she'd said was true.

As they rode the last few miles to Summerfield, Tilda took time to observe him—and Clarissa. There was an easy camaraderie between them, a total lack of artifice or flighty flirtation. They liked each other and were assured enough of each other's friendship that they could fully be themselves. *I want that someday.*

She had time. She was only sixteen. Seeing Timothy and Clarissa together, and Lila and Joseph, and Genevieve and Morgan, gave her hope that one day she would find a suitable husband who would truly love her.

But then she remembered: Clarissa and Timothy weren't a true couple. Even though Clarissa was ridding herself of the scoundrel that was Damon, that didn't mean she and Timothy would be together in a courting sort of way.

Could they marry? Clarissa was the niece of the earl. Timothy was a carpenter. Convention stated that such a match was not possible.

That fact made her terribly sad. Clarissa may have been mean to Tilda, but Tilda still wanted her to be happy—wanted everyone who loved each other to be happy. Surely true love would prevail. Somehow.

She offered up a prayer that God would arrange for a happy match between the two, just as He had arranged a happy match between the children and Summerfield.

For a moment she remembered the clear voice of her governess, Miss Green, sharing a verse at a time when Tilda was feeling pain about being abandoned by her mother: *"Love your enemies, bless them that curse you, do good to them that hate you, and pray for them which despitefully use you, and persecute you."* Miss Green had made her memorize that verse and had told her that even though Tilda was justified in her anger and bitterness, she needed to replace those emotions with prayers that could help her to love in spite of everything.

Tilda had objected. "How can I love a woman I never knew? One who left me with a father who doesn't want me either?"

Miss Green had pulled her into her arms, and she'd felt her breath as she spoke lovingly in her ear. "There will always be people who hurt you, dear girl. Rise above their lack of character and let God put love in *your* heart. That is the right thing to do. None of us deserve God's love, yet He freely loves us unconditionally. *We* love because He first loved us. Do that, and you will always be better for it."

She *had* been better. Despite her father's failings, Tilda had found a way to accept him and even love him. After he died, she'd been brought to live with her godfather here in Summerfield, where she'd finally experienced the love of a mother in Mrs. Weston. God arranged that. God's love had led her to love others, and had brought her more love in the process.

Now, as they returned to Summerfield, Tilda sincerely prayed for Clarissa's happiness. Wasn't that prayer an evidence of love? If so, it was a love that was God-inspired.

They felt the train slowing down. The children's eyes grew wide and they gripped each other's hands.

"Calm now," Clarissa said. "Everything will be fine."

It would. Tilda knew that it would.

The train slowed down, and Clarissa's heart raced.

The children ran to the window as they pulled into Summerfield.

"Look at all them people," Lennie said.

Indeed. Look at all them people.

"Did you send a message to the entire village?" Beth asked.

"Of course not."

"It seems they're all here." Timothy waved.

"It also seems that the Wiltons said yes," Tilda added.

There wasn't time to decipher or delight in it. The train stopped, their door was opened, and the eight of them stepped onto the platform.

The crowd cheered.

The Westons and the Kidds rushed forward to embrace Tilda and Beth. They were introduced to the children, who were so overwhelmed they just stood there, offering an occasional nod.

But then all eyes turned to watch the Wiltons as they walked through the crowd towards the children. Mrs. Wilton clutched her husband's arm with both hands, her eyes locked on the children, her forehead furrowed, but her mouth smiling. She looked on the verge of tears.

The crowd quieted, letting them through. The children peered up at Clarissa, their eyes asking questions. She suffered her own threat of tears, but managed to contain them. "Children, meet your new parents."

Their eyes grew large and they smiled — not just smiled, they beamed. Little Lulu ran towards Mrs. Wilton and wrapped her arms around the woman's legs. The others followed until all were pulled close.

Hang the restraint. Clarissa began to cry, as did most of the crowd, who began embracing each other as if a refreshing rain of love had poured over them.

Beth rushed into Clarissa's arms and Timothy put his arm around Tilda's shoulders. "Well done, ladies. Well done."

Uncle Jack came towards Clarissa and took her chin in a hand. "You should be very proud of yourself. You have done a grand thing here."

Before she could respond, he stepped up and raised his arms, quieting the crowd. "What a glorious day!"

They cheered.

"What a glorious people you are to open your hearts and gather the things these children will need." He glanced at Clarissa. "When my niece sent word that they were bringing four orphans back to Summerfield, and suggested the Wiltons adopt a family, I was obviously surprised. We are all aware of their pain, but now we can plainly see that 'they that sow in tears shall reap in joy.'" He smiled at the happy family. "So much joy — for all of us. For now we have four more members of our family of Summerfield!"

More cheers and applause. Uncle Jack motioned for Clarissa to join him. "We need to thank my niece for her compassionate heart and her wonderful idea."

Clarissa heard the applause, but wished they would be silent. The applause she'd longed for her entire life, now grated because it was not rightfully hers.

She had done little to bring this about except to buy some train tickets and a little food. She turned to Beth and Tilda and beckoned them forward. They came to her tentatively, not used to the attention. She drew them close, one on either side.

"I thank you for the praise, but it does not belong to me." She put a hand on each girl's back. "These girls are the reason a new family was born today. My Beth knew the children from her time in London. She was dismayed to discover they were now orphans, living on the street, trying to fend for themselves."

Empathetic murmurings tittered through the crowd.

Clarissa looked at Tilda. "But the connection that has so obviously sparked between the children and the Wiltons is because of Miss Tilda Cavendish. Thank you for your wonderful idea, Tilda." Clarissa began to clap and everyone joined in.

Tilda looked as if she'd like to flee. Beth kept her there, by hugging her arm to her side.

"Speech!" a few people shouted.

Tilda looked horrified, but Clarissa encouraged her with a nod. "Say something. Tell them why you thought of this."

Tilda hesitated, nodded, then took a step towards the crowd. "Over a year ago I came to Summerfield as an orphan." She extended her hand to Beth, who took it and stepped up beside her. "Beth was an orphan. We both know what it's like to be fully and totally alone." She pointed at the children. "When we saw the children and heard their plight, I recalled the grief of the Wiltons. Suddenly, the need for parents and the need for children meshed together." She took a fresh breath. "Now we all have families who care for us."

"Praise God!" Timothy said.

"Praise Him!"

Clarissa took the girls into her arms. "Well done, girls. Well done."

Mrs. Keening and her husband said their goodbyes and stepped away from Clarissa.

She took a deep breath and said to Timothy. "Before today I'd not spoken more than a few words to most of these people. But now…"

"Now you share a common goal."

"I can't believe how many items were donated. Everyone came together to welcome the children."

"You did a good thing giving credit to Tilda. I know that must have been difficult."

"A few days ago, you would have been right. But since London…everything has changed."

"You have changed."

She looked up at him, hopefully. "Have I?"

"You've… softened."

She shook her head vehemently. "I do *not* want to be soft."

"Being soft does not mean being weak. God has enlarged your heart, making room for the children, for Tilda, and…" He didn't finish.

She knew what he wanted her to say. She knew what *she* wanted to say. But not yet. When and if the time came for his sentence to be completed, she wanted it to be fully meant. And fully and happily answered.

She spotted Damon leaning against the far wall of the depot building. Alone. Disengaged from the happy groups chattering around him. His eyes met hers and he saluted with two fingers.

Clarissa's insides churned with hatred and the desire to confront him right here, in front of the entire village.

She felt a gentle hand on her arm. "Don't."

Timothy's single word of reason determined the victor of her inner battle. "I won't. Not yet." She turned her back on Damon and spoke softly to Timothy. "I will handle this in my own way. I want to warn you that it may seem as though I have forgotten all we learned about Damon, but I assure you, I have not. I need you to trust me."

He studied her face and she marveled at the sweet kindness in his blue eyes. "Of course I trust you. Always."

She vowed not to let either of them down.

"You made quite the entrance," Damon said as Clarissa approached. "A heroine's welcome."

"As I said, it was Tilda's idea."

"Hmm." He stood erect and leaned over to kiss her cheek.

What used to give her pleasure felt like a hot coal upon her skin.

He offered her his arm. "I see you found the girls."

No thanks to you.

"Did they tell you why they left?"

Clarissa's heart felt like it would beat out of her chest. She tapped into her acting skills and managed to speak calmly. "Not really. Beth and I had argued that morning, so I assume that was the impetus."

"Girls have a tendency to be overly sensitive."

To slaps? To groping hands? To threats? To promises of abuse? There was no "overly" about it.

They strolled through the village towards the Manor. Unfortunately, all the usual small-talk that usually filled their time together, was unavailable on her part.

"You're quiet," he said.

"I'm tired. It's been a stressful two days."

"I was surprised you were gone overnight. Where did you stay?"

In a meadow. Beside Timothy.

"No where you would recognize."

"Was Timothy of good help?"

"Immense help. I couldn't have done it without him."

"I do regret not being the one to take you. Will you forgive me for that?"

"Of course."

For that.

***

Lila and Joseph walked the short distance from the train station to the main square of Summerfield. Nana and Rose accompanied them.

"I'd say there's been a good day's work in the village," Joseph said.

"I've rarely seen everyone so excited," Rose said.

"And so united towards a common goal," Lila added.

"Children will do that." Nana said. "And what dear children they are. Lennie, Laura, Lee, and…?"

"Lulu," Lila said. "I heard Lennie say he is ten, Laura is eight, Lee, six, and Lulu, four."

"A fine spread," Joseph said.

"Mrs. Kidd!"

They turned around and found the entire Wilton clan rushing to catch up with them, the children laughing and holding hands, playing crack-the-whip with Mr. Wilton.

The gaggle arrived with giggles and gasps for air. Lila reveled in their exuberance.

Mrs. Wilton nodded to her husband and he spoke for the two of them. "We wanted to thank Miss Weston and Miss Cavendish, but couldn't find them. So we'd like you to pass along our sincere gratitude." He looked across his happy brood and put a hand upon Lee's head. "God gave us a miracle today. We do not take it lightly. These children will be cared for and loved..." His voice cracked and he put a hand to his mouth.

His wife took over. "Mark our words: we will raise them to be valuable members of the community of Summerfield and faithful children of God."

Looking over the lot of them, Lila knew they would keep their promise.

Sitting alone in their bedroom that night, Tilda brushed Beth's hair and could tell by her movement with the pull of the brush that she was close to sleep. "It will be good to rest in a proper bed tonight," she said.

Beth nodded. "I keep thinking of the children and their first night with the Wiltons. I hope they minded their manners at dinner."

"It was probably their first hot meal since their mother died."

Beth turned around on the bench. "I'm so glad we went to London."

"It did turn out well for the children."

"And for us. And for my mum. We never would have found proof about Damon if we hadn't gone."

"If he hadn't forced us to go."

Beth nodded. "That's the odd part, isn't it? That something good could come out of something bad."

There was a knock on the door and Clarissa entered. "How fare my two favorite girls?"

"Tired," Beth said.

Clarissa moved to the bed and pulled down the covers. "It's late. To sleep, both of you."

Tilda and Beth got into bed and Clarissa kissed Beth good night.

She then sat on Tilda's side of the bed. "I need to apologize for all the pain I've caused you this past year."

Tilda was too shocked to say anything more than, "It's all right."

"No, it's not," Clarissa said with a shake of her head. "I've been rude, petty, and spiteful. I begrudged you the love of my family. I made your life difficult, and put both you and Beth in harm's way with Damon."

Tilda had never imagined she would hear such a confession. She'd longed for an apology—for some sort of acknowledgment of Clarissa's slights to her—but now was overcome with the full of it.

"I don't know what to say," she finally said.

"Say that you'll forgive me."

"Of course. Always."

Clarissa stood, leaned down and kissed Tilda's cheek, just as she'd done to her own daughter. "Good night, girls. God bless."

It *was* a good night when God's miraculous blessings overflowed.

Chapter Sixteen

Genevieve draped a shawl over her shoulders and stepped outside ready to head to the workshop.

"Wait!"

She turned around to see Sylvia hurrying down the last few steps to the foyer, a bonnet and shawl in her hands. She caught up with Genevieve, out of breath. "I'd like to go with you."

"You don't have to," Genevieve said as they began to walk. "You must have wedding plans to arrange."

Sylvia handed Genevieve her shawl to hold while she tied her bonnet. "We've talked to Reverend Lyons and alerted Mrs. McDeer that we'd like her to cook up a variety of cakes and sweets to share with the village. Other than that…"

"What about your dress?"

She shrugged and draped her shawl around her shoulders. "I have nice dresses a'plenty. By the time I ordered one or even had one sewn here, the wedding date would be over. This is my second wedding. I see no need for fancy fineries."

"Does Jack agree? After all, he's the earl."

"I know we are challenging convention by making the ceremony simple, but Jack agrees this is the way we should do it." She slipped her arm through Genevieve's and confided, "We simply wish to be married as soon as possible. It's hard to wait."

Genevieve knew she should have blushed, but she didn't. It was refreshing to hear such talk from the older generation.

"So," Sylvia said, changing the subject. "The Wilton children will need some clothes, yes?"

"Yes."

"You don't sound enthused."

"I am. *I* am."

Sylvia stopped walking. "I thought you'd rid yourself of that chip on your shoulder."

So did I. "I'm sorry. Forgive me. I do appreciate any and all help, but I realize the workshop is *my* passion and not anyone else's. What with the children's needs and the fashion parade in a few days..."

"Who has the passion to work at the mercantile?"

Genevieve was taken aback. "Well...Lila."

"Who has the passion to coordinate the furnishings and remodeling at Crompton Hall?"

Genevieve saw where this was heading. "Clarissa. I accept your point."

"Have you ever helped at the mercantile or at Crompton Hall?"

"No."

"Then why do you expect Lila and Clarissa to help with the workshop?"

"They said they would."

"Lila said she would—and she has. But if I remember correctly, Clarissa made it very clear from the beginning she had no affinity for sewing."

This was true. "And you?"

"I am an expert follower when it comes to sewing. Show me what to do and I will do it. But you've seen my limitations."

"I appreciate your help." Genevieve pulled her shawl tighter against the autumn chill. "I thought this was my one important project, something lasting I could contribute to the village."

"Your legacy?"

"That word is too lofty."

"Not at all. For it is a legacy. Without you, the sewing workshop would not exist. Without you, many ladies of

Summerfield would never have had the chance to learn to sew. We are very proud of you."

The power of her praise stunned Genevieve. Was the affirmation of others so important to her?

Once again, Sylvia took Genevieve's arm and they resumed their walk. "Perhaps there is something else bothering you?"

"Not at all," she said. "My silliness suspecting Molly and Morgan is over and done."

"I'm not talking about Molly and Morgan. I'm talking about you and me."

"You and me?"

"When I marry Jack I will become the Countess of Summerfield — a title that will be yours after I am gone."

"I am glad for your new position. Happy for both of you."

"I believe you. Yet…you have virtually been the acting countess since marrying Morgan. You had the responsibilities but not the title. Now I show up, taking the glory away from you."

"I've done little to elicit glory. I don't think —"

"You may not realize it, but it's natural for there to be a bit of resentment mixed with your approval of our match. You've taken on the burdens of the Manor, only to endure a usurper stepping in."

And she is the usurper, Daughter. Don't be so quick to let her take over what we have worked hard for you to gain.

Genevieve shook her mother's voice away. She began to speak but Sylvia stopped her with a hand.

"Just think of what you have accomplished and overcome: New York to Summerfield, single to married, dealing with family secrets and past loves. Not to mention twins."

Genevieve smiled at the thought of them. "I still am awed they are mine."

"And not just twins but a street urchin come to stay."

"I love Beth."

"We all love Beth, but that doesn't negate the drama of her sudden appearance." Sylvia moved to a rock wall next to the road and sat, waiting for Genevieve to join her. "Then there is Tilda, another orphan who has experienced a complicated time at the Manor."

"It was Tilda's idea to bring the London children to Summerfield."

"I commend her for that. But let's get back to you, Genevieve. A few months after giving birth, most of the family abandons you and travels to India. You are left to carry the weight of the entire Weston family *and* the Manor."

It was a relief to have someone understand. "I don't really mind. I just want to do a good job of it."

"Spoken like a brave soldier." Sylvia raised a finger to make another point. "And then Crompton Hall burns and you suddenly have the influx of thirty guests."

"Thirty-four. Give or take."

"What was an enormous undertaking became gargantuan."

Genevieve nodded, and felt her eyes sting with tears. "I tried so hard…"

Sylvia squeezed her hand. "You did a brilliant job of it. You dealt with everything that was poured into your bucket."

"But not gracefully. I made a fool of myself. I overreacted and was petty."

"So what? We pushed you to the point of breaking. You are allowed. The most important point is you did not break, you bent—bent low—but you did not break. You are a strong woman, Genevieve. I look forward to having you as a daughter. Having you as an ally. Together we can run Summerfield."

Genevieve smiled. "I'm not sure Jack and Morgan would agree to that terminology."

"The men may not admit all *we* do, but we know better." She stood and pulled Genevieve beside her. "Now then. Let us go to the workshop where you can tell me which needle to thread with which color, and which button to sew on. Agreed?"

Genevieve hugged her. "Thank you for everything you said. Thank you for being here. I need you immensely."

Sylvia kissed her cheek. "As I need you." She grinned. "All in all, quite a smashing arrangement."

Tilda held Max while Nanny put May to bed.

"You're so good with children," Lila said, bouncing Etta on her knee.

"I love them."

"They love you. Again, I commend you on the idea of bringing the Wilton children here from London. You helped create a family."

Tilda saw her chance to bring up the subject that continued to press on her heart. "I'd like to do more for them."

"We'd all like to do more. Are you planning to go to the workshop later to sew for them?"

"Yes, I'll go. But I have another idea I've been wanting to talk to you about."

Lila's eyebrow rose. "What's that?"

Just say it. "With all of the children being here – they need to be taught. The school is empty."

"Our teacher moved away."

"She's not the only person who could teach them."

Lila's knees stilled. "You?"

"Why not me? I've helped Beth and the children who came to the workshop. I know the basics and am willing to do my own studying to learn more." She pointed downstairs. "There's an entire library of books I can use for reference. I can learn something and share it. Isn't that the essence of teaching?"

Lila grinned, nodding her head. "I do believe it is. But you know this would be an enormous undertaking."

"Not so enormous. The school is there. It just needs a few repairs and a good cleaning. I could order in a full round of slates and chalk. Maybe a globe, a few primer books, some drawing supplies, and —"

Lila laughed. "You're hired!"

"I am?"

"Let's go speak with my father to make it official, but I can think of no reason this shouldn't happen."

Lila and Tilda stood before Papa. "So that's a yes?" Lila asked.

"I believe it is." He winked at Tilda. "Well done. I appreciate your forward thinking. Let us know what you need and we will get it."

"Thank you so much, your lordship."

"Uncle Jack."

Tilda beamed. "Uncle Jack." She turned to leave.

"I'll join you in a minute," Lila told her.

Tilda left them.

"So, Tilda came up with this teaching idea herself?" Papa asked.

"She did."

"She's becoming quite the responsible young lady."

"She is."

He leaned back in his chair and smiled at her. "You're beaming. Is something else making you happy?"

She chuckled. "You and Sylvia. You two being happy makes me happy."

He stood and took her into his arms. "My cup runneth over, darling Lila."

"Our cups runneth over."

Clarissa walked through the garden with Damon. The stress of acting as though they were still close was exhausting.

He plucked a white chrysanthemum and presented it to her with a bow. "A beautiful flower for a beautiful lady."

She held it to her nose, but lowered it, the smell too spicy. "Did you know that white chrysanthemums symbolize truth?"

He hesitated for only a moment, then smiled. "Ah truth. Well, truthfully, I truly, truly love you." He nuzzled her ear.

She deftly turned her head, but offered a smile to dispel any notion she was rejecting him. The rejection would come soon enough. Tonight to be exact.

Since the subject of truth was in play...

She offered a dramatic sigh. "I do wish I knew what sent the girls traipsing off to London like they did."

"Beth hasn't told you anything? "

"She hasn't. She asks me to trust her—which I do. We're all just sincerely glad it ended well. I cringe when I think of how it could have turned out. Very horribly, indeed."

He moved a stray tree branch to the side to allow her to pass easily. "Young girls can be fickle. Who can possibly understand them?"

Certainly not you. "Let's head back to the house and get dressed for dinner," she said. "I have something special planned."

His eyes glowed with mischief. "Will I like it?"

"I guarantee it will be a dinner you will never forget."

Clarissa took extra care as she dressed for dinner. She wanted to look stunning, strong, and victorious. This was no time to appear demure and sweet—not that Clarissa ever sought those roles.

Tonight was a night when she was finally the star of the production. The mistress of her own destiny.

I am the judge, jury, and executioner of the man who has harmed my family.

No, Clarissa. Those positions are Mine.

She started at the inner voice.

"Is something wrong, miss?" Dottie asked as she worked on her hair.

"No. Nothing." But it wasn't nothing. She'd felt a check, like her mother giving her a certain look when she was too loud, or her father pressing a hand upon her arm when she got too dramatic.

Yet her parents weren't here.

God was.

With full certainty Clarissa knew it was Him. She took a moment to remember what she had been thinking before she'd sensed the inner nudge.

I am the judge, jury, and executioner of the man who has harmed my family.

No. God claimed those positions.

She closed her eyes. *So I'm not supposed to make Damon face what he has done?*

She held very still, uncertain what she wanted God to tell her. *Please let me do this. Please help me do this.*

With her last plea, she felt peace. Maybe God simply wanted them to do this together.

"You're smiling. You look happy" Dottie said.

"I am." *Thank you, Lord. I agree to Your terms. You be the director. I am Your actress. Show me how the scene should be played out for its fullest and best benefit.*

"There," Dottie said, finishing her hair. "Is it to your liking?"

Clarissa nearly laughed. "Actually, everything is rather perfect."

"Do you have a dress you'd like to wear tonight?."

"I do. The royal blue velvet."

"A nice choice," Dottie said, fetching it. She returned with the heavy dress draped across her arms. "It's a beauty, miss."

Yes, it was. And more. Clarissa had carefully chosen the high-necked, long-sleeved dress of chiseled velvet that had a train descending from its bustle. This was not a sensual dress, but one emoting strength. It had a slice of straw-colored satin under the V on the bodice and on the underskirt that was open the length of the center front. Black Chantilly lace covered the bodice and edged the opening of the overskirt in extravagant ruffles. Double frills of lace epaulets perched on the shoulders, held by long, richly beaded tassels behind and before.

It eluded elegance, authority, and drama. It was the essence of perfection.

Beth came in the room just as Dottie was leaving.

"Your mum is a dazzler tonight," the maid said as they passed in the doorway.

With a final look to the full-length mirror, Clarissa knew it was true. She finished hooking her sapphire earrings and presented herself to Beth. "Well?"

Beth just stood there, shaking her head, her mouth agape.

Clarissa smiled. "That good, eh?"

"You are beyond beautiful, Mum. You look like royalty."

She chuckled. "If I can make Damon bow low before me then the ensemble has done its job."

"You want him to bow?"

Clarissa shook her head. "Symbolically, dear girl."

"So tonight is the night?"

"It is."

"Do you know what you're going to say?"

"I do."

Beth bit her lip. "I'm nervous."

Clarissa touched her cheek. "No need to be. I will make things right. He won't hurt any of us ever again."

Beth looked into her eyes. "Promise?"

"Promise." *Please God, help me keep that promise.*
Clarissa took the deepest breath her corset would allow.
"Now then. Let us go to dinner."

It was the entrance Clarissa had longed for all her life.

She and Beth entered the dining room fashionably
late, to make certain everyone was in place. She paused in
the doorway as Beth stepped aside, giving her the stage.

Uncle Jack was the first to see her. "Oh. My. Clarissa,
you look stunning."

"Why thank you."

There was a bevy of compliments from the family.
Clarissa accepted them as her due. So far, so good.

For once she was glad her seat at the dining table was
on the far side of the room, allowing her to slowly pass
the length and width of the table before taking her chair.

Damon was quick to hold it out for her. "You look
divine," he whispered.

Clarissa smiled as she shared the joke with the
Almighty. *You haven't seen anything yet.*

With God's help, Clarissa let the entire dinner play
out as though nothing were afoot. She kept in constant
contact with Him, waiting for His nudging. It was hard to
delay, but she came to realize delay was not denial.
Sometimes delay was appropriate — the calm before a
mighty storm.

During the dinner, Clarissa was witty, affable, and
entertaining, doting on Damon, letting his charm ooze out
for all to see, luring him into overconfidence and
complacency.

When the entrée plates were being removed, Clarissa
finally felt the inner nudge, as though she'd been waiting
in the wings for the climactic scene of a production. She
sensed her Almighty director touch her back and propel
her gently forward with a whispered, *Now!*

Her stomach did a little dance as she turned to Dixon and the footmen. "If you don't mind, could we have a moment before dessert is served?"

"Of course, Miss Weston," Dixon said.

Keeping her smile intact, Clarissa added, "Could we also have the room to ourselves, please?"

Dixon's eyebrow rose, but he bowed and the three men left.

"It's not like you to postpone the dessert," Damon teased.

She began to stand and he had to scramble to help her with her chair. "Sit. Please," she told Damon and the other men who had stood in deference to her gender.

"What's going on, Clarissa?" Morgan asked.

"Forgive the bit of drama, but after I'm finished I think you'll agree it is justified." *Justice is always justified.*

She saw Genevieve and Sylvia exchange glances.

"Finished with what?" Uncle Jack asked.

Clarissa strode to the double doors of the dining room and closed them. She turned to face her audience, expertly kicking the train of her dress to its proper place.

"I would like to tell you a story—a love story."

Damon had the audacity to blow her a kiss.

She smiled at him, then continued. "But as is the way with many love stories, this story is full of intrigue." She teased them with her emphasis on the last word.

"Sounds interesting," Newley said.

"Oh, it is." She smiled at Damon. "For the man in this story is very handsome and…and fascinating." She enjoyed the many facets of this word.

Damon took the bait. "And the woman in this story is gorgeous and intriguing."

You have no idea.

Jack raised a hand. "Would you two like to be alone?"

The females at the table quickly shook their heads, answering for her. From the look in their eyes, they guessed what was coming.

Joseph chuckled. "I, for one, feel left out."

Lila put a hand on her husband's and gave him a look. He seemed confused but didn't say more.

Clarissa needed to get to the point. She strolled to stand behind Damon. He put a hand at his shoulder and she took it, letting their hands rest there. "But you see, in actuality, the gentleman in this story is no gentleman at all."

He pulled his hand away.

She didn't look at him but strode the length of the table. "In fact, he is a cad, a rogue, and a gambler." She stopped and glared at Damon. "Isn't that true?"

Damon put a hand to his chest. "Don't look at me."

"And why not? For you are a cad, a rogue, and a gambler."

Damon scooted his chair out. "I beg your pardon?"

"You have more than *my* pardon to beg for. You should be on your knees begging the pardon of every person at this table."

"Clarissa," Uncle Jack said. "You're being rude to a guest."

"Indulge me, Uncle. If you please."

Jack looked at Newley and Damon's mother as though asking their permission.

Newley said, "I for one, wish to hear the rest of the story."

Damon stood. "You condone this bit of drama?"

Newley sat back in his chair. "She has piqued my curiosity. Clarissa, continue, if you please."

Heartened by his permission, she turned back to Damon, her expression reserved even though she longed to pounce on him with her accusations. *Slow and steady...*"So, Lord Silvey. Did you, or did you not, receive a letter from a certain Beemer and Scott, solicitors from London?"

"I have no such letter."

Semantics. "But you *had* such a letter."

He glanced at Tilda. "Prove it."

"Really, Damon," Jack said. "I will not have you speak in such a way."

"What about the way Clarissa is speaking to me? Accusing me?"

Sylvia forlornly shook her head back and forth. "Oh, Damon, what have you done?"

"I've done nothing worthy of this inquisition." He drilled his napkin onto his chair. "I don't have to stay here—"

In a move worthy of a theatrical *dénouement,* Joseph and Morgan rushed to stand between him and the door.

"You will stay," Morgan said. "An explanation is required."

Newley stood at his place. "Return to your seat, Nephew. Immediately."

Damon held the gaze of the entire family as he returned to his chair, retrieved the napkin from its seat only to toss it on the table. He sat back, nonchalantly crossing his legs. "So?"

His mother huffed. "So, now you tell us what was in that letter."

"It was private. I would prefer not to."

"What you prefer is not—"

Tilda raised a hand. "*We'll* tell you what was in the letter."

"How do you know?" Joseph asked.

Tilda looked at Clarissa, silently asking permission to proceed.

"Be my guest."

Tilda and Beth conferred a moment, with Tilda assigned to tell the story. "Beth and I saw Damon receive the letter and realized it upset him. When he threw it in the fire, I recovered it, but most of it was burned away."

Beth looked nervous, as though she would scream aloud at the word *boo.*

So Tilda continued. "It burned except for the letterhead from Beemer and Scott, Solicitors, and a few words saying he was named in the divorce of a Frau

Kostner." She gave Beth an encouraging nod. "When we were in London, we went to their office and found it to be true."

Damon sprang out of his chair. "How dare they share my business with two nothing girls! I should sue for slander."

To her credit, Tilda did not look away. Instead she added, "The solicitor also told us about numerous other married women. And gambling debts."

Clarissa took over. "My, my, Damon. Dallying *and* gambling? Or are they in fact both gambling issues?"

"It takes two to..." Damon let the phrase fade away.

Genevieve sat forward to see him better. "So you admit you...you courted married women?"

A sly smiled escaped. "I don't think 'courted' is the most apt word."

Newley's face was blotched with anger. "Your father would never approve of — "

"My father philandered more than I ever have." He cocked his head and looked to his mother. "Isn't that so, Mother?"

"We are not talking about your father's sins, Damon. But yours." Sylvia looked at the family. "I admit that I knew of Damon's frailties and flaws. As he and I traveled the Continent, his actions caused us to leave more than one city in haste."

"You knew?" Clarissa asked. "Yet you encouraged our match?"

"I thought the whole of Summerfield would be a good influence on him." She looked at her brother. "I thought you could father him and guide him in a way his own father never did. But the fire caused us to move here, and your time was spent rebuilding the hall and..." She looked at Clarissa. "I should have put a halt to the attraction. I apologize for my own sake, and his."

"Damon needs to make his own apologies," Lila said.

The room fell silent and they waited. Damon simply ⸱ed his arms and stared back at them. "I see no need to apologize for actions that have nothing to do with any of you, or Summerfield."

"Then, what about particular actions that have everything to do with us?" Clarissa asked, with a gesture towards Beth and Tilda.

Sylvia put a hand to her forehead. "Oh dear. There's more?"

Damon flipped a hand. "I'm sure they have a list of absurd accusations. I apologize if I didn't let them win at cards, or if I forgot to say please when I asked them to pass me the potatoes. Really now. Here sit two immature girls with questionable roots who have let their imaginations run amuck."

"Enough," Uncle Jack said. "The girls have a right to air their complaints."

"Even if they are false?"

"I guarantee you, the truth *will* come out." He nodded to the girls. "Tell us. We need to hear."

With an encouraging smile Clarissa motioned to Beth. "Go on, dearest. Tell your story. It's all right. It's time."

For the briefest of moments, Clarissa saw Damon's face flash with apprehension.

Beth clasped her hands on the table, then put them in her lap. "First off, I was never sick. I didn't go to London with Mum because Damon told me not to or he'd hurt me. He *did* hurt me, grabbing my face hard, slapping me, calling me a brat. He said I was in the way. And...and he told me I was a nuisance and was preventing Mum from being happy."

Jack stood. "I've heard enough."

Clarissa raised a hand. "Let the girls finish."

"There's more?"

She deferred to them.

Beth turned to Tilda. "You tell the rest."

Tilda rubbed a hand across her forehead, then began. "To tell you the seriousness of the rest, I want you to know that when we were at the law office in London, we told Mr. Beemer the difficulties we were having with Lord Silvey and—"

"This is ridiculous," Damon said.

Tilda would not be dissuaded. "Mr. Beemer felt so strongly about our situation that he wrote a letter of protection for us." She glared at Damon. "Protecting us from you."

"A letter of protection seems a bit extreme," Ian said.

Damon gestured towards his uncle. "It's ridiculous."

Tilda shook her head adamantly. "It is not ridiculous and it is much needed."

Sylvia looked to Tilda and said with a soft voice. "Tell us everything, dear. We need to know."

Tilda looked to Clarissa for support, which Clarissa was happy to extend. "Tell them everything."

Tilda took a deep, cleansing breath. "The day we ran away, we weren't running away by choice. Damon ordered us to leave or he would...he would..."

"This is absurd." Damon stood.

Newley moved behind him and shoved him back in his chair. He looked to Tilda , "Go on, please."

"He said we weren't wanted here, needed to leave immediately, and could never come back or he would..." The next came in a rush. "He would come to our rooms every night and do unspeakable things to us."

Everyone sprang to their feet. Shouts ricocheted off the rafters. The women gathered around Tilda and Beth, drawing them into their arms, offering comfort.

Newley stepped around the chair to face Damon. He put one hand on his shoulder and used the other to point like a dagger. He told him what a despicable person he was, a shame to the family. The other men stood nearby, adding their own choice words regarding Damon's lack of character.

If Damon had shown the tiniest bit of remorse, Clarissa might have felt sorry for him. Instead, he sat stoically, letting their admonishment and anger bounce off him, as if it were all said to a guilty stranger.

This is what I wanted, Lord. Thank you for this.

Damon glanced at Clarissa for one brief moment, but still offered no guise of repentance.

To think I nearly married such a man. Thank you for saving me, Lord.

Finally, Newley yanked Damon to his feet. "You will leave immediately. You are not welcome here at Summerfield or at Crompton Hall. If I ever hear of you even entering the county, I will call in the law."

Damon straightened his waistcoat and stepped towards the doors. He paused to look at his mother. "Mother?"

Sylvia brushed away a tear. "I love you, Damon. You will always be my son. But I do not like you, nor condone your choices. I thought you and Clarissa would be better together than apart, but you, dear son, bring Clarissa down. She is better without you. As are we all."

"They are exaggerating," he said. "You know how people turn against me with their embellishments."

Sylvia's faced sagged, as though the weight of a lifetime suddenly fell upon her. "It can't always be someone else's fault. I ask God to forgive me for enabling you to become this tainted man that you've become. You need to leave. Now."

Damon's expression reminded Clarissa of a petulant boy, used to getting his way. "You don't belong here either, Mother."

"Yes, I do. I have found family here in a way that I have never found before."

"You just want to marry the earl for his money."

Her brow furrowed and she looked at her lap. "Yes, I want to marry Jack, but not for his money or his title. I would marry Jack Weston if he was still a shopkeeper at the mercantile. This is where you and I differ, Damon. Because of Jack I know what true love is. I feel it—deeply. All these women here know what true love is. They have found mates who support them and who will be with them forever."

"Who's to say I don't love Clarissa?"

She shook her head. "The Bible says that true love is patient and kind and thinks of others before itself. I pray you

325

find this kind of love. But I know with my entire being that it will not be found here. Go now. Seek the good in yourself and others. Do good *for* yourself and others. When you do, you'll know where to find me. For I will always be your mother, but I will no longer be your accomplice."

To Damon's credit, Clarissa saw the slightest twinge of regret pass over his face—only to be quickly replaced with his familiar smug smile. With the low bow of a gallant, Damon opened the doors and left.

"We'll see he gets his things and gets out," Morgan said with a nod to Joseph.

Clarissa put a hand to her midsection and took what seemed to be her first deep breath of the evening. She found herself shaking.

"Sit, Cousin." Lila tried to help her towards her seat.

But Clarissa couldn't sit. She couldn't stay in this room, or even in this house a moment longer.

"I have to go."

"Go where?" Beth asked.

She touched her cheek. "I need to get out of this house until Damon is gone."

"I'll come with you."

"No." She looked at their concerned faces. "I need to be alone for a while."

"Are you all right?" Genevieve asked.

Clarissa let out a laugh. "Actually, I believe I am more than right. I am perfect."

The dress Clarissa had worn to dinner—wanting to present herself as formidable—proved to be just that as she walked towards the village. Even after sweeping the train over her arm, the heaviness of the velvet made her feel as though she was trudging through a sloggy mire, trying to reach the safety of the shore.

Frankly, it got in the way of her walk of victory. For what she really wanted to do was run down the drive and jump in the air in an utter celebration of freedom.

For now she was fully free. Free of Damon, yes. But it was more than that, for he wasn't worthy of tainting one more minute of her thoughts.

The essence of her victory was more personal. She was not the Clarissa she was an hour ago. She was no longer a woman who was easily insulted, who felt the need to defend herself at every turn. Now, she felt full inside, as though she had rid herself of dirty water and was filled with the pure, cleansing water of —

She stopped walking. "Of God." She put her hands to her mouth and laughed aloud. "It was You. There. With me. We did it, Father! Thank you! We did it!"

Clarissa turned onto the road to the village. She couldn't stop smiling and knew she walked with a totally unladylike spring to her step.

In the dimming light, she spotted someone riding towards her. Not wanting to interrupt her celebration — or share it — she stepped over the wildflowers and grasses along the road and strode into a meadow, away from prying eyes.

There, Clarissa spun in a circle, her arms outstretched, her face to the darkening sky. "Thank you, thank you!"

But then she got tangled in her train and tripped, falling to her knees. Yet her happiness was unfazed.

She lay down upon the grass and watched the stars come out in the twilight. And she giggled. And then she remembered another meadow, another time when she'd stretched out in the grass and seen the stars.

She touched the space beside her and closed her eyes, thinking of Timothy. Lovely, tender, honorable, delightful Timothy.

She whispered his name.

"Yes?"

Clarissa opened her eyes and saw him standing over her. She sat upright. "You frightened me."

"And you perplexed me." He nodded towards the road. "I was riding and saw you step into the meadow. When I got closer I saw you fall. Are you all right?"

She held out her hand and he took it. But instead of letting him help her up, she pulled him down beside her.

He tumbled and fumbled, then sat with a laugh. "You are full of surprises."

"I am."

"What's got into you? What are you doing out here?"

She was happy to say it. "I just sent Damon packing. The family knows the full truth about him."

"Everything?"

"Everything."

"How did he react?"

She shook her head, not wanting to think of Damon. What mattered now was Timothy. "I don't want to speak of him ever again."

Even in the dim light she could see his face brighten. "You don't?"

She took a moment to put her thoughts into a single phrase. "I feel incredibly, undeniably thankful." She looked into his eyes. "God saved me, Timothy. In all ways."

He took her hand, interweaving his fingers through hers. "I'm glad. For you are worth saving—in all ways."

"I am?"

Timothy took a deep breath. "You're free now."

She was pleased he'd used her special word. "I am."

"Free to ..."

"What?" *Say it, Timothy.*

"Free to...be mine?"

With a surge of joy she threw herself into his arms, making him topple backward onto the grass. As they lay beside each other, she lifted herself up onto her elbow. She peered down at the loveliness of him. Then she glanced heavenwards and asked aloud, "Is this what you want, Father? What You've wanted all along?"

After a moment, Timothy asked, "Is He answering?"

She put a hand upon his chest, feeling the steady beating of his heart "Is this what *you* want?"

He took her hand captive and kissed it. "With all my heart. But with your new-found freedom, you are free to choose."

"Yes, I am."

"So…is this what *you* want?"

The answer came easily. "I think it's what I've wanted since the first time we went to London to find Beth."

"And now, here we are. Finally together."

"Finally together."

His voice softened. "I love you, Clarissa."

"As I love you."

He pulled her into his arms and she marveled at the way her head fit perfectly against his chest. She knew it would be her special place. Forever.

Timothy and Clarissa walked back to Summerfield Manor, his horse walking beside them. Night had fallen, and the moon was hidden behind a bank of clouds. Yet Clarissa felt as if they were walking in the light—a very bright light that glowed from within. It was a light fueled by love and trust and faith.

A memory surfaced. "Do you remember the serious discussion we had over a year ago in the nursery at Crompton Hall?"

He hesitated a moment. Then he said, "Actually I do. You had just snuck back to Summerfield and were hiding at the Hall, away from your family."

His details were right, but they weren't an important part of the memory. "You led me into a discussion about why we are *here*. On earth. We discussed finding our purpose. You said that we each have a unique purpose—"

"The trick is to find out what it is."

"And I said, 'some trick.'"

"*I* remember. I'm surprised you do."

"Don't be. For I have come to believe my life was changed by that one conversation."

"If I would have known that, I would have chosen my words more carefully."

She swatted his arm. "Don't tease. I need you to listen to me. For there is something else you said that resonates in *this* moment, in *this* conversation."

"What is that?"

"You said that coming home is always the right road towards finding our purpose. I couldn't branch out until I returned to my roots."

"And you did return. You went home and made a fine—"

She needed to fully finish it, so she stopped on the road and faced him. "*You* are my home, Timothy. *You* are my roots. *You* are my purpose."

His forehead furrowed with emotion. "And you are mine." He got down on one knee, right there in the middle of the road. "Clarissa Weston, will you be my wife?"

She pulled him to standing and into her arms. Then he lifted her chin and they shared their first kiss.

The moon broke through the clouds, shining its light upon their love.

As the happy couple turned into the drive leading to Summerfield Manor, they heard a carriage coming towards them. They moved out of the way and saw Joseph driving. Beside him sat Damon with all his belongings strapped behind.

Clarissa was torn between wanting a final word and letting him pass. She decided that her best message could be conveyed without words. She put her arm around Timothy's waist and he draped his arm around her shoulders. Together they stood in the moonlight as the carriage moved past.

Upon seeing them, Joseph nodded.

Damon gave them a two-fingered salute and smiled.

"Nothing fazes him," Clarissa said with a shake to her head. "He's probably planning his next deception."

Timothy got them walking again. "Then I feel sorry for him. For without a conscience he is doomed."

They continued up the drive, letting Damon move away in the opposite direction.

Tilda came downstairs and found Beth at the window in the drawing room. The lamps were unlit. "Why are you standing here in the dark?"

"I'm watching out for my mum."

Tilda joined her. "Do you think she's all right?"

Beth considered this a moment. "She did a very good thing confronting Damon, but she has to be hurting about it too."

"She will be fine. Your mum is a very strong woman." As they gazed out at the night, Tilda said, "I'm glad we could tell people what happened."

"I'm glad they believed us."

"You didn't think they would?"

Beth shrugged. "It was our word against a baron's. Who would most people believe?"

Tilda smiled. "The Westons and Kidds aren't most people."

Beth returned her gaze to the window. "I won't feel like it's truly over until I see Mum—" She gasped, then ran into the foyer and out the front door.

Tilda began to rush after her, but saw in the lantern light that Clarissa was not alone. Timothy was with her. And they were walking arm in arm.

The sight of the couple made her smile. She'd seen their special friendship in London and had hoped it could be something more than friendship. Tilda wanted to run to them and find out what had happened, but she held back in the doorway.

She watched as Beth ran into her mother's arms. After the embrace Beth looked up at Clarissa and then Timothy. Timothy took Beth's hand and said something, just to her. Beth nodded vigorously, then wrapped her arms around his waist. Clarissa joined in the embrace.

They're going to be a family.

"Well, well." Genevieve came up beside Tilda in the doorway. "Will you look at that."

"They're together. The three of them. Like a family."

"So it appears."

"Beth is very lucky."

Genevieve cocked her head, then put a hand on Tilda's back. "So are we. For both you and I came to Summerfield as outsiders, but now we are family too."

"We are?"

"Of course, Tilda. And you know what? Sometimes those who come in from the outside appreciate it the most."

She nodded. "I do. I do appreciate being here."

"Not just being here, Tilda. Being family." Genevieve stepped outside and called to Clarissa. "Welcome home!"

Such wonderful words.

"And then Timothy asked if he could be my father and I said yes, of course. Please." She took a breath. "I can't believe we're going to be a family."

Tilda pulled the covers over the two of them. "I'm very happy for you. Truly I am." She settled her head into the pillow. "Did you know I have my own joy?"

Beth turned on her side. "What? Tell me."

"I have family too. Genevieve said so."

"The Westons have always been like family to you."

"But now I am finally like family to them."

Beth turned onto her back. "We are two lucky orphans."

"Orphans no more."

"Thank God."

That's exactly what Tilda did.

Chapter Seventeen

Clarissa sat at her dressing table, staring at her reflection in the mirror. *Today I will be married.*

Her thoughts were immediately transported back to the time she'd been engaged to Joseph—a match arranged by their families.

She stared at her reflection with more intensity. "Who *was* that girl?"

She knew the answer. That younger Clarissa was willful, flighty, and selfish. She'd known Joseph and Lila were in love, but their love had only stirred her competitive nature. Even though she hadn't loved Joseph—and knew he didn't love her—she had agreed to the match as a way to win against Lila. She felt a wave of shame that she had been willing to marry for the conquest, as though vying for a theatrical part.

The part of bride. Wife. Mother.

"Joseph and I would have been miserable together," she told herself. "You know that."

Her reflection nodded, accepting that truth.

"But Timothy and I . . ." She watched her countenance soften, as if the very mention of his name transformed her from the inside out.

Clarissa was suddenly overcome with gratitude. She leaned her elbows on the dressing table and bowed her head. "You are too good to me, Lord. Thank you for the blessing of Timothy. Help me be a loving wife to him and a wonderful mother to Beth. Teach me how to love them more than I already do."

As if hearing her name, Beth knocked and entered Clarissa's bedroom. "Are you ready, Mum?"

Clarissa ignored the question, as she took in the sight of her daughter. "You are so beautiful."

Beth did a pirouette, holding the skirt of her blue bengaline silk dress. It had gold buttons, creating a bib outline on the bodice. "Do you like it? Genevieve made it for me, as a present."

"When did she do that?"

"This week, at the workshop. It's been an incredibly busy week there, what with the ladies wanting to finish their own dresses for the fashion parade and some of us working on new clothes for the Wilton children. She's at the workshop now, making the final arrangements for this afternoon."

"Perhaps it was too much, having two weddings, a fashion parade, and the Harvest Festival all in one day."

"Not too much," Beth said, adjusting the back of her mother's hair. "It's a day no one in Summerfield will ever forget."

Another knock on the door signaled an influx of females. Lila came in first, wearing a delicate lace shawl tied at the bodice and cascading down her front. Then Tilda entered wearing a dark green dress with a pleated skirt she'd borrowed from Clarissa.

Finally the other bride made her entrance. Sylvia's dress was a peacock blue brocade with an ivory overskirt and trim. As soon as she entered, she stopped and sighed deeply. "I cannot believe this is happening. Me, a bride again at the age of forty-eight."

"You *are* ancient," Clarissa teased. "Aren't you a year older than Jack?"

She drew in a breath. "Oh dear. I never thought of that. Men don't marry older women."

Tilda went to her side. "Age doesn't matter. Not if you are truly in love."

Lila adjusted her bracelet. "Papa adores you."

Clarissa felt badly for causing doubt and went to take her hands. "I apologize. I shouldn't have teased you. Today is a glorious day for both of us."

Sylvia drew her into her arms. "It is, isn't it?" she whispered in her ear. Then she held her at arm's length. "Look at you. I adore the taupe color of the silk. And the lace of your overskirt is divine."

"I know I should wear white," Clarissa said. "But there was no time for a new dress."

Lila grinned. "Actually, there *was* time. We could have postponed the wedding a few months. We could have waited until your parents returned from India."

"And the dowager and the colonel," Sylvia said.

"And your brother, George," Tilda said.

"I think not," Clarissa said. "I don't want to go another day without Timothy as my husband."

"I agree," Sylvia said. "I cannot wait to be Jack's wife."

"Then wait no longer," Lila said. "Are we ready, ladies?"

More than ready. Heady.

Clarissa sat in the carriage with Sylvia and Newley, a short distance from the church. They watched as the final few guests entered while the less-than-lucky stood outside.

"Do you realize for the first time in Summerfield history, a widowed Earl of Summerfield is being remarried in our church?" she said.

Newley offered a nod. "To add to the exclusivity of that event, is having the niece of the earl share the day by marrying the love of her life—a village carpenter."

Sylvia laughed. "Never did I think my visit to Summerfield would involve becoming its countess."

"Never did I think I would marry my best friend," Clarissa said.

"Timothy is a fine man," Newley said. "A man of honor and character."

"That, he is," Clarissa said.

"You two brides are certainly bucking convention."

"With pleasure," Clarissa said. "There is no formal guest list, no wedding gowns ordered from Worth in Paris, no men in tuxedos, or dozens of lavish gifts displayed in the Manor ballroom for all to admire."

"Just two couples, very much in love," Sylvia said.

Newley leaned over and kissed his sister's cheek. "I'm so happy for you."

"Thank you, Ian." She nodded towards the entrance. "I think everyone is inside who can fit inside."

"Except us," Clarissa said. "Let us give them the show they've been waiting for." She smiled at Sylvia. "Ready, bride?"

"I am ready, bride."

The carriage pulled in front of the church and Newley got out and helped Sylvia and Clarissa alight.

The crowd oohed and ahhed at their dresses—that were beautiful despite being untraditional. Applause followed them inside.

Now that's an entrance.

Once over the threshold, Newley offered the women his arms—another unorthodox decision. For with Beth and Joseph standing up with Clarissa and Timothy, and Lila and Morgan standing with their father and Sylvia, there was no other relative to give the women away.

Looking over the congregation, Clarissa spotted the rest of their family sitting with Timothy's father in the front pew. Behind them were the upper echelon of the servants from both houses, with the rest of the small church populated by villagers, first come, first served. Clarissa noticed the Wiltons happily claiming the seats next to Dr. Peter and Molly.

Pastor Lyons stood up front with the grooms and attendants. He offered them a nod.

All these details were quickly forgotten as Ian walked the brides down the aisle. More than one villager reached out and touched the dresses as they brushed past. Even that was forgotten as Clarissa's eyes met with Timothy's.

He didn't just smile at her, he beamed. The rest of the world fell away as Clarissa smiled back at him.

Their journey nearly complete, they paused in front of Pastor Lyons.

"Who presents these women to be married to these men?"

Newley smiled at each woman in turn. "I do."

Clarissa moved to Timothy's side. She slipped her hand around his arm and pulled it as close as possible. He covered her hand with his. *May we never let go.*

The ceremony commenced. Words were said and vows repeated, but Clarissa went through the motions, saying her lines and knowing what was being said without letting it intrude on the surge of joy that swelled inside her. Its strength and magnitude was all-encompassing, as if any joy she'd experienced before this moment was a single note compared to this symphony.

Somehow, in the midst of the happiness came another emotion just as intense. Gratitude.

Yet no mere thank-you was enough and she found herself praying that God would know how much she appreciated what He'd done for her.

And then she heard the final benediction of man-and-wife for Jack and Sylvia and knew their time was next. She reveled in the last few moments when she and Timothy faced forward, two people standing before God, two becoming one.

Then it was their turn. The pastor made his declaration: "Timothy and Clarissa, I now pronounce you husband and wife. Whom God has brought together, let no man put asunder."

Clarissa's 'amen' was sealed with a kiss. One of many, that would extend over a lifetime.

The two couples turned towards the congregation, and the crowd expressed their approval with cheers and applause.

Walking up the aisle, Clarissa realized she'd just accepted the most important role of her life.

She was finally a star. Or rather, a very willing co-star.

Jack and Sylvia—the Earl and Countess of Summerfield—stepped into the first open carriage and waved to the crowd.

Timothy and Clarissa entered the one behind.

As the horses pulled them away, Timothy drew her hand to his lips. "Are you happy, my darling?"

She touched his cheek and kissed him, gazing into the blue eyes that somehow had seen beyond the willful girl, the eyes that would watch her as she became more, became all she was meant to be.

"I am beyond happy, my love. For now, I am finally complete."

Tilda and Beth clapped to the music as a dozen men of the village danced in the square, all wearing white shirts with red sashes. They waved handkerchiefs in the air and stomped and danced, ringing the bells that were strapped to their shins.

"They're very good," Tilda said. "Look at old Mr. Granger."

"He's keeping up with the others. I'd like to learn to Morris dance too," Beth said.

"It's not for girls. Just men."

"Tisn't fair."

When the men finished their dance Mr. Mauling began to play his violin and a duo of other men kept rhythm with drums and sticks. Their song was infectious.

"Yay! Now we can dance too." Beth hooked arms with Tilda and they skipped in a circle. Their exuberance caused others to join in until the entire square was awhirl in happy motion.

"Look at Uncle Jack," Beth said.

They watched as Jack and Sylvia, and then Clarissa and Timothy joined in, overfilling the square, taking the dancing into the streets beyond.

"You started something," Tilda said.

Beth took Tilda's hands and they sashayed to the side and back. Again, others followed their lead. Mrs. Hayward and Rose came to join them and a circle was formed.

"Well done, girls," Rose said. "I have never seen the whole of Summerfield so exuberant."

"And I haven't danced in decades," Mrs. Hayward said. She broke off from the circle and hooked arms with Rose. "La di da da, la di da da…"

"You're a good dancer, Mrs. Hayward," Tilda called out.

"Thank you, my dear. But call me Nana. Both of you, call me Nana."

Really?

As they danced, Tilda looked out over the crowd of boisterous, joyful people. *Am I really here? Am I really a part of all this?*

"Come on, Tilda!" Beth said. "Let's try this…"

Beth spun her under an arm, making Tilda dizzy with delight.

❦

"Line up, ladies."

"And boys," Tilda said.

Genevieve corrected herself. "And boys." She looked down the row, taking note of Lennie and Lee Wilton who were sporting new shirts and vests, thanks to the quick work of Molly and Mrs. Keening. The two women had taken it upon themselves to sew for all four of Summerfield's newest residents. The children beamed, taking everything in as though not quite believing their journey from homeless orphan to beloved sons and daughters was real.

Actually, every participant in the fashion parade radiated excitement and satisfaction in their newly sewn clothes.

Lila sidled up beside her. "Look at what you've accomplished."

"What the women accomplished," Genevieve said. "I just got it started."

"Their lives are better, because of you."

"I don't know about that."

Lila took her arm and turned her away from the line. "Accept the compliments, Genevieve. Say 'thank you.'"

Why was it so hard? "Thank you," she said. "Thank God."

"I agree. Thank God for all of this, for all the joys of this very fine day."

"Can we get on with it?" Mrs. Keening asked. "My Ralph is motioning that he needs help with our booth."

Everything seemed ready. "Lila, would you tell Mr. Mauling to start playing—something slower perhaps?"

"No, I won't."

"Why not? I arranged for him to accompany the parade."

"You need to say something first. To everyone."

"I'm not good at speaking to crowds."

"You will be the countess someday. Today will be good practice." Lila took her arm and drew her towards the center of the square.

Genevieve tried to pull away, but realized she couldn't do so without making a scene. What would she say? Last time she'd stood before them, she'd had to humble herself about the gossip issue. What if they remembered that day as much as she did?

As they approached, Jack stepped forward and drew her to the center with him. "Ladies and gentlemen of Summerfield!"

The crowd quieted and gave him their attention.

"Thank you for sharing our joy on this memorable day," he said. "My wife and I, and my niece and her husband could not have asked for a more festive celebration."

"Here, here!"

The crowd cheered and clapped.

"We have so much to be thankful for, for God has been ever-faithful, helping us, guiding us, and enriching our lives. We have worked together, showing our care, loyalty, and love for each other. It is truly a time of plenty and prosperity, a time of the rise of the Summerfields!"

The villagers congratulated each other, their faces glowing with gratitude and hope for the future.

Jack continued. "God has also provided a fine harvest to take us through another year. And He's blessed our village with the addition of four fine children in the Wilton family."

Genevieve saw Mr. and Mrs. Wilton exchange an embrace and wave at their children.

"Speaking of children..." He looked over the crowd and pointed at Tilda, gesturing for her to come join them.

She clearly didn't know why she was being brought forward, but Jack draped an arm around her shoulders. "Because of Tilda here, and her desire and willingness to share her special gifts, I am pleased to announce that the Summerfield school will be reopened on Monday."

There was a cheer.

"All children are welcome," Tilda said. "Be there at eight o'clock on Monday. Together we will learn many exciting things." She stepped aside.

Jack turned to Genevieve, drawing her hand around his arm. "Finally, we have this very special woman who has blessed us by her very presence."

Genevieve felt herself redden. "It is I who am blessed."

"Because of her, Summerfield has a sewing workshop. Because of her, many women have learned how to sew clothes for themselves and others. We applaud your American ingenuity and drive. Bravo, Genevieve."

More applause? Genevieve wanted to slip away. She saw Lila, who mouthed, *Say thank you.*

"Thank you." She suddenly found more words. "So many people have worked very hard to make this happen. So many women have created beautiful dresses." She glanced at the people in line. "Fashion they wish to show you today." She looked at Jack. "May we proceed?"

He waved an arm in a gallant bow. "It is my great pleasure to present to you, the fashion parade!"

Mr. Mauling began a song and the parade commenced.

A victory parade.

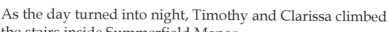

As the day turned into night, Timothy and Clarissa climbed the stairs inside Summerfield Manor.

"I can honestly say I never, ever thought I would be bringing you up here," Clarissa whispered.

He stopped on a stair. "You didn't? I did."

"You did?"

"Perhaps not here, exactly," he said. "But I dreamt of our wedding night, taking you to a place where we could finally and fully be alone."

She suddenly had a fear and drew him into an alcove at the top of the stairs. "I may have lived on my own in London, but I never..."

"I know."

"Have you ever...?"

He shook his head. "I was waiting for you."

She fell into his arms, right there in the hallway, leaning her head upon his chest. *And I was waiting for you.*

She heard someone clear their throat and saw Jack and Sylvia, also coming upstairs.

"It's only ten more steps to your room, Niece," Jack said.

"Leave them be," Sylvia said, "or I'll find us our own alcove."

"Good night then," Jack said, leading his wife down the hallway to his—to their—room.

"Good night."

"Shall we?" Timothy asked.

They entered Clarissa's bedroom and he closed the door behind them. And locked it. "Finally alone." He pulled her into his arms.

"Yet never alone. Never again," she said.

"Never again." He pulled back to look at her." Are you certain you don't want a honeymoon? A grand tour of the Continent? Seeing the world?"

Clarissa shook her head. "There is time enough for that. For now, I just want to be home with you and Beth. You two are my world."

"What a glorious world it is." He grinned. "Shall we see how glorious?"

His wish was her command.

Epilogue

Four Months Later

"Why am I so nervous?" Clarissa asked Timothy as they approached Crompton Hall.

"Because you've put your heart and soul into this project."

Lila and Joseph faced them in the carriage. "As well as months of your life," Lila said. "You have done what I never could have accomplished."

Joseph put a hand on her knee. "You are too hard on yourself, dearest. I am sure the hall would have survived your decorating skills."

Lila laughed. "Survived, perhaps, but not flourished. Clarissa has recreated what was there and improved what was not."

Joseph shook his head. "Indoor bathtubs and water closets. Such luxuries."

" Since such luxuries came from ashes, perhaps we should burn a bit of Summerfield Manor," Timothy teased.

"Perhaps you can find a way to make such changes without the destruction," Clarissa said.

"Now that the Manor will be emptying out again, perhaps I can adapt some extra bedrooms for a different use."

"There you are," Joseph said. "Clarissa, you and Timothy have your next project."

Clarissa glanced at Timothy, and he gave her a small nod. "Actually, we have another project in the works," she said. She put a hand on her midsection.

"A child!" Lila exclaimed. "You are with child?"

"I am."

Timothy leaned over and kissed her cheek. "The twins will have a new cousin to play with."

Lila and Joseph exchanged a look. "Shall we tell them?"

"I don't see why not."

Clarissa beat them to it. "You're expecting too?"

"I am. Etta will have a new brother or sister in late spring."

Clarissa took Lila's hands in her own. "Our children can play together, grow up together."

"The future of two families, right here in this carriage," Timothy said.

They pulled in front of the hall. "I do believe some fine work has been done all around," Joseph said.

Very fine work indeed.

Lila stood in the nursery of Crompton Hall. Finally alone. Finally home.

The new and improved Crompton Hall was very fine indeed. Each room had been toured, with Clarissa and Timothy showcasing the handiwork, and detailing the choices that were made.

Without her.

It was your choice, Lila. Remember how overwhelmed you were when Ian gave you the task?

She nodded at the inner reminder. Clarissa had been a godsend, and—as Joseph had so aptly put it—she had saved the hall from Lila's meager decorating skills.

She sat in a rocker and placed her hands over the new baby growing inside her. They would have two children. What a tremendous blessing.

"Knock, knock."

Nana stood in the doorway holding Etta. Lila rushed to greet them, kissing them both and taking Etta in her arms.

"Come see your new room, sweet girl. What do you think?"

Etta only cared about wanting down, where she proceeded to walk a few steps, before giving up and crawling towards a stack of blocks.

Nana strolled through the room and looked out the window at the back garden. "It seems brighter than before."

"The paint is lighter. Clarissa said a nursery should be all about light."

"I agree." Nana pointed to the right. "Weren't there some low cabinets along that wall?"

"There were, but Clarissa thought they took up too much of the best space in the room."

"Space now available for playing."

Lila nodded. "Clarissa said—"

Nana raised a hand, stopping her words. "I'm hearing a lot of 'Clarissa saids.' What does Lila say?"

Lila retrieved some blocks Etta had scattered and set them near her daughter. Then she sank into the rocker. "Lila says 'well done.'"

"But...?"

Lila sighed. "You read me too well."

"Always have, always will." Nana pulled another chair close. "That being true, you might as well tell me what you're really thinking."

"It's complicated."

"So I gathered."

Lila rocked up and back, trying to sort her thoughts. "I'm very grateful for Clarissa's fine job. The Hall is beautiful once more. Better than it was."

"Better than you could have made it?"

"Far better."

"Is that the problem?"

She hesitated. "I don't know."

Nana waved the answer away. "You do know. Didn't your father-in-law expressly tell you that his wife was like you, that she—like you—had other talents beyond designing the bric-a-brac and furnishings in a room?"

"Yes. He said that." She remembered the conversation that had lifted the burden from her shoulders. "He said Anabelle and I both chose people over pomp and position."

"I think I would have liked her very much."

"As would I. I wish I would have known her. I wish Joseph would have known her."

"But now he has a wife who embraces the same essence of being. You are what he needs. You are what Crompton Hall needs. You are no longer the timid mistress, trying to achieve some lofty measure. You can be yourself, knowing your own talents, gifts, and purpose. People strive a lifetime to know such things."

Etta crawled close and used Lila's knee to stand. Lila took her upon her lap, nuzzling into the sweet smell of her neck. "It does feel like a fresh start."

"Because it is." Nana handed Etta two blocks, which she proceeded to clack together. "Do you remember what I first told you when I came to Summerfield to live with your family at the mercantile?"

How could she forget? "You said I was a rare gem."

"A rare gem sparkling in the sun. I told you I would help polish you to a luscious sheen."

Lila remembered the conversation as if it had been yesterday. It was right after her mother had made belittling comments, making Lila feel dreadful about herself. Nana had lifted her from despair to hope.

Then she remembered something else. "I also remember discussing the fact that gems need to be cut and shaped."

Nana spread her hands. "Have you not been so? The fire, Joseph's injuries, and various dramas within the family and the village have shaped you into the stronger woman you are today."

"I guess they have."

"And who is sitting across from you now?"

Lila smiled. "My darling Nana, who promised to help me become a many-faceted jewel."

"And, as God wills, I hereby promise to be here to help little Etta sparkle. Three generations ready to help and encourage one another, no matter what happens."

Lila felt an inner nudging, then smiled. "Actually...there will be one more who will need your encouragement and care."

Nana's eyebrows rose. "You are...?"

"I am."

Nana sprang from her chair and encased Lila and Etta in a hug. "When?"

"Late spring or early summer."

"How marvelous! I assume Joseph knows?"

"He does. And Ian."

"Do your father and brother know?"

"Not yet. But...Clarissa and Timothy do."

"That's an odd order to the telling, but—"

"They are expecting a child too."

Nana clapped her hands together. "Two more babies in the family! May God be praised."

Fully and often.

Tilda stood at the front of the classroom, facing eight tables that would soon hold two children apiece. And just in case, two benches had been added at the back. Oh, to have them filled too.

She straightened the stacks of slates and chalk on her desk. She'd considered putting a set at each place, but decided the children would find more pleasure in coming up front and claiming their own. A silly distinction perhaps, but Tilda knew how important it was for children who owned little to feel as though something was theirs and theirs alone.

She heard footsteps outside and felt her stomach grab. Yet they were not the footsteps of a child, but of—

Clarissa stepped through the door and gave it a full scan. "Are you ready?"

"I think I have been ready for this my entire life."

Clarissa's eyebrows rose. "I didn't realize you felt such a calling to teach."

"Neither did I. I would never have realized it at all if not for the chance I had to be with children at the workshop. Having to entertain them sparked the teacher in me."

Clarissa sat on one of the benches and sighed. "I've never been in here."

"You didn't go to school?"

"Not here. I had a governess."

"Ah."

"Did you go to school, Tilda?"

She shook her head. "Papa hired ladies to take care of me and they taught me my ABC's and numbers."

"Were they nice?"

She shrugged. "It was their job. None of them lasted long."

"I'm sorry for that."

"It's all right. Though there *was* one special lady. Miss Green was especially nice and taught me far more than the others. I truly believed she loved me. I certainly loved her as the mother I never had."

"What happened to her?"

"She married and moved away."

"Do you stay in touch?"

"We did for a while, but I have no idea where she is now. She certainly could never find me, not here."

Clarissa nodded once and smoothed the fingers of her gloves. "Are you glad you moved here?"

"Of course. Life in Summerfield is far beyond anything I ever imagined. I'm very grateful."

"As I told you before, I'm sorry I haven't made it easy on you."

"The timing of my arrival was unfortunate. I'm sorry I was here, in the way of your homecoming."

"You weren't in the way. I just hadn't learned to share yet."

It was an odd way to put it. "And now?"

Clarissa let out a long breath and took another. "Since Beth and Timothy came into my life it seems the more I have the more I have to give. It would be nice to be the sort of person who gives no matter what, but that doesn't come easily for me." She paused, then added. "You came with nothing and gave of yourself."

"Not really. I came holding a grudge against the world, feeling I was owed something because you at Summerfield had plenty. I took far more than I gave."

"But now you're giving plenty." Clarissa turned towards the sound of children outside. "Here they come."

Tilda put a hand to her stomach. "What if I can't—?"

"You can." Clarissa spread her arms to encompass the room. "You were brought here for this, Tilda Cavendish. You know it, and I know it. So do it."

Tilda nodded. She did know it. She felt it as fully and completely as she had ever felt anything.

The door opened and the two oldest Wilton children peered in.

"Come in, children. Welcome. Find a seat. Class will begin shortly."

A dozen children filed into the room, some bubbly and some tentative, but all willing.

"I'll leave you to it, then," Clarissa said, as she readied to leave.

"Thank you for…for all you said."

"You're welcome. But Tilda? One more thing."

"Yes?"

"Know that Miss Green would be very proud of you."

"I like to think that."

"As I am proud of you."

As Clarissa left, Tilda laughed to herself. The knowledge that others were proud of her made her own pride grow. And her confidence. She could do this.

"Well then," she began. "My name is Miss Cavendish. I have the honor and privilege of being your teacher."

Genevieve stood alone in the hallway leading to the twenty-five bedrooms of Summerfield Manor.

The quiet, empty bedrooms.

She closed her eyes and drank in the blessed silence.

"What are you doing?"

She opened her eyes and saw Morgan standing at the other end of the hallway. "I am wallowing."

"I don't understand."

"I am wallowing in the silence, in the emptiness, in the peace of having our house back after nearly six months."

He came beside her and closed his eyes, mimicking her stance.

"What are—?"

"Shh!" He kept his eyes closed.

She loved how he made her smile. She closed her eyes again. "So?" she finally whispered. "What do you think?"

He pulled her into his arms. "I think it's wonderful that the house is empty enough that I can kiss you out here in the open."

She giggled and kissed him back. "So what do I do now?"

"Rest and relax. Go play with the twins. Read a book. Sew for enjoyment. Take a stroll through the gardens. Play the piano—I haven't heard you play in ages."

"Mamma was the one who insisted I learn how to play—in order to catch a husband."

"If I remember correctly, your playing was definitely *not* a factor in catching me."

"I don't play that poorly."

"Do you like to play?"

"No."

"Then don't play another note."

His suggestion caught her off guard. "You make it sound so simple."

"It can be."

Genevieve thought of the continual battle against her mother's voice. She smiled at the notion of never playing the piano again. *See, Mamma? I have a husband and he doesn't care one whit if I play well or at all. And so I choose…*

I choose…

"Oh, my," she said aloud.

"What?"

"I just realized the extent that Mamma's voice has become intrusive. Invasive."

"You hear her?"

"Too frequently. I hear a lifetime of Mamma's to-dos, should-dos, and don't-dos. Her words hover over me, threatening rain."

He took her chin in his hand and peered into her eyes. "You have survived the storm, Gen. Step into the fresh air of a sunny new beginning."

He was right. It was time to banish everything that had held her captive to the past, everything that kept the old Genevieve from becoming the new Genevieve. The better Genevieve.

"Order your mother to leave you alone," Morgan said.

"Order?"

"Right now. Say it aloud." He stepped away, giving her room.

Although she felt foolish, Genevieve stood erect with her shoulders back, her chin strong. Her words began tentatively, but gained strength. "I… I choose not to listen to your voice anymore, Mamma. You do not know what's best for me. I know what's best for me. God knows what's best for me. And that is enough."

Morgan kissed her on the cheek. "Well done, my darling."

Voices filtered up from the foyer. The happy voices of the family wove their way up the stairs and surrounded her with assurance, hope, and love.

"Shall we join them?" Morgan asked.

"We shall."

Genevieve took the arm of her husband and chose to be happy.

THE END

Dear Reader:

I am sad to leave the people of Summerfield. They've been with me many years and are like family to me. As you can imagine, we have a very close relationship.

I hope you feel the same way.

But…because I am so close to them, and because their story goes on even after the last THE END, I am happy to tell you that Lila's story continues in *The Pattern Artist*. I bring her back as a mature woman with a 29-year-old daughter, Etta (who you met as a baby in this book.) *The Pattern Artist* is the story of one of Crompton Hall's maids who finds the American Dream in New York City in 1911. If you'd like to find out more about Macy's and the Butterick Pattern Company, I know you'll enjoy this book.

And I'm not saying the Westons or Kidds won't appear in other books. I have two series niggling around in my head that I would like to connect to Summerfield. Stay tuned.

I hope you've enjoyed the Manor House Series, and celebrate with me the growth and happiness of all its characters.

May you discover your own unique God-given purpose. He's waiting to show you the details. Just ask.

Blessings and happy reading,

Nancy Moser

The Fashion of Summerfield

GENEVIEVE'S Fashion

Chapter 12: "Jane dropped the skirt over Genevieve's head, being mindful of her hair. It fell upon the bustle and Jane adjusted the cascading lace ruffles and drapery that circled the dress and bustle, but the moment of truth would come when it was hooked. Or not hooked... Jane held the bodice so Genevieve could put her arms inside. The bodice opened in the back and Genevieve prayed the hooks would close... Jane faced her and adjusted the lace collar and edging down the front of the bodice and at the cuffs at the three-quarter length sleeves. There was a satin bow that tied just below the waist in front, and Jane worked on it until it lay flat."

CLARISSA'S Fashion

Chapter 16: "Clarissa had carefully chosen the high-necked, long-sleeved dress of chiseled velvet that had a train descending from its bustle. This was not a sensual dress, but one emoting strength. It had a slice of straw-colored satin under the V on the bodice and on the underskirt that was open the length of the center front. Black Chantilly lace covered the bodice and edged the opening of the overskirt in extravagant ruffles. Double frills of lace epaulets perched on the shoulders, held by long, richly beaded tassels behind and before. It eluded elegance, authority, and drama. It was the essence of perfection."

Wedding Fashion:
TILDA, SYLVIA, LILA, BETH
and CLARISSA

Chapter 17: "Beth did a pirouette, holding the skirt of her blue bengaline silk dress. It had gold buttons creating a bib outline on the bodice... Lila came in first, wearing a delicate lace shawl tied at the bodice and cascading down her front. Then Tilda entered wearing a dark green dress with a pleated skirt she'd borrowed from Clarissa.

"Finally the other bride made her entrance. Sylvia's dress was a peacock blue brocade with an ivory overskirt and trim. As soon as she entered, she stopped and sighed deeply. "I cannot believe this is happening. Me, a bride again at the age of forty-eight."... Sylvia held Clarissa at arm's length. "And look at you. I adore the taupe color of the silk. And the lace of your overskirt is divine."

Discussion Questions:

1. Genevieve's idea of the sewing workshop is a good one, and initially she has a full contingent of helpers. Their interest wanes when they realize sewing is not their talent. Name a time when you were asked to do something you didn't enjoy, or had no talent for. Did you remain with it, or remove yourself from the task?

2. Genevieve struggles with her weight after her twins are born, and subsequently doesn't feel attractive to her husband. If you are a mother, how did you deal with baby weight and feeling normal again?

3. In Chapter 8, Nana and Lila are discussing plumbing and electricity improvements. Nana says, "A body doesn't miss what a body doesn't know." Is this a true statement? What life-improvement did you wish for before it was invented?

4. Genevieve goes days without remembering that she'd not had quiet time with God. Have you ever experienced a time in your life when such spiritual time fell away?

5. In Chapter 13, before speaking to the village about her accusations against Morgan and Molly, Genevieve prays: "Help me only say what you would have me say. Help me make it right." Have you ever prayed such a prayer? What was the result? Did you receive the right words, or feel compelled to say nothing at all?

6. In Chapter 14 Beth points out, "If Damon hadn't been such an awful man and ordered Tilda and I to go to London, we never would have learned the truth about him, and we never would have brought the children to Summerfield. God worked bad for good." When in your life have you witnessed God working bad for good?

7. In Chapter 15 Tilda finds herself praying for Clarissa's happiness—a woman who's treated her very badly. She remembers her governess telling her that we love because God first loved us and we are to pray for our enemies. Have you ever prayed for your enemies? What was the result. Or do you have some enemies you should pray for?

8. In Chapter 16 Clarissa realizes that God saved her from Damon, an awful man. In your own life, who has God saved you from?

9. In Chapter 16, Clarissa and Timothy watch as a smug Damon leaves Summerfield. Nothing fazes him. Timothy says, "Then I feel sorry for him, for without a conscience he is doomed." What do you think Timothy means by this comment?

10. In Chapter 17, Lila helps Genevieve graciously accept compliments by saying a simple "Thank you." How do you handle compliments?

11. In the Epilogue Nana talks with Lila and says, "You can be yourself, knowing your own talents, gifts, and purpose. People strive a lifetime to know such things." Do *you* know your talents, gifts, and purpose? Share what you have discovered about yourself.

About the Author

NANCY MOSER is the best-selling author of twenty-nine novels, including Christy Award winner, *Time Lottery* and Christy finalist *Washington's Lady*. She's written thirteen historical novels including *Love of the Summerfields, Just Jane, Masquerade,* and *The Journey of Josephine Cain.* Some of her contemporary novels are: *The Invitation, Solemnly Swear, The Good Nearby, The Seat Beside Me, Weave of the World,* and the Sister Circle series. Nancy has been married for over forty years — to the same man. She and her husband have three grown children, seven grandchildren, and live in the Midwest. She's been blessed with a varied life. She's earned a degree in architecture; run a business with her husband; traveled extensively in Europe; and has performed in various theatres, symphonies, and choirs. She knits voraciously, kills all her houseplants, and can wire an electrical fixture without getting shocked. She is a fan of anything antique — humans included.

Website: www.nancymoser.com
Blogs: Author blog: www.authornancymoser.blogspot.com, History blog: www.footnotesfromhistory.blogspot.com/
Pinterest: www.pinterest.com/nancymoser1
Facebook and Twitter:
www.facebook.com/nancymoser.author, and
www.twitter.com/MoserNancy
Goodreads:
www.goodreads.com/author/show/117288.Nancy_Moser

Look for *The Pattern Artist,*
a book about Macy's, the Butterick Pattern Company
and a housemaid who discovers the American dream.

The Pattern Artist

1911

Annie Wood! I demand you wipe that ridiculous smile off your
face. Immediately."

Annie yanked her gaze away from the view out of the carriage
and pressed a hand across her mouth to erase the offending smile.

But as soon as the attempt was made, she knew it was
impossible. The grin returned, as did her gumption. She addressed
her accuser sitting across from her. "But Miss Miller, how can any
of you *not* smile? We are in New York City! We are in America!"

The lady's maid sighed with her entire body, the shoulders of
her black coat rising and falling with the dramatic disdain she
seemed to save for Annie. She granted the street a patronizing
glance. "It's a big city. Nothing more, nothing less."

"Looks like London," said the younger lady's maid, Miss
Dougard.

Miss Miller allowed herself two glances. "A city's a city."

If Annie could have done so without consequence, she would
have made them suffer her own disdain by rolling her eyes. Instead
she said, "If you'll pardon my directness, how can you be so
indifferent? We've just crossed an ocean. We're in a foreign land,
another country."

"Hmm," Miss Dougard said. "I much prefer France."

"Italy is the country of true enlightenment," Miss Miller added.

Show-offs. For they *had* traveled with the Newleys to many far-
off places. But Annie could play this game. "I happen to prefer
China."

She earned their attention. "When have you — ?""I haven't, in
body. But I *have* visited China in my mind. Multiple times.
multitudious times."

"Multitudious is not a word."

Annie rearranged her drawstring purse on her lap. "I am excited to be here because I've never traveled five miles beyond the village. Even when the Kidds travel to London for the social season I'm left behind at Crompton Hall."

Miss Miller smoothed a gloved hand against her skirt. "You wouldn't be along on this trip, excepting I knew her ladyship would get seasick."

What?

Miss Miller's left eyebrow rose. "Don't look surprised, girl. Even though you're traveling with the two of us, you are still just a housemaid, here to do our bidding as much as the family's."

Annie was tempted to let loose with an indignant *"I am not 'just' anything."* What about all the special sewing and handwork she did for the viscountess and her daughter? She had assumed *they* wanted her along because of her talent.

"Pouting does not become you," Miss Miller said.

Annie pulled her lower lip back where it belonged, hating that they'd witnessed her pain. Searching for a comeback, she bought time by yawning as if their assessment of her position meant little. Then she had it: "Considering her ladyship kept the contents of her stomach contained on the voyage, is it fair to assume my duties are now over? Am I free to enjoy myself at the Friesens'?"

"Don't be daft," Miss Dougard said.

"Or impertinent," Miss Miller added. She flashed a look at Annie over her spectacles. "There will be chamber pots aplenty wherever you go, Annie Wood."

Annie felt her cheeks grow hot. *Under* housemaids had the burden of emptying chamber pots. As an upper housemaid Annie claimed cleaner duties that involved changing the linens and dusting the fine bric-a-brac that couldn't be entrusted to lower maids.

Except on the ship, when she *had* endured the wretched pot duty.

She drew in a deep breath, willing her anger to dissipate. As it waned, her determination grew deeper roots. Someday she'd rise high enough in the household that the Misses wouldn't dare make such a comment. Someday she'd be their equal.

Until that day. . . Annie revived her smile and returned her attention to the city passing by. She was in America, and she was not going to let anyone dampen her pleasure. No one in her family had ever even hoped to travel so far. When she'd told her parents about her opportunity, they'd scoffed. *"Who would want to go there?"*

She should have anticipated their reaction but refused to let their naysaying ruin the adventure. *She* wanted to go to America. She wanted to experience *everything*. If they were content to live in the cottage where Ma was born, taking in laundry or doing odd jobs to get by, let them. Annie had dreams.

The progress of the carriage was slow amid the teeming streets. On the ship, Annie had been astounded at the number of people gathered in one place. That number was a mere handful compared to the throngs capturing the streets of New York City. Everyone was going somewhere in the middle of amazing missions. "They're so alive," Annie said, mostly to herself.

Miss Miller allowed herself a quick glance. "They look like ants rushing about, dizzy over a bread crumb. They don't realize life is ready to squash them. Like this. . ." She pressed her thumb against her knee and gave it a maniacal twist.

"Excuse me, ma'am, but if not for those busy ants, who would have built these enormous buildings? Who would grow the food that will be in abundance at dinner tonight? Who would do *all* the work a day requires? And if the truth be told, are *we* not ants, doing our work for the Kidds?"

The wrinkles in Miss Miller's face deepened. "I am not an ant!"

"Nor am I." Miss Dougard flipped a hand at the window. "If you can't see the difference between those of us who serve with dignity and those. . . those. . ."

"People who also work very hard?" Annie offered.

Miss Miller hovered a finger in the air between them. "Never group the two of us with laborers who toil."

Two of us. Not three.

"*We* do not toil," Miss Miller said.

"Never toil," Miss Dougard said.

Although Annie knew she should nod and let it go, she heard herself say, "I agree."

The women blinked, and Annie changed the subject before they could dissect her full meaning. "Do you think the Friesen home is much farther?"

As those who did *not* toil discussed the correct answer, Annie let herself enjoy the sight of others like herself who did.

71358466R00218

Made in the USA
Columbia, SC
25 May 2017